Afterlives

A Novel

Philip Tew

Brigand
London

Brigand Press,
All contact: info@brigand.london

British Library Cataloguing-in-Publication Data
A catalogue record for this book is
available from the British Library

Printed and Bound in Great Britain by CPI
Group (UK) Ltd, Croydon CR0 4YY

ISBN: 978-1-912978-02-1

As ever, Bartha Tavasz Agnes, édesem, lélektársam

It is a curious circumstance that death, which always filled his mind with the most gloomy and horrible reflections, and which in his unoccupied moments can hardly be said to have been ever absent from his thoughts, should have been chosen by him as the subject of one of his most popular scenes in the pantomimes of the time.

Charles Dickens, *Memoirs of Joseph Grimaldi.*

Contents

Afterlives

Prologue: Pantomimes

Distraught, Jim wandered through his secondary school, its vivid presence exact, everything just as it ought to be. Seventeen, Jim felt light-footed, yet vulnerable, his stomach insistently queasy. Moving to the exit, an impalpable quality disturbed him, something else not quite correct. He was confused by his melancholy, which persisted despite his youth. Pausing inside the panelled entrance-hall of the upper school, near the door to the headmaster's office, he found the silence uncanny, most unsettling. Above the lighter parquet floor, the dark walls consisted of downward rectangles of mahogany, the centre of each one beaded and recessed. The sombre veneer was gloomy, dismal. Beneath the panels the matching skirting boards were further blemished by darker streaks, scuffed by the soles of queueing schoolboys.

Jim was late for something, quite what for was elusive, mind a blank. Where should he be? Frowning, he tried, but he couldn't recollect. Agitated, first he swept back the long hair that fell straight upon his shoulders, black sideburns flourishing, no longer part-hidden. He thrust his hands into deep blazer pockets, unexpected objects in both, nasty sensations, sticky, unanticipated movements, something alive. Shuddering, his stomach became an echoing void. Every single finger was numb, wooden, lifeless.

Jim had experienced these very sensations previously, as a shadow prowling these corridors, the moment revived, stretched across the years. Surely his conviction was simply *déjà vu*, or a nasty daydream, yet he was unconvinced. Momentarily his mind and body swirled, his thoughts random. He tried to focus. Odd, but it was strange to be so young. Just what or who was he looking for? Might it be Boris, his friend? And if so why? Where exactly was Boris? Hidden? Or, lost? In which classroom was he?

A strange, unwelcome sensation overwhelmed Jim, like deep cold water, as if he were struggling ... sucked downward . . . . Next a further precipitous idea: might he still be sleeping? Maybe . . . yet . . . this was all far too lucid, so utterly realistic, absolutely solid, precisely located, familiar. The mornings he'd been here, always the same, unchanged. Or was it? For a start, he pondered, there was the wood . . . there before his very eyes . . . he might even touch . . . suddenly unable to move his hands, he steadied his body, kicking out, only hearing a dull sound, no sensation in his foot, limbs anaesthetised, rendered immobile. . . . He panicked, felt nauseous, disembodied, dislocated, trapped in a vortex, twisting, struggling. His frame flexed, an involuntarily shudder, and he was awake, back in his bed. So that was it: he'd been dreaming. No longer at school, hadn't been there for years. It was March 2014, unexpectedly warm. He'd left school in 1972, after which an epoch passed, a whole new world emerging. Yet his sense of the past faded slowly, images persistent, as if he might re-inhabit them.

Falling for an instant, Jim willed himself awake, refused his reverie. Consciously he reoriented his senses, locating himself, retracing the awful epiphany of knowing that he was both so old and a failure. Once stirred, he knew he was *ancient* compared to his adolescent self. Yet that lost time lurked within, seeming simultaneously improbably close and so utterly distant, another historical reality. Simply closing his eyes would allow him to re-inhabit every facet of his dream, the hopefulness, and eagerness again. Eyes open, in his wakefulness he knew he'd reached a specific threshold where the past receded ever more rapidly, the imminence of physical decline, and death, a most uncomfortable thought.

Still bewildered, overwhelmed by vivid purple bedlinen, newly-decorated glare of white ceiling, Jim realized he hadn't thought of Boris in forty years. The poor boy died in 1969, during the summer holidays, drowned near Geneva. Jim shook his head, sighed for the passing years, unable to picture his long-dead friend. Jim was more obsessed with the current year, 2014. Only a month previously he'd attempted to ignore his sixtieth birthday, his evasion a futile enterprise. His baby-boomer panic was evident to everyone who knew him well, friends, family, colleagues.

Like most of his peers who'd supposedly matured in a golden age of youth cultures, Jim was once convinced he might stay young forever. Many still appeared to believe they might. One sixty-six-year-old male ex-colleague from his school-teaching days had joined the stand-up comedy circuit, seeking stardom, confident of supplementing his tiny pension by being spotted for the movies, or at least television. He'd never acted. His jokes concerned ageing, impotence, infidelity, divorce and death. He was reading from the script of his own life. Another female academic Jim knew vaguely from time at the British Library, recently, according to a third party, started performing live as a jazz singer aged fifty-nine, equally confident of fame and celebrity. A close school-friend, met first at five years old, had taken to weekly guitar lessons, resumed after a hiatus of over forty years, supplemented by yoga classes. For Jim such ambitions were pantomimic. Trying so hard at their age seemed to him pathetic.

However, Jim felt far from his prime, jaded, nerve ends jangling. He sat up in bed in sodden pyjamas; he suffered an intense wave of vulnerability, his system over-charged with emotional shock, profound nervousness, as if under immediate threat. According to his alarm, it was 06:15 Tuesday 22nd April 2014.

He was not ill, not as far as he knew. Maybe it was his age, or being wasted the previous night. The weekend was very normal, usual routine. Sunday morning, he shared coffee (decaffeinated for him) with his Hungarian partner, Gabriella, or Gabi as she was known. Subsequently he ate lunch at her house. After a half-mile drive between homes, he watched Manchester United lose to Everton by two goals. Monday they'd lunched at a country pub in Essex, near Harlow. A luxury: usually Gabi worked in the City, five long days, leaving at six, returning at seven-thirty. They rarely saw each other weekdays. Last night, Bank Holiday Monday, everything was as it was on a Sunday, relaxed, no impending tasks, no surprises, as he preferred. The only change was a thick late-night mist. Usually Jim felt comfortable and unthreatened in his Victorian terraced house. Although eastern Enfield wasn't the most salubrious, usually it seemed quiet, normal, unthreatening.

Yet, today he was troubled. He ought to feel secure. Was it the thought of Muslim neighbours, the recent murder of Lee Rigby in Greenwich, beheaded hostages in Iraq, or terror attacks, a bombed bus garage in Nigeria, where Boko Haram seized into forced sexual slavery 276 young schoolgirls, or the bombing of a train bound for Karachi? Now other groups like the so-called Islamic State in Aleppo in Syria claimed they could threaten and overwhelm the region, seize Iraq. Did such events unsettle him unconsciously? Each day the world seemed more primeval, menacing.

A large bare-footed figure, he stepped carefully onto the carpet from the high bed, steadying himself. In the kitchen he wondered why his dreams were so often morbid even in the optimistic summer months. It was a strange thing death, he thought, one minute you're sentient, the next not . . . and sighed at this dreary notion. He thought about how most people lose sight of those they've known, and how the past is abandoned, and sighed again. After all, he hated thinking about oblivion, most especially his own.

Chapter One:
Recalling Sue Townsend, April 2014

In his kitchen Jim prepared a mug of tea, decaffeinated, milky, drunk rapidly. For distraction he switched on his radio, the 'Today Programme' at seven a.m., looking through the window at a clear April sky. He found himself thinking vaguely of Sue Townsend, recollecting dismally that she'd died twelve days previously. Now she'd been a genuine success, he thought. He'd heard the news on his car radio and today she was mentioned again on a trailer for a tribute, evoking Adrian Mole, and Leicester. That was another period of his life, but Jim didn't want to think too much about age and decline, or, the reality of her death, so he turned off the radio.

Outside already bright sunshine evaporated the billowing river-valley mist that swirled thickly around the house when he retired the previous night at midnight. Despite being early on Tuesday, bank holiday over, such unexpected, cheerful weather raised Jim's sprits. He went through the ritual of preparing a second mug, humming, ever more optimistic each passing moment. Nothing today could be as bad as his shock on awakening, feeling so very old. He survived that revelation. Yet despite his buoyancy, he couldn't suppress a dark thought that forty miles away around the M25 by car, summer term loomed at his university. That entailed much Jim positively disliked: examinations, anxious students awaiting grades, end of year appraisals of doctoral students' progress, an influx of peripatetic students plus staff members from around Britain, Europe and even further afield. There were exam boards too, and a renewed argument about what he might be expected to teach in the coming autumn term. The latter was the last thing he wanted to contemplate on such a potentially beautiful day. However, thankfully today Jim might pretend he was free, able to work from home, as long as the bloody internet didn't crash yet again.

Unshaven, grey stubble beneath his cropped hair, he limped three metres from his kitchen door to an office situated at the back of his home, keys and a third mug of tea in his hand. He was a large figure, especially around the waist. His start was much later than usual. As he sat at the computer desk, he peered at his diary to reconfirm the date: 22nd April 2014. Briefly he rang Gabi and explained that he was working at home that morning, adding, 'At one I'm coming to town for a late lunch.' She thought Jim a success. They'd argued about his recent gloom and despair. He imagined her sitting at a desk in the City. She was a financial analyst for a major bank. Asked why he was venturing out, he responded, 'I'm going to see Alfred, so I could meet you for coffee later, Gabi.' A typical Hungarian she'd a habit of asking for a justification and challenging matters, even ones that were utterly inconsequential. Jim referred to Alfred, his fellow editor, of a scholarly journal that Jim founded a decade previously with an ex-colleague.

Taking coffee was Jim's favourite ritual, a passion Gabi shared, along with over half the population if the spread of the various franchises was a reliable indicator. Jim pencilled in his editorial meeting later that day, to discuss the journal's future. They were paid nothing, made barely enough money to survive. Jim wondered whether keeping it alive was worth the effort. He sent an email to David, an ex-colleague, currently working high in the mountains in Kurdistan in Iraq, life with low tax and cheap cigarettes. David could even buy booze, which surprised Jim.

Even after a third generous mug of tea, Jim still tasted the residue of last night's gin - not the tonic, in fact never the tonic. This habitual morning aftertaste, as he sat at the computer psyching himself up to start a new project, was something slightly unpleasant, but eleven hours earlier, stimulating, even pleasurable. He'd drunk several large glasses while watching his large flat HD screen, occasionally dozing. In the bright early daylight, this aftertaste seemed to Jim a tad like getting old. Not radically different to the original drink which he'd enjoyed, but belatedly transformed into something far more unwelcome.

At nights, over the years Jim lived alone, television became a big part of his life, although not a dominant aspect since until very recently he'd worked weekdays from eight to eight, with only an occasional break. Few people visited him at weekends in the suburbs. Usually, apart from shopping, he continued writing academic articles, on post-war fiction, generally British. Although after the funding success, occasionally he did so on narratives of older people, real ones they kept in diaries. On weekdays telly followed his scholarly routine. For Jim it represented both a comfort and a substitute for company, but, essentially, an excuse not to find other more demanding things. He could rest, rather than further draw on his mental reserves, which he'd come to believe were finite. So distractedly he just watched what in his youth many older people had dismissed as a 'goggle box.' They believed this intrusive device mesmerized its audience, brainwashed them; a few regarded the rays emitted were downright dangerous, threatening one's health. Recollecting such objections reminded Jim of a visitor stridently criticizing him for watching television, memories of passing moments that he'd sublimated.

About ten years earlier around the cusp of 2003 and 2004, at the end of the Christmas vacation a Hungarian ex-student was passing through London. Jim knew her from his time teaching in Szeged, a city fairly close to both the Serbian and Romanian borders. She visited him in his flat in Tufnell Park, staying for a week and sleeping on the perennial sofa bed, on which during his twenty-plus years in his tiny home he'd put up many visitors. Exacerbating his growing sense of ageing, adding to his apprehension at approaching fifty, despite their proximity she exhibited no underlying erotic desire at all, not toward Jim at least. As never before he felt perhaps at a half century he faced no longer being regarded as a sexual object; part of his life seemed to be ending. Rather, the girl's sole motivation was all about her need to undertake research. Faced with her own lack of scholarly ideas, calculatingly she wanted to draw them from him in a vampirical fashion, draining his underlying energies entirely for her benefit, without reward bar her company. She sought to mine his expertise, desperate for academic guidance concerning the thesis she planned. At that time, she was dark, thin, relatively tall, with short, black hair, as if growing out a crop. She seemed incredibly severe, too serious for someone so young. As Jim remembered when he conjured up that stay, she looked at him through large dark brown eyes with what seemed a profound disappointment. Her prime target was completion of her long-anticipated PhD, about which she'd talked, although the topic Jim had long since forgotten, no doubt literary. That's why she visited. Yet another project concerned with something of little interest to the world at large, almost inevitably all about storybooks, as Jim increasingly dismissed fiction, including the literary sub-genre he taught.

Yet in 2014 on this sunny morning literary criticism was still his profession, just about. On occasion he interpreted for student delectation the fiction of Nabokov, Amis Senior, Spark, Murdoch, Durrell, Pynchon and so forth, British and American Fiction between 1945 and 1975. Increasingly student numbers on his modules decreased, complaints centring on the length of the books. John Fowles' *The French Lieutenant's Woman* was a particular bugbear, as was *The Crying of Lot 49* and *Gravity's Rainbow*, or so Carlin, his boss, informed him at the end of last term when discussing Jim's future. A supposed 'expert' on scholarly identity in academic writing, Carlin was small, smartly suited, furtive in his visual appraisals, like a briefly glimpsed monster. He and Jim loathed each other. Carlin's features seemed unpleasant, habitually avoiding the gaze of his colleagues, not out of guilt, rather fear they might read his underlying intentions. On this occasion his guile seemed redoubled. Carlin spent much of his career cracking what many considered unfunny 'jokes,' mostly less than subtle insults, which criticized people's size, their taste in dress, or their age. His other constant was that he avoided and demeaned research whenever possible. He was certainly not the kind of figure that Csilla sought on her visit; suddenly, Jim could recollect the Hungarian's first name, pronounced 'Chill are'.

After the third night Csilla spoke out, complaining bitterly in her stilted fashion, the words accented, very formal, each one precisely accentuated, each one like a stone thrown, nothing like every-day English. Whenever she spoke it was as if someone had wrenched the vocabulary out of its usual patterns, its flow thoroughly disturbed, perhaps even mangled, battered.

'You . . . .' She paused. Then, she waited a few moments. Clearly, intended as an accusation, a chastisement, she added, 'You watch much, so very much television, James.' She reduced his name to *Jumz*, in an accent akin to a Bond villainess. Initially he simply shrugged and exhaled. 'So, why all this nonsense, James?'

'Csilla, from my perspective it's a bit rich for you to be criticizing me for relaxing. What exactly did you expect of me after a long day working, over eight hours being intellectual or intensely cerebral. You think I want more of the same at home? I want to relax.' At that time Jim cycled to the British Library whenever he was in London, and worked very long hours committed to his research.

'James, I am so *disgusted*. So much absolute *rubbish* you watch, you know, every single night. Really James, constantly, all night long, such total rubbish for too many hours, you watch so much.'

Jim was irked. Her accusation was pure exaggeration. Mostly he returned from the British Library at night at around eight-thirty, his research notes and marked student essays in his bag strapped to his cycle's pannier rack, before preparing food for both of them. His serious viewing habit started from nine-thirty onward, until maybe midnight, hardly a lengthy period. Admittedly, he did little else, avoiding protracted conversation with Csilla, about her topic. He'd no intention of slighting her. However, such lengthy exchanges would result in having to take on board her neuroses, her scholarly slowness, and other specific examples of her academic impasse, such as suffering blank page syndrome. Very definitely he didn't want to think through her project in detail, plan the nuts and all on her behalf. Getting involved would be a huge commitment, another mistake. She'd only blame him later if her thesis were to go awry, most especially if she decided not to follow his advice. He knew he'd still be at fault.

Such situations were bad enough with Jim's own doctoral students, some of whom habitually, and wilfully failed to follow his instructions. Waleed from Jordan, for instance, whose thesis was on modernist, post-war and contemporary travel literature. A large, jolly man of twenty-five, he'd produced contrary to Jim's wishes three longish chapters on a single author, one he liked above all else, and only one each on four other writers included in the original plan, all far shorter. As a result, the thesis seemed radically lopsided. And naturally such an unbalancing begged the question of why it had not been focused solely on his favoured author. Jim warned him before the oral examination, about which Waleed was incredibly nervous. Still he was too doggedly headstrong to follow advice. When the external examiner objected, Waleed became livid. After the examination, in a corridor he shouted for a while at no one in particular. The examiner demanded one of the first three chapters be cut, the addition of a single chapter on another sixth relevant author, requiring Waleed to write this supplement. 'It's only another twelve thousand words, Waleed,' Jim argued. 'You've already written far more words already discarded and you've read the new book as background research.'

'This is a pure insult,' Waleed raged, 'such an absolute affront.' He continued being outraged, stubbornly refusing to alter his thesis. Finally, after weeks of persuasion he agreed, spending the Christmas vacation at Jim's flat, departing just a week before Csilla's first visit. Jim cooked Waleed a halal turkey dinner. He was unconvinced that you could find such a peculiar fowl but did so at a Muslim butcher on Seven Sister's Road. It was smallish yet inexpensive, and perfectly proportioned with firm, plump legs.

Hence during the subsequent visit of the Hungarian, Jim was doubly determined not to be inveigled in any way into any such supervisory activity. Now he was himself offended when his new visitor presumed to criticise him in his own home. Waleed hadn't complained once. He watched anything, only objecting that Jim's television should have a far larger screen, be more up-to-date. 'What did you expect, Csilla? Look, I read all day, or research, or write, and at times even teach. Being a scholar, an intellectual all day long is pretty demanding. So, at night I just want watch mindless pap.' And Jim felt exactly the same in April 2014; or, so he realised considering he still watched very similar programming, much of it American, with lots of police procedurals, feature films and various comedy series. No real change, Jim admitted, no real harm.

'*Pap*?' She was confused, and slightly annoyed, the word far too arcane for her command of English, a skill in which she took great pride. This was a game he played intermittently during Csilla's stay, confusing her by deliberately dropping in on occasion a simple colloquialism, of which she'd never heard. He'd triumphed already with 'snog,' 'ruck,' and 'chuffed.' She asked in puzzlement, 'Grandpa? So, it's short for grandpapa, yes?'

'No, not grandpa. Pap, P-A-P. Literally its origin is in sloppy food for babies or invalids, yes, sloppy, gooey. So gradually sometimes the word might be used colloquially for rubbish, anything crap; almost like shit for brains . . . .' Drawn into his teaching mode, a slippage, ill-advised, abruptly he stopped.

'I expected you would be more . . . well, more . . .,' she trailed off into silence, standing, a thoroughly bookish woman in her mid-twenties, thin, saturnine face, exceedingly short dark hair cut in an elfin bob. She had thin legs, and a reasonable figure, although too flattish a chest for Jim's taste. After more thought she resumed the personal attack, 'Far more intellectual.'

In 2014, a decade later, unable to focus on his work Jim found himself wondering idly about what might have become of Csilla. Thinking back, more of his memory stirred. He recovered more of her past complaint about his uninspiring way of life.

'I thought we might talk,' she opined, 'go through scholarly matters. I hoped for guidance, like a mentorship. I could learn more about Britain, its *academic* life.' Jim simply shrugged and drank more of his red wine, which she refused.

Looking back, he saw a pattern of disappointment clearly loomed large for Csilla. This eager, clever, idealistic academic-in-the-making would not have anticipated such a destiny. No doubt she'd always expect more of people than they could ever deliver in the real world, given mostly they were tired, overworked, and sometimes downright dispirited. For her academia was clearly still some magical realm she aspired to enter, looking for princes rather than the frogs or toads that lay in wait. Jim was expected to offer the condensed equivalent of a London intellectual circle. She anticipated Bloomsbury or Fitzrovia, and encountered something more akin to Tony Hancock in *The Rebel*, a version where the comedian's character, an aspirant painter in the late-modernist mode à la Pollock, hadn't even the courage to move to Paris and was still struggling to start *Aphrodite at the Waterhole* in his suburban digs. What was her surname, Jim wondered? Csilla what? Or, more properly, *what* Csilla since the patronymic came first for all Hungarians? Her first-last name, or in English her surname, he just could not remember, much as he tried, probably because it was something arcane. Not Kiss, Bényei, Bartha, Nagy, Glant, Kalmár, Séllei, Moise, Rácz, and Kovacs, names he'd encountered during his year spent in Debrecen on the eastern edge of the great Hungarian plain. Now they seemed exotic once again, but they'd been commonplace at the time. Nor was it Hajmássy, Galamb, Gábor, Korda, Bartók, Kodály, Liszt, Tarr, Csonka, or Soros, names he knew from more celebrated Hungarians.

As he recalled, she came from Szeged, in which city's university Jim once taught. He travelled by train every fortnight to offer a clutch of classes over two days. He gave up on her name, rather trying to imagine what might have happened to her since their few nights sharing his small portable colour television in his living room with its impossibly high ceiling, which later collapsed. Was she married—had she a partner or given birth to children—or had she lost anyone close? Surely, she had her doctorate, awarded by now? Would she be teaching, and where would she be living? In Hungary he presumed. If not, London, nearby, even? Or perhaps she was doing something completely different? She might even be dead, or murdered, he pondered, a morbid chain of thought. But maybe she had, yet if so, he'd never know of her fate.

So, in a curious fashion losing touch so absolutely was akin to someone dying. Such a separation erased the totality of that person, everything shared forgotten and consigned to oblivion. Those other points of view excised, memories of what had been shared lost, those other perspectives of oneself forever inaccessible, like a divorce without any reconciliation or contact. In his youth Jim had tried to write. In doing so perhaps such undoing, through separation was what he'd been resisting, trying to remedy, putting off the reality, that fear of such loss inscribed in his notes, in the journals, in his poems, in all four of his unpublished novels, all the lost occasions, the passions, places, people, and well in truth mostly the people, all those lost relationships, with the individuals who meant so much to him. How could it ever be put across, the enormity of such a perpetual dissolution that followed one like a shadow? And out of nowhere he wondered whether he might write fiction again, an odd idea, especially as nowadays Jim knew he'd never enough time, or so it seemed.

And now in April 2014 rather than work, instead he worried endlessly about some girl whose family name he couldn't recollect, a passing figure in the complexity of his life. And he started thinking about his television habits again, an easier rumination, which activity had been mostly alone after the nineteen-sixties and apart from the early seventies, when he reluctantly shared his life with his parents. He'd watched alone for years, switching channels endlessly, apart from nights with Cedric in the years before his friend's untimely death, only then would he willingly share televisual experiences. Although thinking back, there was another friend who would die prematurely, in this case by his own hand, poor old Steve Knapper, who often crashed the schedules demanding booze. He'd been a would-be actor and clown, reputedly having been trained in mime by Jacques Lecoq. He taught drama at Kingston University, cycling half-way across London to Waterloo on his bicycle from his flat in Stoke Newington. Back when Jim still lived in the flat in Tufnell Park Knapper would habitually pitch up unannounced, cycling by mostly from a pub or a club, very late at night after closing time. He knew Jim would be watching television, supping a few glasses of wine. Knapper arrived with a mission, to seek and consume Jim's weekly stash of wine restocked on a Thursday night, hidden earlier in the under-stair cupboard of his ground-floor flat. Bought in advance so as to avail Jim of all the bargains. Despite quaffing a high proportion of such purchases, Knapper would always argue vehemently about various matters, including the quality of the wine, the absolute necessity of changing tv channels, demanding alternative programme choices. He reviled whatever viewing Jim selected.

'Anything but that pure unadulterated crap,' he would fulminate drunkenly about both the wine and their viewing, much angrier than Csilla, invariably far more direct. 'Why on earth watch this awful fucking crap?' He hectored Jim, who ignored the gate-crasher, increasingly a serial disturber of his relaxation.

'I'm not fucking turning over. I've already watched half, and now you want me to change channels just to suit your preference.'

'This is shite and I'm your fucking guest,' Knapper often argued, somewhat illogically since his claim was entirely spurious. Once again, he was invading Jim's territory for the wine stash, having run out of money or any drinking buddies prepared to further subsidise his evening's excesses. There was never a genuine invitation actually offered, although admittedly sometimes Jim welcomed his company, however belligerent this interloper proved to be. As Knapper's aggression increased, Jim's response was to turn off the set. He thereby declared the argument over, although it always rumbled on one-sidedly, with yet more recriminations from his drunken friend, while draining another bottle of wine. With the screen dead, he complained volubly about bad hospitality. Sometimes he'd a tale of the evening, as when the police found him asleep, still drunk, bike next to him on the grass centre-point of a roundabout near Battersea Park. They'd told him to sleep it off elsewhere. After which he made for Jim's flat, his capacity to cycle while being almost blind drunk being prodigious.

Now Knapper was dead, Jim mostly watched alone, with very few arguments over programme choice, except when Gabi, or more properly Horváth Gabriella, his partner, came over on Saturday evenings, their sole night together. Jim avoided movie genres he knew she detested: horror, overly complicated thrillers, overly sentimental comedies, and wherever possible all unresolved endings, although sometimes this was hard to judge in advance. However, much of his planning proved academic (in the popular sense) since their capacity to watch together rarely lasted, most films ending as one or the other of them dozed off, sometimes both. His excuse was that he was old, sixty, and things were certainly going downhill in terms of energy. Her tiredness was unsurprising despite being a decade younger; she worked in a major investment bank, driving to the local station before six, returning after seven, every weekday, whatever the weather, whatever her mood. In ten years, he'd never known her be off sick, not a single occasion. Gabriella played a significant role in Jim's life, since their intimacy gave him security. Despite his view that he was a failure, she believed in him, thought him a success. However, they were rarely together. Gabi had her own home where her teenage children lived, who she seldom saw, spending most of her life commuting or working. By the time Jim was awake she would already be at her desk, in an office in an investment bank in the city, the insides of which he'd never seen, cheek by jowl with Liverpool Street Station where they met occasionally for coffee among the raucous crowds of suited, booted city-workers.

Seven-thirty. April 2014, according to his desk diary, white pages open beside the keyboard. What mattered? Did anything really signify apart from the diktat to work, alienated lives controlled by investors, capital, while being royally pissed off?

The abandoned, deflated ball on the uncut grass of his small garden, the residue of last year's apples shrivelled on the tree in the border by the shed, overlooked by his whitewashed office. What of any of it? What might it mean, all that stuff? He wound down the white blind because of the glare of the sunlight obscuring his computer screen, and opened his notes, ready to progress. There were a number of emails, most of which he deleted. One from an Eileen Beckett had an attachment, and the strapline 'Seeking Information', so seemingly weird to Jim, cautious about viruses. He paused, thinking about the name for a second. Deciding he definitely didn't know her, he deleted the missive. Another email from LinkedIn invited him to connect with yet another academic he did not know. He ignored that too. Instead he looked up an old friend, Wendy, an academic who'd retired from London to Kent, according to rumour having inherited a vast fortune from her mother. Recently, she showed him her idyllic and enormous workspace, an old wooden chapel in her cottage's garden, which he toured via her webcam. He frowned. He found over ten pages with 108 people with the same name as her, more than a century of namesakes, or *naamgenoot* in Dutch, a reality which battered one's own sense of uniqueness like a heavy cosh over the head, and which was among the real troubles of the electronic age. On page one was 'a reassurance assistant at Blackpool Council,' which, as they said, you couldn't make up if you tried. On page two another was 'Director of Parent & Family Relations & Student Affairs Assessment' at a college in Albany, New York. Page four offered a 'Compliance Director at Krups.' Not to be confused with Krupp. Jim gave up. He knew he'd just gone through yet another of his classic work-avoidance techniques, all devised intuitively, following a strong instinct. Yet, no guilt involved, not a jot.

He blinked. Seven forty-five. He knew what he should do, but still somehow his mind refused to think about the funding application for a project on medical humanities. He dreaded its mindless detail. Any paragraphs he wrote would only be endlessly revised by some internal review committee chaired by a rival professor, a younger one, still eager about his career and its rapid, unjustified advancement. Sometimes Jim found himself hating such mediocrities, but lacked the passion to do so fully. Instead he wondered idly why so few contemporary novelists used adverbs, the new generation deployed only a few essential adjectives, an austerity toolkit of words. From his bookshelves he took down the novel which Carlin had given him at the end of their last meeting. He'd completed this thin tome without great enthusiasm. He studied the prefatory material again. The book was published in 2010 in Ullapool, something Jim hadn't noticed previously. He sensed synchronicity or uncanniness. The place sounded so familiar.

He looked online. 'Ullapool: a small town of around 1,300 inhabitants in Ross and Cromarty, the Highlands, Scotland.' Had he been there? Yes, seemed recognizable, somehow related to him. He read on. 'Ferries sail to Stornoway in the Outer Hebrides.' Naturally enough, this was familiar, somewhere else visited that he'd forgotten. In 1969 he'd sailed from Ullapool to Stornoway on the ferry for an outward-bound style expedition on the western coast of Lewis and Harris, more properly in Gaelic *Innse Gall* meaning 'isles of the foreigners,' which Jim knew from a school geography class was the largest landmass of the Outer Hebrides, in fact the third largest island after Great Britain and Ireland in the British Isles. He checked on the internet. So, both Britain and the Hebrides were archipelagos, even now such an exotic sounding word, redolent more of South Sea Islands than Scotland or the UK. Yes, a genuine archipelago. He recollected fondly being so young.

In those days Jim had been a black-haired fifteen-year-old, fit, lean, like the proverbial butcher's dog, running everywhere, walking miles. However, he'd been very emotionally uncertain, at times even desperately unhappy, yet somehow despite everything being not in his favour, in the face of his grim home situation, essentially, he remained a hopeful soul, finding the best in people, wanting to embrace life and maturity. On that expedition some of the London-based participants like himself flew back from Glasgow on a rickety old propeller-driven aircraft and in those days, you could smoke on planes, just as you might on buses, trains, tubes, in fact just about anywhere you wanted. He was terrified of flying back then, remaining traumatized by the very idea of being off the ground. Yet, despite his intense fear, conversations on that trip confirmed his wish to go to university, so impressed was he by the other working-class boys he met from Manchester Grammar School who were determined to do so. Previously for Jim this had been only a vague plan, although on his return it became an aspiration he still very much doubted.

In summer 1971 Jim returned to the Hebrides on a second expedition, to Eilean Fladday off the Isle of Raasay, the former's tiny settlement of three stone houses having been abandoned forever in 1965. There was neither electricity nor running water, only a generator and a well, which had still functioned with potable water to the expedition's delight. Without a toilet, latrines were dug, basically one long and deep ditch above which a tent was pitched, one with ventilation. A mouldering Gaelic Bible had been left behind in one of the kitchens of a croft, a forlorn remnant of the crofters' faith. Jim was in the expedition's advance party, having spent several nights in a warehouse in Fort William, before they'd taken a fishing boat with the expedition supplies to Fladday. After leaving the relative calm of Loch Linnhe, the sea was rough as the boat rounded both the Isles of Mull and Skye. Jim recalled the difficult time unloading as the rocking vessel bucked and swayed, but they managed. On landing, a local sheep farmer met them with a shotgun, indignant they were being allowed to encamp amidst the abandoned crofts on land that his estranged brother owned. He was Cain to his brother Abel, although this murderous Cain retained only the grazing rights. After they left Jim presumed their feud continued unabated, perhaps still did if they had both survived into their reprobate seventies or eighties.

Eight-thirty and Jim knew he really ought to concentrate, and avoid memories of earlier times. He should leave that to weekends. He attempted to focus on his original train of thought, but he returned instead to the postmillennial novel he'd been reading. Yes, he went through his own conceit again, retracing the idea. You were so rarely told anything about, say, the colour or texture of ordinary, everyday things in contemporary novels. Few of them allowed much digression at all even in an age of irrelevancies and illogicality. All such writers seemed directed, sparse, full of intention, even while stylistically, attitudinally they were supposedly oblique, opaque, askance. That was the intention. All that everyday stuff was pretty much taken for granted, a collective backdrop, same in novels, same in life. So, what if his shed was a Homebase autumn brown, painted not sprayed, slightly faded, exactly the same as his garden fence. Ignore the purple sheets upstairs in his bedroom, the matt black of the office's electric oil-filled radiator that was superfluous with today's heat. Clearly, Jim still did not want black and white magpies described as such, to quote a novelist friend. However, for Jim the composite narrated fictional world of the late twentieth and early twenty-first centuries was all: Action, Dialogue, Events, Irony and Style. At a guest lecture for someone else's module he indicated them on a 'PowerPoint ©' he'd prepared for students who were paying little attention, texting surreptitiously and openly yawning. Take issues of style, a matter of aesthetic choice with generational implications it seemed. The novel he'd just finished reading had virtually no adverbs on its opening pages, except 'quickly' on the second, none on the third, an adventurous 'noncommittally' on page four together with a veritable rash at the bottom, a 'finally' followed by a 'generally,' with another adverbial rationing on page five, on six a 'usually'. Chapter Two had on page seven 'violently' (of seagulls again), eight 'originally', and another 'quickly' and retracing his saccades, the jumps of textual reading, Jim wondered whether he might or ought to include something adverbial from the sentence or phrase 'How little it meant anything,' which he didn't understand. Was the grammar just wrong? Or, was he being dim?

Without his glasses, he tired of his game, the next page a strain with its tiny typeface. Moreover, his notes would never form the basis of any genuine research. So, what was the point? Well,

well, he thought, as he reviewed his scribbled notes on coloured squares of paper, 'noncommittally' was about as audacious or foolhardy as this novelist was prepared to be, the rest of her adverbs were all very bland. No élan, no vitality, no virtuosity, no zip. Yet he knew that was precisely the point: all post-postmodern knowingness, a requirement to be arch, clever, and self-referential. These latter terms represented words from one of the lists he once used to prompt a mass of students in their discussions, but mostly they preferred being told the answers by him, copying the information he supplied, being entertained by his YouTube recordings, author interviews, looking at downloaded pictures. The modern university was becoming part of the entertainment industry, a pallid version of showbiz, a cog in the same business as the *goggle box*. That term rattled around his head like a pair of marbles! He looked at the recently finished novel again. Page three had the detective as not part of the story, an outsider looking in, acting as another reader. Clever stuff! Admittedly Jim liked the book, had enjoyed re-reading passages well enough, but where was the depth, the breadth, the excitement he remembered from the classics? It wasn't just this novel: all these elements seemed to be missing in most contemporary stuff. His suspicion was that maybe that was true of life itself. Existence had contracted. Then another thought came: unless you were young, perhaps? Even then, maybe not, maybe youth were all endlessly bored, broke, well in debt, anchorless, unable to climb the property ladder, underpaid. That was how it looked from the outside. Momentarily, these ideas cheered him until he remembered his son with partner, and grandson who until very recently had been paying fifteen hundred quid a month for a basement flat in Clapham, and now they were living in Congleton, not far from Manchester. Jim wasn't keen on the north.

With a jolt Jim realised it was already nine-forty, with no lectures planned, no research undertaken. Immediately Jim remembered year on year of his own teaching and publication on post-war British fiction, an area that was of great comfort to him, having lived through most of it. However, recently much of his time had been concerned with managing a funded project and writing a joint book. Both were concerned with real life narratives which had been collected and used in applied social research, looking at attitudes towards older people and their responses. With a small team of staff, other malcontents, Jim applied for funds somewhat tentatively, when their jobs had been under threat after Carlin had discovered a large deficit. Management blamed staff despite their own responsibility for budgeting. Carlin made it clear that Jim was in line for redundancy if the predicted cuts came about. However, fortuitously Jim's team was successful, money awarded, about half a million quid. Even Carlin was impressed. The project had delivered. That was the crucial element, although subsequently Carlin was promoted again, so maybe still more cuts might follow. Did Jim mind having to change course, being forced into going off in a new direction? Well if he did so, as his boss suggested it hardly mattered. As Carlin added Jim would just have to find a new source of external income to survive. Carlin stressed the matter in no uncertain terms. Carlin wasn't required to do so, not as a manager. Without funding maybe more changes loomed, Carlin added. Exactly what these might entail was not fully explained. Jim needed to look at matters from a different perspective, Carlin suggested. Outside a very few prestigious scholars in a few elite universities no one was prepared to pay for research exclusively and intensively committed to narrow literary fields. Such days were gone. Jim knew the implications of Carlin's homily. One could not afford too much time on such research. A book could not take more than a few years, most of the research to be undertaken in one's own time. Who wanted more and yet more academic books on *Jane Eyre*, the Brontës, Dickens, or even B.S. Johnson or Kurt Vonnegut? Certainly not many among the circles that included government, politicians, their advisors, or the bosses they influenced in universities with the snap of their fingers. Such scholarship seemed to be regarded suspiciously, parsimoniously, illiberally, stingily, and with downright hostility by many. Carlin didn't care. He'd only written one book, adapting his doctoral thesis many years previously. Just how had Carlin phrased his objections? Such work was *insufficiently engaged*, not *impactful* or *outward-facing* enough. He spouted the current jargon, reflecting bloody-minded managerialism.

Ten-fifteen and Jim felt slightly, peripherally depressed. He made yet another mug of tea in the kitchen, seeking signs of whether mice had returned after the last generation of intruders had been poisoned. Victorian terraces made it difficult to exclude the squirming little beasts, as they were in effect porous, with gaps between houses in the roofs and beneath the floors. Apart from potential vermin infestation, Jim had other grounds for being downright disconsolate. He'd an underlying worry about the bowel cancer testing kit, sent in the post by his health authority a month after his sixtieth birthday. Challenging not just in terms of the potential health implications if he failed the test, but also the matter of how one somehow might collect a sample of one's faeces. 'How to Use Your Test Kit.' The jolly, enclosed leaflet sported a cartoonish older bloke on its cover who advised in a speech balloon using a plastic bag over one's hand, or a wad of folded toilet paper, or even . . . . This all seemed entirely optimistic, and he wondered whether the leaflet's writer had tried out the suggested techniques. Given his weight Jim could see them all being less than easy.

'How to Use Your Test Kit' had very probably been written by somebody much, much younger than him, and far, far slimmer. Idly he thought of a new hypothetical career advising on older people's day-to-day difficulties, a consultancy about ageing, the subject of his last academic project. Now he knew about it from direct personal experience. These days just wiping one's arse was bad enough at times! Hence, he'd been putting off collecting his shit for medical perusal via the post, just leaving it for another week. However, now it was April and he realized the package had arrived in March, maybe late February even, and lay unopened on his kitchen table. Although the leaflet stated that the unopened the kit should last for months, he knew he ought to get underway, undertake some faeces retrieval, and become an unpaid collector of his own shit. Last week a conference in Brighton had been his excuse, not wanting to take the testing materials with him. And that toilet in his bathroom in the very unexpectedly gay-oriented hotel with garish décor and pink flooring near the Brighton pavilion had proved difficult to use. Some toilet bowls just didn't allow sufficient room for the larger figure. Not a problem he'd envisaged when he was younger and running marathons, thin and agile. Sixty seemed improbable, but there it was, he'd reached that landmark.

Once it happened, the alternative was far less palatable. Yesterday he cycled six miles to the Abbey, but still he was too fat, ate too much food, drank too much wine, too many gin and tonics, and took insufficient exercise. He'd bought a new white cotton formal shirt recently, seven quid from Tesco. Such amazing value, especially with its nineteen-inch collar, so much cloth for the price. He couldn't believe he'd let himself go. Yet he'd seen it happen to others. The appetites remained after intense activity diminished. All part of these awful mechanics of him getting old. Indeed his next project was probably going to be focused on dementia. That was such an inviting prospect, Jim reflected ironically, both professionally and personally! Although it was in exactly such areas where funding might be found, which everyone reminded him. Follow the money, so went the dictum! He said so himself, advising his younger colleagues concerning such an instrumental, pragmatic reality. So much for contemporary academia!

At his desk, perusing online papers, avoiding a new funding application, a surely very complex and demanding process, he was drawn by an online headline about Sue Townsend. He looked at the time on the computer. Ten-forty. He was reminded once more that she'd died a few days before. He remembered hearing a report on his car radio a day later driving back to his university campus from Brighton after his keynote address which had started a conference. Here was the news again in black and white. He sighed, feeling melancholy. He skip-read the first obit he found, online, *The Scotsman* ... born in Leicester ... father a postman ... mother a bus conductor... failed to learn to read at school ... fear of a violent teacher ... taught by her mother when she was at home ill at the age of eight

. . . . Richmal Crompton's *Just William* books. Jim loved those himself, had finished them all about age nine, using a clutch of library tickets at the Carnegie library in working-class north London, his own, his father's and his mother's. Twelve books every visit, in holidays twice a week. Of course, the writer in *The Scotsman* lauded Adrian Mole as an everyman for the times. Jim preferred *The Queen and I* rather than those awful Adrian Mole books in whose creation he'd actually played a very small part a few years after graduation, a time about which he seldom thought, still living in the Midlands, married for four years, training as a schoolteacher, becoming the father of what would prove to be his only child. On his screen he read two more obits: first in *The Telegraph* and next in *The Guardian*.

Back in the late 1970s, early 1980s for around four years Jim knew Sue, then a working-class single mother of three kids living in a terraced red-brick house in Leicester's sprawling red-light district. She'd aspirations to write and, almost miraculously obtained a bursary to script a play for the local fringe theatre, the Phoenix. She'd earlier joined a writing group that the Phoenix housed, later becoming their writer-in-residence. The theatre performed several plays by Chris Challis, a local poet whom Jim knew reasonably well, a role model as far as research and writing were concerned simply because Challis actually published, and Jim hadn't. Like Jim, Sue had been a working-class autodidact obsessed with all things literary, both aspirant writers. They'd shared that elusive passion. As he remembered, the main difference between them had been his transition at eleven to a Tudor grammar school in a London suburb, therefore the beneficiary of a more than half decent education. In contrast Sue had failed her eleven-plus, leaving a secondary modern school for a shoe factory aged fifteen, followed by a series of dead-end jobs. Nevertheless, she'd succeeded where in many ways Jim had failed.

In a flash, looking back at his youth, he realized that in that period clearly Sue exhibited far more empathy than Jim, she felt for other people, whereas he was somewhat self-obsessed in the way he thought many young people still were. There was, for instance, her strong fascination with Daniel Lambert, a Leicester resident during the Romantic Period, so renowned for being so immensely fat his clothes were still exhibited in the local museum on New Walk. Lambert weighed in at over 50 stone, at that point the heaviest person in recorded history. Dead at thirty-nine, his coffin was built with wheels, 112 square feet of wood. Jim remembered the exhibition. He thought Lambert obese, an awful provincial freak show. More recently Jim could begin to empathize as he could never have done at that time. The younger Jim's life was defined by energy, libido, arrogance, self-pity and the dismissiveness of youth. Jim's own ambition to write foundered, maybe because of the emotional deficiencies of his circumstances.

In full flow, Jim forgot to divert his thoughts away from the fact of Sue's death, and instead he chose to continue recalling the better times, the past, when he had hopes as well as energy. He remembered one occasion when Sue twice asked him directly 'What do you want to write about, Jim?' It had been early November 1979, about six months after Thatcher's first electoral victory, an appalling new phase they both agreed. Outside the lights sparkled in the rain as the night darkened. They'd been sitting together in a group after a meeting about a new proposed arts magazine, in a pub long since closed, the Magazine in Newarke Street, opposite the old Phoenix Theatre, Leicester city centre. Sue and Chris Challis had associations there, contacts, something of which Jim had so few. In the pub Jim and Sue were nominally with Challis, celebrated doctoral graduate of the university, published poet, with plays performed, one on BBC radio. He was in the rear bar buying drinks, but by the length of his absence, it looked as though he'd hooked up with some other contacts. A few students from the earlier discussions, five years younger than Jim, were huddled together, ignoring them after the meeting. If they thought he was over the hill, Jim realized, they clearly imagined Sue a dinosaur, being well over thirty. Jim was aching for a cigarette, but he'd quit earlier that year. Sue was puffing away, exhaling the smoke contentedly. When she repeated her question, gently prodding him, he realized he'd been daydreaming.

'I'm not at all sure,' Jim responded. He wanted something to say, to write about, but he realized he wasn't sure what his subject was. Nothing came to mind. His life seemed so small, the world so large. The day before militant Islamic students in Iran stormed the US embassy in Tehran, the capital, taking hostage more than ninety people. After Sunday lunch busily he marked essays submitted by his fifth year English Literature O-level class.

'I know.' She paused to light another cigarette, a roll-up. 'They say one should write from experience.' She smiled. 'Maybe that's just a cliché? I think a writer needs to look for the subtext, even in the most mundane of lives. You ought to be able to write of ordinary working people, those who struggle in life.'

'I've written a novel about a teacher, in a miserable job.'

'Is it going to be published?' Sue cut to the critical issue.

'I haven't tried. It concerns his tribulations, an unfaithful wife.'

'So, is yours?' her eyes brightened at the potential confidence.

'No, I don't think so. I made that bit up to add some conflict and suspense. It's set in Leicester, the first few scenes anyway, later in London. After a grim class he redeems his day, playing with friends in a football match in Loughborough, next gets drunk in a country pub, and a day later without warning he leaves his spouse for London, by train, instead of work.'

'Well. There's plenty going on. Maybe you're yearning for your old life, back in the smoke, and hankering for a new one back there?'

'I guess I might be. Ginnie would never move, hates London.'

'No, really? So, is she a difficult woman?' Sue pulled a face as she spoke. Jim nodded. He realized he was falling out of love with

his wife; that much he knew. In the earlier meeting he noticed
how pretty the young students were. They were so cheerful.

'I'm fed up with her. She lives for work and possessions, new
things for the house.' He grimaced. 'I need to be more creative.'

'Well, that's a conundrum' Sue responded. Looking back Jim
knew soon after that discussion she'd capture the minor absurdities
and pathos of the life of a complete nonentity, one more young
nobody with aspirations, revealing her vulnerabilities in a fashion
Jim could never have imagined doing himself. There might even
be just a touch of himself in what became Adrian Mole, which
she'd come up with the following year, the artistic aspiration
at least, the yearning. Neither of them really believed the arts
magazine would ever emerge, but events confounded them.

In Enfield in 2014 behind and above Jim's office, up in his attic,
buried in boxes, was a signed copy of the initial appearance
of a one-page story concerning Nigel Mole (as Townsend's
character had been originally named) published in 1980 (the
year that Jim's son had been born, hence his distinct recollection
of the date). Young Mole had first been featured in a now long-
forgotten slender arts magazine simply entitled *magazine*, lower
case title, very neo-Beatnik hippyesque typographical culture,
its cover a sketch of a Medusa's head, for some obscure reason
again long lost. Jim helped produce three issues in Leicester
while a postgraduate at the city's only university, for the other
degree-awarding institution was still a polytechnic in those
days, or the *polly* as it was generally referred to locally. At
magazine the editors commissioned the idea of the diary of a
Leicester schoolboy, his ambition to be a writer, thinker. As
Mole would do, like Jim himself, Sue wanted, even craved
publication, and so she set aside her important dramatic work
for a few hours every week to produce something for their arts
magazine, a comic feature. Nigel Mole's provincial schoolboy's
aspirations written in diary form were the results of her efforts.
In the upheavals of the production and distribution processes
Jim was moved from Poetry Editor in the first issue to Deputy

Editor in the second. As Jim remembered, one of their three issues had been laid out manually on Sue's kitchen table, the furniture dipped to remove generations of paint or varnish as was the fashion in the seventies, cleared (and scrubbed) for the task, its large bleached pine surface resting heavily and firmly on its broad knobbly legs. He could picture it now. That was as much as he recalled, apart from his and Sue's hard drinking throughout the process, and her enthusiastic half-chuckle, half-laugh and even more her odd, mischievous smile.

No, there was more. There were only two issues of *magazine* sold. Their third issue was impounded by the printers for bad debts, so never received, or distributed. Even the editors weren't allowed a single copy. That unavailable issue was the one that they'd set out at Sue's house by hand. The people involved in *magazine* formed a vague collective, but the two managing editors (who were required in order for the magazine to qualify for funding) decided to take their nomenclature seriously and spend most of their cash on *magazine*'s launch. Their argument was that they would attract even more dosh through regular advertising. There was very little take-up on that front, but lots of canapés eaten and free wine drunk. Nobody thought of a business plan, had any real idea of what that might even entail. It was very early 1980, but in Leicester the culture was still palpably 1970s among intellectuals, artists and their many wannabe counterparts in the city. Everyone who was anyone like Jim wanted to be a writer, or an artist or photographer (or all three), and cared little for liquidity, apart from Jim who had not been making the critical decisions, not when it mattered. The trouble was that the cash stream had run dry: no more business; no more credit; final full stop; everything over; kaput; all finished; sorry for you; bye, bye; no more being Mr. Nice Guy to a bunch of fucking wasters. The printer's manager was livid, berating *magazine*'s representative sent to beg for credit. Jim endured his tirade, facing the music all alone, suffering the veiled, yet repeated threats of being sued.

Back in those mythical days, when even Sue was simply another such wannabe, he'd been selected by his fellow editors to represent them. Why? He guessed, almost a quarter of a century later, because of his vaguely thuggish looks and leg-breaker's persuasiveness, a term years later a university colleague, who taught creative writing in prison to long-term lifers, used to describe Jim. Apart from Sue the others involved drifted into obscurity. So, *magazine*'s only real legacy was Sue's Adrian Mole. Jim googled her. Just as he suspected, his search confirmed his impression of the when and where, the stages of her success. One doesn't recollect such distant memories with clarity; part of a now forgotten history. Such memories that remained were more intuitive, impressionistic. And more than most he'd a conscious capacity to forget. He put things behind him, effaced them, moved on, and lived in the moment. That was his knack, motivated to find his solution to trauma by an appalling childhood and ghastly father.

As a child Jim would simply not let that awfulness intrude, ruin the moment. Hence early on he'd developed an unerring capacity to live in and for the present, to set nasty things aside. His friendship with Sue Townsend had once had social resonance. For a while people used to be very impressed that he knew her. Really, they'd say, you really know her? You know her well? He did would be his reply, pretty well. This implied intimacy had even provided a conversation piece with some (but only a few) women at parties. Subsequent to their collaboration, Sue had drawn on her three diaries for *magazine* to write a radio play, *The Diary of Nigel Mole, Aged 13 1/4*, broadcast by BBC Radio 4 on New Year's Day 1982. Jim thought of her life, but was more concerned with her death. Here was someone deceased whom he'd known briefly but very well, not that much older than himself. Born in 1946, she'd been an archetypal baby-boomer – well, if one were to split hairs about the matter, apart from the usual longevity of most of that generation. He knew from rumours supplied by people he'd known in Leicester that despite her success Sue had remained a parochial and ordinary, if wealthy woman, buying a large, old vicarage near where she grew up. She was always grounded, in the streets and institutions of Leicester. Wikipedia in its own manner confirmed her localism. Jim read, 'Amongst her honours and awards, she received honorary doctorates from the University of Leicester, Loughborough University and De Montfort University, Leicester,' all of course within a ten-mile radius of where she'd grown up. God, Jim himself, a dyed in the wool Londoner, had grown to loathe much of Leicester, but it had long been part of his life, for almost a decade. Much later he'd gone back for an interview at the other university where in questions at the end he recommended another candidate, an ex-colleague. Jim found himself reluctant to contemplate a return. After London, Leicester seemed exceedingly tiny and inward-looking. Initially that had been reassuring at eighteen, arriving as a fresher, and in a way he missed those times with their peculiar mix of optimism and despair. Youth had been such an odd phase constituted by testosterone, vague cravings, uncontrollable desires and so much misdirection, notwithstanding all the excess of long hair, beards, leather overcoats, and loose flares that had been involved in his day. He cringed inwardly at the memories, although beards were very much back, even among footballers. It was eleven-fifteen with little achieved, he reflected, not even a shave or shower. The drive he'd possessed ten years previously and which once so animated his career seemed increasingly distant, just like the friends he'd lost.

Sue brought home the reality of mortality, the possibility of dying early, well before what he fondly imagined might be his allotted time. Her origins and commitment made him think of Cedric 'Buzz' Biddwell or the 'Bagman' as Jim nicknamed him after his friend's sudden and curious career change. This other close friend was also originally from Leicester. Living alone in north London, he died prematurely, rather tragically in his mid-forties immediately after the millennium. There was another parallel Leicester death, in the last part of the previous century, of Chris Challis. A six-foot-plus inveterate drinker he tumbled (presumably drunkenly) down the stairs of his narrow-terraced house in Leicester, to where he'd migrated from Essex. Jim had almost forgotten him, but once they'd been close, toward the end of Jim's time in the city, when he knew Sue so well. Challis was a poet, dramatist and writer of all sorts – even pornographic stories it was rumoured. When he arrived in the city in the late 1960s Challis lopped ten years off his age and registered as a mature student at the only university at that point. In the hairy, beard-covered and mostly non-computerized sixties nobody noticed his sleight of hand, presumably he'd completed A-levels as a mature student at a point he could claim to have been eighteen rather than twenty-eight. Jim remembered his own facial hair, similarly excessive in the early 1970s. Such a time ago, years long gone.

And now, despite her riches and success, poor old Sue was dead, just eight years older than Jim, getting no further than sixty-eight. To Jim to go at such an age was beginning to represent a premature ending. He might not have longer than that left, not even another eight years, maybe far less. This imminence, the very possibility felt vertiginous, more than slightly appalling. He thought of poor old Cedric, all alone, cursed by his parents with a slightly ridiculous, eminently mock-worthy first name, later found dead in his Islington council maisonette. Cedric had been one of the few who had believed in Jim's intellect, his capacity to write. Jim had dedicated two of his over twenty academic books to his friend's memory, knowing full well Cedric would have much preferred them to have been novels. Cedric's fate was so uncannily like that of Challis in the thin redbrick terrace house he'd inhabited in Leicester, similar no doubt to Cedric's family home, although slightly better proportioned. Jim looked at the photo of the four generations of Dents taken two months after the birth of his first grandchild, Hugo, just before the death of his father. There they were with the baby: James himself, his own son William or Will, and his father Howard Arnold Dent, the latter reluctant to be photographed, thinking it might reflect his hidden struggle with age and illness. Hugo was dangled on his great-grandfather's knee. Even though at present Jim was privileged in being able to spend half the working week in his underpants at home, this was proving a most depressing start. All these dead people, what with him being overweight and unfit, depressing unless he could change his ways and pretty fast at that.

Chapter Two: Objections, Complications, April 2014

Still in his office Jim was further waylaid from actual work by a vague notion that he might write about all these lost souls, former friends, people like Challis and Cedric. He'd memorialize them in fiction. He'd written books in his youth, admittedly unpublished. Such random thoughts wormed into his head, interrupted by a ringing phone. He answered. 'Jim?' said a voice he recognized immediately.

'Hi there, Alfred,' Jim knew not to shorten his fellow journal editor's name. No Alf or Alfie for him. Alfred required formality, status. His call sought confirmation of their lunch meet, which was why Jim ought to have shaved and showered already. He was way behind schedule, and nothing much done.

It was eleven-thirty. Without further thoughts about work, Jim needed to ready himself *rapidly*. As they chatted, he worried about his localized forgetfulness, at times burning his breakfast when a work task took over, pressing ahead unmindful of the sausages cooking in his oven, an occasional charred mishap.

'So, you still on for lunch?' Alfred asked. Jim looked again at the clock. It was already eleven-fifty, if the battery wasn't flat.

'I am, but I'm really busy,' Jim lied. 'And more to do.'

'Working on another project, Jim?' asked Alfred.

'Yes, but it's not an academic one, at least not strictly so.' He paused for effect. 'I'm going to write a novel, about people I've known. They've all died prematurely,' Jim explained. At that very moment, in a bright flash, having thought about Sue, he'd made up his mind that he would use many of the people he'd known and with whom he'd shared crucial moments as characters in a quasi-autobiographical book. He would focus on the dead ones, those who departed prematurely. He'd resurrect them, and breathe new life into them on the page. Thus, he'd fulfil his ambition of becoming a genuine writer, of fiction. Thinking on his feet, impetuously Jim made up a vague outline which he explained to Alfred as it popped into his head, pretending he'd planned it for months.

Pausing after Jim finished Alfred sounded profoundly uncertain, and started laughing. 'That would all be somewhat confusing I would think.' As Jim knew well, Alfred was always contrary, prone to offering an oppositional view. In fact, he never endorsed an idea or plan without first raising some very specific objection or even a number of them when he was at his best. 'You've known many people who died young, Jim?' He sounded sceptical.

'Well, yes, to be honest I have, when I come to think of it.' He could think of at least nine immediately. 'I'll mix the dead with the living, episodes in the past, some in the present. The difficult aspect is to include sufficient comedy, especially about my severely depressed friend, Steve Knapper, who hanged himself. Given it was so bleak, I'm a little worried about how to effectively include him.'

'Well, yes, so you should be. The subject is distressing, extremely morbid! I worry the concept is in bad taste.'

'Look, it will all be approached positively' replied Jim, 'so I hope it won't be morbid. I mean, we're surrounded by death on a daily basis. We just close our eyes to it all. I had great times with all these people. Telling their stories could be therapeutic. The main character, loosely based on me, will recollect the different episodes in random order as they come to him, as if in flashbacks.'

'So, not chronological, then?' Alfred's disapproval was obvious.

'No, I don't think so. Its logic is chance, memory, the narrative controlled by the unconscious mind. Well, that's my idea. It's more of a jigsaw, pieces fitting into place all over the board, a process of accretion.' The ideas and episodes were cascading in

Jim's head as he spoke, a list of potential characters forming. He'd jot it all down on the journey, in a notebook he'd been searching for as he spoke among the jumble in his office, if it turned up. He felt enthused, but sad. 'I feel I should include people like poor Steve Knapper. Do you remember his death?'

'No, not really, I only met him once, very briefly.'

'Oh, I forgot.' Jim assumed Alfred knew Knapper, could share Jim's grief, would instinctively understand his need to write this particular book, to stop the memories fading, from diminishing, and finally altogether. 'My book is a memory palace, quasi-autobiographical, random acts of recollection about real people.'

'Random is not good, Jim.' Alfred paused. 'What's your title?'

'I thought it might be *Gin & Tonic*. What do you think?'

'Oh, no, no,' Alfred responded immediately. 'No, that's so grim, Jim, remarkably unappealing. You'd definitely struggle for readers with a title like that. You might as well print in bold script **"Do Not Read this Book!"** on the front cover. Let's talk later?'

'Sure.'

'We said twelve forty-five at Euston. I was really ringing to confirm that I can be there *promptly*. Will you make it in time?'

'Sure, I can. Actually, I'd better rush. So, could we meet at one, instead? That OK?' After Alfred assented Jim put the receiver back in its cradle. He checked emails cursorily to see whether he'd missed anything important. No. But there was another apparently from a woman who'd sent one earlier, Eileen Beckett. This time there was no attachment. No time to read it though, he realized. Maybe he might do so later. She seemed persistent, which might augur trouble. Although maybe she was a prospective student, he thought. He was really late. Almost twelve already and he needed to rush to meet Alfred on time, and his colleague would need to return to work promptly. His schedules were tight, especially in his new work environment, a private American university. Jim might arrive just after one if he hurried. Still, capturing the moment he savoured his life being far less pressured than Alfred's, time still available at least for some research and scholarship. Not enough, but still some left to think and write, occasionally.

As he showered, he recalled that he could use his free sixty-plus Oyster card, in London one positive aspect of this whole business of getting older, courtesy of Boris Johnson, the blond buffoon, whose very name reminded him of a school-friend who'd died on a trip abroad aged fourteen, who Jim might include. He hadn't thought of him for years. And Jim was about to write again, and not just one more academic work, but a novel, his first real attempt to do so in almost twenty years. He felt enthused about the prospect, a rare quality at this stage of life. The twilight years might prove not to be entirely and irredeemably bad, not simply a steady decline, everything reduced to a struggle to survive. This was a typical baby boomer attitude, just like that eternal youthfulness permeating many of the subjects of his last study, all those old people exhibiting a determined defiance of the real facts of life, denying any decline and refusing death itself. Well, who could really blame them, Jim thought. Like him they'd all once been young and full of beans, and some of them were just not letting go, still thinking they were at the centre of the universe and would remain so for a good while yet, a second adolescence.

As he sat in a train carriage speeding away from Enfield Lock station, for no particular reason Jim found himself thinking of his son, Will, in summer 2003. Jim was avoiding a visit by his ex-wife. Rather he spent his night with Cedric, a friend who lived nearby. During Jim's train and tube journeys he jotted down half a page of spidery notes about those weeks in 2003, setting down the major dynamics underlying the trip of the Wicked Witch to London, by which term Jim referred to his ex-wife, or the Wicked Witch of the East Midlands to give her full unofficial title. She'd ventured south during Will's protracted stay in Jim's flat in Tufnell Park, their son their sole connection after a divorce more than twenty years previously. On another page Jim listed a few other potential characters and episodes drawn from his life and underlining the significant aspects, about eight people in total, all expired, plus Knapper's death also underscored three times followed by three question marks, given that mentally he was still reluctant to explore this event at all. He decided he might leave Knapper out of his account, given the emotional difficulty of the topic. Knapper's appalling fate still unsettled him, made him emotional.

Despite such distractions cascading from the past, Jim managed to reach town for lunch with Alfred, only very slightly late, but forgiven almost immediately. Over burgers they talked of the journal, of Alfred being ultra-busy, the dreadful state of British academia, and the demise of English Studies (the latter lately a favourite topic of Alfred's). Afterwards they took coffee outside Euston Station sitting in the sunshine. Alfred offered another opinion. 'It's not the time to be writing a novel, surely, with all the hassle at work? I just wish I had the time and luxury to procrastinate for a single bloody hour, or even a moment at times. Jim, you're exceedingly lucky to have any opportunity to think, to write.'

'Writing a novel is not avoidance or procrastination.' Jim explained a specific, unexpected reason for his freedom. With a recent change in his faculty, about to be subsumed into another at the end of the academic year, four months away, Jim was outmanoeuvred, ousted. In the jockeying for favour in the forthcoming reorganisation a Machiavellian rival appropriated Jim's role as Research Coordinator. Since teaching was allocated in the previous academic year Jim was unexpectedly free from most daily duties until September, liberated, unchained, a period of freedom beckoning. In stark contrast Alfred's job seemed, even from Jim's impressions gained from phone calls and broken appointments for editorial chats over coffee, crushingly busy, multiple duties as an administrative academic in a private American university, very capitalist, a money-oriented world.

'Your novel,' Alfred suggested suddenly, returning to Jim's ideas sketched out rapidly on the phone, 'the one you mentioned earlier.' By the studied way he approached the topic, Jim sensed his fellow editor had planned his objections, since he even referred to notes on a small pad, 'First, the way you described your ideas, the reader would be meeting people alive again after they've already died, killed off earlier in the book. Have I got that right? It's mixed up, with no forward momentum, little narrative drive. I feel this wouldn't work. The reader would get lost. In truth, Jim, I can't see them liking it much. And, then second . . . . '

'Hang on. As to your first point, I'll tell them when each chapter or section is set, use headings with dates. The overall point is to memorialise those who have passed on actively, rather than just have memories. I can restore them in all their wonderful confusion.'

'So, who are you including? Do I know them at all?'

'No, not really. There are school-friends, a lecturer I knew well, another tutor from my first research degree, or at least I think he died, and a friend from university days. All died early, young.'

'Oh no, they really did?' Alfred said. 'That's so sad.'

'Actually, I might include family members, although of course they've died later in their lives. Anyway, it's drawn from life.'

'Still,' said Alfred, 'it still sounds too grim, as if you're exploiting people's loss or grief.' His tone and face exuded disapproval.

Jim tried to explain his intentions. He could include an episode in the sixties, about an old school friend who'd died, certainly Cedric's death in the early noughties, 2003. There was the Bunting visit with Chris Challis (who was later to die youngish) in early 1980 after the Christmas when Jim's marriage was falling apart, and meeting Sue Townsend in 1999 or thereabouts. There was Jim's own father in 2012, as well as that of Knapper. That was a particularly bad time. 'Maybe the order could follow the protagonist's thoughts and be linked, with death and creativity as the overriding themes of the book, something like that.' Jim knew what he wanted. Each episode would draw upon a significant period in his life, explore the part he played in very different situations, revisit his time in what had been another world when compared with this contemporary technological, post-industrial age. Jim could relive his youth, when he had energy and vigour, but suffered from so much panic and confusion at times, too.

'Going back to my earlier objection, that would be confusing, jumping all over the place, far too postmodern,' Alfred insisted. Jim recognized his colleague's perpetual negativity, most especially when it came to ideas and opinions held by others. 'As a reader how would I know where I'm going, what's next?'

'Well, the narrative regresses from the decision to write the novel, from 2014, its narrator is like me, being sixty, unfit, ageing, a former athlete, who is now overweight . . . .'

'So, very accurate,' Alfred said. Jim ignored his insult.

'The protagonist moves through his life in acts of memory, each episode concerns his (and therefore my) significant relationships with those who have died, various points for instance when he'd been a different self, younger, fitter, better looking, knowing less, more gullible, perhaps with far more illusions.'

'Randomness in effect: how's your reader to make any sense of a book like that? It's so confusing?' commented Alfred.

'Well, like B.S. Johnson's *The Unfortunates*, one follows acts of memory, each jogged out of his unconscious by the act of writing, each one spilling into the next, each largely self-sufficient.'

'Not literally unbound chapters, a book-in-a-box, I trust?'

'No, that would be far too expensive. Anyway, clearly it's been done!' Jim responded. 'However, I'd incorporate a level of randomness, by following the logic of the unconscious. . . .'

'No, I still think such a strategy is far too confusing.'

'I'm not so sure of that. Just remember the protagonist retrieves aspects of his past, some episodes overlaid by earlier memories, but each would be centred on just a day or two, moments that epitomize his life and identity shared with those who influenced him during a specific period, each one different.'

'What type and when?' demanded a curious Alfred.

'Well, after an initial chapter setting the scene, early episodes would centre on 'The Bagman,' an alcoholic, Cambridge graduate who came from Leicester. He lived in poverty off the Hornsey Road. I knew him well. He believed in me as a writer, encouraged me positively, both in creative writing and my academic career before anyone else. Not many people rated me back then, you know. They treated me like an idiot.' He paused thoughtfully. 'Well, another episode might be set in 2003 when my son stayed with me at my old flat, and the second in 1999 when after lunch with the Bagman I cycled up to Enfield to meet Sue Townsend . . . to get her to sign a magazine in which she'd featured.'

'I'd forgotten that you knew her. You two were pretty close?'

'Not latterly, but yes, I knew her pretty well, in the late seventies and early eighties before I left Leicester. Anyway, back to the novel: pursuing the Leicester connection the narrative moves back to late 1979, amid the scene of the protagonist's ruinous marriage, in Leicester, including a subsequent trip in early 1980 to visit the poet Basil Bunting.' In Jim's head the novel was as good as written. 'The protagonist's companion is a long-forgotten Leicester scribbler of poetry, drama and various other odds and sods, Chris Challis, who knew Sue Townsend too, both were drinkers. There are several links, various interconnections. The provinces were vibrant artistically back before Thatcher got a real grip. Then maybe I'd go even further back to 1968 and my schooldays, with a scene centred on a school friend who dies, maybe squeezing in a recollection or two about a film that we were involved in making, me and a group of schoolfriends. That would have the protagonist as a schoolboy, trying to write and act in that film, unfinished of course. In the last phase I would end after my father's death in 2012, moving back to the present, the up-to-date version of the life following the thoughts of the based-upon-me-character.'

'Oh no, Jim, you'll lose your readers. I still reckon it's far too complicated,' objected Alfred. 'And it'll be difficult to write so many different disparate episodes, to make the main character so variable. I mean looking at him as a schoolboy, in an early but doomed marriage, in mid-life, and finally as an old man.'

'So, that's how you see me. Thanks a bundle.'

'OK, an *older* man, then,' interceded Alfred.

'Well anyway, about the structure, Alfred, I just don't agree with you. Readers are far more intelligent than you assume. They'll manage. I'll put the month, dates and years as markers throughout, so that it'll be just like someone flipping back through old diaries, dated photos and journals, like skipping between different scenes as they take your fancy. I'll create a palace of recollections, all interlinked by the reality of death-in-life.'

'It's a very risky strategy for a novel. And as I said it's all potentially very confusing, and gloomy too, very much so. If any reader managed to finish your book, they'd be thoroughly depressed.'

'Well, they'll either like it or they won't, the readers. It's a Marmite situation, each to his own taste. Remember they're proper grown-ups. Most readers, can be pretty adaptable, and resilient.'

'Well, you'll have to change the names.' Jim concluded that Alfred was clearly in a serial objection mode, firmly negative, a familiar stance on many issues, so not really personally directed.

'Only those of the living. The dead can't sue, you realise.' Jim was thinking of other likely candidates. He might add an associated interlude after the school-day episodes, a flash forwards to meeting several old friends, including an old mate he reconnected with in the early 1980s, who had died young, and there was the one whose career died in his mid-twenties, who never worked ever again, still hadn't, living on a legacy in rural Wales, his wife a teacher. Maybe he might fit them in, maybe not.

'Just don't put me in this book, will you. And if you were to, please don't kill me off. I'm sure I'd find that most unpleasant reading.'

'You'll be one of the first characters, Alfred, featured in the first full chapter, your unalloyed, unaltered, intractable, contumacious self.' Alfred snorted, clearly disbelieving him.

'In my opinion any fiction with unremarkable people like me included as characters would be so utterly dull.'

'I could simply include your utter scepticism, a cameo role, a literature professor unaware of his own literary potential.'

'There's that, I suppose, but people wouldn't get the irony.'

'They might. The book could be about the triumph of the everyday?'

'Well, everyday life is far too boring, work, long hours, stress.'

'I might convey some of that boredom, the unpleasant qualities.'

'I've never seen it done, to be honest, not well. And the title you mentioned earlier, *Gin & Tonic*, a truly terrible choice, Jim.'

'Well, the title is unimportant, changed easily enough. I

think I'm going to start with the theme of procrastination, the protagonist's inability to focus, his avoidance of his new academic work, including his refusal to focus on funding applications.'

'Remember, if included I'm not Alfred. Use my middle name.'

Later at home, Alfred's analysis of the rapid demise of British universities still radically depressed Jim, in particular the associated account of the terminal decline of English Literature as a viable subject in most institutions. Alfred predicted it would wither away, apart from in the most prestigious universities. At half-five, back at his desk Jim felt his earlier mood of pessimism lift. Although earlier he'd disagreed with Alfred, now reflecting on this crisis Jim wondered whether his fellow editor's hypothesis might not have been correct. So what? After all who needed three years of learning how to read storybooks? Ridiculous!

Jim thought of Carlin, but the phone rang. Distracted, he answered. As if prompted by earlier thoughts, Jim recognized the voice of his son, Will, to date his only child. Not that Jim ever imagined any others were likely to follow at this stage of life, unlike the ageing celebrity fathers who featured in the tabloids. One wondered about the likes of Steve Martin, David Jason, Paul McCartney, Rod Stewart and David Essex. Jim found the very thought of sixty-plus parenthood pretty dubious, even absurd. Where would you find the energy? Gabi quite rightly would regard any such desire for yet more offspring as a sign he needed to be sectioned.

'So, how's the move been overall, son?' His son had relocated up north four months ago with his wife and son, Jim's grandson.

'Everything's fine,' Will responded. Jim thought how Will had escaped the exorbitant rents of London when the lease on their overpriced flat in Clapham ended. Their move saddened Jim. Will abandoned his post at Chatham House, enabling Kitty to move to the head office in Congleton of the drug company for whom she worked. The pair met while students at Exeter 'uni' as their generation universally labelled such institutions. In London they lived in a rented flat, part of Generation Rent, struggling to find the wherewithal to buy, part of a great exodus away from the capital, while in flowed the migrants. Gabi knew fellow Hungarians packed into houses, up to three sharing one room, remittance money from menial jobs sent home. Jim was troubled, his views contorted by such realities, feeling his liberalism exploited.

'Well, how are you in yourself, Will?' he asked. Over the past few years his son rang him only rarely. 'Aren't you missing work?'

'No, I don't. I feel great. We're all doing exceedingly well.' Will sounded cheerful. Well he might, Jim reflected. Will was no longer working, a man of leisure, his only commitment was as what used to be called a house-husband, although he found that onerous.

'So, you're keeping busy then?' Jim tried to eliminate any hint of disapproval, excising any critical edge, or so he hoped. Jim harboured profound doubts about this role of house husbandry on his son's part, especially as Will abandoned a career path for which he'd given up so much in its pursuance. Jim felt it best to avoid past controversies. 'I'm busy, especially with Hugs to look after,' Will continued, alluding to his wife's nickname for their son, Jim's first and only grandson. 'What with shopping, cooking, washing clothes, and all the rest, I'm rushed off my feet at times,' Will said testily. 'It's amazing how much time everything takes.'

'So, you're all adapting to the new place?' Jim hardly knew what to say. He'd not yet visited his son. They hadn't spoken in almost four months. He had no idea of their new routines. For a long while after Hugo's birth he'd met with Will, who took the baby along to weekly meetings for coffee or lunch, but no longer, not even toward the end of their time in London, which bemused Jim.

'We're all fine. We've not left civilization. We do have supermarkets up here too, and libraries.' Not jobs, thought Jim, but held his tongue on the matter. That was pretty much the end of the conversation, only supplemented by a few more pleasantries.

On the roofs of the houses beyond Jim's garden two crows flew between television antennae, on a nearby tree a pair of jackdaws made an awful racket once more. Jim wondered about an airgun, but realized that someone might report him if he took pot-shots at these winged pests. Will continued 'Look, why I'm ringing is that Kitty's going to have to be in the London office for a fortnight. We wondered if we might all stay over at yours?' Until recently she'd worked at the London branch. Jim wondered. She said the promise was any return visits would be funded by work. He was feeling pressured by his boss, so wasn't keen on the suggestion.

'It's difficult at the moment. Work's not good.' Jim sighed involuntarily. 'Not going well. I've got a lot on at the moment.'

'We wouldn't be any trouble. I can take Hugo out every day. And there's the park nearby, for instance, so plenty of *divertissement*. We'll keep out of your hair, honest.' Jim was reluctant, as he knew he would still be distracted from his work. At the best of times concentration was difficult lately. He'd never been like this when he was younger. Indeed, having started late as a researcher, he'd been driven at times, super-productive.

'I suppose so.' Jim was silent, thinking of all the impending work, stymied by the immensity of it all. A distinct pause in the exchange followed, Jim already inattentive. He was looking up at the afternoon sky, the trail of two jets from nearby Stansted dissipated in the clarity of the proverbial clear blue sky above.

'So, what's so wrong at work?' asked Will, perhaps a little impatiently.

'My boss, Carlin, wants to close my courses, on Post-War British Fiction *and* Post-War Anglo-American Experimental Fiction. He claims they're not popular, insufficiently up-to-date.'

'Perhaps they're not? They do sound old-fashioned.'

'OK, but they're no worse than others. Not as bad surely as the

Brontës, or one on Shakespeare Authorship. Neither are up-to-date or have more students than mine. I'm being victimized.'

'Well why would he make such changes? He must have a reason.'

'Oh sure, but they aren't academic ones, not anything to do with the curriculum. Carlin reckons I have more student complaints than any other module. But you never know if he's either making it up or if he's actually encouraging them to be negative. Certainly, he never shows us any criticisms. There's never any actual evidence. And he says some of the complaints are about the books studied. Apparently, the students don't like long books, which many of my texts are. I believe him about that. He's not making that up. They always complain, every year.'

'Are you making them study exceedingly long books?'

'Well, Pynchon's *V*, Vonnegut's *Slaughterhouse-Five*, *The French Lieutenant's Woman*, and *On the Road*.'

'They're don't seem that long.' Will sounded bemused.

'Apparently, they are, according to most of our students, far too long. Or so the lazy little sods claim on the feedback forms.'

'Have they no shame, no pride? That's pretty poor.'

'Yes, it really is. Carlin says we must respond. Level out the demands on all students. If there aren't long books in Drama or Creative Writing, English should have none. It's all evidence for a real indictment of contemporary university education in literature.'

'So, there's no chance for *Moby Dick* or Proust then.'

'Oh no, none at all. Well, unless you spend weeks on them. One module is called literally 'Big Books' and they do two such novels over a twelve-week period, six weeks each. At the staff-student consultation meeting one of my students complained about too many of my books being over two hundred pages.'

'So, the bottom line is your boss intends to cut both courses?'

'Well, not entirely,' Jim responded, 'but they'll be radically revised. He proposes they should be merged with a course on the late twentieth century period, creating a broad year-long module on Anglo-American fiction from 1945 until 9/11.'

'So, it's not all that bad, really?' his son suggested.

'How can you say that? It'd be terrible. You're not thinking of the changes, new research involved, extra lectures to write, new sources to find so the little buggers won't have to find them themselves, which my boss Carlin seems to expect as a norm.'

'Shouldn't they find sources, demonstrate required skills?'

'Precisely, you'd think so. Not according to my boss. The current areas that I teach will make up only a tiny part of the proposed new module. With the revisions, I'll need to prepare loads of British *and* American texts published after 1975, recent stuff, authors like Richard Ford, Toni Morrison, and a plethora of others I've never read. As for the British it means featuring extra novels that I hate, by idiots like Salman Rushdie and Ian McEwan.'

'Grim in terms of workload, preparation' agreed his son.

'Well, there's more. I'm to be module leader and for another new course. Carlin has instructed me to develop post haste something on Post-Millennial British Fiction about which I know virtually nothing, to offer to the students in October.' He paused for the implications to sink in. 'The module guide must be issued pre-July so they might read the novels over the summer. None do so, but we're now required to offer everything in advance just in case.'

'Oh, I see, a real bummer.' Will paused. 'I could offer pointers.'

'Thanks, but I wonder if I really have enough time.'

'With six or seven weeks, you might just finish.'

'It's still tight. Can you see my dilemma? I'll be running out of time. I'm too old for this.' Jim paused. 'Carlin even loaned me a book to read he thinks I should include, borrowed by him from a young part-time lecturer, and the title was . . . something really weird like *The Existential Policeman.* . . .'

'No, Dad, it's called *Existential Detective*. It's really quite good. An old university friend recommended it. I read it recently.'

'I wasn't impressed . . . it's not convincing . . . . I couldn't work out what it was about. It's confusing.' He thought of Alfred. 'Nothing much happens. So, what do I say for a whole bloody lecture? Nothing stands out, apart from a missing woman. Where was she? I couldn't work that out. What was I missing?'

'Well, that's the point. Think of boredom, tedious life in a small seaside town. Talk about ennui, alienation, a rundown resort, holiday industry in decline,' suggested Will. Jim stayed silent, unconvinced. 'Well, dad we could talk it over if we come down.'

'I suppose we could.' Jim was warming to the idea, plus he knew he'd little choice. Maybe he could use Will's ideas for a lecture.

'OK, I'll email dates. I'll add ideas about teaching the book.'

'You'll make some notes and concrete suggestions?' Jim asked.

'Sure. Are you out on the bike at all?' Jim ignored the query.

'So that's agreed. We'll speak when you come down,' Jim responded, ignoring questions about exercise, cutting off the call. Also, he hadn't mentioned the new novel for some reason he couldn't fathom. Was he worried Will might disapprove, given he would feature. Jim knew what he wanted to write about, all those lost intimacies with people he couldn't interrogate any longer as they'd all died. He'd recreate all the ephemeral, but important moments spent together, set it all down. He thought of the past again, of times with far less work to do, far more leisure time, when he'd been far keener on Will's visits with Kitty. Looking at his large pot belly Jim concluded he ought to service his bicycle and commit himself to discovering the opening hours at the local pool. He thought of former times running over Hampstead Heath together with Will over the years, from the flat, maybe three times a week. In fact, they'd done so even more regularly when Will lived with him over one whole summer, the pair going for a run almost daily. About eleven years ago as far as he remembered. . . . This contact with Will made Jim think once more of 2003, his son staying for three months, being at Jim's for the first time ever for more than a week, which was as long as he was allowed to be there as a child and in his teens, never longer. And that had been a momentous summer, one of decisions made, directions taken.

Chapter Three: Avoiding the Wicked Witch, 3rd July 2003

Thursday 3rd July 2003, precisely 18.04, Jim sat in his Tufnell Park flat staring at the television. He glanced over at his son. Will sprawled in a worn brown leather swivel chair. Both wore shorts and T-shirts, sweating moderately. Unusually there was tension between them, so far unspoken. Jim cycled back from the British Library earlier for a run *and* to cook for Will, who was meeting his mother later. The Wicked Witch was decidedly not invited to Jim's flat. Her nickname derived from an occasion when father and son watched *The Wizard of Oz* together, Will about nine years old. Jim had compared the sharp features of the Wicked Witch of the West to those of his bony ex-wife, amusing his son, eagerly subversive. Instinctively, Will seditiously resisted maternal feminist authority. The term stuck, over time shortened. Wicked Witch sufficed. In his son's company Jim persisted with its repeated, teasing usage.

Today for some reason or other a slightly chubbier, middle-aged Wicked Witch was staying over in town. Jim ignored the reason for her visit. He resisted her malign suggestion, relayed by Will, about coming to the flat. Mother and son would meet in town, Covent Garden. Jim refused resolutely to be drawn into her life ever again. There was too much bad blood, too much bitterness, an excess of pain, at least on Jim's part. Her impending arrival caused underlying friction between father and son. Jim was expecting his friend, Cedric, so convenient Will was heading off.

Having missed previous changes to his son, to Jim Will seemed all grown up, in an instant more man than a boy. He was about to graduate for a *second* time, having just finished his Master's degree in French at Oxford. Since this august institution habitually gave away MAs for payment, or if one was more generous about the practice, as an honorific title, Will's qualification, M. St. or Master of Studies distinguished its nature; real study was required, for which Oxford could charge more fees.

Work was the main reason Will was staying at Jim's place. He had a paid gig, working the summer holidays at a local university, an ex-polytechnic on Holloway Road half a mile away. Will was processing application forms and speaking to students and parents during the so-called clearing process, the time when students tried to find a place when grades weren't as expected. In other universities some tried to trade up when they had better grades, but as Will had put it bluntly, 'Exceedingly unlikely to happen at this ex-poly unless they're totally bonkers or if they've just arrived from Jupiter or Mars!' For Will this temporary post wasn't just a way of earning cash, but a requirement to progress in career terms. His aim was to gain work experience, as he'd been turned down for civil service entry precisely because of such a deficiency, a distinct lack of any paid employment on his profile, indicating little experience. At the time Jim scoffed at the suggestion. He hazarded a guess that this probably did not apply in the case of Oxbridge-educated ex-public schoolboys and girls.

On dry nights they used the small garden as their extra living room, drinking beer or wine in the heat at the evening's end, chatting, sharing their days in a way previously denied them. Jim had split from his ex-wife when his son had been less than a year old, but mostly they remained in touch, close in a rather detached manner. Jim wanted more children, but life hadn't delivered on that desire. He still couldn't find the right woman. He particularly wanted a daughter, at least one, but it was a thought he buried. He wondered what he meant to his only son. Will for his part was uncertain quite what role in his father's life he was assigned. This summer Jim cooked nightly for them, preparing sandwiches for the following day for Will, using Jim's homemade bread and pre-prepared fillers from Tesco on Stroud Green Road. 'Don't eat them when you come back tonight,' Jim instructed his son.

Jim's friend, Cedric, lived nearby. He saw him on Fridays, for which night Will adopted a new ritual: drinking with colleagues until late in a pub near Holloway tube. Jim wouldn't even venture inside, it was so redolent of 'yoof,' with its blacked-out windows, loud live music, late drinking, dancing – all the things he'd once revelled in, but now in his last year before fifty he fled from. He was changing, not yet old, but maybe staid. Theirs was an odd sort of domesticity, since they'd never really lived together before, at least not as far as Will could remember. Father and son were unlike in many ways, products of different areas, class backgrounds and generations. Having grown up under Thatcherism in rural Leicestershire, as a sort of rusticated version of Nigel Mole only cleverer, Jim's now tall, handsome son was also incredibly determined in career terms, something a younger Jim had never managed, not until recently, in his late forties.

Back from Hungary, lecturing at an ex-polytechnic on the edge of Birmingham, Jim started to focus workwise on doing more than the minimum, putting his shoulder to the grindstone in research terms, in his attempt to move back to a post in London. He would need publication, he knew well enough. He totted up his existing stuff in his head: one monograph, another underway, one co-edited book collection in press, eight journal articles and another about his trip to Canada accepted (memoir and criticism), as well as three book chapters and a further three almost finished. He calculated he might soon apply for a readership, assessing what more he would need to publish to do so, and perhaps with some more effort, after that maybe he might go for a professorship.

Jim needed money, shelling out for digs in Birmingham as well as the mortgage on his flat, but such promotion was something he dared dream about only recently. The research exercise freed things up, opening pathways for promotion previously unanticipated. So too had technology, since Jim grasped the importance of computers, the web and email very early, long before most of his peers. Too many academics of a similar age in his field resisted the electronic world entirely, proud techno-dinosaurs. Yet as adaptable and flexible as he thought himself, there had been limits. Living and working north of Watford Gap, even the thought had unsettled him.

'You'll miss the Bagman tonight. He's coming over.' Jim

commented, breaking their silence, and his own thoughts about fatherhood.

'Damn, that's a real shame.' As Jim knew, Will very much liked his friend. 'I haven't seen him yet. Have you two fallen out?'

'No. He's got a new job, one which he hates, makes him reclusive, drinking far more than ever, if that's possible.'

'I have his card,' said Will. The Bagman was their nickname for Cedric Biddwell, a real English eccentric from Leicester, both amusing and literary. Jim's friend reminded him of Wemmick, Jaggers' inscrutable clerk in *Great Expectations*, with his frayed linen and glittering eyes, 'whose expression seemed to have been imperfectly chipped out with a dull-edged chisel.'

'The one he sent me to pass on for your graduation? What was it like? Was it comic? Remind me.' asked Jim.

'Well, sort of. Don't you remember? He had a card stashed away that read "Congratulation on the birth of a baby boy" on the cover, with some real doggerel inside, below which the Bagman signed himself Charles Baudelaire, his idea of a joke.'

'Yes, that's right, the very one. The truth was he was probably too drunk to go out and buy one or hadn't enough money.' Cedric was always desperately short of cash. However, once upon a time Cedric worked at the Law Society on a decent salary. He regaled Jim with tales about its drama society, established by Cedric, opposed by management, and other stories of the love of his life, a co-worker for whom he'd left his wife. For a while the pair lived idyllically on the fringes of Epping Forest. Thin, wiry, an alcoholic when Jim first met him, Cedric worked in a private university opposite Archway Tube, entitled optimistically London Transcontinental University or LTU. Housed in rooms above a Methodist Church, this curious institution was established by Dr Khan, a charming, softly spoken Pakistani academic and former scientist. He wore a short-sleeved jersey beneath his suit jacket even in summer. He'd once been part of his homeland's nuclear programme according to Cedric. LTU was partly a visa factory, although Cedric struggled very hard to bring in legitimate students. He was paid a pittance, but still taught his charges assiduously, even though his official role was designated as a general administrator, like a registrar, but nowhere near as grand.

Jim's first meeting with Cedric occurred because of Dan, a former American colleague at the further education college where both he and Jim had worked, who had been moonlighting as a language teacher at this other curious establishment, LTU. Cedric had been Dan's student, pursuing a PhD on the works of J.H. Prynne, the Cambridge poet, even though its award would have been worthless in terms of accreditation, as this self-established university was not recognized, except by the Home Office for visas to study basic English Language. Cedric had himself created the PhD programme, enrolling himself along with several aspirant, but lacklustre Chinese students eager to add a doctorate to their language proficiency certificates. When Cedric lost his job after some arcane and intricate conflict and the fact that LTU had stopped paying him, he took another position as a clerk in a local company run by a Greek Cypriot couple. Cedric still pursued his academic studies at LTU, and he was even handed a glimmer of hope concerning accreditation. Dr. Khan, the principal, signed an agreement with a small American university, of which Jim had not heard, but they existed on the internet. Cedric had great hopes of submitting his thesis on Prynne to this validating institution. They would discuss such possibilities that night over a few bottles of red wine, and tins of lager, supplied by Jim.

As Jim knew from his own visits to LTU, Cedric was oddly formal at work, with a pompous attitude, entirely absent during the times they spent together throughout the 1990s, mostly in evenings in local pubs. Cedric escaped his wife, who rather tragically he'd returned to after a separation. He despised his new boss, who sold machines and associated paraphernalia for vacuum packaging. Cedric told long tales of the intricacies concerning the supply of plastic bags which compressed food or medical supplies so preserving the contents without refrigeration, hence his nickname of the Bagman. This process impressed Cedric immensely, but not his Cypriot boss, who according to Cedric's account, was filthy rich and yet existed in a state of uneducated ignorance. This combination was anathema to Jim's friend, epitomizing the contradictory, yet prevalent idiocies of capitalism.

Cedric's own wages were so low he found it hard to survive, although initially he could walk to work, which was part of the job's attraction. He would return home for lunch, feed his two mangy cats, even occasionally meeting Jim in the local greasy spoon, the Hercules, Jim paying. Cedric always savoured his food, as he did everything. He truly delighted in life: his drinking; his rollup cigarettes; his long hair in the wind; his skipping, speedy walks along the streets of Islington and Hackney; the very little food shopping he did; conversations with street beggars to whom he was always overly generous; arguing with Jim; telling tall tales; and most of all between quaffing wine and inhaling smoke memorializing his past. Jim felt he should write about Cedric or at least he promised himself one day he would when the time was right. His friend was one of the few people who had appreciated Jim's unpublished novels, although he'd also been highly critical of them. 'Hemingway to your Fitzgerald, Wordsworth to your Coleridge. Do revel in the everyday, Jim, in every bloody second, yes, *carpe diem*,' he would advise his friend. 'It's really all we have. Glory in the ephemeral, discover its ageless qualities, the lessons within which will reveal a million truths. Blake understood exactly this, that if there is anything truly mystical in life, it will be found in the quotidian. Not in God, but in man and his connection with the world of things, especially nature, the diurnal course. We discover the best art celebrates an aesthetic of the unexceptional.' Jim appreciated the support, but he wondered whether he might ever live up to Cedric's expectations. He doubted his ability to match the quality and output of such writers, the ones his friend admired. 'Obscurity has its own rewards. As long as you keep the faith, Jim, and keep writing, that's all that matters,' Cedric advised him.

Yet in other matters, he couldn't quite stick to his own advice.

Four months previously the Cypriot's vacuum bag company had relocated to Cricklewood which resulted in a complicated daily commute that Cedric hated. The experience appalled him. "'Unreal City […]. I had not thought death had undone so [fucking] many." Eliot had it about right, Jim, it's like being fucking dead alive, the whole bloody ritual humiliation: going to work, the effort of getting there, being stuck in the office all day, chained to the desk, enduring having a fucking boss who is ignorant, and who lets his stupid wife tell me what to do, even run bloody errands, all in the name of wage slavery,' he complained at length, a rant. A month into his travels Cedric's wife left him after a fight, of which Jim had not yet heard a full account, but he knew it involved Cedric staying up late into the night. "'April is the cruellest month,'" was his only comment at the time. Cedric was keen on T.S. Eliot, one of a few favoured writers, although his absolute passions were Blake, Ezra Pound and most especially J.H. Prynne, who was far too oblique and esoteric for Jim's taste. The latter poet had taught Cedric as an undergraduate at Gonville and Caius, his days and nights spent mostly debating informally in bars, reading voraciously outside of the syllabus. Finally, he graduated with a third-class-honours in English. 'I was cheated, Jim. I was simply cheated out of a decent grade. And it was all down to being accused of fiddling drinks from the JCR Buttery Bar and the late-night bar. I was victimized, you know, for being poor and working class, basically for being from the lower orders. The bloody yah-yahs all hated me. If I'd have been posh, no one would have blinked, or seen the proverbial mote in the eye.' Subsequently a while after Cambridge, Cedric gained a first-class sociology degree from the Open University, studying in his spare time.

Despite his poor initial degree classification, Cedric still loved literature. He adored language, especially its meanings, with all its possibilities, most of all proverbs and cliché. Increasingly he was drawn to calligraphy. Among fellow students had been Lars Tharp, who'd been an older pupil at Cedric's school and later appeared on *Antiques Roadshow* much to Cedric's irritation, and Alistair Campbell the New Labour spin doctor, who he also detested, the latter with fervour. 'Bloody traitor, that thug. Look at him selling out the labour movement. He went to City Boys in Leicester, and he was a posh kid really, being the son of a bloody *vet*.' The last comment also related to a recent financial disaster, which exacerbated his hatred of that profession. Cedric's debts mounted after paying for life-saving operations on his two cats at a local veterinary surgery, both of which creatures limped on, but only just. His unauthorized overdraft was compounded by bank interest and charges. 'That family never suffered. They must have had money,' added Cedric. 'Yes, and after university that warmonger Campbell became a sleazy bloody tabloid journo, but he couldn't write for toffee in my opinion. Did you know, Jim, I won the College poetry prize when I was at Cambridge?'

Jim nodded. He'd been told so on several occasions, but he'd never been shown the actual poem which he would have liked. Cedric rarely offered Jim his writing, only having real faith in an inner circle of university friends, as if some magical trust prevailed in such Cambridge relationships. Jim respected these boundaries, recognizing Cedric was inordinately proud of his achievement and he'd subsequently spent a large part of his life devoted to its continuance, eschewing the fickleness of bourgeois multinational publishers, not trusting outsiders to judge his art. He despised the recent shifts in publishing, on one occasion declaring, 'The Booker Prize is simply Miss World for talentless writers. It's pure publicity, with mediocrities being transformed into media whores, Jim. Appalling tripe most of it, prizes for idiots such as Rushdie. Go to work on an egg sort of chap, simply a bloody self-advertiser now. "The superior man understands what is right; the inferior man understands what will sell." Confucius, Jim, Confucius.' Cedric expected genuine writers to endure poverty if that's what it took for their art to develop fully. Obscurity was a virtue in his eyes, celebrity a curse. 'The next thing we know, that talentless Alistair Campbell, the goon, will be writing fiction. Heaven forfend!'

Cedric's own name initially bemused Jim, an appellation almost designed to be utterly outmoded, to attract teasing and bullying, which at school it did, as Cedric admitted to Jim. For Jim such naming was tantamount to parental abuse, selecting a moniker almost guaranteed to be derided. What on earth were his parents thinking of back in 1957 when naming him, Jim wondered? Hence with alacrity in the late sixties Cedric rechristened himself Buzz after Aldrin of the moon landing, which became his schoolyard nickname. His parents had both died recently, within months of each other, and left him debts he felt he should honour. Both worked in a Leicester shoe factory, pretty much Sue Townsend territory, but they never managed to leave their extremely badly paid employment until the factory closed in the mid-eighties, leaving them on benefits after their meagre redundancy payments ran out. As their son complained, 'The bare minimum was all the bosses offered. Stitched up like wriggling smoked kippers, a pair of them.' Cedric loved his now departed parents deeply, never blaming them for his family's relative poverty, regarded as a matter of class oppression. They'd rented a tiny red-brick terraced house, frontage on the street, small gloomy back yard. For leisure, they frequented a working man's club in town, the Nottingham Oddfellows Club abbreviated to Notts Club. Jim played a few occasional football games for the latter during his time as a student and later after graduation a young schoolteacher. Young Cedric attended one of the city's best grammar schools, its alumni included the Attenborough brothers. Conveniently the school sat beside the university of which their father was principal, living in a grace and favour house later housing the Law Department.

Living alone, without his wife's contributions, already Cedric was slipping deeper and deeper into debt, and he seemed to be descending psychologically, his behaviour entirely erratic, spiralling out of control, with absenteeism, frequently calling in sick, missing meals, getting drunk earlier and earlier in the day, even on workdays. Generally, he was becoming gloomier. And, more recently he was oddly aggressive. There was nothing much of him and he was losing more weight. Jim fed him when he could, inviting him over, but Cedric stopped coming when Will arrived, even though they were fond of each other. Jim sensed Cedric would be ashamed if the boy was confronted with his decline. Jim was pleased on one level that Will was going out, as he would be spared seeing the state of his friend and Cedric only agreed to visit Jim when he heard Will was to be out. Lately Jim cycled to Cedric's on Fridays and gave him lunch on Sundays whenever Will was either out or away. 'I'm going to shower, OK?' Will asked since the bathroom contained the sole toilet, about to bolt the door.

'Jim Dent,' he replied as the phone rang.

'Hello, Jim?' Cedric sounded fuzzy, uncertain, as if he'd forgotten whom he'd rung, 'it's Buzz.' Cedric's tone was muted, slurred, sounding drunk, very much so. 'Would you mind coming over to my place tonight rather than me going out? I'm under par, been off sick today,' which admission Jim recognized a bad sign.

'Alright, but are you well enough for a visit, Cedric?'

'I am, at least I think so.' He sounded uncertain.

'Should I cycle over?' asked Jim, uncertain whether Cedric would make any sense, worrying the evening might be disastrous.

'Yes, please do. I'd like the company to be honest.'

'So what time would suit you, Buzz?'

'Shall we agree on nine?' Jim worried Cedric would be incoherent later. It was only seven-twenty and he sounded pissed.

'Do you need anything? Medicine or food? I'll shop.'

'Well, I'll need some bread and milk, if you could, plus a tin of beans, but just a small one.' Cedric's needs were modest.

'Shall I bring wine for me and beer for you? I'll buy them later.'

'Oh, please do. I'll put it on my tab of debts owed to you.' This was a fiction maintained by Cedric, to not feel too bad. Jim expected nothing back apart from comradeship. It was a ruse that allowed Cedric to sustain his peculiar sense of pride, equality and fraternity.

'I'll see you later.' The line was dead even before he finished. Cedric wasn't a great one for long telephone conversations, even in his prime, associating the mechanism primarily with work. He preferred people in the flesh, talking at them, with them, about them, amusingly. He refused email. Will emerged wrapped in a large pink towel and sat on his seat.

'Tea?' Jim asked, getting up slowly from the sofa.

It was made in the small galley kitchen, the back door left open because of the heat. They sat in the garden shaded by the huge tree. Next door where the old Irish couple lived, a mass of vegetation choked every inch of the long garden. At night foxes keened, a peculiarly child-like wail, as if tortured or anguished.

Jim reflected that his son was already twenty-three. At that point in his own life Jim had been about to take up his first teaching post, at an all-boys secondary modern school in Leicester, which he grew to hate fervently. Will was born three years later.

'I'm out soon,' Will said. 'You entertaining the Bagman here?'

'No, I'm off out too tonight, for a drink with him.'

'You going anywhere exotic?' his son chuckled at the thought.

'Oh no, he changed the plan, wants me to visit him at his place, which is a bit grim. He's been off sick again all day today and perhaps all week by the sound of things, a bad sign.'

'So, is he "sick?" Or is it really the booze that's affecting him?'

'I should think so, but of course eventually the two can merge; an awful inevitability about the slide toward illness.'

'I suppose that's true. It will get worse, but hopefully not yet. He's a few good years left, surely?' asked Will, who as Jim knew, was an optimist at heart. Jim wasn't. Will continued, 'Well offer him my regards. I haven't seen him yet, not at all so far this summer.'

'No, honestly I think he's avoiding you. Don't take that the wrong way, but he's under strain, really not feeling himself. He hasn't told me why, although he did say the wife moved out the other day. Some sort of argument I suppose. And I suspect he hates commuting to work. That's just not Cedric's kind of thing. I think he really doesn't want you to see him so low.'

'Hasn't that happened before, the two of them splitting up?'

'I think it has, but I'm not sure. It's difficult to tell. She travels a lot, being a typical Kiwi, always off on a trip somewhere. She's hardly ever been there over the Christmas period, so he usually comes over here. On her trips, Cedric occasionally joins her, but not often. They once went off together to Alaska.' Will, who by now was dressed, raised eyebrows to reflect his incredulity.

'I can't imagine the Bagman somewhere so remote, so harsh.'

'Me neither,' said Jim, beginning to think of Lyman Andrews, once his tutor at Leicester, who'd supervised his first research degree. Lyman told a tale of frequenting a bar in Alaska and going to the *men's-room* to find a knife in his back, having been so drunk he hadn't noticed being attacked. Jim hadn't thought of him in ages. He'd have to pass on the story to Will, but not yet, not while the boy was in a hurry, not while the Witch was waiting. He presumed that alcoholic Lyman was surely long since dead.

'Well, I'm off,' Will cried with such gusto, it pained Jim, feeling a twinge of abandonment. 'See you later. Enjoy yourself,' he added, without either side mentioning the purpose of Will's evening.

Jim took the paper and sat in the garden reading its right-wing propaganda. He thought of his father, Howard Dent. The two of them had argued bitterly in the summer of 1970. Jim had been sixteen and Howard tried to force him to carry on with his summer job as a cable drum maker in a permanent capacity. As ever he'd been aggressive, with his confrontational manner, fuming about Jim's decision, what Howard regarded as a refusal to see his perspective. His father expected Jim to leave school at that very moment, arguing that he would have done that much better financially by staying on at work, that he was already earning far more than some of his teachers, even those in their early thirties. Of course, in a sense his father was right, but that was to miss the point totally, Jim felt. There were other far more important things in life, and Jim was insistent on being allowed to experience them, and the sixth form and university were part of that route, the one he'd mapped out for himself. Today he wondered what might have become of him had he heeded Howard's advice. Probably he would have been unemployed after the factory closed in 1999.

Chapter Four:
Soiree Chez the Bagman, July 2003

July 2003, after Will's departure to meet the Witch, Jim cycled the four minutes to the local Morrison's for that night's provisions. Around nine he headed for Cedric's flat, sweat trickling down his forehead and back, hot, the substantial weight of that evening's drinks stowed in his maroon rucksack, maybe three and half litres of booze, plus Cedric's supplies. He thought about his son having drinks with his mother somewhere in town, about that time. The sky was still light. Jim loved dusk in summer. Dressed in an old grey sweatshirt, baggy green army-style combat shorts, and suede grey-black trainers, Jim stood ten minutes later, cycle held by its blue leather saddle, at the front door of Cedric's Islington Council maisonette off Hornsey Road. The area was as grim as the neighbouring ones were expensive, the wealthy living cheek by jowl with the dispossessed, property-gentrifiers living bravely alongside the criminal class, street gangs, beggars, and the poor. Cedric would qualify as the latter, despite his Cambridge degree.

Jim knocked vigorously for a full five minutes, his knuckles slightly sore, wondering about a wasted trip. On occasion Cedric would fail to answer, a possibility Jim weighed up. Jim had been trying hard not to think about his ex-wife, of the intense dislike he'd harboured for her for over twenty years since their divorce. Still no response to his hammering, but he knew to wait. Cedric had no functioning doorbell. He and his wife had even refused central heating when its installation had been offered by the council gratis. 'It would just entail another bloody expense, with all that gas to pay for. I can't be having that,' had been Cedric's curious explanation of his rejection of modern comforts. Instead his living room was freezing for much of winter, apart from when he burned packing cases, palettes, and occasionally coal on special occasions in the old-style grate. Jim heard a vague shuffling sound inside. A pair of eyeballs belonging to the Bagman appeared at the letter box, bloodshot, strained, and suspicious. More time passed after the grey-green eyes had disappeared, a chain rattled, and slowly and tentatively the door opened. 'Oh, it's you, Jim.' Cedric looked, exceedingly drunk, already lolling. He was clearly *pissed as a rat* as Jim's friends referred to such inebriation during their schooldays.

'I brought your food: sliced wholemeal, beans, back bacon, and skimmed milk. And some booze.' Jim anticipated and knew Cedric's preferences; he would complain volubly if you mistook them. Jim manoeuvred the bicycle into the small hallway. This area was too edgy for Jim to risk leaving his machine outside, especially in the dark. Inevitably it would be stolen in a heartbeat, by one of the ghostlike characters who emerged from the ether in these council estates. Jim avoided clipping Cedric's skinny hairless leg with a pedal, visible below his camel trousers, stained, worn slightly too short. Cedric's thin and pale bony ankles and narrow sockless, feet were visible in clumpy blue leather shoes with huge thick soles and heels.

As Cedric turned Jim was shocked by his large bald pate, which had further expanded and made Cedric look like some clichéd medieval monk, amid the long curly brown locks of which he was clearly proud. This natural, God-given tonsure was far bigger and rounder than Jim could remember from his last visit. He felt shocked. Cedric would hate losing his hair. In every way he was an unashamed, unrepentant hippy, a 'long hair' as some once referred to them, every aspect of his bearing and wardrobe redolent of the early seventies. Part of the squatting generation, he'd lived in a previously empty Georgian terrace in the very late seventies in Stoke Newington, at the tail-end of the decade when the area had still been an awful dump, almost completely un-gentrified. Maybe five years previously the Angry Brigade had defined the area as cheap, yet counter-cultural, dangerous and revolutionary.

Jim had lived nearby, briefly inhabiting a rented room in 1980, his landlord a young bearded guy buying a two-bedroomed flat who was employed by the Inner London Education Authority and the Greater London Council to write short plays for kids in schools and on summer play schemes for them to perform. Real rubbish as far as Jim could ascertain, sub-standard pantomimic stuff, with the emergent left-liberal message that the world could be easily perfected with love, kindness and public funding. An Arts Council grant had been involved, which Jim thought overly generous. The purported dramatist's girlfriend had left him. Jim's rent had been required to top up his mortgage payments. This was Jim's first London residence after leaving his severally unfaithful wife, abandoning his child, baby Will. As long conversations revealed over the years, Jim and Cedric's paths might well have crossed years before, since Cedric had apparently known and still derided this joker who aspired to be a bard for the young, alluding to him as a talentless little shit. Curiously Cedric and Jim lived in the same areas for years without ever meeting. They knew very much the same territory in Leicester, in London, and even had some acquaintances in common. 'Are you OK, Buzz?' Jim asked, which Cedric ignored. He staggered into the living room wordlessly, which was pretty unusual. Recently he was rarely so drunk so early. It would appear that when relieved of work, still angry, Cedric filled the void, starting to drink all day long.

Jim moved his cycle into the kitchen, its surfaces strewn with dirtied glasses, cutlery, bowls, one with the remains of pilchards on toast, hardly touched, cold, congealed, from a day or two earlier. Cedric's cooker was a relic, a grill high above filthy gas hobs, greasy, fat in the aluminium foil that lined its grill-pan. Jim balanced his bike against the cooker and sink, the latter full of utensils and used pots and pans. The domestic chaos was spreading, as was mould on leftover scraps on the plates. Jim carefully rinsed two glasses with a slight shudder, drying them with a soiled dishcloth and followed his friend into the main room.

'How are you?' Jim persisted, worried Cedric might be seriously sick. In the small living room, the only one Jim knew without a television, he placed his bag on top of a pile of sheet music on a stool before the upright piano, taking out two bottles of red wine and a four pack of the supermarket brand of extra-strong lager,

Cedric's favourite tipple. 'You want a beer?' His companion simply nodded, so Jim handed him the cans and a glass. Despite the warmish night, there were the remains of a fire in the grate, discarded wood smoking, and a few embers glowing. Cedric seemed to find timber endlessly from building sites and elsewhere, and a few burnt coals that he bought expensively in tiny bags from an off licence where he obtained Red Stripe lager heavily discounted, well beyond its sell-by-date. The first drink revived him. He turned very deliberately toward Jim. The latter knew the signs of an impending revelation, a long, convoluted account of the perfidies of the capitalist class, or the *rentier* class or just the bourgeoisie. Jim loved Cedric's narratives, peppered with arcane quotations, full of venom and occasional spite.

'They sacked me the other day, those bloody awful Cypriots, the husband told me not to bother going back. Such bastards! So I've left.' Adeptly he flicked his first cigarette butt of the session into the ashes in the grate. Outside the light had dimmed and the night sky darkened the unlit room full of shadows.

'So, what happened?' Jim sought to situate the crisis.

'It was down to that fuck-face, Mrs Cypriot Capitalist Running Dog, the wife.' Cedric was not at all racist by any means, but he hated philistines and bullies, and for him she clearly qualified on both counts. 'That fucking woman, she kept sending me out on errands, endlessly, to buy this, to look for that, sometimes a dozen times a day, maybe more. First cigarettes, then chocolate, next milk, followed by crisps. Later it'd be chewing gum. That would be five separate visits to the shops, I kid you not, not one. Even when I was really busy with work, such a silly, selfish, stupid, ignorant fucking cow. I was missing orders and queries, we were losing business. And that journey, most days the trains were late, long delays. Cricklewood Station, but the office was well beyond that. I just hate the place, difficult to get to, nothing to do there apart from work. Lunch was bloody tedious, nowhere to go. I was just sick of it all.' Cedric was frustrated, even a tad resentful. 'And that sodding journey! It was either Upper

Holloway to Gospel Oak, where I nearly always just missed the sodding connection. Long wait, change at West Hampstead, change stations, take the train to that unnameable destination. Or catch a bus or walk to Tufnell Park tube, which is fucking miles first thing in the morning, one stop to Kentish Town, and change to a train for your ultimate destination, although as I said there was a long walk at the other end. It had been taking me well over an hour, each way, every bloody day, sometimes almost two, and I was still late. It was fine when the firm was local, a ten-minute walk, a simple matter, with a reasonable amount of exercise, not a fucking sodding route march. Lunch hour was meaningful, it was still mine. I could even come home. There it was well . . . just . . . just awful . . .,' he trailed off, drinking more lager. Cedric was seldom lost for words

'Where exactly is your new place of work.' Jim couldn't visualize the area. He quaffed red wine while Cedric seemed to cogitate. He had an odd look when drunk, both his eyes and mind unfocused, almost as if he were attempting to look inside himself, peer into his own skull. Automatically Cedric gulped more lager.

'You go from the tube up Cricklewood Lane,' he continued, his voice slurred, 'along the bloody Edgware Road going northward, off to the left, near the North Circular. "In every voice, in every ban, / The mind-forged manacles I hear [...]."' Cedric was fond of Blake, quoting his work illustratively. He thought Blake a *true bloody genius*, a phrase he repeated emphatically. 'I would have taken a bus, but that's another expense to be added. My boss only ever pays retrospectively. Well, I walked a distance equivalent to going from here to Highbury Corner, maybe further by a few yards.'

'So quite a daily trek then? And the place itself, just an office?'

'No, the office is above a small warehouse, on an industrial estate. Much better than our last premises, but the area is nondescript, bleak, out of the way. I detest it. Foul place.'

'And your actual work, the duties?' asked Jim, genuinely curious.

'How might one put matters accurately? It was humdrum, banal, wearisome, tiresome, or simply bloody deadening in a truly mind-curdling fashion all day long. Take your pick. Or imagine all of these qualities, incrementally. Roll them into one, all together. Such utter tedium. The kind of appalling routine that rots your brain, reduces it to pap, makes you a dullard, the curse of the working classes, eager lambs slaughtered in multitudes.' Cedric rolled and lit another cigarette, the smoke wafting across the cluttered room. He smiled, waving one bony finger for emphasis. 'Finally, she asked me to return her fucking library books and I told her I was no-one's factotum. And she didn't know what I meant! She just looked at me. *Johannes factotum*, I repeated, adding *jack of all trades am I not*. Still she had no inkling. So, I let loose both barrels, metaphorically speaking. Told her she could *fuck off*! "I was angry with my foe: / I told it not, my wrath did grow."' More Blake. As Jim knew Cedric was always in his element conveying stories of the everyday. Jim tried to persuade his friend to write prose, a novel, but Cedric remained faithful to his poetic muse. Such storytelling was a social function for Cedric, an everyday practice, indulged over drinks, amidst debate and discussion. Cedric remained a verbal raconteur only in terms of an oration, a master of the anecdotal mode. Next, he emphasized every syllable in each of the next eight words, wagging two forefingers as if conducting their delivery, a performance, which naturally it had become. '*I am not your fucking servant, you bitch.* That's what I said, word for bloody word, and then she told the old man who sacked me, on the spot, uxorious bastard. Then he rang and asked me back three days later. They couldn't cope without me.' Clearly Cedric relished his employer's dependence upon him, pride in this fact permeated his very tone. 'So, I agreed to return, probably a mistake, because I was sick again, that grim commute, the whole kit and caboodle sickened me. I managed ten days until this Monday. I haven't been back, four days. I just can't face it. Plus, the boss wasn't paying me my fares as agreed. I consented to work in the new, relocated premises only if he paid my fares.'

'Well, have you asked him to honour that promise?'

'Sure. But he denies he agreed long-term. He claims our arrangement was only for the first two months, which is pure bullshit, a fiction, but what could I prove, given it was a verbal agreement? They're simply peasants, the pair of them. They're two vicious nasty peasants, just like some of those awful money-grubbing characters in Claude Berri's film sequence, utter vicious, selfish little bastards. Have you seen his movies?'

'No, I don't think I have, not that I can remember.'

'Well you should. You absolutely must. They're called *Jean de Florette* and *Manon des Sources.* Get them out from Blockbuster, Jim, really do. I've seen them in there, in the international section. The star of the second is an absolute beauty, Emmanuelle Béart, who exhibits an extremely Gallic loveliness which I think you in particular would appreciate.' As Cedric knew well, Jim once had a French fiancée, who moved to Wales. She deserted him after an argument on the telephone. Jim had no new address after she moved again. She hadn't contacted him in the ensuing six years. So he knew about abandonment and betrayal well enough. 'Cricklewood Library was built on land owned by All Souls College, Oxford, you know. I hoped to spend some of my lunchtime in that institution, reading, but it was a bloody hike, just to get there and back in an hour would be improbable, unless one sprinted, unlikely for me.' Cedric smiled at the joke at his own expense.

'So, can you, and will you sign on now you're not working?'

'Could do, except they'll say I left gainful employment as they term it, of my own volition. I should have left when he moved the whole outfit. I could have signed on then, easily. I'm kippered.'

'Yes, but he's not paying the fares as promised,' Jim interceded.

'They'll still make things difficult, as you well know.'

'Sure, that's given, but if you can't get there, to Cricklewood, if literally you can't afford to, you can make that case.'

'I'll try, I suppose.' Jim knew that tone. He probably wouldn't.

'You must. He's changed the circumstances, your boss; introduced unacceptable conditions of service.' There was something of the barrack-room lawyer about Jim, a dedicated class warrior, which pleased Cedric, this identity pivotal in their friendship.

'You're right, I know, Jim. First thing, I'll go to sign on.'

'I've bad news. Will told me the other day. He's decided not to do a PhD, even though there's guaranteed funding, at Oxford.'

'Well, that's a real damn shame.' He lit another roll-up.

'I'm very unhappy about his decision,' Jim said. 'Wasted opportunity.'

'Look, Jim, remember it's not your decision. You can't lead his life, Jim. It is Will who must choose which prospects to pursue.'

'True,' Jim admitted, but it did not make him feel good having to do so. Cedric was right, he felt, but it didn't damp his irritation.

'We shouldn't do what people want us to do. When we do, it leads to pain, often misery,' said Cedric with conviction. 'How would you have liked a similar response from your own father?'

'True again. You're right, I suppose.' Jim paused. 'What about Myrtle, is she coming back?' Jim referred to Cedric's wife, originally from New Zealand, an antipodean hippy a decade older than her husband, about whom Jim harboured suspicions concerning her absolute loyalty to his friend, given she hated his drinking.

'No, that perfidious person won't be returning, ever. Currently she is staying with some friends of hers whom I've never met, somewhere close to her shop, and I've not been invited. She won't tell me where she is, won't see me, claims I'm violent, and is telling everyone about my propensity for violence, even our mutual friends.' He sighed. 'She'll retrieve her housing association place, end the sub-let I suspect.' Despite being rehoused by the local authority, somehow Myrtle had managed to retain and sublet her previous miniscule dwelling near the Angel, a combined bed-sitting room flat, close to Essex Road where with friends she ran an upmarket hippy bric-a-brac and second-hand shop, an enterprise they described as a collective. 'She has taken herself off the lease of this maisonette, which has caused me untold trouble as she did so officially, telling the council by letter, again claiming I was violent, labelled me a wife-beater, so now they're hassling me.'

'For what reason? You do pay the rent, don't you?'

'Mostly I do. Ostensibly they say it's for having too much space for a sole occupant.' Stopping his words abruptly, Cedric reached for a letter on the shelf by his chair to the left of the dead fire. Jim sat to the right, by the metal doors that if opened led into a small garden. 'In truth probably because they think I'm some patriarchal wife-beater who deserves to be put out on the street. There you have it: the Socialist Republic of Islington!' He shook a letter in the air angrily. 'This missive states essentially that I do not require or deserve a two-bedroomed property as a single person, which is bloody outrageous. Why would things be any different with her departure? I still have guests, and anyway the second bedroom serves as my study.' This was news to Jim.

Despite having known Cedric for over a decade, Jim had never ascended Cedric's stairs, never been invited to do so. He always used the small, iffy toilet by the front door. When Myrtle was around, mostly the pair met in pubs, or at Jim's, seldom in the couple's maisonette. 'Where would Dave Moore stay? He comes and stops over every month.' Dave was an old Gonville and

Caius friend, an architect of whom Cedric always spoke fondly.

'A study, you mean you have a desk up there?'

'Yes, in the second bedroom. Have you never seen it?'

'No.' Jim wondered why they'd never spoken of the matter.

Cedric staggered to his feet, balancing the remains of a cigarette on the lip of the tiled mantelpiece. 'Come and look.' He lurched toward the door, each movement an exaggeration. Upstairs Jim glimpsed the tangle of sheets on Cedric's unmade double bed, and in the next room was a forest of books on shelves placed around all the walls, floor to ceiling, with others set at right angles reaching into the room, so there was only a corridor of access, making the space more of a library. This was the only tidy, ordered room in the house, still dusty, but no clutter apart from notebooks on an old desk by the window. Cedric gestured with his hand. 'Where do the council imagine I can store all of these books if I'm moved into a tiny flat? How can I study and write?' He switched off the light and descended the narrow stairs. Jim followed, wondering just where Dave Moore would stay, certainly not in the study, unless he lay on the strip between the shelves on an inflatable mattress. As with many details of Cedric's life, such matters were slightly improbable, almost bizarre.

They sat again, Cedric retrieving his butt, Jim asked, 'So why did Myrtle leave?' Usually with Cedric one was never this blunt, and he could sense his friend was wondering whether to respond, or see if he preferred another lexical, rhetorical tangent.

'Over there. Look at that stereo, over there; you may have noticed it on your way in. Just look at what she did to my sound system.' By the wall was a stereo system, a solid stack, with a turntable, its playing arm with stylus wrenched free, hanging loose.

'Vandalised, she's ruined it, and I so love music as you know.'

'But why did she damage it? For what possible reason?'

'Well, let me set the scene.' Cedric emphatically put together his makings, rolling a paper around some tobacco for a further cigarette, poured a second can of lager, as if to tease Jim by stalling, rolling his eyes before his next utterance. 'So, where would one begin? Now you know Stroud Green Road, of course.' Jim nodded, knowing when not to interrupt the flow. 'Well there's an excellent junk shop in the direction of Crouch End, although I know you're not an aficionado of such establishments, as I am. Well, the one I favour had this very sound system in the window, reasonably priced. It was something which I desired, something I have always wanted and could never afford. As you well know I'm short of cash, so I asked the proprietor whom I know to save it for me. I saved for weeks on end, and found some items the shopkeeper wanted and with part barter, part cash I purchased it over eight weeks, I obtained my goal of possessing this gem of audio equipment. It had such a wonderful sound, with tuner and record deck, really great speakers. But look at it now, utterly ruined.'

Jim examined the broken object, in a sorry state, probably irreparable. Clearly, it was originally high quality, once state of the art, he could tell, although now superseded by several generations of technology. Jim knew given his father was a hi-fi obsessive. Yet, still perfect for vinyl records of which Cedric possessed so many.

'It's a real shame,' said Jim, comfortingly he hoped. He couldn't afford to offer his friend one as a gift. 'Why smash it up?'

'We'd been to a party together, great evening, even she agreed. I was in such a good mood, despite this cretinous job. Myrtle went to bed when we got back, tired. So, I chilled, prolonging the positive moment, ironic given what was about to occur. I played some Beatles albums, mostly the early ones.'

As Jim knew, Cedric loved the group, had done so since childhood, and was a mine of arcane facts concerning the Fab Four.

Cedric staggered to his feet, and whispered, 'Taking a *wazz*,' using a term for pissing which Jim knew well from his Leicester days. One past Christmas Cedric claimed every single Beatles song was a masterpiece, making up an oeuvre unparalleled in popular music, and on another occasion about six months previously he'd insisted that *A Hard Day's Night* ought to be regarded as one of the best-ever British films, a comic masterpiece, praising its writer Alun Owen as an underrated genius. Cedric returned from his ablutions and carried on his tale as he sat, 'Well, to continue, next thing Myrtle complained, shouting down from bed. Said it was far too late and I was keeping her awake. It was barely two a.m. And I had enjoyed the night greatly, I wanted to savour the moment, capture my mood, its essence. And without warning Myrtle is shrieking down the stairs like some bloody fishwife. She came down, turned my music down, and we argued. She was emphatic about her having to work the next day, on the Saturday, but as I said I bloody didn't have to and I'd already spent the week working at that awful bloody office. I just wanted to chill out. So when she returned to bed, I turned up the sound. Blow me the next thing she came down in a complete fury and ripped the bloody arm off the deck, scratching my copy of *Sgt. Pepper*, for God's sake. So, I hit her, once, more a kind of slap, across the face, just the once. That was all. It was nothing more, I assure you.'

Jim couldn't picture Cedric hitting anyone hard, he was so gaunt. His friend continued, 'She screamed and barricaded herself in the bloody bedroom. I had to sleep in this chair. She left early the next day. I heard her, at about six. I haven't seen her since. She rang, insisting that I go out when she returned the next day for all her possessions, every single item, took the lot.'

'And there's been no contact since?' Jim demanded nosily.

'Nothing substantial. We've spoken once on the telephone.' Jim had rarely known Cedric be so direct in describing an important event. Jim was shocked at Cedric's candour.

'So, what comes next? Maybe reconcile, after a cooling-off period?'

Jim wondered why Cedric abandoned had his 'true love'. He had told Jim tentative elements, but never its totality, never alluding to the emotional underpinning, the what and the why. Cedric sat back, preparing himself, composing his thoughts as he smoked. He pursed his lips quizzically, weaving his fingers together.

'It's unlikely my wife will ever return, or that I would allow her to do so. There's a fuller context I must explain. I met Katharine at the Law Society Drama Group, such a beautiful woman, and eventually after our affair blossomed and deepened I left Myrtle. To be frank I'd endured enough. Her son Leon moved in with us, and he stole from me continually, money, items to pawn or sell, all to fund his habit, to pay for the next fix. He was a junkie, completely hooked, on heroin, injecting and smoking smack, the whole nine yards, track marks, theft, and whatever else one cannot imagine.'

'Where was his father? No longer around, I suppose.'

'No, long gone, some sort of waste of space, apparently. Leon was stealing my books, records, anything of value and I got fed up with our married life being undermined by the little shit. And yet Myrtle idolised him; she couldn't see it was driving us apart. Katharine loved the drama group I set up. That was when I fell for her, during a lunchtime reading of Jean Anouilh's *Antigone*, in the original French. She had a beautiful flat, in Chingford overlooking Epping Forest and I moved in.'

Jim had grown up in the River Valley below, in the once heavily industrialized area of north-east London. Once the clusters of factories had seemed part of the very landscape itself, dense, pervasive, but they had been decimated by Thatcher. He knew Chingford. Cedric seemed an improbable inhabitant, although Dickens' Wemmick popped into his head again, his stories and jollity, recollecting the character's tiny Gothic house with its moat, his pig. Cedric in Chingford offered a contemporary north London version of an idyll. Still there was something absolutely Dickensian about Cedric's life, Jim realized, only without it being intended, and despite his friend residing in early twenty-first century London.

Cedric continued his bucolic recollection, 'That was the very best time of my life. We shared walks in the forest, mile upon mile of trees, deer, wildlife, real genuine countryside so close to town.'

'I know. We went there when I was a child, for picnics on bank holidays. I loved it.' Jim remembered fondly such gatherings.

'Well, this went on for over a year, a perfect time. I resettled. I was enjoying work at the Law Society, for the first time.' Cedric paused, in part for effect, in part because his emotions were clearly welling up inside him, visible. He shed a few tears which he wiped away, and lit another cigarette, the ritual punctuating his performance.

'So, what spoiled everything?' Jim dreaded what might transpire.

'Leon died, of an overdose. Myrtle kept ringing me at work, saying she'd kill herself if I didn't go back. It broke my heart, but I did so, foolishly.' Jim sighed, questioning the perhaps misguided real sense of duty and loyalty. However, he said nothing given Cedric clearly bitterly regretted his decision.

'And what about Katharine, what on earth happened to her?'

'Less than a week after I left, she took an overdose.' Cedric caught himself in a huge sob, controlling his emotions stoically. Jim was astonished that Cedric had never mentioned this personal catastrophe. He wiped away a few more tears. 'However, fortunately she survived, thank God,' he waved an arm in the air, gulping for air for a second or two, 'but it was all very touch and go. In truth, she very nearly died, so the doctors told her. However, Myrtle insisted I shouldn't visit her, that I should leave my job immediately. Naturally enough, they understood and released me. I didn't want another suicide on my conscience. Later Katharine went back to work, unharmed by the gossip. In fact she was promoted.' He paused. 'She married a new colleague, ironically the one that replaced me. I suppose she's happy. After that it's been downhill all the way for me.' He laughed dryly. 'So there you have it, the life, the times and the troubles of Cedric "Buzz" Biddwell.'

'Well, really so sorry to hear your . . . I suppose you'd call them tribulations,' Jim responded. 'It must have been an awful experience.'

'Yes, but it was all for naught. Look where I am now. What's even worse is in the intervening years Myrtle never really forgave me for my unfaithfulness, hated me, and somehow, she still manages to blame me for Leon's death. Not that she says so, but I know nevertheless. Now it's come to this.' He shook his head.

'How on earth did she find out about Katharine?'

'Mutual friends, ex-colleagues, one pieces together a pattern of events in the chaos, a natural rhythm in the discord.'

'You really do have to get yourself back on your feet. Come over and see Will. Like I told you, he's staying the summer, job at the university in Holloway Road. He'd like to meet you again.'

'Yes, we'll see.' Cedric gazed into the distance, unfocused. Suddenly he suggested, 'You miss out on so much in life, Jim, by being alone. You should always reach out to others. I've noticed, you never talk to beggars. They can tell one so much about the human condition, if you listen.' Jim hardly knew how to respond.

'You always give them money, even when you've none. Is that wise?' Cedric said nothing. 'Do you think you'll see Will?'

'If I find the time.' The last remark seemed incongruous for if

Cedric wasn't working he'd all the time he required and more.

Lately, he barely ventured beyond his front door when not at work. So, it was pride, a matter of not being seen at his low-point. Jim couldn't fathom how Cedric survived financially. He worried about Cedric because he suspected that his friend had no intention of signing on, had little to support himself. Yet, Cedric would be deeply offended if he offered him money directly. Jim wondered what lay ahead for Cedric, hoping for the best despite circumstances.

Will would never see Cedric again. Jim's friend would ask after the boy when he came over for dinners and lunches that autumn. Will never made it into the Civil Service as planned. Eventually he found a job at Chatham House, although first he'd worked for a publisher in Oxford. They produced curious illustrated books for *aficionados* on military history. From his university in Birmingham Jim purchased cheaply a second-hand computer for Cedric, fully operational, but Cedric showed little interest in his new possession. Jim suspected it wasn't used. Cedric still mourned the record player, which stood in his cramped living room, unusable, a reminder of that traumatic break-up. On occasion Jim also bought the two of them lunches in the Pillars of Hercules as Cedric labelled their favourite café, always lamb casserole if available given that Cedric was entirely a creature of habit. That had been the cause of their falling out, in October when Cedric had wanted to visit another second-hand shop on Stroud Green Road. Jim had twisted his ankle in a rabbit hole on a run at twilight across Hampstead Heath, so he was limping, struggling to keep up. He took Cedric in his car to a nearby café, parking around the corner. As soon as they entered this establishment Jim decided it was not a good one, which seemed to be confirmed after waiting five minutes to order. He noted that that the menu was limited, everything was with chips. Jim suggested moving on, and immediately, a hung-over Cedric flare up, irritable, evidently hungry. In one movement, he rose and stormed out. This was a side to Cedric Jim had never encountered previously. By the time he followed and reached the pavement, Cedric had walked away as rapidly as he could. Jim peered after him in the distance, lost among the shoppers, glimpsed, invisible again, irrecoverable.

Subsequently Cedric stopped answering his phone or his door whenever Jim pedalled round on his bicycle. On the third occasion through the half-open letter box he could hear an exhalation or two behind the wood. So, he gave up. And work was increasingly demanding: he'd been appointed reader, and there were more classes to take in the second semester. A few months passed without a thought of Cedric, but at Christmas he cycled round and posted a card, adding a brief note. However, there was no response to his request that his friend might ring him, and that he would be welcome for Christmas, which Jim was to spend alone.

In the New Year, in 2004 as February arrived Jim thought of his fiftieth birthday in about two weeks. Celebrations reminded him of Cedric, particularly as Will would be in town all weekend, taking Jim and Kitty to watch Tottenham against Leicester on the Sunday. Jim decided he'd send Cedric a formal letter inviting him for a meal on the Saturday at the Pillars, followed by a drink or three for Jim's birthday at the flat. He posted his missive through the door thinking of his friend's eyes peering out intently from inside, aware of Jim's presence, refusing to acknowledge him.

Two weeks later, early evening, the day after his birthday, a Tuesday, Jim about to drive back to his Birmingham digs, a class at nine next morning. He stood shaving. He heard his doorbell, and answered, shrouded in his dressing gown, face half-shaved, wiping away foam with a faded pink towel. There stood Myrtle, Cedric's estranged wife, a total surprise. Her visit was unprecedented. He frowned. He'd no idea that she even knew where he lived.

'Hello,' she said, uncertain of herself. The array of oddly coloured clothes suggested they'd originated from stock in her shop, recycled quasi-junk (Cedric's term) that she described as bric-a-brac.

'Hello,' he said, curious about her purpose, slightly embarrassed.

'Look, it's about Cedric.' Jim wondered if he were to serve as a go-between, not something he wanted. 'I don't really know what to say . . . .' Jim was intrigued, immediately imagining that either his friend had been arrested or needed help with money. Yet given the recent troubles, why would he send Myrtle? She went on, 'I'm afraid I'll simply have to blurt it out. The bad news is he's died. There's no other way of putting matters. It's awful. He's dead.'

'Dead?'

'Yes, they found him last Friday. A neighbour worried, hadn't seen Buzz. He was out of sight, for a week or more. Someone called the police, who forced an entry. They found him where he always sat, by the fire, apparently natural causes.'

'So, he's really dead,' Jim repeated, dumbfounded. 'How?'

'They think possibly a stroke or brain haemorrhage, or so the police suggest. There was a *post mortem*, inconclusive. He was emaciated, hadn't been eating. Finally, no one really knows.'

'Oh, my God, he's gone! I really can't believe it!' Jim stood stock still as if overtaken by a seizure himself, blinking, stunned.

'Cedric was also troubled by his massive debts, with compound interest levied by his bank. The loans were spiralling, and nothing was coming in. He'd stopped working, refused to sign on.' Jim sighed, but he'd guessed as much. 'The last treatment for his bloody cats left a black hole he never really conceded was a problem. He never recovered. They'd cut off his phone, gas and then even the electricity. The council had issued a summons for his eviction.' Jim looked at her with an accusing stare, but she seemed oblivious to his judgment of her potential culpability.

'So he'd stopped arguing, gave up?' Jim asked.

'Yes.'

'To do all that to someone in this day and age, it's shocking. The so-called Victorian values, those hypocritical bastards in the fucking socialist republic!' His grief had a particular target: it greatly angered Jim more than anything that Islington Council would have achieved its aim of seizing back Cedric's home. Jim sensed a deeply troubling chasm opening in his daily existence, like an unexpected sinkhole, full of emotional turbulence, so disturbing to him, so overwhelming that he stopped being able to listen properly. In fact, he really couldn't follow or make sense of Myrtle's words, just saw her mouth moving, up and down, around and around, the lips, the spittle, the wrinkled corners of her mouth. The sound became a blur, fluctuating. He knew she'd mentioned a funeral, made out the word, but the rest went as if through his ears and out again. Nothing registered apart from the fact of his friend's death, and that the previous day was Jim's own birthday, and that his grandfather had died years before on that very same day, on his fifteenth birthday in 1969. Jim's aunt called the hospital. The family was arguing while preparing their visit. Jim's grandfather had been a mere sixty-one, dying of an industrial disease, unable in the last months to walk to the corner of the road, twenty metres from his home. Those few moments after his aunt had listened and sobbing, relayed the awful news had been seared into his brain. He'd felt unreal at fifteen being told of that earlier death, and again did so in Myrtle's presence, her reporting of his friend's, her husband's death. Jim felt as if her were drowning, swept away by the uncanny, equally hallucinatory, and chimerical nature of the moment. How could this be? He was nonplussed,

'Well, you're busy shaving, you're probably off somewhere nice. I'll be going. I thought I should tell you, you two being so close. Incidentally the police said he'd opened your letter, but we don't know whether he read it. He had it on his lap. His letter opener was beside him, on the floor. The letter was still in its envelope.' So perhaps there had been no reconciliation, his message probably remained unread, Jim thought. He would never know, never be able to speak and laugh with Cedric again. He could find nothing to say to her, simply grunted and nodded. 'I'll let you be,' she added. 'God bless.' She walked down the driveway to the gate where she turned briefly. 'See you next week?'

Jim was completely numb, so stunned he still said nothing more. He thought vaguely of how unbelievable death is, that it all must end. She walked off toward Holloway Road, in the direction of Cedric's place. All of a sudden, as Jim recovered his senses partially, he realised she'd been referring to the detail of the funeral, had invited him, and he didn't know where it was to be held. He'd lost the detail. None of it had sunk into his consciousness, not a word, just a blurred sensation of them. He went to the pavement, but she too had disappeared. Maybe she knew someone else in the street. But he could hardly go knocking on doors in a state of undress, so he went inside, sat down. After a while in a daze he finished shaving and then cried uncontrollably. He thought also of Fruity, a friend with whom he'd fallen out, the pair refusing to talk, each as stubborn as the other, unwilling to renew contact. He knew that unconsciously that's why he'd written to Cedric. Jim and Fruity had been still estranged when Fruity had died of cancer, although still his father had invited Jim to the funeral. That had been a painful occasion. And now it was Cedric, and another ceremony Jim would probably miss, as he'd work to go to, no time to track down Myrtle, no contact details so he might ring her, and he couldn't even think of the name of her shop so as to ring up with his query. 'One day I'll write about you, Cedric,' he told himself aloud. 'One day I'll set it all down, well at least some of it, some of your life, our friendship.' He thought of his chum intently and remembered Christmas holidays spent together, a festival they often shared, while Myrtle travelled, and Jim was mostly single. There they'd be like two old bachelors, a real-life comedy duo with its own particular brand of intellectual humour. On one occasion after Jim's cooker blew up on Christmas Eve, when Myrtle was on the other side of the world visiting home, Cedric and he had cooked the turkey at Cedric's maisonette on Christmas morning, ferrying it round to Jim's place in his car, the baking tray perched on Cedric's lap, his pencil-like legs shielded from the heat by a swathe of newspapers and some cardboard they had found somewhere, the smell of meat and hot fat everywhere. Why they didn't eat at Cedric's place Jim couldn't recall precisely, probably because of his central heating and a bigger, better television, colour, unlike Cedric's. Cedric had persisted with a black and white portable for a while for which he paid no licence, until that had packed up completely. It was never replaced.

That was how he would remember Cedric, in the happier times, the festivals, the holidays, whenever both of them could get away from wage slavery. Jim had difficulty in bringing himself to think of life without his friend, aware of the large part Cedric had played in the unfolding of the days, the weeks and months, and eventually the years of that period of Jim's life. Now those shared times were at an end, had halted so abruptly, a sense of which engendered his shock. And how would he tell Will? He might be devastated. And in that moment, Jim realized that Cedric was one of his closest friends, had helped him through some exceedingly hard times. Now it had become impossible to tell him of his appreciation, his love for him, unless his spirit was out there somewhere, swirling amidst a plethora of everyday things, the cafés, the pubs, the junkshops and the urban sprawl of Hackney and Islington where Cedric spent so much of his adult life, or would it be out there in the fringes of Epping Forest, where Katharine probably still lived, thinking of her former lover. Jim sighed, opening a bottle of wine in Cedric's memory. He would delay his departure to early the next day and just sit quietly thinking of all they'd said and done. There was for a start the Saturday four years previously when Jim had tracked down Sue Townsend, Cedric had played his own part on that day too, entertaining Jim as ever, and as late as ever in getting to the Pillars of Hercules . . . .

Chapter Five: May 2014 & Sue Townsend, March 1999

Early May 2014, later in the week when Jim met Alfred in town, on the Friday Jim sat in his other office, at university, one he rarely used. Its shelves were stacked with books he seldom consulted and were also weighed down by multiple copies of the two journals that he edited. He avoided the thought this might represent his only legacy, a pair of academic publications read by a handful of people. His office overlooked a courtyard. Originally post-appointment on the first few visits in his more productive days, Jim found the vista attractive, but no longer. Why he'd become quite so disillusioned with his profession so rapidly during the past three or four years seemed a mystery. Alfred had stirred a few thoughts with his downbeat assessment of where English Studies found itself as a subject. The more particular question that struck Jim was the matter of where he was in his career. He was at the peak of his potential; his research had secured appointment as professor some years before. Upward was only senior management, and he was not the type to pursue such a route, he knew that much. Apart from a book based on the funded project concerned with diaries kept by older people concerning their lives, he had to admit, for the very first time, since starting his doctorate in 1995 aged forty-one, he was struggling with research and publication. Until very recently his enthusiasm for his career begun belatedly had been undimmed.

Perhaps the problem was his age, the fact that he was sixty, for his perspective on work of any kind had shifted. Everything was slowing down and that even included his plans for a new projected novel, his *Gin & Tonic*. He only had some scrappy notes and plans for about three of the various episodes he intended to include, a list of other possibilities, which consisted to date of a word or two each, and maybe a page of details he'd scribbled on the train and tube journeys either side of his meeting with the sceptical Alfred. And despite trying very hard to remember the past, the facts of which seemed to have passed through his mind much like water through some unresisting sieve, many past events were far too painful to contemplate. To think of such former times also involved registering the contrasts with his current condition: the rapidity of the ageing process, his physical stiffness, occasional memory lapses, lack of fitness, and his added weight. All of which seemed overwhelming at times, if you stopped to ponder the matter concretely and too closely. Far better just to get on with life.

Moreover, he was further distracted after the morning's earlier confrontation. He'd driven into work early just for a meeting with the boss which had ended ten minutes ago. Jim was still agitated. Everything Jim had outlined to Will and which he'd so feared was still going to happen, despite his vociferous objections. Carlin had refused to budge, so Jim's only remaining option would be to go to the union, or take out an official grievance. Both would entail far too much effort and work. Ever crafty, Carlin seemed to sense as much. Even before their meeting Jim had concluded that neither option was viable. The result as far as Carlin was concerned was that three areas which had been discrete modules were to be merged into one spread over the whole year, with the post-millennial burden still upon Jim's shoulders. He would struggle like some mighty Atlas, as Cedric might have termed matters. Jim's only concession was that he had until mid-August to finish the new module guide, irrespective of a plethora of current duties, despite innumerable reports to write for the funded project, which his team had just concluded.

Added to these duties was his plan to write *Gin & Tonic*. That he'd like to complete this task over the summer meant even more work to make any progress, and it would need a good deal of effort. As he knew from other attempts years before, novels did not write themselves, whether everyone has one in them or not. It would entail determination, which was off-putting. If such a book were to be at all feasible, in truth he ought to push forward with notes and research as much as he could while term continued, well before the summer holiday began. He'd saved all of his leave days because he desperately wanted a vacation in August to recharge. As he aged he needed quality time away from the job, away from mental effort. Increasingly genuine relaxation was required, preferably on a beach somewhere, like holidays taken at his little *dacha* at Lake Balaton in Hungary. He didn't want to have to spend his vacation yet again catching up with work for which the university scheduled so little time, but expected as its right. Why on earth should he do it all like a slave (Cedric's term)?

However, Jim wondered, was not doing so really feasible? He looked through his current black desk diary and the new red one for the coming academic year. He'd require nineteen leave days for August, another four for the last week in July. He could do that on what was left. He calculated he'd twelve weeks for various tasks: the preparation of both modules, involving reading of novels, research and writing, maybe fifteen new lectures; preparing two module guides; his end of year interviews with and reports about eight doctoral students, which required independent academic interlocutors as witnesses, so he would have to reciprocate; checking end-of-year PhD student reports of all other forty faculty staff; after this preparing the faculty annual audit report on everyone's PhD students to be submitted to the university; odds and sods left from the previous funded project, including reports; various meetings and lunches with colleagues on journals and of scholarly societies; and, a conference paper he'd promised.

And naturally there would be a load of other stuff he'd not anticipated, as he well knew from past years. So, if he wanted to write his new novel, maybe it would prove difficult to take half of August as a real holiday. He sighed. He checked his emails, one from Eileen Beckett again. Being on the work computer he opened it. She was from Newcastle originally, and wanted to know if Jim knew either her mother, Lauren, or Chris Challis. Jim recalled them both, but there was no indication why the daughter had contacted him. He thought suddenly again of the Bunting trip in early 1980, a cascade of memories just right for his new novel, Lauren included. Back then as a school teacher, he'd been on such a treadmill, working weekends and evenings to keep up. There were later periods when life was not as pressured. He missed those. Later, certain compulsions compelled him to work. He remembered the time after 1997, doctorate awarded, when he'd been desperate for a job in a university, he so wanted the salary, the time before he departed for Hungary. He'd worked part-time at Cambridge, supervising final year dissertations, writing freelance articles for a curious financial journal run by the brother of the novelist, Will Self, another writer friend of Jim's, one he'd known before his successes. Living in the Tufnell Park flat, Jim had survived well enough, albeit occasionally very broke and with debts that had to be cleared, but never as bad as Cedric's later ones. Jim had been far less busy, with oodles more time to himself, able to write fiction if and when he wanted. However, Jim hadn't done so. It was not something that he'd kept up during that period post-divorce, despite earlier advice and encouragement from friends like Chris Challis and Sue Townsend, losing touch after Jim left Leicester.

On the other hand, Jim had been ploughing ahead professionally by turning his thesis into a book, and simultaneously writing his part of the next one concerned with Post-war British Fiction, his magnum opus, perhaps. That second volume had originally been a joint project, planned with a collaborator, Bernard. He'd suffered from a massive breakdown of some kind, before settling in California, from where his new wife had arrived, the underlying cause of his crisis. That had been a difficult moment, letting Bernard down gently, telling him he'd been ditched by their publisher, otherwise the editor would have cancelled the contract, which was true. Nevertheless, Jim remembered the time fondly, a period when Cedric had still been on track, ever optimistic, as weird as ever, but always writing, and talking avidly with Jim about his academic work. There had been none of the later aggression, or the long withdrawals, Cedric's later impoverished imitation of Howard Hughes. In fact in many ways it had been Cedric who had inspired Jim to keep going, to push ahead in academic scholarship, and later to take the risk in going out to Hungary for a lectureship, unable to find his first post after completing his doctorate in Britain. He remembered specifically a time inching toward the end of the last millennium, when he and Cedric often dined together, when Jim naturally enough paid for both of them, his friend being completely *borassic*, real piss poor.

On Friday 19 March 1999 a very light, intermittent drizzle fell in Holloway. At around midday Jim was waiting for Cedric under an awning outside their local café on Hercules Street. He was worrying about the fact that two years after completing his PhD he still didn't have a job, and was still subsisting on part-time teaching, some freelance journalism, and private tuition. He was coaching three foreign students who were struggling to finish their own dissertations, one Master's degree and two doctorates. He was forty-five and felt life should be far more secure, less hand-to-mouth. Even Cedric appeared to have more stability at LTU. The short road on which this eatery stood had recently been designated one-way; and Jim noted that periodically some drivers either ignored or missed the signs, driving with determination in the wrong direction, including the Italian owner of the establishment. One vehicle almost knocked Jim down when he'd cycled over from Cedric's. His friend was to follow on foot. Cars lined the road, on the side of the café at almost ninety degrees to the curb, sticking out into the street at a slight angle, lined up like wayward sardines. As a consequence a wide thoroughfare was drastically narrowed, which had earlier left him little room in avoiding the offending female driver, totally oblivious of Jim's anger. He'd been ready to berate her as she parked, but out of the Range Rover stepped the café owner's better half. Jim smiled. 'It's one way now, you know, everything is supposed to go in the other direction.' He pointed out the new sign indignant about her transgression.

'Bloody Islington council!' the matronly Italian woman replied.

Having settled himself inside by the front window, his cycle locked in view on the street furniture protectively guarding a scrawny tree, Jim was reading a copy of *The Independent* that someone had discarded. He was on the obituary page. Lee Falk, the creator of Mandrake the Magician had died, whose weird comics he remembered from childhood, amazing adventures of *Mystery* and *Magic*. This curious figure wore a top hat and tails, a stage costume, and his sidekick was Lothar, a dethroned king of an African tribe who walked everywhere barefoot. Concentrating on the newsprint was difficult as the Care-in-the-Community brigade who frequented this cheap, long-established eatery had appeared outside to surround the tables under the awning. All were smoking and being incredibly noisy, as they often were. Two stood further out in the open, a light spray on their clothes. One chubby-faced large girl in her thirties with crooked teeth had a crazed look beneath her blonde fringe, another was a curiously intense grey-haired young slender Italian guy who always wore a suit with a white shirt. As Jim knew, he flew off into intense rages without apparent reason. Had he been sane he would seem handsome, but somehow his demeanour and the intermittent fury altered the entire effect. He was periodically ejected by his compatriot, Marco, the owner, a fanatical football supporter who gloated over England defeats and victories for Italy. Perhaps once a week on average, Marco would point to the young guy babbling in his suit, dismissing him like an amateur referee at a game of football on a local park, an *Arbitro* or *Direttore della gara* sending off a player.

Well-known by the café's regulars—exceedingly so according to Will—Marco was obsessed with Italian football, tossing out terms such as *Gli Azzurri* and *Serie A*, of which few were familiar, only devotees of Channel Four. He supported passionately from afar Torino, or Associazione Calcio Torin, local team of his hometown, their flag flying outside. Inside were team photographs on the walls, with a curious memorial to the Superga air disaster in 1949, which saw all twenty-seven passengers and four crew killed. Returning from Lisbon the plane hit the wall of the Basilica, wiping out Torino's entire first team. 'Far, far worse than the Munich Disaster. Torino, they had won the last four league titles,' as Marco would tell anyone willing to listen, and a few others who wished they hadn't been so regaled, in the accent of a foreigner long resident, Cockneyfied, but with a singsong quality of the Italians, where every word sounded slightly oh so *clip-ped*, out of synch with the local babble. The interior was a visual assault, an unexpected cultural immersion, so incongruous in sloppy old Holloway where everything was between being run-down and a barely incipient gentrification. 'After the disaster Turoni, who were top of *Serie A*, and only had four more league games left to play. They played the Primavera, the youth team, and as a respect to the dead so too did all their opponents Genoa, Palermo, Sampdoria, and Fiorentina. The Primavera won every match and Turino had their fifth *scudetto* in a row, still a record.' Jim knew the rest almost by heart, he'd heard the tale umpteen times, their coach, a thirty-seven-year-old Englishman, Leslie Lievesley, among the dead. And the wall at the back of the Basilica of Superga had never been restored as a memorial to the victims. Only the injured Torino players who hadn't travelled survived. One further player missed the whole trip, unable to renew his passport at police headquarters. Such is fate. All the other footballers in their prime were killed in an instant, *a tragedy* said Marco.

The event occurred prior to Marco's birth. To cap everything, according to Marco's account, the Italian national side had lost ten out of its starting eleven. He regaled everyone with the tale, repeatedly, becoming more Italian by the second, his gesticulations more exaggerated. 'You know they were so traumatized by the death of our players that the team went to the 1950 World Cup by liner, not by plane. It was so long a voyage, which was why they did so badly,' continued Marco in 1999, as if the tragedy of almost fifty years previously had occurred the day before, outlining his football tale again, to an unsuspecting postman who'd innocently wandered in five minutes before. Jim concluded the entire narrative was gross exaggeration on Marco's part, an embroidered personal myth that took on a life of its own, rooted in fact, but developing its own momentum. It would take an age to check up everything in a library. If he remembered he might look it up on the internet that was installed in his university library. There might be something, perhaps, although he had doubts.

The previous year, summer 1998, Marco had installed a bulky television, on a shelf specifically added by a local builder who lunched in the establishment, for viewing during the last World Cup which had been held in France, and they had dutifully watched the hosts beating Brazil 2-1 in the final, Lilian Thuram with both goals. Marco regretted the addition, for already Italy had gone out to France in the quarter final, o-o at ninety minutes, penalties after a goalless extra time, going down finally 3-4, spot-kick misses by Albertini and Di Biagio, as opposed to just one for France by Lizarazu. In that final phase Marco was unable to watch, following just the commentator, and he cursed each miss and its taker in Italian, the air blue. The result left him inconsolable, literally in tears, blaming specifically the Scottish referee, Hugh Dallas. 'I never, ever trust them, those Jocks, never ever again. Those . . . bloody Jocks!' he spat out the last two words with utter contempt, furious, pop-eyed. Amazed, Jim laughed raucously.

In an instant Jim was banned for life from the eatery, so Marco insisted even on the next day, until finally he softened, influenced by his purse, and a rumour that Jim had begun to frequent a nearby rival, the Hope Dining Rooms, close to Islington Library. Jim's offence had been to follow his cackle with whooping, at which, amid his tears, Marco had complained melodramatically, 'You fail me, you are killing my heart,' whether to Jim or Italy would never become certain. 'Just killing my hope, I feel I am finished, like some dead man.' Given Marco's actual heart was dodgy, angina recently diagnosed, Jim wondered what might to transpire as he walked away. He imagined his banisher clutching his chest and keeling over, stone dead. However, Marco survived. Jim suffered a fortnight's exile. For a few minutes after the banishment Cedric stayed behind to finish his mug of tea, and despite his laughing too, Marco forgave Jim's friend, agreed he could return after a day. Two weeks later Marco ushered Jim formally to a table, Cedric having parleyed, nevertheless for weeks Marco sulked like an infant having lost a favourite toy to a rival whenever Jim was dining, but the mood finally dissipated, normal service literally restored. 'You are such a very cruel one,' he occasionally added, at times reminding Jim of his transgression

On occasion Cedric conversed animatedly with the mentally challenged, Care-in-the-Community individuals, who made up a regular group in the Pillars, pretty much a daily occurrence, apart from an occasional ban when their *transgressions*, a term Marco stressed, disturbed the other paying customers. Marco was too fond of their revenue to exclude them totally, and generally they spent far more than the average customer on each and every visit, with cokes, coffees, ice creams and sandwiches as well as a meal. Jim considered them a real *bloody nuisance*. Their mindless babble, their constant arguments over nothing more than who would sit where, and who could read the menu first, all of it irritated Jim immensely. Cedric was amused by such people, maintained they were victims of society, calling them *the unfortunates*. If Jim mentioned their antics as a source of frustration, he would be reminded that according to Cedric's interpretation of their plight, these poor people were martyrs of Thatcherism, examples of all those emptied from the asylums to reduce the burden on the public purse.

'Remember,' he'd been told by Cedric, 'this scheme allowed the redevelopment and refurbishment of substantial properties, in most cases either by producing chichi flats, or they built whole new estates after demolition. That was the real intention. Thatcher chucked the insane out onto the streets to line the pockets of developers, estate agents and the rentier class, all parasites.' Certainly, these Hercules Street former inmates were generally harmless, like overgrown children. However, as Jim pointed out to Cedric, Jim knew of cases where people were killed by those released, and the families of such perpetrators had persistently begged for them to be sectioned, not objecting to incarceration if they received appropriate treatment, some sort of psychological help. In vicarious fashion they actively sought asylum for these maniacs. Today, Jim studiously ignored the nonsensical squabbles, wishing fervently that they would depart, fuck off elsewhere. Both their hilarity and rancour were raucous.

As he waited for his friend, an article by Boyd Tonkin caught

Jim's attention, entitled 'New literary festival aims to take books to high-rises.' According to Tonkin a London-wide festival called *The Word* planned to take writers to the people that coming weekend. Jim traced the words of part of a paragraph with his finger: 'However, if you want to call the central box office and make a booking, think again. There isn't one; all tickets will be sold by local venues, whether it be the Enfield Civic Centre for Sue Townsend and Terry Pratchett, or the Surbiton Assembly Rooms for Peter Carey.' Clearly, Tonkin had cut and pasted this effort hastily from a press release, but there in his compilation was a vital personal link that intrigued Jim. So, Sue Townsend was visiting Enfield, he thought, going to the place where Jim had grown up and been educated. Instantly, he thought of his edition of *magazine*, back in the flat, with Mole's first appearance, and in that moment, Jim had a bright idea, one that lit up his otherwise aimless day, offered him a purpose. If he could get hold of a ticket, he might cycle up to Enfield, where he could see his mother first, and combine that trip with an opportunity to persuade Sue, if she remembered him after almost nineteen years, to sign a copy. Her signature would make the copy unique, maybe worth a tidy sum, or worth putting away for the future at least.

Money was always on Jim's mind since he was forty-five and basically jobless. At least even when he was in work it was part-time or casual, without a career path or guaranteed salary. In terms of grown-up employment, he wondered whether his part-time teaching in universities really counted. Still, he had completed his doctorate on B.S. Johnson two years before in 1997. He'd a contract for his first book with a university press, one based on his thesis, but this remained unfinished, even after two months spent in the library at the Free University in Brussels, paid to coach two former Erasmus students toward completion of their dissertations. Nevertheless, he had one article in a Hungarian journal based in Budapest, with another coming out in a different Hungarian journal based in Debrecen where he'd visited for a major conference in 1997. Not much to offer with regard to job applications, hardly any real strong points on the curriculum vitae. Publish or perish was the cliché, but with the government's Research Assessment Exercise or RAE it had become increasingly the dictum for all those seeking entry into his putative profession. As if designed to dispel Jim's renewed negativity, Cedric arrived looking positively happy, as if his step was sprung-loaded that morning. 'He's got the bloody goggle box on again, I see, and it's really blaring, and no sport,' he commented disapprovingly, theatrically shaking his head. 'I really wish he wouldn't.'

'Usually, he only has it for the soccer,' Jim explained. 'Marco's obsessed with the Italian league, has it on every Sunday.' Such expression of the owner's passion for football would surely irritate Cedric, not believing pubs and cafés should have televisions, although he considered what he persisted referring to as a *wireless* set was allowable if tuned to Radio 3 or 4 or the World Service.

'Lazio or Juventus will win this year almost inevitably,' Cedric observed unexpectedly, for as far as Jim understood his friend knew nothing of football. After Jim ordered the new arrival a tea and a lamb casserole, Cedric went up to the counter and to Jim's amazement persuaded the wife to turn down the volume.

'Well done,' said Jim and as his friend sat he showed him the Tonkin piece, explaining carefully the context of his intended visit.

'She's not much of a writer,' Cedric responded, 'though lots of people do like her books. At least she's from Leicester, and more importantly she's genuinely working class. Still, go for it. What do you have to lose? Only the calories expended, and you do that anyway, constantly, cycling, all that jogging over the Heath.'

'You see that Lee Falk has died?' asked Jim, changing the subject.

'No, I didn't. Let me try to remember all I know.' He furrowed his brow and rolled another cigarette, his long hair over his eyes as he hunched in his seat. 'He was the creator of Mandrake the Magician and the Phantom, both favourites of mine. Did you know that during the last war he served in a branch of America's Office of War Information, which conducted a full-scale propaganda campaign home and abroad?' Jim shook his head. 'They produced Rosie the Riveter in poster and cartoon versions, the icon now so beloved of feminists started off in support of war production. And here's a curious fact. Falk wrote many plays. They featured Marlon Brando, Charlton Heston, and Basil Rathbone among many others. We live such tame lives, don't you think, Jim?' Cedric paused as if to consider their obscurity, then held up his right index finger as a signal of a competition. 'And for a new challenge, Jim, I quote anonymously: "To hell with circumstances; I create opportunities." Who wrote that?' Jim was familiar with this testing of one's intellect in this way. Guessing obscure quotations was a literary game which Cedric had introduced to Jim's life, about which he was ambivalent, since invariably he lost. Cedric guessed a good half of the ones dug out by Jim.

'So, who said that, Buzz, a writer I'd know, or one I should?'

'In my view, you'll never guess, so one you do not know.'

'I guess it's someone modern by the sound of it.'

'Well it is someone almost contemporary, but they are dead.'

'Well, give me another clue, one's not enough, is it? Too broad!'

'No, I think probably you're correct. Well, the person in question died in the nineteen-seventies, the early seventies.'

Jim wracked his brains. 'So, when did Hemingway die, could it be him?' he murmured to himself. Recently he'd been interviewed on LBC Radio by Lorraine Kelly about the author, when he worked briefly at a television production company in Soho in 1997, better times financially, although only temporarily so. Currently he struggled with fewer part-time teaching hours.

'He died in the early sixties,' Cedric responded. '1961. Hemingway said, "Courage is grace under pressure." A great line; he knew that less is better, paring down the words, just as Orwell said.'

'Just like Raymond Carver.' Jim offered a writer that currently he greatly admired, aspiring to write like Carver, albeit in stories with a London setting, about the inhabitants of Holloway and Islington, friends, acquaintances, and neighbours. He'd just finished one about an identity shop, set in the future, where one could download a new personality, new skills, all hotwired directly into the brain. Cedric was about to read the finished version.

'It's not him. Although certainly it's true Carver is dead.'

'I didn't think it was him. Compare his style to Orwell's advice about less, "if it is possible to cut a word out, always cut it out."' Carver did that. A true genius, and died so young,' said Jim.

'From lung cancer, aged fifty.' Despite his own comment, automatically Cedric rolled another cigarette, continued talking as he lit up, smoke exhaled between phrases, 'He died sober. Toward the end he foreswore the drink, little good it did him. Probably abstinence made him miserable. Funnily there are many premature deaths among writers. Subsequently their literature is a matter of recovering the life. Coleridge, Keats, Byron.'

'Rupert Brooke, H.P. Lovecraft.' Jim added to the list.

'Yes. Actually, Jim, I don't want to disillusion you,' said Cedric, 'but, thinking about Carver, there is a well-established report that an editor at his publishing house had to pare down everything written by Carver, reduced everything, changing the whole emphasis, inventing that supposed Carveresque minimalism that is so well-known and admired by such as yourself, at least that was the case in the early days. Some even say that Carver never learned to distil his work, always needed help.'

The comment made Jim think of a secret he kept from

Cedric, that in truth lately he balked at the notion of brevity prevailing, of avoiding any expansion of a scene by not adding a plethora of details, the addition of various ways of saying something. Covertly, even though he tried to follow his friend's advice, the opposite was the style Jim truly admired.

Lately he'd been re-reading Waugh's *Brideshead*, which Cedric despised. Good writing surely, thought Jim. While Cedric ate Jim scanned a short passage from the novel, where during Eights Week a rabble of womankind arrives, hundreds drinking claret cup, eating sandwiches; all the frivolity distressing to Charles and Sebastian. Cedric would disapprove, but secretly Jim liked Waugh's style, his use of lists, the sardonic asides.

As Jim swallowed, he wondered where Cedric derived all the information he offered the world, much of which Jim hadn't ever guessed at. Yet such gems would usually prove to be accurate enough, bar some occasional minor exaggeration for effect, and Jim wondered too what earthly purpose or end such gobbets could serve collectively, this compendium of obscure facts. He guessed Cedric was simply a literary aficionado, one who had an endless capacity for all matters connected with his passion. Despite his doctorate, at times Jim felt he was in the presence of an unsung master, hidden in a nook off the Hornsey Road, suffering anonymously in the city, a symbol for their age and its indifference, its mania for image and celebrity. He would pump Cedric for another clue. 'So, what's the nationality of your original mystery person? Maybe it's another American, like Hemingway and Carver? Couldn't you offer me some clues, obliquely,' Jim asked trying to pry something else out of his friend.

'No, I'm not playing ball with that. To tell you the nationality would make it just far too bloody easy. You have to work at it, just like a riddle.' They ate in silence for a few minutes, Cedric reading the paper, Jim still mulling over the literary riddle.

'So, what was the quote again, the original one?' Jim demanded.

'"To hell with circumstances; I create opportunities."'

'What about Evelyn Waugh?' Jim's mind felt like a void, echoing

'No, it is certainly not, you're nowhere near, not even warm.'

'Well, if not, maybe it could be E.M. Forster.'

'Better. A goodish attempt at a guess, although again it's a no. Not even very close. Hemingway also said: "I drink to make other people more interesting."' They both laughed at this one. 'Plus, he also said "Happiness in intelligent people is the rarest thing I know" which is a true enough observation in my experience.'

'What about a woman, say maybe Elizabeth Bowen?'

'Again, that's an excellent try, however, definitely not.'

'Oh, I'll just have to give up.' Jim was irritated, feeling stupid.

'Make just one more guess, and I'll tell you.' Jim thought hard.

'Well, what about Barbara Pym.' Cedric put down the newspaper on the Formica surface of the bench at which they sat.

'Another good try, but you'll find she died later in the 1980s.'

'O.K., then tell me, please. You promised you would.'

'Well,' he paused longer than required for effect. 'Bruce Lee.'

'Oh, Buzz, that's cheating, especially as he's not even a writer.'

'Well first, I didn't say it would be a writer, not at all. You presumed it might be. However, second, you were correct in your presumption. As well as acting Lee wrote poetry, about which he was very serious. "Be formless . . . shapeless, like water."' Jim was amazed. Cedric always surprised him with his arcane reading and research, like some benign, contemporary wizard. 'First Lee's tragic early death at thirty-two and later his son Brandon died very young, aged twenty-eight, in a firearm accident while shooting *The Crow* in 1993.' Jim nodded, although he'd never heard of the film. 'It featured John Polito, who was in *Miller's Crossing*, another really great movie, written by the Coen brothers.'

'Who directed *The Big Lebowski*. I so loved that film.'

'Yes, agreed, I think it's just brilliant.' Cedric paused and smiled to himself. 'They're rumoured to be doing a film based on the *Odyssey*, which I anticipate eagerly, I really hope it is good. You know that despite losing its star *The Crow* was a critically acclaimed film, and it was finished using special effects after Brandon Lee died. Death can be inspirational, or it's claimed. Some say Joe Orton's murder was the inspiration for the Beatles' song "Maxwell's Silver Hammer." Personally, I don't believe that.'

'You know, I heard that once, a few years ago, when I was living at the Angel next to the Island Queen, in the same road as Orton was murdered,' Jim said, knowing Cedric coordinated urban space largely by reference to pubs even though more recently he rarely ventured out apart from work, and even that seemed to be becoming an infrequent journey. Cedric informed Jim that there was once a drinking club in that pub frequented by thespians late at night where John Lennon himself rubbed shoulders with Gielgud. And he added more information, relaying that the Angel was steeped in the spirit of revolution, since Tom Paine had written large parts of the *Rights of Man* in the Old Red Lion in 1791, and that Lenin had drunk in another pub in the vicinity, as earlier had Marx. And, according to legend, an inebriated Marx stole a policeman's helmet, but Cedric didn't believe a word. 'How do you know all this stuff, Cedric?' His friend simply smiled, like Carroll's contented cat. 'Let's order dessert.'

At lunchtime a day later, Saturday 20th, Jim stood in a mezzanine area inside a concrete extension to the vulgar aluminium-coated tower-block which housed Enfield's local authority. He waited for Sue Townsend to finish signing some books, prior to her reading later. So far, he kept his distance. He hadn't approached her, feeling nervous about doing so. There were children everywhere. Sue, in her early fifties, looked tired, jowly and certainly carrying far more weight than he remembered. He approached when the last person disappeared. 'I don't know if you remember me, but I'm Jim Dent,' He said. She peered at him.

'I know the name and naturally I recognize that voice of yours, virtually unchanged, although maybe deeper. Come closer, my eyes aren't so good.' He sat opposite. Her local Leicester accent was unmodified. 'Oh yes, you've hardly altered. I think you're somewhat thinner than I remember you in your Leicester days.'

'It's all the running. I jog all the time, almost every day.'

'Well done you. It's a great if you can sustain the effort. I remember you were a great sporty type back in the day. I should do more exercise, what with my diabetes. My eyesight isn't great, deteriorating.'

'I'm very sorry to hear that. It must make life difficult?'

'I can still write, finishing a new book, *The Cappuccino Years*.'

'You know that's a great title. Look, I was wondering if you would sign this for me. I kept a copy.' He produced the first issue of *magazine* from his shoulder bag to sharp intake of breath from the celebrity author, and a wry smile that had been familiar to Jim in the past. She was peering at the offending page very close to her face. 'Do you remember this, Sue?' he asked, knowing she would.

'Oh, do I? Certainly, I do. I haven't seen this in years.' She laughed with that sardonic smile. 'This was the very first start, although I hadn't an inkling of what was to follow. I have one or two of these stashed away somewhere.' She read a few lines. 'I'd written so little at this point. I didn't realize. When was it? 1980? Before that, I was so poor, and it grinds you down, fixes you in a single location, unable to move, to develop. Having nothing with three small children was terrifying. I used to feel very guilty. This story was the start of a change, my transition, one for my family. Later Mole virtually took over my life, you realize, dominated it.'

Jim nodded. He'd forgotten how pleasant Sue was, always straightforward, generous with her time. She took out her pen.

'Here?'

He nodded again. 'Yes, that'll be just right.'

'He's been good to me, has good old Mole.' She paused. 'What I mean really is that I can't complain given all the success he brought me. We never imagined all that when it started, did we?'

Jim shook his head, recollecting the once unknown writer.

'Of course, although he was Nigel back then, as you well know. Just look at this, it's only a page, two-thirds in fact, if you discount the illustration.' Jim could see the page. In Sue's first brief story Mole's dog was being sick on his homework and the provincial adolescent lit a joss stick in a futile attempt to feel that he might become intellectual. She captured provincial aspiration.

'Very few people know where he began, very few were privy to his origins.' She sighed wistfully, Jim thought. 'Really, Jim, Mole had such a tentative beginning. I remember wondering what I'd write for you all, whether it was any good, would read it to myself. Just think.' Jim recollected the second offering that he'd dug out that very morning, headed 'NIGEL SEARCHES FOR LEICESTER'S INTELLIGENTSIA.' In the second the very status of an intellectual is conferred ironically enough according to young Nigel by watching Malcolm Muggeridge on television.

'They were happy days, weren't they' he said nostalgically.

'Are you staying for the reading?' Sue asked, making him feel sharply guilty about his planned escape back to Islington.

'I'm sorry, but I'd arranged to meet my mother. She lives in Enfield.' Jim's statement wasn't entirely true. He'd already visited her that morning, had some tea together. Now he wanted to work on an academic article back home once he cycled back.

'Is she widowed, Jim?' Sue asked sympathetically.

'Oh no, my father is still very well, very fit, in fact. I just don't get on with him at all. We avoid each other. So, I meet her over here in town sometimes, so as to avoid him. They live near the industrial part of the borough, two or three miles away, once thriving, although recently the few remaining factories have begun to close.' He was still feeling guilty about rushing off. 'Sorry to rush, but she'll really be expecting me, my mother.'

'Well, it's mostly kids dragging their bloody parents along, who are clearly bored to death. We're forced to do so much by our offspring. Are you still a socialist, Jim?' she asked, out of the blue.

'I suppose I still am.' He was uncertain. 'I don't trust this Blair character. I met him, after canvassing for Islington Labour Party, doing my bit as one of the foot soldiers, fighting off the local SDP defectors, knocking up voters. When I met Blair, I couldn't warm to him. I didn't trust him then, or that wife of his, and I still don't. He's a populist, a revisionist, clearly on the right himself. He'll be even more trouble as he gets into his stride.'

'I think I tend to agree. Nevertheless, the Tories had to go, the vermin, as Aneurin Bevan once described them.' Jim had his doubts about such partisanship. 'So instead we had to support Blair.' Sue sounded as if her doubts were growing. 'I'm totally unconvinced about this bombing of Yugoslavia, they're even going for civilian targets. Just think under a Labour government we'll probably be targeting civilians by the look of things.'

'Yes, I voted for him, but very reluctantly. Look at all this propaganda about Serbian oppression against the Kosovo Albanians. Blair's a warmonger, and a war criminal.' Jim told her about one of his students, a Serbian girl from Novi Sad, in tears last week during his discourse analysis class. They had been studying Blair's speech on the crisis, listening to a recording of the announcement of the bombing, looking at the appalling bias in its language. Blair's speech-writer had loaded this invective with pejorative terms whenever referring to either Milošević or the Serbs, he had written them on the whiteboard: 'vile oppression;' 'death and barbarism;' 'siege;' 'hideous;' '"ethnic cleansing;"' 'massacred;' 'broke his word;' 'massacre;' and 'repress.' He added Blair's claim: 'Britain is a peaceful nation; we are a peaceful people who take no joy in war.' Paradoxical. Sue seemed to recognize Blair's warmongering and the poor young woman's distress.

'It's awful. I hate this bloody bombing,' said Sue. 'They'll be killing women and children next, without remorse, full of glib excuses.'

They were quiet, feeling the betrayal of their youthful socialist ambitions, both unwilling to further contemplate the war Blair described as a 'fight for peace.' Both hated him and what he'd done.

'Well, maybe I'll vote Green next time,' said Jim without conviction.

'I was hoping for a resurgence of the genuine left,' responded Sue. Jim left his own doubts of such extremists unspoken. 'I hoped that over the coming years the socialist arm of the Labour party would garner support, be succoured, and regain its authority. Somebody has to care for the poor.' She was thinking of her youth, of her early adulthood, of childhood even, a poverty just as Cedric had known, a dispossession that was alien to Jim who'd been brought up in the relatively affluent south-east.

'Yes, very true. Any good Leicester news? Do you have any of the gossip, and scandal, Sue, about people we knew? I hardly ever see anyone from the old days, and lately I never go back. My son, Will, is nineteen now, and at Exeter University, so I visit him in the South-West occasionally. There's no excuse or time left for a Leicester jaunt, and not really enough money. I'm working part-time'

'Shame. My, he was just a baby when I knew you, as I remember.'

'Yes, he was just born, only four months when we split.'

'I'm sorry. I didn't know your wife at all. Well, kids do grow so much, and so quickly. However, you asked about Leicester news. Yes, actually there is some gossip, a sort of very minor tragedy and scandal. Could you come outside while I have a sneaky cigarette, and I'll tell you all?' She was ever the storyteller, building suspense. 'I'm trying to give up, but it's really hard. I admit I do allow myself just an occasional one now and then.'

'Once a day, impressive self-control. I couldn't manage that.'

'Well, maybe several each day. Are you coming outside?'

'Yes, I will. My bike is out there, so I can retrieve it.' The two of them got up, went down some stairs and wandered out slowly to a grass area to the side of the building. It was sunny, but still chilly. Sue moved slowly, cautiously, with great effort. She withdrew items from her bag, first some posh-looking cigarettes. Her lighter was expensive too. She lit up, dragged in the smoke. He envied her, remembering such moments of pleasure. They'd punctuated his youth. He missed a cigarette with a drink. Outside in the sun he declined with his palm the offer of one of her tailor-mades from her enamelled tin. 'As to fags, I quit nine years ago.'

'Well done you, for a second time. I'm surprised given you were such an inveterate smoker as I recall, always one on the go.'

'My old school is over there,' Jim pointed to the grounds of the lower school, once a country mansion, changing the subject.

'Oh, really, is it?' she responded, clearly not at all interested in his alma mater. She inhaled, coughed, but persevered, sucking in more smoke. Jim kept quiet, sensing she'd something specific to relate. 'So, as I seem to recollect, you were close to Chris Challis, very close buddies for a time?' Jim hadn't thought of the Leicester-based poet for years, not once.

'Well, yes, I suppose I was for a while, just before I left Leicester, for the last two years of my time there.' Details flooded his mind, images, words, places, people. 'I met Ginsberg at his house once, and together we went on a long trip up north to interview Basil Bunting.' Challis had possessed a huge old white American-style car with power breaks, tiny steering wheel, covered in white leather, which he called the Great White Shark.

In the last week of 1979, after Jim's car packed up and the trip was in danger of being cancelled, Challis offered to accompany him, and drive them to the North-East in the Shark. The previous summer they'd shared an informal food and drinks reception at Challis' house, held for Allen Ginsberg who'd been booked to read later at the student union, the earlier gathering in the improbably small terraced house where Challis lived, given the volume of guests. Dope cakes were the order of the day, still very much a legitimate part of the hippy zeitgeist, even sold in shops and cafes on the quiet in places such as Hay on Wye, where he'd once taken Will in his youth, driving down from Shrewsbury where Jim lived briefly.

'I remember him mentioning that visit, about when we did *magazine* together. Everyone knew that monstrous car, a huge old thing. Chris was into cars, whenever he had enough money. Well, clearly you've not heard poor old Chris' fate?' Sue asked reflectively. Jim half-noticed her use of the past tense, a curious detail.

'I haven't seen him in years, not since I left Leicester in 1981.'

'He died, two years ago. I thought you might not have heard.'

'He's not dead, surely not? Two years back. No one told me.'

'Well, sorry to bear bad news He was found at the bottom of his stairs; he'd been there for days, tumbled down drunk, they presume. He'd died before the body was discovered. There was an inquest, but the verdict was predictable enough: accidental death.'

'Poor Chris, I'll miss him,' said Jim even though they'd not spoken in years. 'And to think of it, what an awful way to go.'

'I agree, it was a really grim end.' As Sue spoke, Jim thought of the terraced house in which Chris had lived, initially forgetful of the street's name, although he could place the exact spot. He remembered too the strange dark brown cat that actually at certain times when it was cold used the upstairs toilet to crap in. No one ever believed Jim about this natural oddity, but he'd seen it with his very own eyes, on at least two separate occasions. He'd been convinced that a trick was involved, the animal must have been trained to do so, but Challis had vehemently denied being involved in training the creature. He'd claimed the cat must have copied him. Jim remained sceptical, radically unconvinced. 'Was he in the same place, on Prospect Hill? The terraced houses overlooked what was literally a deep valley used for their gardens.'

'That's right, the place near Spinney Hill Park.' For Jim a flood of other memories overwhelmed him, of playing football nearby.

'You used to live below Chris, near Needham Street.'

'You have a good memory, Jim. I wasn't there for that long.'

'Regarding Challis, he confessed he'd acquired the house from a girlfriend, a rich student, which I found unlikely.' Jim suspected Challis was covering up nefarious dealings, perhaps a fraud.

'No, he was telling the truth. He really did. It was originally bought for a hippy chick in the late sixties, for a really posh *bird* as they called them in those unreconstructed days. She was an almost aristocratic student called Posh Pandora something or other that I forget. She was rumoured to be able to use a title if she so wished, Lady Pandora. The father had been a viscount or an earl, although long gone, dead from the drink and buried, money left to the children, but with strings attached, a trust fund. Her trustees bought the place for her, and somehow, she ended up going out with Challis. According to others she was attractive in a hippy fashion, but pretty thick, so not much good in her studies, always struggling. She met Chris, bright working-class boy, and hey presto her grades began to improve meteorically.'

'So presumably this led to a reciprocal arrangement?'

'I think so. Chris helped her with pretty much all of her degree, gratis, while getting a first in his own. He had free accommodation, initially as her unpaid lodger, but after a while it became clear that they had become what we used to call an item, acting as her lover and unofficial tutor on tap. When they split up, he stayed on. Although the malicious rumour was that on occasion he beat her up when he was drunk, once or twice, and according to those accounts that she left finally, completely fed up with him. I think she just upped sticks and went back to London, personally.'

'Well, certainly he was a big guy. He used to work out, with his Bullworker.' Jim remembered the expanded biceps and chest.

'He was and yes he did. You do recollect all the little details. Now you've reminded me, I remember all that daily routine of exercise. Yet he was a gentle soul all of the time I knew him. I knew about the supposed incidents because Pandora was friends with Clementine, another hippy babe, the one my bloody fellow ran off with, leaving me in the lurch without money and with three kids to fend for. Anyway, he told me about Challis' supposed dark little secret, which I still find hard to believe, although admittedly there's the whole subtext of pornographic photographs of young students that isn't so salacious, yet in truth not all that shocking back in the day, during the sixties and seventies.'

'How come she let him stay for so long without recompense?'

'She gave him a tenancy without rent. Prices were so low back then and she was loaded. Later the trust signed it over to him.'

'Really, did they?' Jim was surprised. In his circles people didn't go around giving away assets like houses. 'It was still worth something.'

'Yes, they really, really did. Remember she was so stinking rich, so wealthy she was part of a set that is hard to even imagine, with so much money. The rumour was that she'd arrived at Leicester because she was too thick for the best universities and everyone suspected a donation would have been involved, some promised bequest. As to Challis' supposed wife-beating, I think personally she just left to go to the smoke, as you might call it, because she fancied a change. She probably lived in a squat, to be trendy. Back in Leicester a single black eye became an urban myth.'

'How could you give away a house?' Jim repeated, incredulous.

'See it from the trust's perspective, Jim. The value of a terraced house would have been small change for a proper trust fund. And back then, in about maybe 1970 or 1971, you could buy a house of that kind, in that area for maybe three or four hundred pounds, possibly even less. By the time Challis was assigned the house rent free, they would rather avoid the maintenance costs and ongoing commitment, so made him responsible.' Jim thought of the six thousand he and his wife paid in the south of the city in 1978.

'You make a good point.' Finding another perspective was hard for Jim, given he had rigid values instilled in him as a child.

'Even good wages in Leicester for an ordinary worker were

only about fifteen quid a week, for a man, even less for women,' she added. 'I earned less than ten quid a week. They were tearing such houses down by the acre, clearance schemes.' Jim remembered this process of so-called regeneration as an undergraduate, seeing row upon row being condemned, the residents rehoused, the council clearing out the squatters who sprouted like weeds, huge yellow bulldozers going in, flattening entire streets, and lastly the residue that was not burnt acridly on site being ferried away in immense tip-up trucks, entire communities vanishing. The higgledy-piggledy flats that had replaced the narrow terraces were being demolished themselves. Jerry built, they'd lasted barely thirty years.

'Challis couldn't have been that old when he died.' It was a chilling thought and Jim guessed Challis to have been ten years older than him, tops, although he'd been very secretive about himself. From what he could recollect from their long conversations on their journey, Challis was originally from Ingatestone, a small commuter town in Essex, and he'd been employed as a roadie with a then relatively unknown band, Genesis, when he first visited Leicester for a single night, 14th February 1970 at Leicester's Students Union. After the tour ended in July he decided to return, determined to study at the university that autumn. Something definitely drew him back. Quite what, Jim could not imagine. Maybe he must have met a cute, young babe?

'Well, that's exactly the point, Jim. Everyone believed he was fifty-one, which is no age at all, because they were told so by Challis. More recently there has emerged a strong rumour that when he first arrived in Leicester to register at the university, he subtracted ten years from his age. With all those beards, and all that long male hair, no one really noticed. And he carried it off well if he did so, for years. So according to the rumour, he actually died aged around sixty-one, although that's still very young.'

'I knew a tutor that Challis also knew pretty well, Ian Hilson, who was killed in his thirties, when he was about to marry for a third time. That was so awful; he seemed about to put his life back together on the personal level after several fairly acrimonious splittings-up. The irony was that he'd just met a new partner, a nurse, who was a really nice person. I met her.'

'What happened?' asked Sue, curious about all Leicester-oriented matters.

'A motorbike doing over a ton went through the windscreen as he turned onto London Road, hitting Ian's car full force. Rumour was the impact turned the vehicle over twice. The motorbike rider and his girlfriend survived, badly injured. Ian was trapped. I was with Challis when we heard the news. This is the real point, I remember he was taken aback, literally speechless. You know, I'd never believed in that word until that occasion.'

'Actually, to be honest, looking back I liked Challis a great deal, Jim, whatever other people said about him,' Sue added. 'It's just I didn't realise how much at the time. He'd a lot of people against him, and maybe even as friends we didn't offer him enough appreciation. I know many people in Leicester who couldn't stand him. Most claimed he was a fraud, without talent.'

'The university's English Department treated him pretty badly, rarely offered him any work' Jim said. 'His face didn't fit. And yet he did publish, successfully. And his plays were performed at the Phoenix, and one even broadcast on the BBC, on Radio Four, I think, which I heard. Although I can't exactly remember the title.'

'Maybe those who objected to him were jealous, of his creativity. There were a number of plays. The BBC one was *The Ten-Foot Play*, another for the Phoenix Theatre was called *Coca-Colonisation*. I remember the titles because they were so typical of the man, so Challis, to choose something so whimsical, stupid, even though he was totally serious about his writing. It was always his main mission throughout his life. He wrote well.'

'Do you think so?' Jim had his doubts, even at the time.

'I do. You know, Jim, Challis infuriated those who were against him, he upset their small-town mentality, and I say that as a local myself. They thought him an interloper, which annoyed them given his local prominence, what with Arts Council and other grants and the paid poetry readings and the fact that his plays were performed. They wished he'd just go away, especially those who weren't getting any attention or any success. Personally, I didn't think that way. He was among the first people who encouraged me to write, one of the very first to do so. I know he could be peculiar, and he liked his drink, but he was a sensitive guy too, Jim. Did you know him well enough to sense that hidden side of him?'

'I suppose. You're right about his sensitivity. I was fond of him, yet never admitted it at the time. He took me under his wing.'

'He did that. He didn't harm many people, not badly anyway.'

'You know that when I worked with him once on a project, he was developing photos, using his hands, which were very soft, hardly any sign of labour. And I remember thinking that those hands were incredibly wrinkled for a man of his age. I have no clue what we were doing, just that it was in the student union, the basement. You tend to forget most details, but that stayed with me.'

'Well if your instinct was right, maybe I was wrong, and he did lie about his age. To be honest I had thought it was just more malicious gossip, almost like an urban myth. But from what you say it may be hearsay which might actually be based on a real impression. Well, I must perform soon. One has to sing for one's supper.'

'Well, good luck with the reading. Knock them dead.'

'Have you any paper on you, something to write on?'

'No, not on me.' Sue pulled a pad from her pocket, scribbled on a page with it very close to her face, folded on completion.

'Oh dear, I was thinking that the Jim Dent I knew was a *real writer* full of commitment. Like Challis, you showed some real promise at least as far as I recall. You seem far more detached these days, far less radical, and far less committed to anything creative.'

'Life's been hard. Work demands so much.' He hadn't told her about his doctorate, his change of emphasis to academic writing.

'Yes, but you wrote some good pieces once, so you ought to try to keep going. And writers, they always carry around a notebook, that's one of the rules, Jim. And the Jim Dent I knew was interested in everything, and passionate about things. Today I'll excuse you for once, if only for reminding me of my Adrian, of his early days, when he was still a Nigel. What times they were, Jim, with such hopes and struggles. Writing was your mission, too.'

Jim didn't like to tell her he'd long given up on writing full-length fiction. Six volumes, three unpublished novels, two novellas, and a collection of short stories, stood on his shelves at home, each one with a soft binding like a thesis, as if in preparation for some final oral examination. He sighed inwardly about wasted effort. Sue continued, 'Well, here's my number. If you visit us again, ring me. It's been so good meeting again, Jim, someone from the old days, from when I was just starting out. I'd be pleased to see you if ever you visit Leicester. Try to write again. Remember: always carry a notebook, without exception, as you used to.'

Jim rode away heading for home, a vigorous eight-mile ride, thinking that during the time he'd known Sue, Will was conceived and born, even though Jim's marriage was falling apart, a split increasingly inevitable. First, he discovered his bride stole from him, change he stored in a jar, saving for Christmas presents. After five months the amount had reduced, because daily Virginia was pilfering from his stash. Next was her half admission of an affair before their wedding with an acquaintance of his. Jim was troubled, Virginia blasé and defiant. During this period he'd been closest to Challis. As Jim continued to pedal he tried not to dwell on his awful marriage, the betrayals, and gradually he focused on what were initially a few vague impressions of the

Bunting trip they shared, which recollections became a torrent. He must write it up, he thought, maybe compose an academic essay about Bunting, include his meeting, draw on what he'd written back in 1980, perhaps take a quote or two from the university arts journal, the name of which he couldn't quite recall.

He decided he must find out later; that is, if it had survived his many moves over the years. He knew that a whole load of stuff was once left behind in a cellar in a house in Dudley co-owned at one point, and that had stood empty for fifteen months or so after which he departed. All that stuff was now irretrievable. At least the experience taught him two essential truths: first, don't look back, better to just live for the present; and, second, throw out all the clutter, as at least half the junk which we cling on to is superfluous as regards our real requirements in life. He should have learnt that lesson earlier, might have cleared out the emotional entanglements, quit his marriage sooner, before 1980, maybe have avoided it altogether. If he had, his life might have been palpably better. . . .

Chapter Six:
Christmas Eve, December 1979

Over the weekend of 2nd and 3rd May 2014 Gabi was away for a trip to Hungary, visiting her ailing father, who was dying very slowly, withdrawing inwards, profoundly affected by Parkinson's. After driving her to Stansted early Saturday morning, by ten Jim climbed with difficulty into his loft via a rickety ladder. He retrieved papers and notebooks. With free time he sought inspiration, to progress with writing his new novel. With a large cup of tea, at the dining room table Jim went through everything he'd found relating to the past: old diaries; various publications, poetry he'd written as a youth, poems published in regional magazines; short stories from his first novel, originally entitled *Swallows in the Sky*, which incomplete typescript lay on the maroon tablecloth. Several extracts appeared publicly in a student Arts magazine at Leicester, *Luciad*, which he co-edited while a postgraduate.

After an hour Jim abandoned the written record, or as much as he'd retrieved easily on his single climb, and instead he pored over photographs found in his bedroom cupboard, stored in plastic bags and albums, another pile of detritus from the past. He chuckled at the long hair, the flares, the collarless shirts, and his mullet hairstyle. There he was with shorter hair in a dinner jacket with make-up, at a fancy-dress party in the marital house, a Victorian terraced villa, bought in the mid-seventies. He remembered digging over and sieving the entire back garden, clearing it of the habitual rubble builders always bury, even Victorian ones. He recollected the lawn he laid, the apple tree planted to the right. He sat making lists of people and places, going out to his office to look up maps online, finding the various streets, tracing Challis' dwelling in Spinney Hills, and Jim's own home in that southern suburb of Leicester. He spotted all the various parks where he'd played football in and around the city. He thought hard about the substance of his life there, having lived almost a full decade in

Leicester, from age eighteen to twenty-seven and ten months.

After making more tea, for several hours Jim sat at his dining room table, staring into space, thinking about what had occurred in the nineteen-seventies and eighties, to him, to the country, to the way things were, to the British way of life. The late seventies just before his divorce seemed such a different world, even though he'd lived through those years. He sighed. He recalled his wife's hidden infidelities which emerged in autumn 1980, the myriad lies she'd spun previously, her unwillingness to share a bank account, and her failure to pay in any single month for half their living expenses despite her higher salary. Jim was too immersed in his attempts to be a writer to see the emerging picture of her untrustworthiness, the craven selfishness that characterized her. He wondered about Cedric in 1979, whether he might have visited Leicester at Christmas or New Year to see his parents. Jim thought of those in the city who might have been mutual acquaintances.

In about 2000 Jim learnt from a particular conversation that Cedric knew of Challis, heard him declaim his poetry in a pub. Cedric was unimpressed by the performance, and certainly he regarded the man as a figure to deride. At the time in contrast Jim admired Challis, and yet apart from the account of their trip together to see Bunting, he'd written almost nothing about this earlier friend. In truth he probably hadn't considered him as anything more than an acquaintance, not before the trip, nor even in its aftermath. Challis and he hadn't been that close and yet together he believed they shared some remarkable experiences. Naturally it simply seemed like ordinary, everyday life at the time, nothing that exceptional in the flow of humdrum events in a dull provincial city. Although, as he reflected in 2014 and much as Cedric would have reminded him, such places are where you might find all the mystery and wonder of life. Also, there was the reality of the awfulness of Jim's domestic life in the background, which depressed him, deadening his imagination, further dulling his appreciation of simple things. That relationship made him far too inward, feeling solitary even among a crowd. At the very end of the seventies, over its final Christmas his marriage was deteriorating fast, like a car crash in slow-motion, yet difficult to anticipate or control. This was the beginning of the very worst of it all, and curiously this decline seemed to accelerate ironically when his car failed him. Naturally that was only a passing impression, but one that seemed very real at the time, as if he was deflated by the vehicle's betrayal. At the time he thought himself a committed writer, of poetry first, fiction next, all of which clearly his wife despised. Retrospectively, Jim wondered why she ever bothered with their relationship, given she rejected profoundly so much of what he was committed to, plus the lies she told, and her secrets when revealed even shook her usually loyal, unquestioning parents.

As Christmas began in Leicester on Monday 24 December 1979 Jim tasted great disappointment. His gold Hillman Avenger, which he'd loved so very much, failed him mid-afternoon. Fortunately enough, it broke down almost outside his home, shuddering to a halt ten feet away, exhaling loudly, followed by nothing. He turned the key fruitlessly, flattening the battery. With Virginia, he lived in a terraced house in a leafy suburb near the racecourse, south of the city. He struggled with the booze and groceries to the door, with a brass doorknocker, no bell.

Virginia was three months pregnant, expecting their first child. The previous week an ultra-sound scan conjured up a blob of unborn child on a crude print-out they were given. You could make out limbs, but no clue as to the sex. Jim decided his firm preference was for a son. To date there was no agreement on names, although Virginia offered those of two of her first-term university boyfriends, from autumn 1972 before she hooked up with Jim in February 1973, the month of his nineteenth birthday. Jim was intensely annoyed at her suggestion his son might memorialize another relationship of hers. His life was otherwise more relaxed, having finished his first term in a temporary post, teaching as a fractional English teacher in a mixed comprehensive Upper School in Leicestershire, south of the city. He taught in a brand-new block, recently opened, with performance space and library. He loved that environment, much better than his previous two years at York Boys' Secondary Modern, a grim site, and a most negative experience, about which he avoided any continued reflection.

In his half time away from work the previous term he'd sat assiduously at his desk in their bedroom, at the end of the marital bed, every day with a notebook and his wife's portable typewriter before him. He started keeping clippings of interesting items, curious news stories from newspapers and magazines, but they vanished. Whenever he left the house Virginia disposed of them. They argued bitterly about her presumption; she informed him categorically that she wouldn't stand for this clutter in their bedroom, a gross exaggeration as he'd limited them to a small open wooden box originally containing tangerines. For the purpose and to maintain cleanliness Jim varnished it inside and out.

'All that junk you keep, it's useless. Why can't you remember what you're going to say and make notes, like a normal person?'

And when the weather started to turn, cold both inside and outside, Virginia realised that the gas would be lit in their bedroom all day long at least twice a week. She complained bitterly of the expense, shrieking at him, working herself up, reaching a crescendo of complaint. Her idea was that Jim should go to the university library, but in October, the weather still warm, he found it far too distracting, gaggle upon gaggle of teenage girls, half-dressed, exhibiting their young bare flesh, healthy, nubile, exuding indiscriminately their underdeveloped, yet emergent and insistent sexuality. He preferred writing at home, even though at times the amount typed or scrawled proved to be minimal. When the weather cooled Virginia balked at the extra expense, not that she paid anywhere near half the bills. Today she'd offered nothing toward the cost of the shopping, and, as usual, would *forget* to do so.

He turned to his typewriter on the desk in their bedroom, where he'd retreated after packing away all the shopping he'd paid for.

Like many people he knew in Leicester who wanted to write
or be creative, especially those attached in some way to the
humanities departments at both the university and the *polly*,
Jim was struggling to find his voice or subject matter. After a
year at the 'polly' training as a teacher, Jim spent the previous
summer typing out on a portable his first novel, *Swallows in
the Sky*. He adapted the title from John Keats' 'To Autumn', a
favourite poem at school - how did it go? He found his collected
edition on the shelf in an alcove, identified the correct page,
and reread the last line. 'And gathering swallows twitter in the
skies,' he read, finding his choice in retrospect unconvincing.
He realized now his first idea produced a most pretentious
title, which would put off potential readers. One tutor he knew
well, Ian Hilson, read Jim's typescript and he said he liked
it generally, stating that certain parts showed very definite
promise. The word meant much to Jim at the time. Virginia was
unimpressed. Only a big advance would have placated her. Jim
and Virginia became friends with Ian during a long car journey
down to a posh wedding of mutual friends in Kent, a top hat
and tail affair for the groom and best man. The newlyweds
were a couple who just graduated, the year before Virginia,
two before Jim, so in 1974 when Jim was twenty. Together with
Virginia and Hilson, all three stayed at Jim's parents. Recently
Hilson promised he would send a note with further suggestions,
supplementing those initially given on the phone. Jim was
delighted. Hilson made a definite *promise* (that word, again) to
go through the whole typescript together if and when he could
find sufficient time. Jim knew he was very busy, so he respected
the offer, utterly delighted at any positive response. Hence Jim
decided to wait before further revisions. He felt putting his
newly-acquired friend under pressure would not have been
appropriate, and might sour the putative friendship, although
he hoped they might bump into Hilson in a local pub over the
holiday period, when he might give him more advice informally.

To be a writer had long been Jim's major ambition, from aged
about eight or nine. He'd no real idea of what such a commitment
entailed, but he'd been insistent about his sense of his future

in this sphere. One thing he'd known even at nine had been that a writer needed a proper typewriter, preferably a portable. He'd seen that even in his precious DC comics in the office of the Planet where Clark Kent worked. When pestered one Christmas by Jim, repeatedly, his father had obtained one for nothing, with new ribbons bought very cheaply. It was a huge decommissioned typewriter from the offices in the factory where he worked as a maintenance carpenter. This object served as monument to the age of iron and steel, its volume reminiscent of some immense machine tool, hammering out letters from thin air. With Jim's tentative strike certain keys stuck. It was nothing like the beautiful Smith-Corona Corsair he'd imagined when preparing his Santa list. However, the monster served a purpose, demonstrating that becoming a writer would clearly be far harder than he'd anticipated in boyhood. Yet in his teens he managed half-decent poems for his age, no prodigy, just school magazine stuff. Even now as the seventies drew to their close at twenty-five going on twenty-six, Jim didn't seem to have the experience, especially having spent the past seven and half years in this tiny provincial city. Jim realised he missed London, but Virginia was a local, from a village twelve miles away and was dead set against going anywhere else in the world. Imagine, he thought, she'd only applied to a single university, the local one, and as a back-up Leicester's sole teacher training college at Scraptoft on the north-eastern edge of the city. Jim hated such provincialism. He wanted to travel, to live elsewhere, but soon there would be a baby, making such things increasingly unlikely. He should've realised when he met Virginia, but his libido countered common sense, her hippyish long ginger strawberry blonde hair and Mary Quant mascara blinded him to the myopic and provincial nature of this young country girl, neither a real traveller nor a hippy chick at all.

He knew Virginia would complain whenever he tried to write, but he snuck upstairs anyway. She was in the kitchen, singing to herself, while cooking something or other. He was just glad that earlier before today's mechanical breakdown that morning he'd completed shopping for the whole holiday, especially with all the guests expected. The engine had refused to function just after he'd taken a brief afternoon jaunt to buy some extra booze and food in case of other unexpected visitors, various items that were an afterthought on Virginia's part. If they were to need anything more, he could walk the hundred metres to Flynn's, the corner store, and then another hundred metres to see Gordon and Ellen, married neighbours and friends, the husband a colleague in the upper school where Virginia worked in Leicestershire. Jim wanted to ask Gordon, who knew all the gossip, about Flynn, who was rumoured to have left his wife for a teenage girl less than half his age. Some said she was already pregnant. Jim would ask Gordon for a lift to the Cradock, their local pub with its old-world charm and thatched roof, on Knighton Road, near the awful secondary modern where Jim started teaching two years previously, which crushed optimism, his excellent teaching and good grades entirely overlooked.

About a week before in the Cradock's large back bar Gordon sat next to Jim amidst a crowd of around a dozen friends. Gordon was in a car pool, sharing costs with Virginia and another female colleague, who they all called Moggy for some reason lost in her infancy. She lived along the same road, as it curved toward London Road, whose name continually reminded Jim of home. Huddled together in a corner, in a quiet wavering whisper Gordon made a confession that soon after he'd bought his Fiesta specifically for driving to work, he'd failed his test, just before the summer term was to start. 'When was that,' Jim asked.

'About eight months ago.' Gordon had thinning curly hair, squeaky voice, tremulous, with more than a touch of a Kentish burr. He sported facial stubble, never a beard, never clean-shaven.

'So, what happened? You've been driving much longer, in the carpool. *You only had a provisional licence, not a full one?*' Jim whispered, the last question being entirely rhetorical.

'Well, yes, naturally I had to drive in without one. There was just no other way of getting there, once I'd accepted the job.'

'What, so you've been driving every day of the year without passing your test, I mean driving without a full licence?' Jim was so flabbergasted he repeated his query in his incredulity.

'Yes, but who on earth would know?' Gordon was unperturbed.

'Well, they would if you'd been fucking stopped,' objected Jim.

'Unlikely. It's only to work and back, and most of the journey is along the M69, which is almost brand new. They opened it in 1977, only two years ago. Most days it's empty, both carriageways.'

'I know, I've driven along the road myself using my *full* licence.' Jim paused to think. 'You say you only drove to and from work, but you use the car to come to the pub, and for shopping. You go to Oadby Kwik Save by car every week. I see you there.'

'Oh, well, they're both less than half a mile. I can drive perfectly well, I only failed on reversing around a corner. That's not required on our commute. I passed everything else.' Jim was astonished.

'And what about when you came to the track to see us training?'

'Well, another tiny local trip, hardly counts, less than a mile.'

'Well, the police might think differently if you'd been pulled over. It would have been an automatic ban. So, let me get this clear. You're telling me you've been driving around without a licence.'

'Well I had a provisional. I had an infinitesimal chance of being stopped, most unlikely,' Gordon responded, ever the optimist.

'Look, almost anything could have happened. An accident, for instance. Remember, things do go awry, eventually they always will. If you keep doing it you'll bloody well get caught. Your good fortune could easily run out.' Jim remained aghast about the whole scenario. As radical as Jim might fondly imagine he was, there was something peculiarly moral about his rebelliousness, inherited from growing up as part of the skilled working-class. Gordon was on the other hand a farmer's son, his parents living on a small holding, near a tiny village without a policeman, unless one was drunk in the local pub. Gordon even drove tractors as a child. 'Remember technically your insurance is rendered invalid.'

'Well, maybe previously, but not anymore. You are now completely wrong.' Gordon smiled widely. 'That's my good news. My luck held out long enough. Last week I passed my test, on the third try. Don't tell the girls, they might find it shocking.'

'Did you drive round to the test station, alone?' asked Jim.

'Yes.'

'Didn't they notice, the examiners, when you pulled up?'

'No, I left it parked nearby, told them my wife drove me, that she was coming back in an hour after shopping in case I failed,' Gordon responded. 'Not everyone is as suspicious as you, Jim.'

'With good cause. However, I'm truly amazed. I wouldn't have taken you for a master criminal, Gordon.' At Jim's attempted quip, the offender stood, turning to their friends, grinning.

'Drink?' he asked them, 'I'm celebrating.' All the while he was winking at Jim, briefly putting his forefinger to his lips, laughing.

'So, what's the big secret, Gordon?' asked Moggy.

'Nothing much,' said Jim, 'merely a matter of road etiquette.'

'Well, I feel very safe when he's at the wheel. Gordon is always a cautious driver, very reliable, doesn't take risks' she responded.

'Maybe he had a good reason not to.' Jim couldn't help chuckling as the newly qualified chauffeur bought a round, surreptitiously celebrating his successful driving test, passed belatedly.

Later as Jim's least favourite holiday of the year approached, he sat at his desk thinking about the dynamics underlying that afternoon's conversation. Mentally Jim admitted he envied Gordon his roomy, Arts and Craft semi-detached house, currently something out the financial capacity of Jim's own marriage, especially now he was fractional with only sixty percent of a full salary, a fact Virginia was daily and repeatedly berating him about. Her resentment reached a crescendo after the confirmation of the forthcoming birth. At certain moments Jim coveted his friend's Leicester-born Irish wife, Ellen, an accountant, smart, dark-haired and perpetually good fun. Jim was anxious about the viability of his planned trip to Newcastle to interview Basil Bunting, being suddenly without a vehicle. The jaunt was arranged through a poet friendly with Aidan, a colleague of Jim's wife. Another aspirant, would-be poet Aidan was originally from the North-East, hence Bunting. The outcome was to be published in the university literary magazine, *Luciad*. Jim was about to become a research student, his thesis on American literature.

A frowning Virginia appeared at the top of the stairs, peering at him through the door. 'It's about time you hung the tree, are you coming down?' Both sets of parents would arrive the next day, staying together that night in the cottage in which the McAndrews lived, owned by Virginia's maternal grandfather, a seventy-nine-year-old veteran of the Great War, who lived in his own adjacent cottage, street access to their garden though his. He despised Virginia's father, thought him a buffoon. The grandfather was referred to universally as Guppy, which was Virginia's babyish rendition of Granpa, according to family myth.

Since their wedding in 1976 both sets of parents had become firm friends, all four individuals eagerly anticipating Christmas together and later becoming grandparents. Earlier in the morning over breakfast in preparation for the shared festival,

Virginia underlined the television schedules in the *Radio Times*, offering him her selected viewing, with on BBC1 at 3:00pm for her parents the Queen speaking to the Commonwealth, followed by her own favourite, Larry Grayson in *Generation Game*, with Isla St. Clair (although Virginia far preferred Brucie, unlike Howard), and after an early evening meal on the box at 8:45pm selected for his parents *Christmas with Eric and Ernie*, with special guests David Frost and Glenda Jackson. Jim hated the idea of all three. He'd gone through the double Christmas and New Year issue, its cover a sentimental cartoon of four children using snow to make an unfinished snowman against a pillar box that dwarfed them, its twin letterboxes looming like vacant eyes. Two of these figures had a Wellington boot each, one yellow, the other blue, that stepped outside the frame of the drawing into its white border, all very *postmodern* playfulness, a term Jim had heard but never yet used, uncertain of the concept's full and precise meaning. He'd rather have watched the Beatles' *A Hard Day's Night* at 3:00pm even though broadcast in original black and white, and some classical music on the same channel, but he was overruled vigorously by Virginia. She'd reminded him they would have guests, and he just couldn't be allowed to monopolise the only television set. On Boxing Day the first underscoring was at 6.00pm, *Jim'll Fix It* on BBC1, which entertainment threw Jim into despair, a yodelling buffoon and inevitably an appalling posse of kids hanging onto the clown's every word and deed, an always must-see show for Ginnie.

Virginia stepped into the room. 'Are you not listening to me? Just where does your mind escape to? You know, Jim, it's high time you grew up. You'll soon have real responsibilities,' at which she pointed to her belly. She added, 'Where will any of this constant scribbling, cutting out stories from newspapers and interviewing old fogey poets get you anyway? It's an utter bloody waste of time. And you've just been initiated again as yet another bloody eternal student. What do you need another degree for?' Virginia was shocked in June when he resigned from his full-time post. Her subsequent objections and remonstrations continued, six months later, which Jim felt wasn't entirely in the festive spirit.

Far more festive than his wife's mood was the drinking undertaken by Jim and their crowd that night, with no car to drive. With the perfect excuse not to do so on his part, he'd squeezed into the back of Gordon's now legally-driven Fiesta. After a short time standing in the Cradock, a huge pub, the clientele all packed together, each and every bar completely mobbed, even the glum, bare public one to the left of the front entrance, all eight of them had ended up in the Clarendon off Queen's Road, a favourite haunt of university staff and students. Tonight, most of the latter would have already returned to their parents, celebrating in various cities, towns and villages all around the country. Sure, Jim thought, the Clarendon's two bars were crowded, but spare seats remained. Perched on a stall in his usual spot at the bar was Lyman Andrews, a minor American poet, bi-sexual poetry critic of the *Sunday Times* and about to be Jim's tutor for the planned part-time research degree in American Literature. He nodded at Jim, but continued his animated conversation with the large landlady, Kath, also in the corner where the bar was hinged for access. She was Lyman's habitual drinking companion, apart from when he was chasing a Leicester crowd of working-class male youths, some underage at sixteen or seventeen, who frequented the other smaller bar. Lyman and Kath's main delight was deriding other drunks, locals, sad old men who frequented the far bar. The pair threw insults at them as they patiently waited to be served. Both were already well pissed, and above the hubbub Jim could make them out, calling for refills volubly, bullying Kath's skinny husband who'd be serving all night, even after hours. Probably half of Leicester's own returning students were in the Cradock, thought Jim, at least most of those who lived within a few miles.

Standing at the back of those clustering at the bar for service, ordinary mortals without Lyman's influence, Jim worked out that this would be his first Christmas spent with his parents since that of 1972, his first year at university, during which he'd returned home mid-December. When his father came back from the cable factory he'd been surprised not only that the backdoor was unlocked, but that Jim was inside, on the sofa, the television on, sound up. Jim scrutinized the cover of the Christmas *Radio Times* as his father entered the living room, peering at Morecambe and Wise as circus performers, Bruce Forsyth as the ring master with whip and top hat, Lulu in a Pierrot costume ending with a row of frills at crotch level, a conical hat perched on her head, all posed around a stuffed lion in a tiny version of the big top. Jim and Howard hadn't got along for years, so this was an awkward encounter. 'What you doing here? You're supposed to have left home, *for fucking good.*' Howard opened the exchange with an aggressive accusation charged with a curious anger and sense of finality.

'The university lets out our rooms during vacations, used for visitors, unless you're foreign. Even then they move you and charge more. There's storage, but only a single suitcase each.'

'Outrageous. That's a bloody cheek, they charge enough.'

'It's in the contract, apparently. Students stay term time only.' In fact, Jim asked specifically. He anticipated difficulties at home. The pair had argued monumentally on his first day at university.

''Well, I don't know about that. Let me make one thing crystal clear.' He paused for effect. 'You don't live here anymore. It's not your home.' Howard held out his hand. 'I want your key back.'

'I've nowhere else to stay.' Jim pulled his single key from the fob pocket of his jeans, even though it was going to make life difficult.

'Well, I suppose you could stay this once until New Year, but after that, just you bugger off for good. I don't want to see you back again. You don't live here. You're not welcome. Use that huge brain you think you have for once and find a solution. Maybe you'd be better off working instead of idling. The problem's yours, not buggering mine. You can stay somewhere else. We'll still contribute to your upkeep, since your mum wants that.'

'I know, I'm grateful,' Jim replied; he detested such dependency given his father's ever-present aggression toward him.

'And don't just watch that bloody goggle box. Give me that, came today' Howard said indicating the *Radio Times* which he took, staring at it's the magazine intently. 'Rubbish! Can't stand that man,' which dismissal Jim knew immediately referred to Bruce Forsyth, featured on the cover much to Howard's annoyance, born the same year as him, same birthplace, Edmonton, similar upbringing. According to Howard the entertainer was 'a talentless sod.' Later Jim suspected his father was jealous; Forsyth attended the prestigious Latymer School, while Howard had failed his eleven-plus. He remained sharply bitter, his mother's disappointment obvious many years later.

In 1979, seven years on, Jim could recall the exchange, the attendant emotions as if endured the day before. His father was economical with the truth, paying only half the recommended parental contribution. He insisted that to pay the full amount was a ridiculous expectation, penalizing them for his mother working. So, in January when Jim returned for his studies, he arrived at his hall of residence the first night it opened, an empty block apart from Sonny, an African third-year who wore a variety of bow ties and a suit, who obviously thought Jim was common, since he blanked his presence entirely. To distract himself in the echoing darkness, Jim read a newspaper, lying on the thin mattress of his narrow bed. The United Kingdom had just entered the *European Economic Community* which excited Jim, who imagined one day he might work somewhere interesting abroad, maybe even Paris.

The following week Jim met Virginia again, only previously a passing acquaintance. Jim was seeking another girl. As he rapped, opposite Virginia opened her own door, and their relationship turned rapidly into more, Leonard Cohen playing mournfully in the background. He sang plaintively of a Gypsy boy, of a girl being taken home. The following night Virginia and Jim watched *Last Tango in Paris* at the ABC cinema in Belgrave Gate, her choice, somehow this trip to the movies further cemented the relationship. Virginia made him feel wanted. Hence Jim would spend the Easter vacation at her parents' home, with unprotected sex in an ancient hay store at the bottom of some fields, but that was fine since she was on the pill. The next summer he moved early into a rented student house, Jim working in a carpet warehouse for twenty pounds a week, cycling across the city every day, sandwiches in a tin in his gas mask bag, cigarettes in its outside pouch. Virginia joined him in October, failing to find her own room, for sharing proved a cheaper solution by far.

Six years later in the Clarendon amid the festivities Jim fished out a pound note to wave, hopefully drawing a barman's attention in the smoky atmosphere, and a figure loomed at his side. Challis was wearing his cowboy hat, boots, and a tasselled tanned suede jacket, shoulder length hair, moustache and long sideburns that almost met on his chin. The taller man leant on Jim's shoulder, fishing out a cigarette from a pocket in his jacket to offer Jim. 'I've given up,' Jim explained, 'three months ago.'

'Wise move. How are you?' Jim told Challis about the car's malfunction, the endangered trip, to see Bunting, Jim's difficulties in writing and in part others in his marriage, insofar as he revealed that Virginia was hostile to his ambitions to write, opposed him undertaking a research degree, and preferred him working. Challis was horrified, supportive in a vague fashion. Jim's novel, as its author explained, centred on a couple, the relationship modelled on his own marriage, but with a difference. 'What's the draft title?' asked Challis, who nodding seemed genuinely interested.

'Currently, it is called *Swallows in the Sky*,' Jim replied.

'Mm? And why did you make that particular choice, man?'

'It's adapted from Keats, taken from a line from "Ode to Autumn."'

'It does very little for me, man,' Challis commented. 'Stirs nothing.'

'Well, the swallows in Keats' poem gather at its end before leaving the cottages, the birds about to migrate, winter is imminent. My central character is unconsciously preparing to leave, unaware of a crisis. He's about to split from his wife.'

'"The whole mad swirl," is better,' suggested Challis. Jim looked at him quizzically. 'Or maybe just have *Mad Swirl*? It's from Kerouac, the sainted bum, from *On the Road*. My gift, a new title.'

'Well, maybe,' Jim responded without the least conviction. In the other bar he could see Sue Townsend, a local playwright he knew, a woman in her early thirties, writer-in-residence at the Phoenix Theatre. She waved; Jim waved back. He liked her. Down-to-earth, she was unpretentious. 'It's Sue,' he said to Challis. He knew her well. He waved too, a Churchillian backward V-sign. It was far too crowded to switch bars, too noisy even to shout hello effectively.

'Not often you see her over this side of town,' noted Challis.

'True,' agreed Jim. They were firmly in university territory, one of the three or four pubs dominated by its staff, students and ex-students. Jim continued, explaining his plot to Challis, that in his novel the young wife was unfaithful, having sex with a colleague, doing so surreptitiously. After which at about a third of the way through (or maybe it could be half) the pair split up. Next the male protagonist was able to return to London where he stayed trying to reinvent himself, find another life.

'Maybe try "Raggedy madness and riot" or *Raggedy Madness*?' Challis suggested. Jim's expression exhibited so much disapproval, face pulled so evocatively, there was no further comment. Challis laughed. He really should have remembered what Jim was explaining, for he'd already been Jim's second reader, of just two chapters, nowhere near the whole novel. Challis had not only forgotten the title, he appeared to have forgotten his advice, his objection that the narrative was too linear, far too static. He advised adding some movement, more dialogue, more digression, more characters, more scenes, less inner self, far less tortured soul. Jim thought perhaps Challis had been stoned while reading, hence his forgetfulness. Tonight, by the time Jim finished his further tale of woe, of the treacherous car preventing him from visiting Bunting, he was just about being served, which now included buying in addition to drinks for himself and his crowd of friends, another Challis pint and cigarillo. 'That's really uncool,' was Challis' arcane response to Jim's litany of complaints about the death of his beloved Avenger endangering his trip north, and concerning his spouse and her lack of support for his creativity. Challis gripped Jim's hand. 'You know, I could help you, definitely.'

'How? Bump her off? I couldn't afford the fee.' Jim laughed, his comment reflecting how deeply unsupportive she'd been about his novel, as well as the research degree, his writing poetry and anything else not directly concerned with earning money.

'No, not your wife, man,' Challis said smiling. 'I can offer help in two other ways. First, my wondrous mechanic who'll fix your car *and* second, I'll drive you myself to Newcastle, my man, there and totally back to your home in the Great White Shark.'

'Travelling in what?' Jim thought he misheard him.

'The Great White Shark, my sturdy, reliable automobile.'

'You'd come with me all that way, drive me there?'

'Sure, I'll take you, the full round trip, our own road trip of just under four hundred miles. I know because I've performed there, a poetic gig. Think of it, man, on the road together.' Challis' absolute passion was and always had been from time immemorial the American Beat writers. He often quoted them. He did so for Jim, for his elucidation. 'I seek holy lightning, my quest to find a holy con-man with shining mind, a sorrowful poetic con-man, seek a dark mind. That's you and me together encountering what you might well call the mad swirl of everything. Good karma, man.

'Do what?' Jim didn't comprehend the relevance of any of these references. 'Who is it?' Challis raised an eyebrow.

'That paraphrases Kerouac my friend, like I indicated previously. According to the sage, in the words of Jean-Louis, one's life ought to be utter spontaneity, with travel, man, the road, it's the key to everything. Chance meetings, offers, they map your way.'

'Oh sure,' Jim said unconvinced by curious poetics, or that Challis would accompany him up north. 'Great ideas, but when things got tough he lived mostly at home with his mum, Gabrielle-Ange.' Jim had researched Kerouac, not as extensively as Challis, but he grasped a few hard facts about Challis' idol. 'Let's face it, if the truth is told, Ti-Jean was at heart a mummy's boy!'

'That's unkind, man. Sure, he'd maternal issues, as Burroughs warned him.' Challis seemed offended. 'He idealized the maternal, the road like a retreat to the womb. Yours is a cruel slander.'

'A case of *regressus ad uterum* then?' Jim said ironically. 'Actually, you can't slander the dead, Chris, legally speaking.'

'So are you interested in Bunting?' Jim nodded assent. 'What's involved, man? Are you undertaking an interview?'

'Yes, it's all been set up, already agreed through intermediaries.'

'Well I'd be delighted to accompany you, it'd be hip. Look, as for Bunting, he's a key figure for a scholar of the beats, which is me, situated in the United Kingdom, as we are. Bunting knew Snyder, and he was close to Ginsberg, advised the dude on poetics. Ginsberg once had a gig with the new generation of British poets, 7,000 people at the Albert Hall, the International Poetry Incarnation, June 1965, such a great occasion. I was there.'

Jim knew nothing of the seminal moment, being eleven at the time. According to Challis' later account he was eighteen or nineteen at that time. He continued, 'Same year at Morden Tower Book Room, which was the very first reading which involved Bunting with Ginsberg. Lawrence Ferlinghetti and Gregory Corso would follow, both reading there. I couldn't ignore a chance to meet Bunting: in large part the Beats revived his poetic commitment, inspired him to take up that art again, to write *Briggflatts*. Bunting *instructed* Ginsberg, who said of the Modern Tower night that as a poet he acquired *more* at that reading from Bunting than ever Ginsberg would have learned at a hundred fucking universities. What an opportunity you have been blessed with! Who put you in touch with Bunting, with the main man? He's a poetic genius.'

'Richard Caddel who knows Bunting; Caddel is a friend of a colleague of my wife, a guy who writes poetry. I know him well, we can trust his word, he's a poet.' This was offered as a credential, as if it might serve as evidence of his general good character.

'Damn me, small world. I know Caddel, man. His first gig was music. From Gillingham, twenty miles from where I grew up. I saw him play. The dude got into poetry at Newcastle University, just published a fifth book. I heard him reading, exchanged our poetics. He's into Zukofsky, Creeley, Carlos Williams, cool guys.'

'Chris, you know more than me. I've never met the man.'

'So, when can we go, Jim, to see the daddy, this dude Bunting?'

'Maybe after the New Year? I have to be back before school starts. Otherwise I'd have to wait until the next half-term. I can't get any time off teaching during school term, stuck with that.

'That's a bummer, man. Let's go in January, soon as we can. I'll ask my lady, the delightful Holly.' He pointed her out. She stood in the other bar among friends. 'I think we could leave on Tuesday 8th, back Thursday 10th, interview on Wednesday 9th. If Holly agrees, you book a slot with Bunting, get his agreement.'

'Apparently, he hardly ever goes out, according to Caddel, or so my friend reported. Bunting's a virtual recluse.'

'Still, it's best to ask, to set it up officially. As to petrol we'll go half each, agreed?' He shook Jim's hand, Challis' skin soft, warm, and wrinkled. The offer surprised Jim, so much so that slightly tipsy now he was convinced the ever-cadging Challis would actually accompany him and serve as his Beat chauffeur.

'Cool, that's really great, Chris. Where should we stay?'

'Just leave that arrangement to me. I have an ex-babe in Newcastle, lives in a great big house with a Scot who worked in Leicester for a while.' Challis' network, which was notoriously wide, was celebrated, and included John McVicar, once dubbed "Public Enemy No. 1" by Scotland Yard. Challis had known him ages. The poet and the prisoner corresponded, Challis' favourite modes of communication. McVicar liked Challis. They become friendly when Challis taught him while incarcerated in Leicester nick. Jim joined Challis and the old lag to celebrate his parole in 1978 in a dodgy club on London Road just below the level of the university, where the road sloped toward the station, definitely Lucky Jim territory, where eating people was still very definitely wrong.

On that Christmas Eve in the Clarendon Challis disappeared with his cigarillo lit into the other bar to join Holly. Jim handed out drinks to his crowd, telling Virginia news of his good fortune, the revival of the poetic odyssey northward.

'He'll never keep his promise,' she responded. 'He's drunk, bound to be. He'll have forgotten by tomorrow.' She disapproved of Challis, who only worked a few hours teaching at the university's Adult Extension College, the WEA, supplemented by selling stories and, according to gossip, photographs to semi-pornographic magazines, and maybe even, according to rumours, by selling vastly overpriced 'weed' to gullible undergraduates.

'I think you'll be proved wrong.' Her assessment was to prove erroneous. Going solely by appearances, Virginia was a bad judge of people, too self-absorbed to notice any underlying qualities. As Jim looked across the smoke-filled room, he decided to walk to the telephone kiosk and phone Matthew Evans, an old school-friend from a Welsh family, a Baptist, parents hailing from Swansea where Matt had attended university, changing courses twice, finally dropping out, too much time spent playing piano with bands in local pubs, into the groove of the scene.

Outside in a red call box smelling of piss Jim shuffled through his change, before ringing Kingston upon Thames, an area of London about which he knew little. He hated ringing friends and family in homes he'd never seen, either physically or at least in a photo. It was a curious phobia. Another was sneezing, whether by himself, or by others. Jim hated this activity, especially when his otherwise affable father-in-law, Godfrey McAndrews, sneezed, for he managed to turn a simple involuntary act into an elaboration, a drama. It became a statement: here I am before you, take note, here's Godfrey, a force of nature, handkerchief waving like some flag and kaboom. Jim thought of Virginia, only to find he was trembling, not pleasurably, more a horrible quivering.

Why ring Matt? He knew his friend would reassure him concerning Jim's marital resentments. Jim knew Matt disapproved of Virginia, one of the few who'd been honest about the issue of her character. In June 1976, around the time of their marriage, during the long drought, among its ferociously long hot days, followed by boiling nights, midnight often as warm if not warmer than a normal British summer, Matt had stayed for two nights before Jim's wedding. At that time Jim and Virginia lived in a rented flat on Florence Avenue, behind a women's hairdresser on a corner near to the County Cricket Ground. Virginia was at her parents' place, at some hen night she'd organized. Matt arrived, complaining of losing himself in the Leicester streets, and as usual the rooms reeked of hairspray, of bleaching agents, the air saturated during the day with muttered gossip, old women's complaints rinsed blue and lavender. One bus route circled through Aylestone, a sorry area, factories cheek-by-jowl with tiny workers' houses, a cut through between main roads, spokes out of town. Convenient though for the match days when Virginia watched cricket on summer's evenings until dusk, mostly with her visiting father, continuing another of their long-established family routines. After returning in Matt's car from the Cradock, they purchased beer *en route* from a local off-licence on Saffron Lane, near where Joe Orton was raised on what was now a particularly grim council estate. Over beers Matt offered stark and definite advice. Jim shouldn't marry Ginnie. She would prove unreliable. She was a train-wreck, a disaster waiting to happen.

'It'll be a complete catastrophe,' his friend warned. 'The truth is I've rarely known such a selfish, myopic woman.'

'I can't cancel, too late now,' Jim objected. 'She's not that bad.' He thought of their better times, not the tantrums and worse.

'She's awful, terribly self-centred, unreliable. Jim, it's never too late. We'll go to France, I'll drive.' Jim shook his head. Matt added, 'You'll regret it, you will. She's no good. It won't last.'

'Look Matt, I want a family life, I need some stability.'

'Just like your parents, except remember that they're miserable, ruining their lives, mutually assured misery.'

'I know,' but curiously it was such a home life that left Jim needing support, a characteristic he sensed about himself as soon as he left home. That night he didn't want to confront the issue, yet Jim was overcome by the revelation, which entailed recognition that his friend was being entirely serious. Looking back, he knew that Matt's judgment was correct, and that in his pre-nuptial state Jim faced a real choice that night, a critical one. Yet it was one he avoided, he lacked the courage. He knew as much looking back. Now in his current mess he pondered his desire for his friend's advice. At the time of his wedding he'd been unconvinced anyone could feasibly expect him to take a different path so abruptly. How could he take such dramatic, abrupt action, with a public betrayal, broken promises? 'I can't jilt her at the altar with all the money that's been spent,' he'd said lamely. His true fear was he'd be alone.

'Why not? We're talking the rest of your life, no chance of happiness. Is she what you really want? Or need? Do you trust her?' Matt was unusually fervent. Inwardly Jim wavered, but his friend's warning altered very little. Still he married her.

Now over three years later in the short time in which he waited for Mat to answer, standing in the call box he more than half wished he'd listened. Currently he was facing, so he concluded, the ruinous marriage Matt had predicted. As Matt had distrusted Virginia, now Jim did so. Yet even now Jim sensed he couldn't give up on a six-year relationship, believing surely there was much that could be retrieved, a reconciliation now a child was coming. In that scorching summer of 1976, back when Björn Borg had been about to defeat Ilie Năstase in July, in that June the juggernaut of wedding costs had spiralled, mostly parental spending, and on the very night Matt tried to rescue him, many of the McAndrews' guests had already arrived at local hotels. Most of Jim's own family were planning to travel up the next morning from multiple locations. Jim felt there'd already been far too much momentum to contemplate calling a halt to the wedding. He dreaded the recriminations, having to admit he'd been wrong in his choice. He knew he'd pull on his unfamiliar grey suit and hope for the best; still confident things might work out for the best, that was his to be his destiny, a vague hopefulness against the odds. That night back in June 1976 if he'd attempted to divine his own future, his sense was of an optimistic one, without the conformity and hostility that were daily coordinates in his current life. He guessed any such future potential of a rosier kind was destroyed well before the marriage itself, doomed by Virginia's wilful sense that betrayal and secretiveness were acceptable, that she could achieve whatever she wanted, most of it pretty sordid when scrutinized.

Tonight, December 1979 dialling Matt's number, Jim was sinking swiftly; Matt was right. Jim had less and less to hold onto, a sense he didn't have what some people still described as a *good marriage*, far from it. Additionally, the child's impending arrival in June perturbed him. Clustered together such half-thoughts were overwhelming. He was convinced his friend might help, but the call went unanswered, answering machine kicking in. Silent, wordless, Jim left no message. Just anticipate the Bunting trip, he reflected, returning to the warmth of the pub. It would be strange to spend time with Challis, since he hardly knew him, not the man himself. Everyone saw an image. Yet, what was he really like, the hidden, private self? Wasn't that why fiction and poetry mattered? They offered a glimpse of things unsuspected, both the awfulness *and* the best of people. That might well apply to Bunting. What were his inner qualities, his private self, the best and the worst of the man? The opportunity of glimpsing such qualities, even a scintilla, thrilled Jim. Yet he worried Challis might spoil the trip, with his obsessions, but it was too late to revise their arrangement. Without Challis he simply couldn't go, which was the mad, swirling crux of the matter.

Chapter Seven: Lauren, Basil Bunting, January 1980

Christmas was over, parental guests returned to their respective homes. A drunken New Year's Eve ensued, followed by a new decade, the eighties. People talked of a renewed optimism, but Jim thought only of the awful new Prime Minister, Thatcher. Neither she nor her government augured well, despite her being a woman, on which fact many fixated. It was 14.15 according to Jim's new digital watch, a festive gift from his mother, with its shiny chrome casing offering side buttons he hadn't yet mastered, on 08-01-80. In the middle of the street Virginia pulled a borrowed Mini to a halt gingerly, ice scrunching beneath its tyres. They stopped outside 67 Prospect Hill in Leicester, Challis' home. Everywhere the buildings were a typical dark-redbrick, which sometimes so depressed Jim. The colour once weathered seemed nondescript, yet utterly dour and miserable. The weather hardly helped. There was deep snow everywhere, in the streets, on the roofs, smothering Spinney Hill Park, even the bushes and trees. Jim had rung his mother-in-law to beg for a loan of her ancient white vehicle, a move forced upon him since Jim's Avenger was still being repaired just around the corner, or so he hoped. It had been towed to a garage near Challis' favourite and closest pub, the Rifle Butts, a traditional, extremely basic red-brick hostelry, little changed from its late-Victorian origins, much like the rest of the area. Virginia asked, 'Are you sure you're going through with your silly jaunt? The two of you must be utterly insane. It's total madness, just look at the weather.' Earlier there were pictures on the television news of pickets outside a Texaco Depot somewhere up north, during an industrial dispute staying warm by gathering round a jolly-looking brazier. Jim wore a dark green duffle coat, long blue scarf, matching woolly gloves, jeans and brown Dr Martin boots.

'I will carry on whatever the weather, if Challis is willing.'

'With this weather you might get stuck somewhere in the middle of nowhere, unable to get to a phone.' She sounded half-concerned.

'Sure, it's a risk, but the road is mostly motorway until Leeds, plenty of emergency phones on the hard shoulder. We'll be fine. I worry far more about petrol shortages than bad weather.'

'What about the journey after Leeds?' she asked.

'A-roads, I think, through Darlington. Challis has been before.'

'Look, I won't park, since I might get stuck,' she said. The snow was thicker by the roadside. Jim stepped out gingerly onto ice, frozen slush, rutted beyond the narrow, melted strips made by the passing tyres. 'I'll keep the engine running,' she said. Jim went to the rear, pulling out his bag from the vehicle's tiny boot. He tapped on the driver's window which his wife wound down.

'Hold your horses, while I check Challis is at home and make sure he hasn't changed his mind,' Jim insisted. He didn't want to trudge home if his travel companion had pulled out.

'I haven't all night, you know. Things that have to be done.'

The front door sported a small lettered brass plaque, announcing the occupant, 'Dr Christopher R. Challis.' After Jim had rapped his knuckles on the wood and repeatedly pressed the bell that he suspected might be buggered, Holly answered, dressed in a white towelling dressing gown, hotel logo on her left breast, long blonde hair wrapped in a towel, bare-footed.

'Is Chris in?' Jim asked. Holly assented. 'Is he still coming?' he asked, half hoping they might cancel, plead travel difficulties.

'Nothing as banal as bad weather would stop the Lion-heart. I've just finished wishing him on his way, charging his inner battery with delight to give him strength for the journey,' A strange sexual innuendo was evident in her manner of delivery, almost a parody of a younger, dyed platinum blonde Fenella

Fielding. Her behaviour caused Jim to reflect on the oddness of the couple. His driver's girlfriend might well be younger than Jim. Even from outside he could smell bacon, its odour wafting from the rear of the house. He waved Virginia away and entered. Books and papers lined the shelves found in every room. Challis was in the back-living room, eating a sandwich, a joint smouldering in a large glass ashtray.

'We still on for the trip up north, are we?' Jim asked.

'Naturally, this particular lion's heart is ready.' Putting down his food, he tapped his palm on his chest, twice, slowly.

'I didn't make out any large white car outside.'

'The Great White Shark is being especially prepared at the local garage, around the corner, where you left your vehicle. You ready, man?' Jim offered thumbs up, both simultaneously. They were delayed by Challis finishing the remains of what had clearly been a late breakfast, and further ablutions, and snogging between Holly and her departing beau, all of which was most embarrassing for Jim. Challis carried a leather Gladstone bag like some transcendental magician, six-two, back straight, stepping gingerly in his Cuban heels, long hair waving in the breeze. They reached the redbrick workshop set off a broad cobbled back alley in a side street, where Challis greeted the proprietor, who waved at Jim, having met him when he left his own vehicle for repair a week before. He wondered idly whether Challis might have encouraged a delay on repairs to the Avenger to ensure his participation in the trip.

'Any progress on my car, my good man?' Jim asked the owner-mechanic in greasy overalls, pointing past him at his Avenger.

'It's the parts, mate. I'm still waiting for a delivery. The snow hasn't helped, nor the holiday, and these bloody strikes. Some areas are really short of fuel, so no vans, no trucks.' The gearbox needed rebuilding, not something Jim properly understood.

'The Shark?' asked Challis, 'Is she ready?' The man pulled back a large dark green tarpaulin carefully, dramatically revealing a model the like of which Jim had never before seen, its white paintwork waxed and gleaming, the chrome highly polished, included a huge, broad bumper containing four headlamps, and lines of the metal along the sides above black buffed wheels.

'What on earth is that beast?' Jim asked, impressed. The vehicle's lines were elegant, chrome trim on white paintwork added swagger. Admittedly no tail fins, but the expanse of its bonnet threatened power, the inward curve of its back lights stylish.

'Chrysler CH Sedan, the so-called Chrysler by Chrysler, a 1976 model,' said the master-mechanic. The local warble accentuated oddly the final syllables of certain words, 'the last year of production in Australia. After that, Mitsubishi took over.'

'Wow, it's quite some car,' Jim responded with genuine admiration, sucked into boy's stuff Virginia would have derided.

'You're right. It is a real wow this model,' the man added, again his Leicester accent undermining his obvious enthusiasm, and although a socialist at that point Jim could not shake off his dislike of the peculiar intonation. 'Front disc brakes, power-assisted steering, tinted power operated windows, Hemi six-cylinder engine, three-speed automatic transmission, all as standard. This one had leather seats added, which I reckon could be Kangaroo skin. And with the Hemi-6engine: 6-cylinder, 6 overhead valves, and still almost 30 miles per gallon, a real beast.'

'Are we right to go, man?' Challis asked. 'Topped up?'

'She surely is, soldier. She's full up and I've put some extra fuel in two spare fuel-tanks in your trunk, just in case.'

'You're cool, man,' Challis said to the mechanic, adding to Jim, 'We are blessed by the muse responsible for travel and associated writing, she has deigned to allow us our superlative mode of transport, a carriage fit for gods.' Challis handed over bank notes and what looked like a large translucent bag, apparently full of weed. He climbed into the driver's seat, placed a card on the dash, started up on his first attempt and waved at Jim to join him with a half-cupped hand. Off they throbbed, in the CH Sedan, Challis' Shark. 'Mind a personal comment, man?'

'Well, no, not really.' Jim felt nervous, perplexed.

'You don't have much of a clue about women, Jim, do you?'

'What do you mean?' The left-field comment was unexpected.

'Well, you seem embattled. You need to woo them, preen their fancies. It keeps them interested, always guessing. Keep the whip hand. You're too honest, too straightforward. You're just you.'

'I'll have to think about that, mate.' He wasn't sure he understood.

'Crazy. I reckon you should, at length, my good friend.'

They both lapsed into silence driving out through the narrow streets toward the M1 motorway, not an awkward pause. Both were talked out for a while after the festivities. Challis switched on the radio. Reaching the motorway, Jim noticed the sleek light grey surface stretching northward, the snow not settling due to the volume of traffic, lights from lorries playing out in front of them, illuminating the snow flurrying thickly as they drove. The heater warmed the vehicle uncomfortably until Challis adjusted the flow of air. With a flourish he switched on the radio.

A Cockney voice sang of relationships, of talking things out, a girl saying he doesn't care, of his being unaware and of his weakness, a jaunty tune with poignant words. The singer's accent that made Jim think of home, of North London, of the past and he was beginning to decide it might be his future too. He couldn't see his life spent forever in and around Leicester. He wondered whether Challis was happy living in the city, but he didn't ask. The snow seemed to be ever thickening, some settling on the road's surface, not quite a white-out, but visibility was far from its best. Curiously such whiteness added a shimmering quality to the sky, hypnotic. As they drove nothing seemed normal, the fields and entire landscape was being transformed into something singular, undifferentiated, rendered unfamiliar, the difference almost magical with a vast expanse of snow across the hills and fields, in the sky, exuding a brightness from the layers of snow settled uniformly across the trees, bushes, streams, houses and factories. Jim remembered a similar, more localized first-ever metamorphosis in his childhood back garden, aged about three.

After almost another hundred miles of motorway as the Shark approached Leeds, Jim was definitely impressed with the vehicle, which was fast, quiet, comfortable, warm and stayed on the proverbial road. He'd just awoken from a nap. 'So where did you find the Shark?' asked Jim, yawning. He was slipping into the vocabulary that sustained Challis' fantasy world, part suburban commuting belt of his youth, part Hunter S. Thompson, part Beat, and part maniac. Challis consulted the cardboard on the dash. On it was pasted on white paper on card the route beyond Leeds, each road and town typed in green ink with estimated mileages. On its reverse was the return trip to the M1, the direction in red ink.

'No, Jim, I never sought the Shark; in truth she found me. This holy vehicle crossed the globe for me to be its owner.' He was smoking a joint he'd pre-prepared while he drove one-handed. As they went up the carriageway onto which they had just turned, a light snow was being wiped from the screen, the Shark's clunking wipers audibly struggling, the volume of slushy residue increasing. Jim pulled a sceptical face. 'It was karmic; the machine was destined to be mine, for the ferrying around of Holly, and of my good friends.' He placed his hand briefly on Jim's shoulder. 'The Shark came from Oz with a rich grad student, who shipped it over to travel around Europe during his stay. You might ask why he didn't buy a car in Blighty, which you and I would have done locally if we'd found ourselves transposed in similar circumstances to the antipodes, but the Ozzie mind is differently configured, mentally, particularly as his brain was that of the wealthy variety. Three years later PhD completed successfully, he owed the Lion-heart a great deal of money. I supplied his needs.' He twiddled the joint indicatively. 'Since he couldn't afford the shipping costs, I paid him the difference, with some in kind,' at which Challis jiggled his joint again, 'and the Shark came to Daddy-oh the Lion-heart. Seemingly this represented a financial transaction between two mortals with feet of clay, but naturally far greater forces were at play.'

'So, you refer to greater forces, well, how exactly do you tune into them?' Concerning others without a spiritual gift, Jim was utterly prosaic at heart, a pragmatist, the son of Howard who as a jobbing carpenter during his working life had hung office doors, fixed locks, laid out huge shuttering for concrete to be poured, each creating a base which would be surmounted by massive machines. Everything when he'd grown up was instrumental, a matter of skills, logistics, getting things done. Job over, you could proceed to the next one. And Jim himself had briefly been a cable drum maker that achingly boring summer of 1970, a fate his father intended as semi-permanent, anchoring Jim's life in tedium, albeit very well-paid boredom.

'Man, as Neil Cassady would say, it's a matter of fate, kismet, written before it occurred, the work of disembodied spirits. Cassady was into Buddhism and other interesting shit. So was Kerouac. You should explore those areas of your soul, Jim.'

'Well, speaking of matters of soul or spirit, my maternal grandmother knew all kinds of travellers, spiritualists, all manner of similar folk, and she thought I had a definite innate gift, that of seeing the dead, of foresight and the ability to curse people.' Jim was reflecting on an aspect of his self that his father sought to suppress, hated fervently, discouraged his mother-in-law referencing.

'Heavy stuff. An unexpected dimension, way off beam, weird, unexpected, man. So, we're referring to visions, and ghosts, man?'

'Well, no, not exactly. As a very small child, three or four, I saw people no one else saw, everywhere, always faces at night before I slept. I was convinced I'd lived before, glimpses of other lives.'

'Man,' responded the ersatz Beat. Jim didn't know quite why he told Challis, since it was an aspect of his personality Jim mostly hid of late, buried in one dark corner of his brain, closed in a casket, a secret interred in its now grave, now an unconscious element only accessible through dreams and his writing.

'And I saw colours, swirling energies in rooms, a shroud around certain people, a white fuzziness. It freaked my parents out. They refused to believe me. Discouraged all and any reference.'

'Uncool.'

'Anyway, I knew things instinctively. So, do you remember the Cuban missile crisis, 1962, when there was almost nuclear war?'

'Naturally, I do.' Challis according to his account would have been fifteen. 'Really bad vibes, thought we'd fry. You know Ginsberg produced a cut-up from the Kennedy-Khrushchev speeches: "the purpose of these manoeuvres is offensive weapons."'

'Well, I was eight and my father freaked out all day long, weeks on end, shit scared, as if being terrified achieved anything, convinced that he would die any minute, that everyone would, stymied by fear. I told him it wouldn't happen, that I knew I had a definite future, that I wouldn't die at that point and nor would he.'

'What did he say?' Challis was captivated by his tale.

'Told me to shut up, didn't believe me, said I was far too young to know anything about anything, I was a snotty little brat.'

'From the mouths of babes and all that. . . .' Challis was clearly thinking about something. 'Do you still have the gift?'

'Well, occasionally. Sometimes, but nowadays just impressions, faintly received, often a jumble, random thoughts, words or images. More like a flash of associations.'

'So, what's my future?' Jim hated being asked like this. Challis continued, 'Maybe an academic job, publication, novels, fame?'

'Remember, it's not to order . . . .' Jim allowed his mind to drift.

'Anything?' asked Challis. Jim shushed him, trying to concentrate.

'I have to focus, to find the zone.' He drifted off, thought again of the snow, its whiteness, the hum and throbbing sound of the heater, the slurrying slush of the tyres, the clack-clack of the wipers. Ahead ever more snow was settling on the road surface, so Challis slowed. Jim glimpsed tiny back-to-back houses in a nondescript northern town as they passed through, outskirts, centre, outskirts. He turned his thoughts inward, slowing his breathing as if somnolent, so he might meditate. Suddenly in a flash he saw an older Challis sprawled out as if unconscious, then a book with his name, hardback. Jim next had a vision of Challis driving a Cadillac on a freeway, which faded; Jim seemed to sense Challis again, a lifeless body in Prospect Hill, an awkward position, alone, the house cold, Challis abandoned, no Holly, no one else. On occasion his visions were literal, accurate, others more a matter of impressions, symbols. 'You'll publish at least one academic book.'

'Man, I knew it.' His voice conveyed his delight.

'And this will sound strange, but I sense that on at least one occasion you'll be driving a big Cadillac and doing so around America.'

'I'll be on the road! Oh man, there's also going to be a job in the States, which is my secret dream. I've never admitted it to anyone else apart from Holly. Jim, you are the bearer of excellent tidings.'

'Well, hold on, I saw the car, but really nothing much else. There might be a job, but in truth I didn't see one.' In fact, as he thought of the matter Jim had a distinct impression of the opposite, that any such employment anywhere in the world would decidedly not play much, if any part, in Challis' future. Jim was possessed by another appalling insight, that there was far less left of that life than Challis himself might imagine.

'The two go together. Why else would I be in the States?' Jim guessed another reason, but said nothing. There would be no academic employment, he felt certain, no such collegiate adventure.

'Maybe your trip is to do with the book, which I can assure you, will be a most important one, a good publishing house.' Jim made up the last detail to avoid his friend's mounting frustration at his unconscious dream of the Promised Land not being confirmed and validated, irritated that Jim was not the bringer of the psychic map of his route to the American Dream.

'I suppose it might be.' Challis only wanted concrete success.

'Research, maybe.' This was now Jim in guessing mode, using his natural intelligence, not acting as a mystic. He decided he needed to censor this whole vision and most especially the matter of the prone corpse, which might have just been an idle fancy, simply symbolic, maybe representing the death of Challis' literary desires, indicative of the state of his aesthetic talents possibly. Over the years Jim had learnt never to offer bad news, and mostly he refused his gift, of late only drawing upon it to try to fathom difficult situations for himself, but he'd long ago discovered that the gift rarely if ever gave insight to your own personal, sexual relationships, since there were too many energies and passions involved, drowning out the underlying perceptions. Given he was a committed socialist, Jim's supposed powers also embarrassed him. Lately he increasingly sought to avoid them, fearing that he would be reduced to a late night parlour game, offering mumbo jumbo advice at dinner parties. Challis lapsed into silence, daydreaming of transatlantic campus life.

Further north the weather deteriorated but slowing again they ploughed on through more A-roads beyond the motorway, almost literally, although the Shark showed a tendency to slip and slide along the last section of the journey, the snowed-in streets of Newcastle. Finally, they arrived, their destination a long row of impressively large semi-detached Edwardian houses, a street lined with mature trees, gardens full of snow topped bushes. Challis parked. He left the Shark slightly askew to the kerb. The pavements were thick with snow and ice. They approached a wide door with a windowed panel to one side. The bell was of the brass kind that one pulled, and Challis having done so, the pair waited. The door opened, and there stood Lauren, an ex-colleague from the appalling secondary modern boy's school, York Boys', the Leicester school named after the road on which it stood.

'Lauren?' Jim said, but immediately Challis was kissing her, almost intimately, long enough to make abundantly clear they knew each other well. Jim felt distinctly disappointed, and was surprised. He sensed perhaps there had even been something between them, maybe even a sexual encounter along the way. Jim felt a pang of jealousy. He'd known her since university, but he'd never associated her with the lion-heart, surprised she knew him.

'You two know each other,' asked the hipster, also clearly intrigued.

'We do,' Lauren said. Challis looked curious, expecting more information, a dishing of dirt. 'Don't stand there. Come in, I'm trying to keep in the warmth.' She said nothing more, leading them to a large third floor room they were to share, two single beds.

Much later, at about ten, after several rounds of drinks in various pubs in the town centre where the local girls wore skimpy clothes skittering on high-heels between the bars and clubs, they decided they'd walk back. While doing so they retrieved yet more booze from an off-licence. Even with his coat Jim was frozen, and yet he and Challis seemed grossly overdressed amidst the half-naked totty buying take-out booze for later, stowed in handbags. Currently around a large dining table four of them sat awaiting dinner, the wine already being served by a new friend of Lauren's, Billy, a fellow member of a Maoist-inclined socialist splinter group. They advocated immediate revolution as its primary goal, by any means. Her husband, Mike, was a locally-based Scouser, a teacher poet who knew Caddel. Mike had met both Bunting briefly and Challis, in the latter's travels on numerous occasions. In fact Jim was beginning to feel like a supernumerary, the trip not entirely his own, its centre of gravity shifting, more toward Challis, who was its centre. 'He's a weird old buzzard, Chris, almost eighty now, born 1900. He won't let you record the interview, unless he knows and trusts you. For anyone else he insists you take notes. And he probably won't let you even photograph him.'

'Curious,' said Challis, disgruntled. He'd brought several cameras.

Lauren was in the kitchen with her partner, another ex-colleague of Jim's, John Brown, a bearded Scotsman, with brown, sandy hair. Jim liked him immensely, but both were drawn to Lauren, rivals for her attention, despite both being married. She was coquettish, a short blonde cockney, teaching French, slightly chubby, but not fat. A handsome French beau was once in tow, but was no real obstacle. Jim had known her in the years after university, like so many of his generation of students both stayed on in Leicester, partly because housing was so damned cheap. Long before Lauren had lived in the same house as Virginia, part of a girls' hall of residence, both friends of a woman with whom Virginia shared a room until the Easter. Homesick the roommate interrupted her studies, returning to Malta where her father ran a brewery, a fact which mightily impressed Jim, a detail never to be forgotten.

When first a colleague, Brownie, as everyone referred to

Lauren's current partner, was doing up a large Victorian house, a virtual mansion, with his wife, a tired brunette with whom he'd two children, one of each stripe. Resident until about a year before, he abruptly left the unfinished residence for Lauren, sharing her room in a shared house, the former French fiancé uncomfortably in residence. This scenario became a minor staffroom scandal, of guarded conversations, exaggerated whispers, daily updates, some in favour, others scandalised. Jim thought it was none of the staff's concern anyway. They moved on from their previous scandal-mongering about one of the deputy heads who had moved in with one of the younger mothers of around thirty; her three sons were pupils, the Womack boys, all behaviourally problematic, the eldest in Jim's class aged fifteen, barely in attendance. The deputy-head's visits for pastoral intervention clearly took a more intimate turn.

Admittedly Jim had previous, as it might be termed, with Lauren, two years previously to be more precise, a drunken night toward the end of his teacher training year, so ancient history. Weeks in advance Virginia had booked two tickets for Jim and herself for a school staff party to be held on a large canal boat, but she found herself too ill to attend, with vomiting, diarrhoea, for a time unable to leave the bathroom. There were no refunds, since externally-catered food was involved. Ginnie was too mean to sacrifice her investment. Hence over the phone she sought a companion to replace her, someone prepared to pay a discounted rate of fifty percent, and she came up with Lauren at the eleventh hour. Since neither Jim nor Lauren taught with or knew any of the other attendees, they gravitated to each other in the warmth of the evening drifting through rural midlands countryside which possessed its own particular charm. A turning point and a country pub were reached, several kisses beneath the darkening sky, out by the canal side, hedges and trees becoming silhouettes, as if unreal, clipped from dark paper and pasted by a child upon the scene.

Hours later around three in the morning Virginia found them together in Lauren's bed, his wife let in by another former housemate from her hall of residence, a somewhat tactless action, even thoughtless Jim considered the next morning, guiltily hung-over. In Newcastle Jim reviewed the episode, awkward again since although he'd claimed at the time he'd simply passed out, too drunk to go home, crashing in a convenient bed for the night. In fact he screwed Lauren. This briefly requited encounter was so much better than any of the couplings with his wife over the years, so much so he was less than enthusiastic on that front ever since. He was also wondering whether Lauren might admit their brief tryst tonight, given the fact that during the subsequent two years as colleagues at York Boys' she acted as if this particular indiscretion had never occurred, as if Jim were an acquaintance. At the Newcastle dinner party, by the time food arrived, they were all very drunk, and Brownie had some loud advice for his visitors. 'Take this poet a gift, maybe a pen. I've a splendid set unopened from Christmas, the doppelganger of one that I already use.'

'That's *very* generous, Brownie,' Jim responded.

'Think nothing of it!' The drinking continued. Jim was later photographed by Challis asleep at the table, chin on his chest. When he woke with a jolt, they were all laughing at his narcolepsy.

'Upstairs, Jim,' suggested Lauren. She put him in a smaller room, away from Challis He undressed, clambering into bed. She sat, kissing him on the cheek. 'Good night, Jim, sleep tight.'

Hours later he awoke and found a glass of water on the bedside cabinet, which he drank. His brain ached. His neck felt as if someone had been trying to rip off his head, he was nauseous, thinking of bottles of Newcastle Brown Ale, the flowing red wine. He turned, finding Lauren snuggled into his body, her pale skin almost white, her mascara smudged, and her lipstick patchy. She stirred. 'What on earth are you doing,' he whispered.

'You drank my water.' Her response made little or no sense.

'What are you doing here, Lauren?' he whispered. 'It's all

very cosy, but with Brownie around? Isn't it rather risky?' She said nothing. Gently he prodded her. 'How did it happen?'

'Sorry. Don't you remember last night at all?' she asked. 'Us?'

'Not really, only up to you dragged me up here, putting me to bed.' She smiled, slightly embarrassed, and blushed mildly.

'You kept falling asleep at the dinner table, a lightweight. No stamina when it comes to drinking, I see, not like the others.'

'Well, a long day. So, what happened? Brownie might find out.' His ex-colleague was another very big guy, just like Challis.

'Unlikely. The pair of them are wrecked, completely stoned. Brownie and Challis went at it hammer and tongs, probably a few lines involved too, until they collapsed. I wasn't sleeping with Brownie in that state so I came to you, for old time's sake. Brownie won't be awake yet. No chance at all. He's stoned.'

'Did anything happen, between us, earlier, you know?'

'Did you know you snore, Jim, loudly at times, and frequently.'

'Sorry.'

'When I punched you, it stopped, so you might find yourself a little bruised, on your back, plus a few scratches too.'

'Is there anything else to tell? Why the scratches?'

'If anything else transpired, it doesn't matter if you can't remember what occurred. That's for me to know. What's out of mind is out of harm's way, Jim. Don't tell Brownie we shared a bed, OK?' Jim laughed nervously. 'You want breakfast?' she asked.

Breakfast was awkward for Jim. He relaxed only after Brownie went out for cigarettes. Challis arrived, cheerful, and full of energy, not like a man stoned until the early hours. An hour later Jim and Challis stood at the open trunk as the mechanic had called the Chrysler's boot. 'Fuck me, man!' said Challis, peering in disbelief at the peculiar mess inside. Jim was beginning gradually to feel better after mugs of sweet tea and several sausage sandwiches. Externally Challis still looked completely unaltered by his further excesses, having consumed a volume that awed Jim.

'What?' asked Jim, unfocused, brooding on the previous night.

'It's wine, frozen wine and broken glass, a real mess. I bought two bottles of Hungarian bull's blood wine, Bunting's favourite, and I left them in there. It was so cold last night they've fucking exploded, busted glass as the wine expanded. Amazing, man.'

Later that afternoon the pair stood wind-swept outside a grim but almost new council house in Washington New Town, the whole estate perhaps less than ten years old, if that. The Shark looked incongruous parked amidst the rectangular prefabricated dwellings and streets, the latter with Fiestas, Cortinas and more than a few derelict old wrecks. Yet it felt nondescript. Jim stood with a bottle of whiskey he'd bought in his hand, a replacement gift. A figure shuffled toward them, made out through the glass. Bunting answered, smaller, thinner, and older than Jim anticipated. Here was the great poet before their very eyes. His grey hair was greased and combed back in 1920s-style, he sported a greying beard, pointed below his chin. He wore a wide-coloured open shirt over a dark-grey buttoned cardigan. The visitors were ushered inside an L-shaped living room with modern French doors, boxes of books stacked everywhere, a treasure trove, thought Jim. He worried that Challis might attempt a modicum of pilfering, so kept him in his sights, concerned about the possibility. He thought his companion might seek a souvenir to memorialize meeting a man many regarded as England's greatest modernist poet.

'I have not lived here long,' Bunting explained. 'Moved after marital discord.' They all sat, Jim on a box. There were only two chairs. 'So, to what do I owe this honour, that of your visit?'

'An interview,' Jim explained. 'I was told you had agreed, by Richard Caddel, who said he confirmed the visit.' Bunting nodded.

'An interview concerning exactly what?' he asked unexpectedly.

'Well, we'd be interested in just about every aspect of your work, your life, and your take on poetics,' Challis responded.

'Well, that's rather broad,' Bunting commented. 'Are you thinking of any specifics? Could you not offer something more focused to prompt me, offer some guidance?' Jim wondered if he might be toying with them, indulging in a subtle joke or put-down.

'Well,' Challis paused, 'What's the state of your consciousness, your philosophy of life?' As he spoke he took a portable tape-recorder out of his bag and carefully unwrapped a cassette tape. 'First, in what do you fundamentally believe, man?'

'No recording, it's something I do not allow,' Bunting explained firmly. Mike was correct about what was not permissible. 'You need to remember the scene, the essence of what is said. You may jot down notes, those are perfectly acceptable to me. I dislike verbatim records. Unedited they are utterly inconsequential, always mundane.' He lit an unfiltered Player's cigarette, not offering one to either of them. The tobacco smell was pungent, pleasant. 'So, let me ask again, what exactly are you after?'

'When did you become a writer, from childhood?' asked Jim.

'Childhood, that's a good start.' He paused reflectively. 'I was born as people rejoiced in the relief of Ladysmith, which perhaps will serve to date me. Victoria was still on the throne, reigning over an empire, soon to be replaced by her son.' From Jim's gift he poured himself a generous whiskey into a tumbler, which he sipped tentatively at first, neat. 'I was at a kindergarten, which was its pompous name, once fashionable, more a local school run by a Miss Bell as I recollect. She read to us; my favourites were *Grimm's Fairy Tales*, 'Two Bad Mice,' E. Nesbit, and I loved stories. At five I knew I wanted to write poetry, an instinctual desire. My father read to me and my sister, Joyce, snippets from Wordsworth, and other worthwhile poets. I cannot remember them all. Joyce and I had a governess ... a Miss Wraith, I believe.' He laughed to himself, perhaps at the name. 'We had maids, my father was a doctor. He belonged to the Fabian Society, and to the Lit & Phil, that is to the uninitiated the Newcastle Literary and Philosophical Society, which had lectures and all manner of cultural events. It still exists, running its library, the largest independent one outside London. However, sadly I'm sure not as popular as in its heyday. In my youth some lectures drew well over 500, astonishing. No radio, no television, just the cinema to compete with back then, and the churches. Even Pound visited the Lit & Phil in 1919, a lecture on troubadours. He told me later, for by then I was living in London, of course, after I left prison for being a *conchie*. By 1919 I was at the LSE, growing my beard, which was nothing like yours, though.' He peered at the hirsute Challis, with what seemed initially a disapproving gaze, but smiled.

'Where is your inspiration, your motivation,' asked Challis.

'Oh, that's easy since subject matter is everywhere, the pen like a chisel on stone, in among the shards you will find lying there your poems. On the page say less is my dictum for any serious poet. Discard your words. Brevity is the key.' He sipped more whiskey, enjoying being centre stage. He wiped his beard, lighting another cigarette. 'Now as you may know my parents were Quakers, I followed suit. I went to a Quaker School, wonderful place. I discovered Whitman, a copy of the *Leaves of Grass* half-hidden in the library. His verse was a revelation.' As Bunting continued, Jim furiously scribbled, and by now miraculously Challis' patience was rewarded, sparking up one of Bunting's cigarettes, puffing away together as if they'd always been best of friends. A few more fingers of whiskey were poured. Bunting told of being a conscientious objector in the

First World War, of T.S. Eliot who he'd fallen out with, of various women and young teenage girls in his life. He also remembered his time in the Canaries leading up to the Spanish Civil War. In 1936 he'd played chess with Franco, when the latter had been governor, from where he began his military rebellion. At this point Bunting returned to London, via a boat to Southampton, an unpleasant voyage, little food, fog. By this time Bunting had a wife and children, and he moved near Hampstead Heath.

'Leigh Hunt lived nearby,' Jim commented, 'And Lawrence too, much later.' Jim cursed inwardly for his stupidity in adding something so mundane, so obvious. He felt embarrassed momentarily, especially in the presence of such a great man. Bunting responded, as if gliding over Jim's idiocy, or so it felt.

'I disliked Lawrence as regards his disposition, his personality,' Bunting said. 'He locked me out on a window ledge at a party, in Paris as I recall. On another occasion he secretly slipped hashish into a pie that made me appallingly ill. He could be such an awful jackass. However, I admired *Sons and Lovers*, such a marvellous book. Philip Heseltine appears in *Women in Love*, as Julius Halliday if my memory still functions. Yes in the twenties Heseltine was arrested in Kent for riding a motorcycle, naked.' They all laughed at the circumstance. 'He was caricatured by Huxley in *Antic Hay*.' Bunting got up, 'Sorry for the interruption, nature calls.' He shuffled up the stairs to relieve himself.

'No goggle box,' whispered Jim, 'only radio, valves I'd guess.'

'He's a relic of the past,' Challis responded, 'and a human archive, but he's not giving us much of any real aesthetic, poetic interest.'

'No, you don't think so?' Jim found him fascinating, but clearly going by his tone and facial expression his travelling companion had not been impressed with the older poet.

'Oh no, there's only been tedious stuff so far, but I may be able to use the setting in my piece,' Challis whispered waving his arm around the square room with its low ceiling and off-white paintwork, 'and he has made no offer of a drink so far.' He pulled another face. 'I want to get him onto the Beats, man, as soon as I can. All we have so far are some forlorn rags of growing old.' Jim had no idea who or what Challis was alluding to, although he guessed somehow it must be from the Beats. On his return Bunting was more intriguing, maybe even for Challis hoped Jim, as Bunting ran through his life, including his friendship with Pound, the antipathy toward Bunting from Eliot, possible causes for that negativity, and Bunting's time as an intelligence officer in the Second World War, moving on to his marriages. Jim was mesmerized. However, Challis was beginning to look distracted, and really bored. He yawned, and interrupted the older man's flow.

'So, you met Ginsberg, Snyder, and the Beat poets?'

Bunting peered at him, his eyes piercing, a look of disappointment. 'Yes, I did,' he replied with an obvious lack of interest.

'And they started you back on the poetic trail.' This was a statement of fact from Challis rather than being a personal query.

'No, no, no, that's quite wrong. *They* did not. Let me be clear, my resurrection in poetic terms came after a visit in 1963 from a very young Tom Pickard, just about seventeen, but with great energy and commitment to the poetic cause. I became enthused again, and I started writing once more. And then yes, I did discover that the Beats were among my admirers. Because of such support, there were Arts Council grants, one to reprint *Poems 1950*, which I hear even the Beatles bought in first editions.'

'Really?' said a sceptical Challis, now slightly more impressed.

'Well, life became far better by the sixties, for the fifties were an awful grind, a dispiriting period for me. By the sixties I was writing *Briggflatts* and became convinced that it was the best thing I'd ever attempted or achieved in verse.' He invoked his long autobiographical poem that captivated so many in poetry circles, in the fourteen years since its first appearance, Bunting himself a cult for many. With another whiskey he became far more animated, a twinkle in the eyes, smoking more, like a younger man. 'The poem is my autobiography, every word, no need to say more. I told Jonathan Williams so when he wrote asking for factual details of my life. What has that to do with the public, just give them *Briggflatts*, a copy each, perhaps, or one per family?' He smiled at the thought. 'When I was a child we were read to as a family, by my father, a remarkable man. My parents gave me Quakerism, not the religion concerning which I have long harboured doubts, but its spirituality. *Briggflatts* took a year to be written down; *Tintern Abbey* a day, but of course Wordsworth refined his impressions, reshaped his thought, a much longer task.'

'You like Ginsberg, his verse, "Howl?"' asked Challis, plaintively.

'As I recall, I first met Ginsberg at the Morden Tower. He loved *Briggflatts*, talked of my poetry in America, proselytizing on my behalf. He helped me with funding from the Academy of American Poets to read in New York. They put me up in the hotel where Dylan Thomas died, a filthy hole. I was most unhappy with that arrangement. Despite the adulation from some, Thomas was a useless excuse for a poet. No real talent, writing drivel, and not a pleasant person. However, I liked Ginsberg, himself, the man, but not really his verse. He gave me a copy of his book, which I have somewhere.' He got up and went to a box, rummaging around. 'Here,' he said triumphantly. 'Even its start exemplifies what I mean, all about best minds of a generation, the madness, images of starving, hysteria, nakedness; in truth I find it mostly prosaic, and well, not truly poetic. All that excess, with angel-headed hipsters, a starry dynamo of night. Certainly, his verse possesses energy, offers its own voice, a genuine vision, but he remains far too sprawling, too much like the worst aspects of Whitman, only attempting to be even more mystical, too consciously, pushing even more of the self, and less of nature.' He continued, explained his opinion in detail, praising the Black Mountain poets, subtly deriding

Ginsberg's "Howl," while Challis looked increasingly appalled at such revelations of Bunting's aesthetic judgments that conflicted with his own. Bunting concluded, 'I dislike the idea of gurus, of any breed. That's where the Beatles went astray.'

'Have you read any Kerouac?' Challis demanded.

'I can't say I have. I would think Tom Pickard would have done so, very probably.' With that thought, he told the tale of Pickard's first visit to him in his marital home, in the sterile years as he referred to them, working as a sub-editor on the *Newcastle Daily Journal*. Pickard arrived by train, a long-haired seventeen year old in the early-sixties, telling Bunting that he'd heard he was the greatest living poet. 'I had been the foreign correspondent in Teheran, and I was reduced to being a journeyman, slogging away to maintain my family. Poetry came second, they were wilderness years.' Before he became fatigued Bunting told them of his war, intelligence work, followed post-war by time in the Foreign Office, undoubtedly gathering information, serving as a spy, much of his time spent in Persia, where he found his second wife, Sima, who was thirty-four years younger than him. Jim calculated that made her about forty-four as they spoke, so incredibly young at the time of their marriage. After those nuptials the FO let Bunting go, about which he remained bitter, later working as a foreign correspondent gathering news for *The Times* and Jim guessed for the British authorities on the quiet. Jim thought of other writer-spies: Graham Greene, Ian Fleming, John le Carré, Elizabeth Bowen, and most probably Lawrence Durrell with his successive British Embassy and British Council postings. Jim hadn't anticipated Bunting being a part of that nefarious, duplicitous world.

Finally Bunting reached his recent separations and divorce from Sima in 1977, describing his various digs over a few months and how he had eventually arrived in his current dwelling, which had been found for him by the local authority, part of an Arts Council intervention, poets to be resident among the people of estates. Challis had once introduced Jim briefly to the writer Jack

Trevor Storey who lived in similar fashion in Milton Keynes, the difference being that Storey had come to love the city for its optimistic modernism, making it his permanent residence. Bunting had no similar feelings about this estate perched on an otherwise desolate hillside by a main arterial road. 'So, it came about I moved here, to 127 Stridingedge, Blackfell, Washington New Town, through the auspices of the Northern Arts Council. The house was offered by the town council. My, it's an utterly bleak place, some inhabitants are grim, but at least my neighbours are kind. Most Sundays they bring me food, a roast dinner. The house is roomy, albeit the environment is hideous. You could have a competition for hideousness without finding anything much uglier. Tom comes over to see me,' Bunting was referring to his youngest son, 'and he's trying to find me somewhere better, perhaps a place in the country, near a pub.'

'So, you feel cut off here?' asked Jim sorry for the man of letters, almost eighty, separated from the worlds he knew, surrounded by people cleared from nearby slums, crammed in an area with few amenities, made far worse by sleet and snow.

'This weather – I'm unable to go out. I so enjoyed the fell country buried under its drifts of snow, trudging through them, back to a warm fire.' He paused, muttering, 'Each birth a crime, and each sentence life.' Smiling, Jim recognized a sentiment from 'Briggflatts.'

'And the local people here?' asked Challis. 'Friendly?'

'The children can be delightful, but I speak with only a very few of my neighbours. There's woefully little with which the young ones can occupy themselves. There is one local supermarket, with half decent wines and strangely an excellent range of cheeses. One adapts, survives. I have visitors, such as your good selves. However, I live on two small pensions, more meagre than the one allowed by the state, in a house which is not mine, in an intentional slum-in-the-making. Really, after sixty years as a poet, I haven't even a house of my own in which to die.' Challis and Jim looked at each other. Tremulous and angry tones mixed in Bunting's voice. Already he'd drunk more than half the whiskey.

'Might I take a photographic record?' asked Challis, forestalling further melancholy. He pulled out a huge professional camera, his Leicester trademark. Incredibly, given Bunting's antipathy to recordings, he assented. Challis' flashed away, maybe twenty occasions. Afterwards they parted for Leicester, wary more snow might trap them in the north-east, Jim unwilling to revisit Lauren and Brownie. 'I miss my chick Holly, man,' Challis insisted. Jim acquiesced. Jim pictured Lauren, as Challis drove, he held forth on the scandalous nature of Bunting's dismissals of Ginsberg, sacrilegious according to Challis' aesthetics. Jim was silent.

Yet more snow descended. Jim worried about the drive back. He thought of Bunting in his splendid, unexpected isolation. Jim calculated he might never see Lauren again, or hear from her. Their lives would diverge. Jim might yet fix his marriage. Although he might not. Poor Bunting, he thought, solitary, abandoned, old, among people in the middle of nowhere who'd no idea of his significance. Few would ever read a poem after school, and certainly nothing by Bunting, some old codger, an oddity given his diction, clothes. Jim shivered. What did it all amount to, relationships, writing, one's aspirations, the whole life thing? Although he wasn't that keen on the alternative, not yet, not for ages, he hoped. He still possessed the optimism of youth. His thoughts turned to schooldays, the film they'd tried to make in 1968, when Boris died. Jim wondered about how they'd been. All that energy and enthusiasm, yet still tinged with uncertainties. For Jim that time felt completely different from his present life, freer, yet stressful in different ways. He and his school-friends had ambition, but they knew so very little of the world, they had no real experience of loss, of that certain irrevocability ... of eternity, of events like death itself, which was only for the old . . . surely.

Chapter Eight: Filming, Summer 1968

Back in May 2014 already Jim had lost three days to meetings and various other supposedly necessary administrative tasks. They came at the point he hoped he might start some extensive writing. He managed maybe another ten or twenty more lines of notes about the schoolboy film they'd made in 1968. Instead of more creativity, he ended up spending two days at his university, and another in town sorting out the bank account of the ridiculous journal he helped run, forced to meet Alfred yet again at the branch in Russell Square, adding him as another signatory. Otherwise without funds they would have ground to an immediate halt. The previous signatory had left academia, emigrated, immediately losing all interest in any such associated activities. Gabi was back, so he had only the afternoon on Saturday 10th and the evening of Sunday 11th to address the matter of the novel. It was insufficient time, especially as progress on paper was so limited. Yet he was very active mentally, sifting his memory for different scenes to illustrate his themes. Plus, he held a firm idea how he might approach the task of composition, but again it still needed more time for further development. He checked his emails, with yet another one from Eileen Beckett. She was persistent, so was probably a prospective student seeking supervision. He virus checked it with difficulty. Reading through he saw that she noted he hadn't responded, apologized for another 'intrusion', explaining she wanted to find out about her mother's past, specifically her relationship with Dr Chris Challis early in the 1980s. Jim thought he might know the woman she referred to, of course he did. But surely by then Challis was with his long-haired blonde who lived with him, Jim uncertain of her name, and he was not with this stranger's mother who apparently also knew Jim. Or, so Eileen wrote, and so she thought. It was ancient history he decided, people and places long lost, a long-forgotten, peculiar past. Really, he didn't want to think about certain painful episodes again, not his marriage, the birth of his son, the divorce, not on such a nice day with the sun out. He deleted the emails.

Currently, while thinking back, he sifted the past only for plans for his new book. In doing so he was trying hard to pinpoint his own first tentative artistic ambitions, which—apart from a few poems published in the school magazine together with his voracious love of reading as a child and adolescent—had actually involved a film project shared with other boys from his grammar school in Enfield, back in the late sixties, during the summer of 1968, the year after the so-called Summer of Love. Jim had almost shoulder length hair back then, and as an early developer, sideburns. He spoke to Gabi about this phase of his life, but she showed no real interest in his teenage self. She laughed at the photos, dismissive in particular of his tonsure. In 1968 Jim was concerned primarily with the script, but out of necessity he acted in the film as well, most of them did, except Boris, who was too shy despite his height. Nor did Ray who was the cameraman, or so Jim recollected. He decided he might check on who did what and why, and who decided matters. Maybe he'd ask Matt. He'd surely remember.

Looking back from 2014 it seemed so difficult even to imagine what they were all like as teenage boys, or what animated them. He wondered why the film focused so determinedly on bombs, terrorism, and Welsh nationalism, concerning itself with a race not especially renowned for its political violence. On the Saturday he made his call to Matt and pumped his friend for his recollections. Matt was fairly certain Jim was correct in supposing they undertook the shoot in the summer term of 1968, writing the scripts as they went, mainly improvising, but making some notes which hadn't survived. He was surprisingly tentative, suggesting they might meet. Jim guessed he wouldn't say much on the phone because of the pipe bombs, the two they actually exploded, such massive blasts, surprisingly so. Forty-six years later Matt was still nervous concerning these events. Jim was reminded by Matt that Welsh nationalism was his passion at the time, his family originating in and around Swansea. Coincidentally Matt was to visit his parents in Enfield the next day, so he agreed to meet at a local Wetherspoons pub for supper. They'd go through everything in person, a meet arranged. Jim would work up some notes from their conversations and draw upon Matt's memories. Jim's own chief impression of being fourteen was of a rebellious streak in many of his peers, all still full of undirected vim. Jim felt optimistic, eager to confront his authorial task, thinking about what he could recollect and piece together. These events were a core part of his friendship with Matt, that and their earlier and different commitments to the Scouts. Yet, the film had also entailed loss, of a sort they couldn't have previously imagined.

As Jim remembered, one morning before school during breakfast listening to the radio, he decided consciously to be more interested in the wider world, paying closer attention. Vietnam was nightly on the news. He watched with growing horror, disgust. There were the Phong Nhị and Phong Nhất and the Mỹ Lai massacres the previous winter and spring. On March 17 a violent demonstration in Grosvenor Square against the war, after which Martin Luther King was assassinated, followed by Bobby Kennedy. Enoch Powell made his Rivers of Blood Speech. Ted Heath dismissed him from the Shadow Cabinet. Jim's father was outraged. King's killer James Earl Ray was arrested at Heathrow Airport, flying to Rhodesia. That confused Jim mightily. King Constantine fled Greece, immediately replaced by a military junta.

Jim didn't really understand the underlying dynamics, but he wanted to. What was the pattern? He and some new friends had the idea of a film, yet such momentous events seemed to have hardly impacted on the others' adolescent minds at all, given their initial suggestions for the film's topic, which were for an updated *Romeo and Juliet* (the play they were reading) or a car chase. Boris pointed out they had no girls available for Juliet and they were far too young to drive on a public highway. They were to meet later that day at lunchtime, so as to make a firm decision, after which they would begin shooting the project, the following Saturday.

However, the morning of Saturday, 1 June 1968, designated Day One of the Film Project during the previous week, arrived and their topic still wasn't decided, as they'd planned it should be.

The meeting on that Saturday was to usher in the brief era of the pipe bomb and of the film about Welsh terrorists, or *freedom fighters* as Matt insisted they ought to be called. However, on first gathering that morning there was another tetchy debate over the issue of topic or subject matter. Plans for the film project began first at the tail end of their third year as the holidays approached. Boris loomed large over them, literally as he was taller, almost by five inches, boisterous, yet chubby, and originally christened Charles. Oxlade, another classmate, discovered that Boris Karloff attended their school and unofficially rechristened their lanky classmate Boris, initially a sarcastic nickname. He embraced his pseudonym, mimicking the actor for laughs. In an interim period between exams and results they all had plenty of free, unstructured time. Teachers disappeared mysteriously, but no one in authority seemed to worry. Magically discipline became less severe, some masters even allowed pupils in their charge to talk very softly in classes, so more ideas were exchanged, plans hatched, with new friendships and groupings forged.

One morning, just after registration, in the previous week during the first period two third year classes marched the quarter mile over to the lower school to play cricket for the entire day. Of the sixty-two boys, twenty-two of them were allocated as players, two as substitutes, three more scoring, two others acting as umpires, one chosen from each class, a group of six, three at each end, to move the huge wooden screens behind the bowler's arm according to the dictate of whoever faced the ball, and the rest spectators, sitting in the sun on the grass beyond the boundary. A number of them from Jim's class lounged near the huge, half-buried concrete air raid shelter at the side of the field, itself covered in grass, its huge iron door firmly padlocked. Boris was slyly, but gently kicking Matt and Oxlade in the backside and giggling as he did. 'Let's plan the film,' he hissed in a stage whisper, 'come on.' So, while their team was batting they hatched their plans to meet at the weekend, a group of eight, some like Boris padded up, ready to replace a batsman if required. Later, he was delighted with his day, as seventh batsman scoring a creditable fifty-three in their subsequent victory. He was asked about playing for the school, but as Boris confessed to Jim, he was too terrified of the ball, particularly when fielding. So, he couldn't catch, not such a hard object. Jim admitted the same phobia. So like Jim Boris decided not to move from athletics, however good batting well had felt. Earlier their history teacher and form master told them about a national competition for anyone under sixteen who could produce a short film of between ten minutes and half an hour, the two criteria being *quality* and *originality*. Matt was eager, and so too was Boris. Being their friends Jim and Ray thought they might as well be involved too. From a host of others about four were persuaded to sign up and actually join them.

At the weekend a motley group of schoolboys huddled in the garage to the side of Matt's large whitewashed, detached corner house near the centre of Enfield. It bordered the Willow Estate, the original building with curved metal window frames like a grounded ocean liner. Beyond a rickety porch, the front door led to a jumble of rooms, including an extension to the left, the bottom of which was Matt's massive bedroom, huge windows front and back. When Jim originally met Matt in the first year, there'd been a large puppet theatre to one side. It had been in that very room during a performance of part of *Under Milk Wood* that Jim first kissed a girl and felt her breast, a small right one, through her jumper, his arm reaching at first tentatively around her back.

Jim knew well all the areas of Enfield, being a subject of parental conversation. His mother worked at Northern Metropolitan, an estate agency very near their home. His father considered Briggs, its owner, to be a total crook. Briggs had been known to rook gullible old people, for instance, who had been thinking of selling to move near a son or daughter. 'What do you want to achieve?' Half had possessed no idea of their own property's true current market value, so they became easy prey.

'If an old couple needed a thousand to buy somewhere cheap, somewhere like Suffolk, Norfolk or Cornwall,' his mother explained to her husband the previous evening, 'Briggs will immediately offer the cash they need, rushing through a rapid, lightning-quick sale. He'd spend maybe a few hundred on renovations and sell the house on within the month, for three or four thousand. He's no conscience at all, very much the wheeler dealer.'

'You ought to tell them,' retorted her husband. 'It's crooked.'

'I can't. I daren't. He might catch me and I'd lose my job. And I could only warn one couple, after that I'd be history.'

'Isn't it illegal,' interjected Jim from the doorway, having been about to enter the lounge a few minutes previously.

'That boy's a bloody idiot!' objected Howard. 'Illegal?'

'Don't start, Howie, please. He doesn't understand anything, that's all. He doesn't mean anything by it. Do be quiet, Jim.'

'He's a fool, or a bloody moron, that's what. Haven't you anything better to do than snoop on our conversations?' Jim shrugged. His father turned to his mother again. 'Little imbecile,' he muttered. Jim's mother sighed. 'Briggs, does he need carpenters at weekends, for the renovations?' Jim's father asked, being it had been his trade since he'd left school at fourteen in 1942, with the Germans bombing, and V1s soon to descend.

'I'll ask,' she promised, but Jim doubted she would. His mother knew all the areas of Enfield and she mapped them out according to property values. When Jim told her on the previous evening where he was going the next day, knowing he'd visited previously, a number of times, she'd asked for a description of the house, particularly the number and size of bedrooms, mystifying Jim. 'Well, they have money,' she commented. 'We sold a smaller one in the vicinity recently, fewer bedrooms. Well, who'd have thought it, with five bedrooms their house must be worth five or six thousand,' she added. She was thirty-four, a few days from her thirty-fifth birthday, and that made her slightly depressed.

'Is that a great deal, mum?' Jim asked, although he was not financially innumerate, just unworldly, because the bigger picture had meant more to his young, inquisitive mind, hence a growing interest in politics and the economy. On the day before he'd understood that inflation had been drifting upward to about 4.7%, a fact he'd gleaned from his daily dose of BBC Radio 4 (replacing the Home Service the year previously), because his mother had always banned pop radio stations in their home on weekdays. Music was to be enjoyed only in his own bedroom on a Sunday after his judo club, before a late lunch, his special time. After lunch he would listen to comedy and drama on the radio. Before doing so he quizzed his mother about money and wages.

'Well, your father is lucky to make £40 a week at the Cable, *with overtime*, and that's before stoppages,' she informed him, reminding herself. At home money or a shortage thereof was a frequent topic of conversation during the many, often volatile exchanges between his parents. His father had an additional part-time job evenings and weekends pumping petrol at the local garage, pocketing extra cash for repairing flat car-tyres with inner tubes.

Some of the group of boys were also familiar with Matt's house not far from Enfield Town centre, the coterie of them who for a few months had dodged certain classes, scurrying round, joining Matt in his rebellion, when he'd refused to attend school. Boris usually led the way, long legs snaking toward his destination, the others scurrying after him, twice the steps. They had talked endlessly, of school, of teachers, of parents, even of girls, and of sex and drugs and rock and roll. The shared musical taste went well beyond the charts in the main, nothing like 'Young Girl' by Garry Puckett and the Union Gap, although Boris had pointed out the punning obscenity in the group's name. Ray said it was the singer's real name. The rest laughed at him. They all approved of the Small Faces, though, and definitely the Stones new single, 'Jumping Jack Flash.' The others were less certain about Boris' penchant for 'Do You Know the Way to San Jose?' by Dionne Warwick. Secretly Jim liked that song too, but said nothing.

'This will be a classic of the future,' Boris insisted, but they never played the single again. They were all virgins, but some like Jim had kissed a girl or two, felt their breasts, maybe more.

Currently in the Evans' family garage six virginal schoolmates sat on boxes and foldable chairs among the household detritus, an eighth expected, but late. Oxlade was missing, still expected. Ray with his high unbroken voice, snubbed nose and choirboy good looks was explaining the specifications and availability of their history teacher's camera, which he presented like a trophy in its leather case, 'It's a 1966 Kodak Super 8mm motion picture format, eighteen frames per second, 200 feet of film and sound cartridges. Pretty good, don't you think? Whenever Churchill's not using it, he says we can have access. That's most of this summer. He'll give us dates when he wants it back to record several family occasions, like a forthcoming wedding.'

'Cool,' added Boris 'That's generous'. Dark hair shook with silent laughter, grey school shirt with collar beneath his cable-stitched blue jumper. Jim thought the latter uncool for the weekend.

'Let me know them, I can draw up a roster,' said Jim. He was wearing hipster trousers, a new thin belt, short sleeved shirt, and black suede desert boots. He felt trendy, and was hoping that some girls might be involved, but so far the gender balance was unpromising, all boys, all from their school. Still, he reckoned the film would be something with which to fill up the days during the summer break, a chance to see friends regularly. Earlier his mother had given him some money for fares, and lunch if needed. He walked two and a half miles to save the money.

'I'll have to be the cameraman,' said Ray immediately.

'So self-appointed,' responded Boris, prodding Ray.

'No, I'm not,' said Ray defensively, 'Churchill insisted.' They believed him, since he was the teacher's favourite.

As their teacher had stressed about the competition, entries submitted came in two categories. They could be, he explained, either a factual, documentary-style submission, or, alternatively, an imaginative, dramatic, made-up one. At the Film Project Day so far only Sean favoured the former approach, the others all preferring a drama to be written by them. That much they'd already decided, so they would need to come up with a story they realised, but they were stumped. 'We need a good narrative,' Sean insisted 'that's why a documentary is easier.' They all agreed about a strong story, but coming up with one proved tough. Still they weren't having a factual film. Too boring they thought. Originally access to a camera had been their key stumbling block, but the self-same history teacher favoured some of them who were in the top form, especially that group including Jim, Ray and Oxlade who were in his basketball team. This was a real passion on the part of Churchill, donor of the camera, as he'd once visited or lived in America, a fact which had impressed the boys. 'He's given us some old film stock, suitable for a super eight camera. But, we'll have to buy some more. They sell it in town.'

'How much does it cost? How are we going to get money to buy them?' asked Sean. He was considered a real swot, but had a genuine capacity planning the logistics of any project. Matt simply declared they ought to make a film about Welsh nationalists, stated so confidently and enthusiastically. There was a shaking of heads. Matt was the ideas man, the driving force, or so he thought, expert in supplying optimism and energy.

'What about something like bob-a-job, to raise the funds? We could hire ourselves out to do chores and make some money that way,' suggested Boris. Heads nodded, for like Jim most of them were in the Scouts, and raising money was a norm.

'Good idea,' said Matt, a sea scout like Boris, curious in a landlocked borough, although there was admittedly the River Lea and the Lea Valley reservoirs. These bodies of water were not far from where Jim lived, in the industrial, deeply unfashionable eastern part of the borough where the lower classes lived, in Ponders End, Brimsdown, Enfield Highway, Enfield Wash, Enfield Lock, Turkey Street, and Freezywater. Of the group of boys involved in the film only Jim and Ray came from that side. Instinctively Jim knew the rest would be nervous about going over to his area, even unwilling, with its reputation of being rough. He wasn't concerned, for he'd grown up there and could look after himself. Jim worried about fitting in, and found himself wondering whether Ray felt the same, but he didn't dare ask him. It might mark them both out and he daydreamed about such fears, worried about being ostracized. 'Well, what about the Welsh nationalists?' Matt demanded. The others were reluctant.

'We need is a storyboard,' Sean suggested to blank faces. Boris awoke with a start, the involuntary shudder of unprompted awakening.

'A story what? A board?' he asked. 'What on earth is that when it's at home?' Boris was far more open than the rest about any gaps in his knowledge. His very size afforded him a certain bravado

'One word: storyboard. Well, it's a description of scenes, visual and written, like a cartoon of what you're going to shoot, with daily schedules,' Sean explained. The rest had no clue, so they were prepared to believe this apparently well-informed boy, who seemed to have all the right vocabulary. Jim enjoyed learning new things, reading voraciously from his local Carnegie library. He made a mental note to look this up, to find out more, and about film scripts. He wanted to write something really good.

'I was reading about it in the library, when they made us go there for half a day last week,' said Sean. He was referring to the small school library, where if there were several staff absences a class could be banished under close supervision by prefects, different sixth formers every hour allocated during their free periods, which freedom the younger boys envied, these hulking individuals many of whom seemed just like men.

'So, what exactly should it be about, this storyboard?' Boris queried. 'Anyone have any good, concrete and workable ideas?'

'Well, what about Welsh Nationalist freedom fighters?' repeated Matt, motivated by his Welsh origins, both parent having moved from Swansea just before his birth, most of their relatives still in South Wales, in Cardiff and Swansea, mostly. Clearly he wasn't going to give up on the idea. The others didn't look that keen, but had no concrete alternatives. 'Does anyone else have any ideas?' In truth he was trying to silence them.

'Well,' said Ray hesitating, 'it should be an adventure?'

'Of what kind, exactly?' asked Matt dismissively, to head off any such rival ideas or suggestions. He knew what he wanted.

'Like *Zorro*,' Ray continued. Jim felt he should remain neutral, see what transpired, since he couldn't yet think of an alternative.

'Too lame,' Boris responded. 'We need something original.'

'Anyway, *Zorro* is copyright, so we could never use it if our film was a real success,' Sean added. 'We couldn't win.'

'It's hardly likely that we would make something that was viable commercially,' said Boris. '*Zorro* wouldn't even be accepted for entry.' The others wondered about 'viable,' whether it meant what they thought it might, whether it could be used in the way Boris thought. They stayed silent, even Sean. 'Well, our idea might win a prize and to do so it must be original,' Boris continued. 'Churchill said so. Remember *Zorro* just wouldn't qualify for the competition; our version wouldn't have a chance.'

'What about crime, maybe, a young soldier, back from Vietnam,' Jim proposed, drawn into the exciting exchange of ideas.

'No,' said Boris, 'too complicated. There's the whole issue of American accents. If we did them, they wouldn't be convincing.'

'What about a bank robbery?' said Ray. 'That'd be easy.'

'Well, that's already been incorporated into my idea for a storyboard, that's part of my idea,' Matt responded. 'You see, this group of Welsh freedom fighters will have to commit a crime to acquire the money for their bombing campaign. The plan for this and the meetings make up the first part, interior scenes. They could be shot anywhere. The hold-up comes in the second part of the film. They commit a bank robbery, guns, and stockinged faces. We could use the Barclays in town,' Matt replied. 'No one would know it's not in Wales. And the third part is their first bombing, of a mainline train line, cutting off national communications.'

'Yes, we could use some sawn-off shot guns,' Ray added.

'They might prove hard to find,' Sean responded. 'Even using fake ones, we might get into trouble. I think avoid firearms.'

Jim decided he wouldn't mention he could easily obtain a real sawn-off shot gun if he really wanted, one which belonged to one of his uncles by marriage, Dennis or Dennie. He'd been rumoured to have used the gun nefariously, holding up a remote sub post office in a small town in Bedfordshire. However, Jim never mentioned the matter to any school-friends. He honoured the close knit secretiveness that certain of the working-class had in bucketsful. Jim already knew to say nothing, deny everything concerning any such issues. He'd been labouring with his extended family at a shop-fitting job in Edmonton in the Easter break, involving his three uncles, two by marriage, his father, Jim himself, and another local lad a few years older than Jim. At noon two of his uncles disappeared for a while. When they returned over three hours later, continuing with their work, Jim's father took him to one side, at the back of the shop. 'Whatever happens, they were here the whole day. Do you understand?'

'Sure thing, dad,' he said casually, 'Sure I do.'

'You need to be certain,' his father admonished him. 'Remember, they were here all day, whoever asks, even the law. You say nothing. You're young enough they're not allowed to question you. Understand? Remember. You up to keeping schtum?'

'I am, dad. You know you can rely on me.'

'Well done. Good boy.' It was the only paternal praise he remembered.

Sitting in Matt's garage Jim realised that whatever their own status, as far as his mother's family were concerned now he'd passed the eleven-plus, he was to focus on obtaining a decent education. That was his mother's ambition, to avoid the factories, any criminality, and poverty, all the things her family and those around her had known and endured. She wanted Jim to mix with a better class of person, rise by his talents and knowledge, not brawn and violence, although both ran through his veins whatever intelligence he possessed. His mother wanted him to acquire respectability, but he remained ambivalent about that ambition.

'Where will we shoot the outdoor scenes if it's supposed to be about Wales?' asked Boris. 'We have to be practical and find somewhere.' For no apparent reason he was laughing again, very quietly.

'Enfield, of course,' said Matt, surprised when his suggestion was derided. 'Use areas of Enfield that look like Wales.'

'That's stupid,' said Beamish. 'Enfield isn't at all like Wales.'

'And if people knew it looked like Enfield, they'd think it was set there. And what on earth would they be doing in Enfield, Welsh terrorists?' asked Sean sceptically. 'It'd spoil everything.'

'No, it wouldn't,' Matt replied. 'Can't you see that?'

'I know,' interjected Boris. 'I have an idea. I can see how it can be done in Enfield. We can fit it in easily. Use Enfield and set it there, because the terrorists are *undercover*, *pretending* to be students, at Middlesex Poly. Really they're here ready to bomb London, hiding, lying low, lulling us into a false sense of security. We'll do indoor scenes here, in the garage. It'll be the place where their terrorist cell meets,' Matt elucidated. Jim began to feel the idea was a good one but was still uncertain of his role.

'Exactly! That was my brilliant idea, already!' Matt was joyful Welsh terrorists remained centre stage, while claiming the scenario.

'What's a cell?' Jim asked, reluctantly, but wanting to know.

'Yeah, what does it mean, a sell?' Beamish demanded.

'It's the term, for an undercover group, of revolutionaries or bombers,' Boris confirmed. 'They work in cells, which are small groups, so no one knows who they are.' Jim couldn't see why the size of the group would make any difference, but he said nothing.

'So why use bombs, and in London?' asked Ray. He found the idea unimaginable and Jim tended to agree. 'Surely it's just too fantastic.' Boris laughed again, out loud this time, but initially said nothing, snorting. He was doubly amused by their ignorance.

'My mother told me that for the fiftieth anniversary of the Easter Rising in Dublin back in March, a group of former IRA members blew up Nelson's Pillar in Dublin,' Boris said. He'd an Irish mother, English father. 'She said you should never trust the Micks,' he continued. His mother had driven ambulances throughout the war, which gave her a peculiar authority in this group's eyes; even though they felt she was incredibly ancient to have a son of Boris's age, being at least in her mid-fifties, if not older, although they never mentioned their feelings to him. 'And the Welsh do have nationalists too. My Dad told me.'

'Exactly, they do. And they did some bombings,' said Matt. 'Back in the 1950s according to my mother, some Welsh republicans tried to blow up a water pipeline that runs from the Claerwen Dam in mid Wales to Birmingham, to stop the English from stealing our Welsh water. We just imagine that this resistance has been revived, like it was in Ireland, spread to the young in our revolutionary sixties. That's our scenario. We just have to believe that the Welsh have taken the fight to the capital, under cover, and they're robbing banks for their funds.'

'Sounds workable to me,' said Boris, 'so let's get writing.' This activity was another attraction of the film project for both the absent Oxlade and for Jim in particular, the script. Both had writing aspirations. Both were clandestine poets, afraid any such admission might sully their reputation as sporty types, both able to look after themselves with their fists if required.

'I can,' offered Jim. 'I can write.' He was eager for the role.

'We don't need a script yet,' objected Matt. 'Just ideas, which we storyboard later. First, we clear out some of the junk, create enough space in this garage, for the shooting.' They all groaned.

'Not my idea of fun,' said Boris. 'Cheap labour for your folks.'

'Look, I'll ask if my parents would pay us, some money to fund the film stock,' added Matt. 'And ask for your bus fares and if you walk here there's some more cash.' Jim groaned. All the rest lived far closer than him, even Ray, so he had to walk the furthest.

'Ok, then, I'll help,' volunteered Boris, moving forward awkwardly, all knees and elbows. He stayed very jolly, his shock of black hair, long on top, shorter at the sides. He often laughed, sometimes silently, a range of private jokes animating his frame. 'Then we can go to the park, perhaps, and have a few laughs over there.'

'And what about Oxlade?' asked Ray. 'Where is he?'

'If he's still not here, he's not interested' insisted Matt. 'If he's late, it serves him right. So, *Cymru Am Buth*!'

'Yes, agreed, Wales forever,' Sean translated before anyone asked. He too had Welsh forebears, just like Matt.

On the following Saturday, the eighth of June, *Cymru Am Buth* started in earnest. A larger gang of nine boys reconvened in the tidied-up, empty garage, space cleared for shooting the first scene. During the week three of them, the terrorist cell members, had been learning their lines, cobbled together by Boris, Jim, Matt and Oxlade during lunch breaks at school, at Matt's place. They chose the older-looking boys to participate in the *acting*, Boris, Matt, Jim, and Oxlade. Surprisingly Boris was reluctant, too shy despite his considerable size. Oxlade also declined, but took to wearing sunglasses or his shades as he referred to them. A youthful Beamish was co-opted for a minor role, as was Broadhurst. As Boris was going away on a trip, as was Sean, Oxlade appointed himself as co-director with Matt, and Ray remained cameraman on the basis of understanding the camera and having the trust of Churchill who'd loaned them that precious item. In truth, only he had the technical capacity to operate the machine.

Toward the week's end they'd been excitedly discussing and playing Donovan, who'd entered the charts with 'Hurdy Gurdy Man,' and they'd agreed he was a good musician, in the folk-rock tradition. Matt derided the charts which they'd been discussing, as first he played a John Mayall album featuring Eric Clapton and then Savoy Brown's first album. Matt's especial ire was directed at all the crap, as he considered such music, from people like Solomon King, Roger Miller, Cliff Richard and Des O'Connor.

'Fucks sake, who buys all this crap? We're supposed to be living in the swinging sixties,' Oxlade remarked. 'Last year was called the Summer of Love, the start of a Hippie Revolution.' He was an avid reader of the *International Times* or *IT*, an underground paper supported by Paul McCartney and Allen Ginsberg. The boys hoped Oxlade would bring a copy to their second Film Project Day. He hadn't disappointed them. According to Oxlade from 1967 the police or *pigs* successively raided the *IT* offices. 'The filthy scum is trying to close them down. It's an establishment attempt to prevent resistance, stop youth finding their voice.' He showed them the cover, a long-haired chick with a tight-fitting, ribbed jumper, boobies prominent. 'She's cute,' Chris commented, pulling a face. They all giggled, their laughter increasingly infectious. It took them time to calm down sufficiently so that they might continue to scrutinise the picture.

'"May 31 June 13, 1968, *it* 32,"' Oxlade read. '"Paris alternative society now. UK 1/6, Paris free."' So, nothing in Paris. Cool.'

'So, we pay and the French don't.' Boris' frame was in animation once more. 'Silly, we're subsidising the Frogs.'

'What's inside?' Matt asked, purporting to be bored by the whole affair. Promptly Oxlade passed the paper to Boris, who smirked.

'"Poets may feel *IT* is giving them a raw deal. We have a fat file of poetry received over the past months. For the time being, we are not using any poetry. [...] Meantime, don't send any more poetry until further notice,"' Boris read out loud, trying to sound as adult, as authoritative as he could. 'That's curious.'

'Bummer,' said Oxlade, 'So we can't send in our poetry.'

'Why? You'd think they'd want that stuff?' asked Ray.

'It's because everyone and his aunt wants to publish poetry,' said Boris. 'To be a poet the only qualification is a pen and a sheet of paper, and stupid ideas. You don't have to be a good poet, and the length is not off-putting. Anyone can manage a few lines. They've probably a huge pile of rubbish in the corner of their office, a mound of maudlin, meaningless drivel.'

'Look,' said Jim pointing to the page, 'Are those hippy small-ads.'

'Yes, it says *Personals*. Shall I read some,' suggested Boris.

'Oh, yes, please. I'd really like that,' said Broadhurst, a new addition to the team, travelling all the way from Barnet.

'"Three Oxford students interested whether girls really answer erotic ads. Box 32/5,"' read Boris. 'Sounds intriguing.'

'No, it's dull,' said Oxlade, 'These ads are bound to be full of blokes seeking chicks. That's boring. They do that in the local paper.'

'No there is one chick. Listen. "Girl with gorgeous body would like to model for appreciative artistic photographer. Box 32/28."' Boris chuckled suggestively. '*Gorgeous body* . . . .'

'Let's write to her,' Broadhurst suggested, 'offer her a part in our film, her gorgeous body, *naked*.' They all laughed smuttily, uncontrollably, except Sean. Boris shook with merriment.

'We haven't enough money. If we were to I think she might well agree to take part,' Sean said primly, 'but not otherwise.'

'But it doesn't mention any money,' said Ray. 'Where?'

'It what's called "implicit". By "Appreciative" she means she expects payment from the photographer,' Sean added a touch bombastically.

'And "model" possibly means a prostitute, or hooker.

Apparently, they're called that in Soho,' Boris said to deflate Sean's pomposity, still chuckling as he spoke. 'According to what my dad told me. And I'm not sure how he knows.' They missed his irony. He passed the journal to Jim. 'You read next.'

'Look, an Arts Lab Restaurant,' embarrassed about the previous lewdness Jim changed the subject, reading a third page ad, 'open late Thursday, and until 2 a.m. Saturday and Sunday.'

'We should all go together,' said Oxlade. 'It'd be cool.'

'Yes, we ought to,' Boris added. 'When we have some money.'

They'd never let us in,' responded Sean. 'We're too young.'

'Speak for yourself,' Boris objected, but they sensed Sean was right. Other than Boris they were too small not like men.

'Here we're in Swinging London, too young to enjoy it,' said Oxlade, speaking them, 'doomed to forever miss out on the fun.'

'Well, it says "The restaurant will develop some unique cooking methods,"' Jim read. 'Like what? Would it be genuine curries?'

'No, it refers to drugs probably,' Oxlade concluded.

'In the food?' asked Boris, dubious. 'How could you?'

'Maybe it'd be like frying cannabis leaves?' said Ray, without a single clue as to what might actually be involved.

'No, it's more likely to be code for dope baked in cakes and biscuits. I read about them. They add it to the ingredients and it makes you very high,' Oxlade informed the group.

'Oh, look,' said Jim indicating another ad with the naked

torso of a woman, flowers painted on her thighs and naked breasts, '"The Way Out Club." Weird. It's a magazine with sex ads. Listen to this, "Wife swapping, girlfriend swapping." .'

'If I'd a girlfriend, I wouldn't swap,' said Boris. 'I'd keep her, hold onto her really tight. They're stupid these hippies.'

'AC/OC … .' Jim continued, clueless as to the meaning.

'What on earth is that? AC, OC?' asked Oxlade, which surprised them. He was the man of the world, the most fashionable, with his *shades*, and even he was flummoxed by this contraction.

'I've no idea,' said Matt. Jim nodded in bemusement.

'No nor me, I've absolutely no idea,' Jim said aloud. He was going to continue reading, but another reference to transvestites puzzled him, so he paused. His thoughts were soon interrupted.

'Shall we proceed with our film? Can we do something? You can read the stupid smutty ads later,' Sean suggested primly.

'Well, I've got something that might help,' Oxlade said pulling a thick wad of papers from his army surplus gas mask bag.

'What on earth is it?' asked Boris. 'Looks boring.'

'No, it isn't. It's stuff from various guides to making explosives. I researched it in various chemistry books last week. Adrian helped me.' This was a friend of Matt's who hadn't turned up on either day. 'So, we can make a real bomb for special effects, just like the films, but maybe even better,' Oxlade added.

'You'll get us arrested,' commented Sean, looking troubled.

'It would be part of the originality. Let me look.' Matt took the sheaf from Oxlade, perusing them for a few minutes before adding, 'We can do this. It's simple stuff to find and buy. Easy, meaning we can record an actual explosion." Jim was doubtful, but said nothing. Later that day the three rehearsed, elaborating, setting the scene in their minds. The cell was planning to blow up a train. Matt persuaded Jim to wear a moustache fashioned of horse hair and stuck on with some pungent glue of whose true purpose Jim remained doubtful. For a subsequent scene the boys had in mind a huge railway viaduct where they could shoot outdoors later if the summer weather held.

'We need to plan for continuity,' said Sean. Faced with blank expressions, he explained, 'You need to be wearing exactly the same clothes for the next scene that occurs on the same day. We could shoot something that happens the next day before the outdoor scenes. In fact, we could film all indoor scenes first over the next few weeks in here, then the outdoor ones after the school trip.'

Boris and Sean were scheduled to leave for Lake Geneva, Switzerland, canoeing and so forth. They were excited, leaving on June 21st and returning July 6th, both legs by plane from Heathrow.

Their flights made Jim think of his own school trip to Cannes by boat-train through Paris in 1966. His front tooth was knocked out in the dormitory at the lycée where they stayed, a freak accident with a Coke bottle upon which Jim rested his chin and which caught the corner of a metal bed frame, exploding like a rocket. That autumn Jim was to have his final treatment at the Eastman Dental Hospital on Gray's Inn Road, his temporary crown replaced by a permanent one, on a gold post drilled into his jaw. He'd hated the treatment, the discomfort, and pain. He refocused.

Matt was trying to convince them they could build a pipe bomb and let it off as a special effect, but several remained dubious. Sean apparently had agreed to take charge of continuity, building up a list of details of each scene. He'd keep them until the holiday, when filming would have to be halted in Boris and Sean's absence. With Sean making notes and diagrams, Ray pointing the camera, others simply watching the drama that unfolded before them, the team managed three takes of the scene, the second abandoned with more horseplay when Jim's moustache fell off and finally settling for only three because they were made suddenly aware that their film-stock had virtually run out. After filming, they returned to *IT*, responding to its hippie small-ads. Jim started, "'SPREAD IT – Mike Seymour is Basil Brush.'"

'Who is that?' asked Sean, 'anyone have any idea?'.

'Not a clue. This is equally strange: "Male Austrian, 21, looking for an odd girlfriend."' Jim added, 'I don't get it.'

'Me neither. *Odd*? Not old? Why an odd girlfriend?' asked Boris 'What a weird thing to want in a girl, oddity.'

'He gives his address in London, S.W.3, with full stops,' Jim added, 'His name, it's Norbert Korba.' He spelled it out for them when they asked, ending, 'K – O – R – B – A, Korba. No idea. Strange.'

'It's such a funny name, that one has to be made up,' said Oxlade. 'It's surely some kind of joke. Or is it a code, like the ones you read about in spy novels or thrillers? Perhaps they're coded messages.'

'They could be hippy spies. The last one, we could write back, pretending to be some weird babe,' Boris added. 'Let's do it.'

'That'd be boring, man,' said Oxlade. 'In fact, that's uncool.'

'Here's another good one,' read Jim. 'It's in capitals,' he said, shouting, "'DO YOU WANT TO GET MORE OUT OF YOUR SEX LIFE?"' They all sniggered, even Sean on the sly.

'That's one for you,' Matt said to Sean, who blushed, face a deep purple, 'and there's an illustrated something or other, too.'

'An illustrated what?' asked Ray. Matt peered at the page again.

'It doesn't say,' Matt replied. 'There's something missing.'

'Maybe it's another coded message?' Chris suggested, but not seriously Jim realised, as he was pulling another of his faces, twisting down his lips, suppressing raucous laughter.

'Well, let me finish,' Jim continued. 'This is funny.' They ended raucously when he read the rest, '"MEN, IT CAN BE DONE. There is now available a sound and successful method of improving virility and increasing man's vital dimensions [...] guaranteed."'

'What's that,' Boris quipped, 'an example of the hard sell?' They had a difficult time stopping the waves of contagious laughter convulsing them, each spasm wave upon wave growing tidally.

'Penetrating comment!' shouted Oxlade adding fuel to their comic conflagration, their near hysterical mood.

About a month later on Saturday 6th July just six of them agreed to meet for an outdoor shoot at Clay Hill where the massive railway viaduct loomed over the landscape. On the day it was drizzling fitfully, with periods of sun penetrating the cloudy skies, punctuated by an occasional short shower. The weather wasn't the reason for Sean's or Boris' absence. Jim heard an appalling rumour, the one about Boris. Ray confirmed just before the shoot, with a replacement for Boris, that Ray too had heard the rumour of Boris' demise. They'd both been incredulous, disbelieving the very possibility. Neither of them knew for certain, but they soon would. They were waiting for Matt, who approached, pulling a cart which contained what appeared to be a crude short piece of pipe, the sort used for drains. This was the bomb, or so they presumed. Matt knew Boris' family, so he might know more, whether it was true or not. 'So, what happened, have you heard anything about Chris?' Jim asked Matt, reverting to Boris' real name.

'He seems to have drowned in Lake Geneva, at night, cold water, got into difficulties' Matt said, emotion in his voice. 'They'd gone for a swim after dinner; they might have had something to drink first, some alcohol.' There was an intake of breath, and a few gasps.

'So when they pulled him out, he was dead?' asked Oxlade.

'No, the body went down, away from the shore, still not found.'

'How grim is that! But how did it happen? He was a good swimmer, very strong,' said Ray. 'He was big and strong.'

'Yes, he was,' agreed Matt, 'an extremely strong one. They're still searching apparently, but there has been no sign of him. They dragged that part of the lake where he was last seen, but I suppose there might be strong currents. Lake Geneva is huge, like a small sea. Naturally enough, his parents are devastated.'

'They would be,' said Ray. 'It's a terrible thing to happen.'

'We had a special service at our church with prayers dedicated to him, on Wednesday evening,' Matt explained. 'It was awful.'

'And Sean?' Jim asked Matt. 'Was he there, when it happened?'

'No, but he's pretty cut up. That night he stayed in their dormitory, at the school where they were staying, where Boris slept.'

'Grim,' reflected Ray again, at a loss as what else to add. At this point they went quiet. Matt broke the silence.

'Sean is back. I saw him at church. The party all came back a week early,' he continued, 'there was a vote, it seems.'

'There'll be a huge hoo-hah at the school, with the governors involved,' Ray added. 'It means trouble for someone.'

'Shouldn't we cancel the film?' asked Jim. 'You know, stop filming out of respect for Boris, to honour his memory?'

'No, we should carry on for Boris,' Matt insisted firmly. 'We'll dedicate it to him. We should try to finish shooting, for today at least. Doing so will be our lasting memorial to him.' So that afternoon in the brightening sun they shot scenes of themselves scurrying around with the cart, just like Keystone cops, all so tragically comic. There was little silliness or outward verbal humour that day, just a shared determination to finish the task.

Next followed the explosion, the bomb went off, a huge flash, a massive bang set off on a mock-up of a train track that wasn't really very convincing, just two planks painted grey for the rails and some other wood. These objects flew off into the air suitably enough, thrown fifty metres or more, the film-makers having scampered behind a huge hedge. Mud and stones rained down over them, but fortunately the impacts were minor. They couldn't have risked damaging the real train line, although they'd talked about the possibility, with Matt keen on the authenticity this offered. Common sense prevailed to a degree. However, they risked trespassing on land beside the railway line, shooting scenes of actual track, of passing trains, until a distant police siren approached, blaring ever louder. Eventually they scuttled off, hiding half a mile away in nearby undergrowth, laughing nervously.

After fifteen minutes of whispering, they abandoned the cart, making their way individually, so as not to draw attention. There were two scenes left, which they promised each other in that undergrowth they'd complete, but the momentum was lost, each engulfed in private grief, unable to carry on, but nothing would be said in the coming days. The next autumn the school governors banned all foreign trips for the foreseeable future. Among the friends, no further filming was ever contemplated, discussed or planned.

Although the boys remained close, until the sixth form ended, for years they were to remain quiet about the great Film Project and most of all about the pipe bombs. At the time they'd have blamed the fear of being punished for the explosion, and for the trespass, but later on it would have been explained variously as a matter of more interest in girls, commitments for some in part-time or summer jobs, and the allure of late nights out in pubs.

However in truth a conspiracy of silence continued, for different reasons, which were concerned with their unspoken, inexpressible grief, unexpectedly shared by boys so young. And what they avoided was a premonition of the fact that the friendship with Boris was destined to be forgotten, their recollection of this poor virgin fading. And with him dead before his life had really got going, even the memory of that would wither; he was destined to become a faint memory, a footnote to their collective past, mostly unremembered, only memorialized in and by their unfinished film which was lost. Boris never had time to develop his creativity. They avoided that fact for a while at least, just a few hours that day of the bomb. To finish the project might have meant facing the prospect of admitting something about themselves they'd rather not have faced in their youth, that much they did at that particular juncture would be forgotten later in life, the detail shadowed as if obscured by a huge spider's web, the freshness of their enthusiasms only reduced to a matter of their naiveté.

Chapter Nine: Howard, 2012

Jim's thoughts of the past led him to recall another phase, his Master's research degree on Kurt Vonnegut in his twenties. Matt mentioned it when they met in Waltham Cross for supper in a local pub in the shadow of Queen Eleanor's memorial. He was visiting his parents, and Jim sifted his friend's recollection of 1968, the film project and Boris. Surprising how much he recalled, most forgotten by Jim. What did Kurt Vonnegut write about fate, consequences, and death in *Slaughter-house Five*, the novel that made his name? *So it goes.* That was it. Every time someone died, Vonnegut wrote: *So it goes . . .* successively . . . . . He himself died in late 2007, aged eighty-four, a fair age for a life-long chain-smoker and drinker. Jim watched him indulge in both to excess after enduring Vonnegut's crappy old play in a fringe theatre in Battersea. While sitting in the bar with his shy French girlfriend, Arnaldo, uninvited the writer had joined them, ogling Jim's companion. Vonnegut refused to talk about writing, only about France. Of course, presumably on his first visit Vonnegut was captured in the Battle of the Bulge, later almost killed aged twenty-two by the allied firebombing of Dresden, his most famous novel circling that event. Jim completed his degree during a difficult period, struggling with stress and depression, isolated, desperate for a partner, never finding the right one. Jim lived close to the Regent's Canal in the early 1980s, his flat in the very street where Joe Orton was bludgeoned to death by Derek Halliwell in 1967. At the time the playwright was thirty-four, increasingly successful and his talents publicly recognized. On the morning of his death a chauffeur arrived to drive Orton to a meeting with film director, Richard Lester, to discuss the rights of and options for *Up Against It*, a script Orton originally submitted to Brian Epstein for the Beatles. The driver discovered two bodies. When resident in the area Jim read accounts of Orton's life, borrowed from the Islington Central Library, ironically the very institution whose books from 1959 he and Halliwell 'defaced' or more accurately artfully modified with obscene collages, altering the covers of over seventy books, for which they were imprisoned for six months in 1962. One account of the life that Jim read was destined to be turned into a film, which in part captured the grim nature of Islington in the 1960s and 1970s, a dubious area. Jim heard an urban myth that Orton's murder inspired the Beatles' song 'Maxwell's Silver Hammer.'

The Angel as an area, along with those adjacent ones, was still working class when Jim arrived in 1981, although it always possessed a bohemian and artistic side. One of Orton's neighbours was the so-called queen of Soho, Elena Salvoni, manageress of the famous French restaurant L'Etoile, in Charlotte Street, a favourite of diners such as Sean Connery, Peter O'Toole and Ella Fitzgerald. Near Jim's flat stood Chapel Street Market, which he frequented, an open-air affair with stalls lining both sides for its entire length and well beyond into the side streets. The market was thriving, a bustling place which Jim first visited with his maternal grandmother back in the late fifties and early sixties as a child, when it was haunted by the writer B.S. Johnson. This tragic figure would die nearby, not far from Jim's flat, just across the Essex Road, in a side street leading up to St Margaret's Church. Just forty Johnson committed suicide in 1973, slitting his wrists in a warm bath, Roman-style. He left behind two young children, a wife from whom he was estranged, and what ought to have been a promising future. However, according to rumours Johnson had probably been depressive, even psychotic. The death was still a mystery of sorts. Johnson had fallen out of favour, partly his suicide, in part feminism. Jim thought his eclipse added to the tragedy. On his return to London Jim was trying to reread Johnson's novels, but they were difficult to find, turning up periodically in second-hand shops.

Jim mused on his father's death, and what followed. He settled the estate, visiting banks and building societies with his widowed mother, and organized the funeral, with Matt officiating over a secular service. Jim talked about his father's death with Gabi over coffee during their weekly shopping trip. It was Saturday, 17th May 2014 according to the *Times*, which he read, sitting together in Esquire's in Harlow after shopping in the Asda superstore. Soon Gabi would undertake a jaunt around various other shops, while Jim ate breakfast in Frankie & Benny's two doors down. First, they talked about his plans for the novel, slightly confused as to where his notes might be taking him. He even admitted his difficulties in writing. 'Maybe it's your father,' she suggested, 'the whole thing is about losing him, the whole project.'

'Why would it be about him, my father?' Jim asked, slightly bemused by her suggestion. He believed it was about Knapper, the one dead friend he couldn't bring himself to write about.

'If you're not sure of where you're going, maybe you are simply avoiding all your thoughts about your father's death. You're circling that reality, which I believe you really want to confront.'

'He isn't relevant. Anyway, he didn't die prematurely,' Jim was irritated by her sub-Freudianism. 'That's the central theme, *premature* deaths.' Gabi pulled back her long dark hair, regarding him intently. His response slightly irked her, he could tell.

'Well, he thought he was dying too soon, didn't he?' she replied without pause. 'He wouldn't eat food on its sell-by date, even at the very end. He believed he might go on for a lot longer if he was careful enough. He thought he would have at least another ten or twenty years.' Jim was stunned by the simplicity and truth of her observations. Of course his father had thought this, and so too did so many of the baby-boomers, such as the people who had participated in his own ageing project, fostering a belief in their own eternal relevance and by implication continuing youth. They all acted as if still teenagers, exploring new things as he and his fellow filmmakers had in 1968, with many of the same naïve values.

'Yet Knapper did die young,' he whispered, thinking both of this friend and of Challis, noting that the latter had little choice in the matter, whereas Knapper brought about his own demise.

'And that all happened at almost the same time, just weeks apart, wasn't it? Bang, bang, like two shots to your body and mind, bang, father, dead, bang, bang, Knapper, and next thing they're both dead. That was a really horrible summer for you, last year. Don't you remember? Remember: you had that student complaint, the one Carlin took so seriously, but later dropped. You've been different since then, you know, less positive.' Jim knew she was right.

'Well, Carlin has gone now, no longer our boss.'

'Oh, so he's left, for somewhere else? That's so good, isn't it?'

'No. He's still there. He's just been bloody promoted.' She groaned. Jim continued, 'Number three in the whole bloody university.'

'No, I just don't believe what they do. How did that happen?'

'I don't want to talk about it. His leaving party from our faculty was yesterday, before the graduation party. Very few attended, but I went along dutifully, not sure why. I didn't intend to.' She shook her head. 'I wanted to confirm that it was really happening. The promotion somehow made me feel such a total failure.'

'I'm sorry about that.' She stood and kissed him on the cheek. 'But you're no failure, think of all those books you've written. You have a good salary, Jim.' He sighed, thinking of the fiction he'd wanted to publish, not scholarly books which very few read. 'I'm off,' she added. As Jim knew, nothing much would get in the way of her weekly shop, only disaster or multiple deaths, maybe a terror attack. 'I'll see you later at the car.' He nodded.

Over breakfast he made a few more notes on the back of an envelope he pulled apart for the purpose, writing slowly as he ruminated on the idea of a new novel, seeing it as a challenge. He thought first of the framework, and of his parents. As Jim recalled and Gabi could testify, their health difficulties began before 2013, for in autumn 2009 Jim had moved away from Tufnell Park back to Enfield to be near them as they aged. Certainly, they'd squabbled more, seemed afflicted by a series of minor ailments, but fundamentally they appeared to be coping well enough. However, in spring and summer 2012 the façade put up by his parents finally came tumbling down, although in truth his metaphor was wrong. It was less a crashing of a wall of bricks, more like the ripping apart of a set of theatrical flats upon which the frontage of a building had been painted, but now stood vandalised, revealing the huge gaps. The monumental building constructed at the centre of their marriage had been that of his father, and the narrative as far back as Jim could remember was that Howard Arnold Dent should be seen as strong, a man of good judgment, and should be obeyed. As Jim had known from a young age, when, already aged about nine, he could work out the machinations of people and events, the truth was that Howard was wilful, neurotic, bullying, like a monstrous child, a monster baby, as Jim often thought of his father right from childhood, right up to the present day. Yet the man looked benign, always had. Well-dressed, capable of being garrulous with strangers, in company he was charming, often generous, although not emotionally. At home he was always a radically different man, seeming caged, enraged by his own failings and those of others, angry at his fate, held back by having been viscerally retarded, as if trapped in an earlier mental stage at least on an unconscious level. At eighty-three he still lacked the capacity to quell his emotions if someone happened to disagree with him, even on minor issues. In fact in Jim's opinion his father had worsened in this respect. Howard's rounded face, and bald pate still managed to offer a vision of youthfulness, his skin smooth and unwrinkled, his hands like those of a much younger man. Until March Howard, with the assistance of Jim's mother, managed to maintain their conjuring trick; until then Howard still appeared to be healthy, even fit, but a single fall from the toilet put paid to any lingering illusion, blew away the smoke, leaving only the shattered mirrors, the manner of their continuing trickery revealed for all.

In December 2009 Jim moved into a terraced Victorian house bought on a new mortgage in the district next to the one in which his parents lived, where Jim had grown up. He could assist them as they aged. He knew they were struggling despite their constant denials, and gradually Jim began to shop for his mother on a weekly basis. His father became increasingly nervous about driving. Outwardly the pair pretended that absolutely nothing was changing, his father beaming to himself on anyone's arrival, scrubbed up, and perched on his leather chair. But if the visitor happened to be Jim, he frowned. Within minutes Howard would become as argumentative, as aggressive as ever. Since Jim left home in early January 1973 there'd rarely been an occasion when his presence hadn't caused a massive argument, hadn't aggravated his father. Howard was prone to flying off into rages, sulking, storming out of the house, shouting, very often literally screaming. Howard had always been the same, throughout Jim's childhood, like some constantly unstable volcano, like having Vesuvius in your back yard on 7 April 1906, the eruption that caused the 1908 Olympics to be held in London, at White City alongside the Franco-British Exhibition. At this long-demolished stadium Jim and his parents watched Kipochage 'Kip' Keino run a mile in August 1967, beaten into second place by Jim Ryan, whose world record had been three minutes fifty-one point one seconds. Everyone at White City anticipated another new record, and so the occasion was tinged with huge disappointment, even though it was a most exciting race. Jim watched it on YouTube, one of the miracles of the internet, with its capacity to allow recovery of long-forgotten public events. When he mentioned the occasion, Howard insisted Keino won, that Jim was mistaken, misremembered. He'd only been a damned bloody child at the time.

Of Howard's decline there were a few clues, the occasional glimpse of a bag of incontinence pads, the mornings when it was clearly a struggle to make Howard presentable, even by ten a.m. unshaved and in pyjamas wet with patches of urine. As a routine Jim cycled the half mile to his parents from his new home. Both houses were in the Lea Valley, whose river had originally snaked down through open countryside into East London, at Limehouse Basin. Once huge and broad in winter when flooded it had offered a natural boundary between the Danelaw and the rest. Subsequently it'd been canalized, feeding huge reservoirs, and yet more of its water siphoned off for the New River which meandered down to Sadler's Wells and the New River Head, a testament to a mammoth engineering feat. The River Lea had once brought wealth, with many factories springing up in the mid to late nineteenth century, with workers drawn from the land in adjacent counties, especially during the agricultural depressions of the late nineteenth century, like his father's family, the Dents, from around Standon in Hertfordshire. Most of Howard's family had worked in the various enterprises, the jute mill, and the power cable works, the precious metal smelting works, the often foul smelling glue factory, the small arms factory, and later the various electronics factories. Once the area had boasted swathes of industry, heavy and light, mile upon mile of massive sites, the landscape also dotted with various pubs, cafes, various yards, suppliers of tools and parts, repairers of vehicles, providers of fuel and lubrication, freelance metal workshops, and myriad other smaller enterprises including local shops, banks, sea food stalls, flower vendors, paper sellers, as well as bus drivers, train operators, patrolling policemen, teachers for children, lollypop people for the young to cross the road, builders, mechanics, all servicing the behemoths of industry, their workforce, and all the families and friends.

This array of activity had long dominated, was so immense and entrenched, so much part of the local lives that Jim's father thought that such edifices, monuments to working men and capital, would last forever. However, by 2012, the time of his illness, they'd very largely gone, bulldozed years before and redeveloped. Thatcher had long finished her scorched earth policy attack upon the unions and the industries that nurtured them. International finance was being shifted across the globe where labour seemed eternally cheaper. The area Howard knew so well from boyhood and throughout his working life had undergone a rapid transition, much of it dying before his eyes, barren areas, empty for many years before its sudden recovery, newer enterprises springing up, bakeries, large retail outlets, offices. When Howard went into his decline, all of the old factories had long been demolished, the sites cleared, their machinery sold off and sent to the far-east, following that trail of transnational capitalism. A whole way of life and work vanished as if exterminated out of sight, no contemporary Bruegel the Elder on hand to record the dreadful martyrdoms. By the time Jim's mother called him frantically on Saturday 24th March, that way of living only survived in the memories of its survivors, those in retirement, others who had been made redundant. Toward mid-morning Jim answered his mobile in the small Tesco supermarket in Enfield while half-way through the weekly shopping with Gabi.

At his parents' house there was a gaggle of neighbours in the hallway, one from next door together with his wife, and an ex-workmate of Howard's from over the road, his father clearly having been tidied up before anyone was called. The heads crowded. There was a palpable panic as if it might be tasted. Howard was still lying with his head in the shower, a pool of blood in its tray. Jim's mother hovered, anxious. 'What's happened?' Jim asked no one in particular and from the jumble of responding, overlapping voices he managed to ascertain that his father had fallen as he tried to clamber onto the toilet and he'd bashed his head on the way down, on the shower tray most likely. That much was evident. 'Well, it looks much worse than it actually is.' Jim explained, 'The head bleeds profusely. Such wounds often look worse than they are. And this won't be the first time you've bashed your head?' The last remark was directed at Howard, who nodded vaguely. Everyone else seemed mesmerized by the scene, so Jim stood back, and searched for an old tea towel in a kitchen drawer, which he soaked in warm water. He returned to his father and gently bathed the likely site of the wound. 'It's virtually stopped bleeding,' he told the assembled throng. 'Look.' His father had a frightened look, pale, slightly out of breath, panicky. 'Nothing to worry about, Dad,' Jim said reassuringly, more in hope than certainty.

'We've called out an ambulance, James,' said the Maltese next-door-neighbour. His wife was looking out of the front door, keeping both eyes on the road, a round woman, body inflated.

'I don't think he needs one,' Jim said, looking at the wound. 'He's just shaken. He'll be OK.' Jim was more concerned with interrogating his mother, to find why the accident occurred, what was at the bottom of this event. Was his father struggling to even walk to the loo? Jim hadn't suspected such a disability.

'They're coming, look, they're on their way,' said the ex-workmate, Frank, who'd spotted the blue flashing light.

'I see,' Jim said, the light visible as the ambulance pulled up outside, a gaggle of children watching from the other side of the road. After he was taken away, Howard was kept in overnight, given sedatives and discharged. He continued using his exercise bike housed in the large garden shed, but decreasingly so, week by week, as if shaken from his resolve by the fall.

Howard fell again on 18th April, down the stairs frontwards, bruised, but otherwise physically uninjured. He was breathless, with pains in his chest and, after Jim sat talking to his father, he asked his mother whether they should take him to hospital. An hour later they were all three into the local casualty or A&E department, one threatened by cuts. At this hospital for years his father had been chairman of the hospital radio, set up with younger friends. While waiting perched on a plastic chair Howard was reminiscing, talking to his wife, cheerful to be at the site of so many happy memories, unperturbed by the surroundings which were so utterly familiar. Formerly, he went around the wards collecting requests. Jim remembered visiting the original studios which his father helped build, near the morgue, and being confronted by bodies under a sheet serving as a shroud, one taller stiff showing its feet. Howard had greeted Jim. 'What a wonderful spot,' Jim complained, indicating two dead souls, the recently departed.

'Don't worry about them,' said Howard. 'The dead aren't worried about anything, they're past caring.' Throughout his life he was a staunch atheist, hating all religions, their exponents and followers, for what reason Jim had no inkling, still didn't. He'd always suspected that it was connected with the war, narratives of which dominated Jim's childhood. However, there were always those who refused to broach the topic, even in his family, as if dark secrets are better interred, left undisturbed, the trauma sublimated.

Howard was in the dark for almost three weeks, feeling physically better, until the diagnosis, after which he was full-time in an oxygen mask. They sat around the bed. 'Pulmonary fibrosis,' he whispered. 'Poor devil over there has it. It's incurable, he told me, but the doctor himself said nothing to me.'

'So, you might well have ages,' Jim suggested.

'Yes, maybe, yet maybe not much time.' Howard sounded gloomy.

'Well, do remember that you might,' said Jim.

'Great, but it gets you in the end.' Howard thought for a moment, self-absorbed, for once in his life justified in so being. 'What's the word for how long you've got, the medical term?' he asked his son, who had to think for a moment. 'What do I ask?'

'Well, you might ask what your prognosis is.'

'What?'

'Look, just ask the doctor "What's my prognosis."'

'Yes, thanks, son. Well, *prognosis*, that's it, *what's my prognosis*,' Howard repeated to himself in rehearsal for his big moment.

A day later when Jim visited again with his mother, the consultant did his rounds. His father fiddled with a radio and headphones. He'd all manner of electronic gadgets in his locker, brought by a young friend from his hospital radio days, Les, who charged up the television with funds, a pay-by-watch system. The consultant approached, a rotund Asian man in his forties, and after a brief conversation about how Howard felt, whether he was comfortable, Howard piped up, 'Well, doctor, what's my prognosis.'

'Well, that's difficult to say.' He looked uncomfortable.

'You've no idea, then?' Howard was typically forward, accusatory.

'Well, unfortunately you were diagnosed late, so that's not great. It'll be months, maybe a year if you're lucky.' For the very first time Jim felt sorry for his father. Howard looked gloomier.

'I see,' he said, looking in accusatory fashion at his son, as if he might be responsible. They made it clear that Howard could return home and on 15th May he did, sleeping downstairs in the dining area, on a new bed in the foot of the L-shaped open lounge, near a small window overlooking the bins and beyond the garden.

Gabi and Jim visited together on 19th, again after their Saturday shopping. They had an idea that a Hungarian helper might be arranged privately, staying gratis at Jim's, to assist his mother who was clearly struggling. She looked wan, drawn, and agitated. Howard was not convinced by the concept. He made his views clear. He hated being downstairs 24/7, thought the look of the bed—a short one which Jim had had to order specially— ruined their home of which he and his wife were inordinately proud. They loved the kitchen extension and another for a front porch, both planned by Howard, all of which allowed them to squeeze in the downstairs shower and toilet. An oxygen machine had been delivered the previous day and Howard was under a mask, breathing heavily. Somehow, he'd managed to move the television, despite his condition, and it was blaring, tuned to a channel that Howard ignored. They tried their suggestion again. He reacted furiously. He wasn't bloody having a helper, they could cope perfectly well, thank you very much. They were just fine. They'd take care of things perfectly well. When Jim tried to persist, offering the opinion that this was untrue and his mother could not cope, and really needed help, Howard shouted, 'Mind your own fucking business! If we need help we'll ask the Macmillan nurse!' Jim desisted. The old man would only become agitated again. On further visits Jim noticed that Howard, an avid follower of football, a Spurs and England fan, seemed to be rapidly losing interest. He was again mournful, depressed. The European Championship Finals were on, but on 15th June Howard had the sound silenced completely for England against Sweden.

'Are you watching, dad?' Jim found the silenced match bizarre.

'No. I'm really not that bothered anymore. I don't know that I'd even see the final, even if we do progress. So what's the point? This is all far too grim, more than I can bear, I can't breathe. You're worried about the match. I can't concentrate on bloody football.' He indicated the breathing mask, which was agitating his skin, literally. Jim felt the life was going out of him, not offering even a real argument, not really, just as few glares.

'You'll be alright.' But Jim didn't believe in his own words.

'Where did I go wrong? I didn't smoke, ever. I didn't drink much.' This was true, or at least after Howard was about to reach forty and his wife gave him an ultimatum about drunken nights out and about with friends. 'I was careful about my food.' To Jim this seemed like an understatement. After the 1960s and the success with the links relating smoking and cancer, the health lobby had moved onto food. Howard avoided almost everything such journalism proscribed, confused about contradictory reports that reached him. A life spent after forty with low salt, low fat, high fibre, avoiding red meat, sugars, artificial sweeteners or additives, E-numbers, and only a little alcohol. Jim's poor mother was chastised on numerous occasions, accused of trying to kill her husband by offering him ice cream, although at other times this was exempted, particularly Ben and Jerry's. 'And now I'm dying before my time, before some of those sods I know who didn't look after themselves at all. Where's the justice in that? All that keeping fit, being careful about everything, and I'm going to bloody die before my time.' Jim thought of all the individuals he'd known that'd really done so, suffering a very early demise, right from Charlie at school and that young woman, one of a crowd of drinkers he knew in the Clarendon pub in Leicester who died of leukaemia back in maybe 1977 or thereabouts, aged only twenty-two. Still his father expected to live at least as long as his own mother, who survived well into her nineties, ignoring the gender differential that often prevailed in matters of longevity.

'It was work that caused it probably. They used to call this condition carpenter's lung,' Jim said. He'd looked it all up online, not just webpages, but downloaded articles from some American medical journals. He'd undertaken similar research the time of his father's extreme confusion in the heart hospital after having a valve repaired seven years previously, offering the consultant a piece of his mind about visible clocks and other such recommendations found in the latest American research. 'You were unlucky, it was all that dust.' Jim was remembering the drum shop in the factory where he'd worked, not as bad as his father's carpenter's shop next door, but at times pretty grim.

'Never . . . not from work, I don't believe you. There were filters.'

'You'd worked there ages before that was done, dad, long before they fitted anything. They weren't bothered for years.'

'They did so. As ever you're just plain bloody wrong.'

'Oh well, suit yourself.' Jim was tired of arguing with Howard, who although increasingly apathetic as his condition worsened still maintained an emphatic obstinacy toward his son.

Saturday 16th June saw another fall in the toilet, his mother so frightened she'd failed to remove the incriminating evidence. Their adaptation to Howard's plight was revealed. The pair were using an ancient, rickety office chair on wheels, with a frayed brown cloth seat, holes in the fabric that had been in the third bedroom for years, the box-room where Jim had first slept as a child. This had long served as Howard's tape recorder, electronics and computer room. His mother was evidently pushing Howard to the toilet, despite hardly having any strength in her thin frame. This was their system of transport, rickety, unstable, and perilous. Howard refused any suggestion of a wheelchair. 'You've not been using this?' he asked his mother, incredulous at yet another secret they were keeping from him. His father was determined not to depend on Jim, couldn't see the despair of his wife, her physical weakness, and the abject quality of their lives. They were terrified someone might intervene, Howard unwilling to change, even contemplate intervention. 'Well, have you?'

'Your father, he told me what to do. What choice have I?'

'This can't go on. This isn't really suitable, it's totally unsafe. And it's wearing you out, mother.' Gabi and Jim lifted Howard, a heavy-weight, putting him into bed, every movement painful.

After more discussion Jim called Matt, who coincidentally was staying again over at his own aged parents' place, the site of much of the film project. He was now a Baptist minister on the outskirts of Oxford, from whose main university he'd obtained his divinity degree only a few years previously, a very late graduate. After a short wait Jim and his friend took Matt's estate car and Jim bought a cheap commode, something Howard was still resisting tooth and nail. His now frail voice still rose from the bed complaining, rejecting the whole arrangement. Jim sensed any mention of Hungarian helpers would make him apoplectic, so the Macmillan nurse was called. On his return with the commode, Jim worried for his mother. Everything looked beyond her, physically, mentally, emotionally. So insistent was Howard, despite the facts, that together the pair could cope unaided, Jim was concerned that through pig-headedness his father would kill off his wife, as well as himself. Yet, Jim sensed Howard's energy was waning, and a day later it was clear even the commode was a struggle, a task well beyond the ageing couple. Exhausted, his mother could no longer lift Howard. That afternoon the Macmillan nurse agreed Jim's mother was unable to cope, and that Howard would go into respite care in the first available home for a week. A few phone calls later he'd been booked to travel on Wednesday. Tuesday night he didn't even watch England take on Ukraine, one of the hosts of the Euros, a nil-nil draw. Jim watched at his parents, Howard oblivious of the outcome. Afterwards Jim concluded matters were grim.

Jim cycled over to the care home near Forty Hill, an area where Jim's friend, novelist Jim Crace, had grown up. He once warned Jim about describing *black and white magpies* if he ever wrote again. Jim thought of his friend's success. He was published before Jim knew him, two books, after having been a journalist for over a decade. Jim's father was in a hospital bed, looking happier, wearing headphones, fiddling with a portable radio on his lap.

'There's no telly,' Jim said, thinking of football.

'I'm not bothered with the goggle box. You waste your life looking at that contraption,' Howard replied negatively, but seeming as if generally he'd perked up, 'Personally nowadays I prefer the radio.' Jim thought that his father had lived so many years without television, maybe the first thirty-five, and he'd reminisced once enthusiastically about listening to a radio in a big mahogany cabinet during the war, which Jim recollected vaguely from childhood visits to his grandparents. As his father talked to his wife, Jim sat looking at his newspaper, *The Telegraph*. His father appeared as if he might keep going longer than the events of the preceding Saturday seemed to indicate, especially if they were to keep him in the home. As Jim suspected, the respite period was very likely a prelude to a longer stay, getting him acclimatised, more used to the idea, to wear down his resistance institutionally. Jim guessed this was the Macmillan nurse's plan. Jim hadn't warmed to her, too much of a control freak, but medical staff were often like that. Certain types were attracted to jobs with lots of vulnerable people. In Jim's youth these had been referred to as weirdos, later recognized as paedophiles, drawn variously to youth organizations like leaders in the Scouts and Boys' Brigades, social workers in children's homes, priests in the Catholic Church in particular, and even teachers in language schools for young foreign students.

Back in the early eighties through a group of friends in West London, one of the women was the magnet for Jim, he knew one such predator. This guy worked in various language schools off Oxford Street, preying on innocence, exploiting his gullible, sometimes virginal female charges by the dozen every summer, some as young as thirteen. Jim disliked him mightily from their first meeting, but many of their crowd seemed to find him charming, even turning his penchant into an ongoing joke. Given his posh first name was Menzies, he was referred to as Mingis the Dingis , a vulgar joke celebrating his sexual preference for overly young and varied females, victims of his libidinous desire. The woman, a friend of Mingis, reciprocated Jim's attraction, although it was unfulfilled. She would marry a carpenter who beat her on occasion.

Jim also once worked with another even younger chap from a village near Norwich, who as an English language teacher pulled a similar stunt in the early eighties, unrepentant and shameless about his sexual exploitation of continental teenage girls, many seemingly under age. His repeated comment had been 'Once they bleed, it's time to feed them this,' pointing to his penis. As Jim reflected, currently both men would certainly be regarded as paedophiles, as outright criminals. And rightly so in his view.

Jim worried about parental finances, especially if a long stay loomed, more than twelve months, but there was nothing he could do. His father was secretive about all matters of money, apart from talking endlessly about his occupational pension, another source of great pride, rescued for him by Jim when his father was threatened with redundancy aged about sixty. Jim wrote for him a letter accusing the employer of 'constructive dismissal,' a phrase he advised his father to bandy about. He also suggested a strategic approach that he'd devised. It was about the only time in his life that Howard listened to him, the only time he followed his instructions, almost to the letter. His mother was about to leave, taking advantage of a lift from a friend arranged earlier.

'Lest I forget,' she said to her husband, 'Is there anything you want from home, Howard?' He waved her away with irritation.

'Leave me alone, don't bother me.' Jim promised to bring her back later that afternoon; she would take a cab home in the evening, as that night he and Matt were attending a lecture about poetry and faith by Rowan Williams at the LSE. Jim would bring her again on Friday, but he was working the following day, his parents' sixtieth wedding anniversary, married on 21st June 1952. When she departed Jim turned to his father, smiling.

'Are you looking forward to tomorrow, dad?'

'Silly question. Why would I? For what bloody reason?'

'It's your wedding anniversary, the sixtieth, your diamond one.'

'I *know.*' Yet, he'd clearly forgotten. He sighed. 'The food here is bound to be bad. It was awful enough in that damned hospital.'

'This stay is intended to give mum a rest, help her recover.'

'She doesn't need any bloody help. We can cope on our own.' Jim was astonished at his father's continued refusal to face reality.

'If we were to find some help for you it'd be easier for mum.'

'No, I'm not having it. I told you, your mum will look after me.'

'She can't cope, dad, the strain's too much. Even that

Macmillan nurse you like agreed. That's why she organized your stay.'

'Did she?' He looked bemused, uncertain, part persuaded.

'Yes.'

'As far as I know, I've come here to get back on my feet. That's what I agreed. I'm here to learn to walk again.' A few years previously, following a heart operation in a central London hospital, Howard had literally done so, after his post-operative delirium, Jim walking his father twice daily up and down the corridor from his bed, eventually to the lift, cycling from the British Library to so do, further every day, on discharge, up and down the back garden in Enfield. Jim cycled the eight miles from the flat, taking the train home at times, on other occasions also cycling back. His father lost his belief for a while back then, but never his ability to flare up. That was summer 2005 when Jim first met Gabriella, as she'd introduced herself, postponing the first date so as to assist Howard in hospital with walking exercises, lessons as Howard thought of them. They worked eventually. Within four months he was back to his old self, Jim almost relieved when Howard became as objectionable as ever. At least he survived. Outside the pub opposite Jim encountered two blonde daughters in their thirties of a man recently admitted to the bed next to Howard's, a patient his father befriended, and who went down to the operating theatre that very afternoon. It was a sunny day and Jim unlocked his bike. He went over. In sunglasses they were drinking lagers, in pints, and smoking. One was attractive, hence Jim's initial attempt to pass the time of day with the pair.

'How is he, your father, how's he getting on?' he asked.

'He didn't make it,' the, prettier, slimmer daughter said.

'I'm very sorry to hear that.' Jim felt he'd intruded, ashamed of having flirted, uncertain of what to say to her.

'Don't tell your father,' the chubbier woman said. 'It might depress him. He'll need everything to seem absolutely positive for his recovery. Believe me, I'm a nurse.' At this Jim couldn't resist looking at her cigarette. He was a reformed smoker and at every opportunity seized he proselytized the virtues of quitting. She added, 'I know, but there it is. We all have to go eventually. I just wish my dad could have survived longer, God rest his soul.'

On his return to the ward Jim didn't bring up the women's deceased father, he'd not willingly mention him ever again, and did so only once. On his return the next lunchtime his father asked about this chap and Jim suggested he might have been sent to another ward after recovery, or even to his local hospital. They took a walk and he finally reached the lifts, maybe fifty feet. Howard was pleased with himself, confident again about going home. He was exhausted after his return to bed, but doubly jubilant. Thankfully for Jim's conscience, Howard lost interest in the guy who disappeared from the ward after one day, the bed being reoccupied the same night, someone else to speak to.

'Your stay is designed to give you both a break, a proper rest.' Jim tried to reassure Howard in 2014 about the care home, eager that his father should relax, accepting the new situation. Although his parents had few alternatives, Jim was surprised Howard agreed to the plan. Somehow the Macmillan nurse persuaded him to the move with minimum resistance, probably because of the walking lessons Howard anticipated, a residue of Jim's therapy.

'No lessons in walking?' Jim realized this curious experience would not be repeated. His father was effectively bed-ridden. Was Howard losing it mentally, or had the nurse misled him so he'd agreed to this home, to get him there, easier for her, Jim wondered. He disliked this busy-body, her intrusiveness, but the strategy worked. He was surprised Howard believed her.

'No, like I said, they wanted to give you both a rest; to see whether you liked it here. It's a trial. To see if you can fit in.'

'I can tell you I won't like it. I don't want to stay. It's full of old people; I don't like them.' Howard's mother was the same, never regarding herself as old, even in her nineties, referring to the others where she attended a lunch club as 'fogeys,' a word popular in Jim's youth, an unpleasant term, exceedingly prejudicial.

'I know you don't.' This was entirely part of the problem, Jim knew. Once again, he explained that his mother couldn't cope, the Macmillan nurse agreed, and Howard was likely to be here a while, to recuperate, because there was a bed available. None of it seemed to sink in. I'm going out tonight with Matt, Matt Evans, from school, don't you remember him?'

'Who?'

'Matt, lived in Enfield Town. We're going to see Rowan Williams.'

'I've heard that last silly name. I must know him. Wasn't he one of those bloody useless grammar school kids?'

'No, he's not one of my friends, Dad. Rowan Williams was the Archbishop of Canterbury until he retired, he's Welsh, a poet.'

'A church type, a poet, what on earth do you want to have anything to do with him for?' His father went quiet momentarily. 'You off to work?' He asked without preamble. Jim wondered why.

'No, not till tomorrow. That's why I'm not bringing mum here.'

'So, you're going out, with some woman?' his father asked, seeming to forget his relationship with Gabi, returning to Jim's earlier comment, distracted by his condition, his unfamiliar surroundings.

'No, with Matt Evans. I told you, I was at school with him, his parents live near your sister, Joan, in Enfield Town, same road.'

'Don't bloody mention her,' he growled. 'Jim, give me your promise. When I go, don't invite any of them to the funeral. Just promise me that.' Howard had long had a troubled relationship with his sister, a falling out over money years before, but their mother had prevailed and contact continued until her death in August 2002, aged ninety-five. After the funeral there was a violent family confrontation, one of those internecine wars fought by some of the Dents, whose skirmishes served as some of the coordinates of Jim's childhood. Jim was at home in Tufnell Park, just back from university in Birmingham where he worked, nine at night when one of his cousins called. Nothing Jim said calmed the situation caused by his grandmother's will and years of acrimony. He gave up, battle lines already drawn. Neither side could ever again communicate, the children as foot soldiers, the retired parents the generals. After the battle, a prolonged Cold War, but in this domestic version each side simply ignored the other.

'I've promised already. I promise again, on my mother's life.' His father pulled off the oxygen mask to emphasize his next requests.

'No death notices either, absolutely nothing in the local papers. I don't want them to know. I don't want them gloating, including bloody Joan.' By 'them' he meant his sister and her family, most especially her husband, Mark, whom Howard despised. Already he'd made Jim and his mother prepare a document for him to sign, stating his wishes in that regard, binding them as witnesses to honour those demands that none of the Tremletts were to be notified of the death or funeral, that they be ejected if they were to arrive, and that the event should be stopped if they were to refuse to exit. Jim doubted the legal status of this declaration, concluding it was worthless, but it had mollified Howard. The whole matter was an obsession of his father's, the fourth time in as many days that he brought up the issue. 'Arrange a quick funeral, it will be over before they've heard,' his father added. The mask was replaced. This was an entirely new train of his thought, a stratagem for his final skirmish in the Dent version of the Thirty Years War, to be played out by this particular general, even after his supposedly early death, by proxy.

'Of course, but that's some time off, dad.' Jim was confident his father would survive months yet. He looked robust enough.

'Just promise me.' He grimaced beneath the oxygen mask.

'Of course I do. What's wrong? Are you in any pain?'

'No, not really, just this breathing. Everything's an uphill struggle.'

'I'm sorry.' His father was silent, putting on his radio headphones again, oblivious of Jim. 'Look, I'll be off now,' Jim said.

'OK.' Howard was unenthusiastic. 'When's your mother coming?'

'Tonight. She'll be back later. Tonight, like she told you earlier.'

'She should be here now, with me. Are you fetching her?'

'No, I'm off out, I told you, with Matt. Mum's here later. I'll see you Friday, all being well and definitely on Saturday.'

'Don't bother coming. I just want to see your mother, not you.'

'I'm bringing mum over here on Friday, it's all arranged, Dad.'

'Well, I'd rather not see you. Just drop her off.' Jim sensed both his usual venom mixed with distraction but he was upset. His father continued. 'I'd rather you didn't visit. I don't like your visits, never have.' Howard always possessed the capacity to be spiteful, indiscreet, and plain ignorant at times. Clearly Howard was goading him, trying to inflict pain to offset his own suffering.

212

'You know, after all these years, this is all like water off a duck's back for me. The simple matter is that I'm coming over, dad, because I'm bringing mum here, so I might as well see you. I'm not driving here and going off somewhere else to wait for you to finish. You have no real say in the matter, to be honest,' said Jim trying to be firm rather than respond with anger as Howard clearly intended. Jim decided he wouldn't rise to the bait.

'Suit yourself, I'd rather you didn't come. I don't want your company.' Jim went toward the open door. 'This respite care is to help your mum, not me? Not for me to get back on my feet?' his father asked in an annoyed tone, glaring at him.

'No, not just her, it's for both of you. So, I'm off. Bye.' He waved, but his father ignored him. Howard was preoccupied with whatever sound was travelling through the headphones and with his thoughts. He looked as if he was puzzled by something or other, mulling over some conundrum, struggling with its parameters. Jim cycled home, worked on his computer and showered, part of his preparations to meet his ecclesiastical friend at the LSE for the lecture, a quick drink first if Matt managed to arrive on time. In his youth he was often late, just like several mutual friends. They were all as bad as each other. At times Jim joked, unoriginally, that they'd be late for their own funerals. He was almost always punctual, which he felt others took as him being needy, a weakness.

After the night out, in the middle of the night the phone rang, Jim's mother. 'They just rang me.' Jim looked at his radio alarm. Four-twenty. He was slightly hungover, Matt and he drinking wine after the lecture, discussing their lives, anticipating retirement. 'They said he'd gone, James,' she added tearfully.

'Who rang? Who's gone?' Jim had no idea what she meant.

'Some foreign woman, ringing from the care home, said your father had gone. Jim, I think that he must be dead.'

'Are you sure?' Jim was aghast, this would be so sudden. They'd just settled his father in the day before, fifteen hours had lapsed.

'That's what she said. He's gone. She kept repeating herself.'

'Give me time to shower. I'll come over on the bike. I can't drive, not yet.' Later during the blur of that day, he reflected on his father's death. Jim stood in the office of the care home manager, about to see the body, which he'd agreed to. His mother refused even to go to the care home, traumatised by the loss of the wedding anniversary celebration, the final legacy of the Macmillan nurse, who Jim suspected cared little. When he'd spoken to his mother earlier, she revealed she visited Howard twice the previous evening, four cab rides. On the first Howard was angry, accusing her of abandoning him, indifferent at her departure, on the second occasion he was increasingly desperate, demanding angrily to be taken home.

'I told them not to close his door,' his mother said, 'but they did.' His father could never bear sleeping in a closed room, the door had to be ajar, his radio on. The woman manager admitted the nurse on duty administered morphine, admittedly prescribed, but Howard had never taken any, for just as he'd been suspicious of foods that might kill him, Howard tried to minimize medication, wary of them all. An aspirin was a personal weakness, the pathway to renal failure. Jim knew his father had been querulous and had been quietened, probably forced or cajoled in his confusion to take the stuff. He'd lasted less than twelve hours in their care. Jim visualized the scenario, the staff unable to cope with his father's vehement tantrum, the shouted demands, the viciousness, the vitriol, the insults, the profanities, and next a liquid cosh. Jim sensed that nothing could be done. Howard had died between twelve and two, between the supposedly hourly rounds which had been stretched. Jim wondered why they decided to ring his mother in the middle of the night, almost as if panicking.

Upstairs Jim looked at his father's body laid out on his last resting place, the hospital-style bed. Howard looked calm, at rest, finally silent. In the manageress' office Jim spotted a name on a whiteboard, J. TREMLETT, written in careful capitals in black.

'What's that board for?' he asked her, pointing.

'It details the residents, their rooms, the floors,' she replied. Jim worked out where Joan was related to his father's room of maybe thirteen hours, where Howard's corpse still waited in the bed until its collection later that afternoon. 'Oh,' he said, taken aback by the synchronicity of the moment revealed by this revelation. He realized that his aunt was virtually in the room above his father's, resting a few feet above her brother as he died. It was as if from beyond the grave their mother, Jim's grandmother, had been exerting her indomitable spirit, trying to bring the two together for a final time, a force for a reconciliation that would never now occur. He stayed silent, highly conscious of promises made to his father. Jim would not enquire after his aunt, not in the circumstances. He supposed he owed Howard at least that much loyalty however mad his father's last request.

At his mother's home Jim felt uneasy, uncertain what was next, daunted by all the tasks. 'He looked peaceful,' Jim reassured his mother truthfully and a week later, as instructed, a funeral was arranged in haste, the Tremletts uninvited. His mother was insistent, Jim doubtful. At the service at the crematorium Matt delivered a non-religious service, Jim a speech, as did Will. Hugo gurgled on his mother's knee, oblivious, a blown-up copy of their photo set before the congregation of over a hundred, friends, variously from the cycling club of Howard's youth, his tape club, the cable factory, the hospital radio and, additionally, a swathe of Jim's maternal relatives gathered more in support of Howard's wife than to celebrate his life. The wake was in a modern, local pub in Innova, a new development with hotel, offices, storage facilities, offices, a school, low-cost housing and MOT testing station for commercial vehicles hidden by trees, bushes and shrubs.

The next day, Jim went numbly through the process of registering the death in Enfield Town, began to plan the process of probate which his mother wanted him to organize. He started to feel as if a weight had been lifted, that finally a burden had gone. He felt guilty about this response, but, as genuinely upset as he was, there was nevertheless an uplifting of sorts. He was freer than he'd been in years, perhaps ever. On the Saturday he was relaxed, somewhat sad, but relieved. He worried more about his mother, of making sure she recovered, that she was nurtured, and they might create conditions whereby she could begin to regain her strength.

The phone rang abruptly. On the line the wife of a colleague, a youngish novelist for whom Jim smoothed the way into his lectureship at his university. The two had met at an arts festival in the Hungarian part of Serbia, in Novi Sad, where during NATO's three month bombing a number of bridges were destroyed, one raid injuring seven civilians. On their visit many ruins were visible, some as they drove over one bridge, a temporary replacement. The call was unexpected, he hardly knew the woman. She spoke of Knapper, with whose estranged former partner the novelist's wife shared a childminder. Even though talking on the phone, she asked him to sit down, which he found a curious request. According to her account, a few days before, maybe on the day of his father's funeral, Knapper hanged himself, an awful shock. He thought of Knapper's ex-partner, now married. Their son was now in secondary school, in his early teens. Knapper's death and his son's plight made him think of a younger school-friend, Conrad whose father died of cancer in his early fifties, when Conrad was around sixteen, an immense shock to his system. The novelist's wife continued her tale. 'Neighbours were worried and so contacted the police. They broke into the flat. Grim I'm afraid: they found his body hanging from a door frame.'

'No. I can't believe it.' For a moment Jim was speechless, unable to respond coherently to such an awful tragedy. Intensely paranoid Knapper destroyed his address books, diaries, erased all numbers on his mobile. Jim and another friend, David, had to contact people, made speeches. After his earlier optimism for Jim it was an appalling period, the conjunction of two deaths, a sense of desolation at his friend's untimely passing. His guilt at having been so busy with his father, so much so Jim felt he hadn't tried hard enough to reach his friend, whose depression was evident, but its depth unsuspected. He'd thought Knapper was agitated, depressed about his lecturing, just not his usual self. Why had it come to this?

Afterlives

Chapter Ten: Home Truths, May 2014

Sunday 25th May 2014 at 7 a.m. found Jim once again sitting in his office overlooking the garden, blinds up, an overcast, dry day. Naturally he'd much on his mind, with a double two-year-anniversary looming. Gabi had reminded him recently, a Hungarian trait since they honoured the dead, visiting graveyards as entire families. His father's death was followed by poor old Steve Knapper's suicide, a blow so closely after his father's funeral. These interwoven events still seemed utterly unreal to Jim, particularly Knapper's demise. The subsequent year was still rather indistinct, only fragmentary memories recoverable. Jim wanted to speak to Matt, but as he dialled, he remembered Matt was sailing in the Hebrides, probably well out of mobile range. His friend's voicemail kicked in. Any message would be far too limited to explain his emotions, so he stayed silent, ending the call. Up popped a thought of David over in Kurdistan, another good friend of Knapper's, but when Jim had Skyped David recently, like Jim, he avoided talking of their mutual friend. The matter was far too raw presumably. Maybe David shared Jim's sense of culpability, which would not diminish even though they both knew there'd been little they could have done. He could picture Knapper at their last meeting vividly, every freckle, every line in his face, the touch of grey in ginger hair and most of all the slightly trembling fingers that wouldn't be stilled. Both wore shorts, sitting by a riverside café half a mile north of Tottenham Hale on the River Lea, their cycles propped against a bench. Knapper had buried his hands in his pockets. The sun was hot, the sky cloudless, seeming to loom low over the river. A hundred yards away kids could be heard jumping off one of the locks, bombing the water, shrieking. The pair's shared table was rickety, the chairs rusty, the slats unpainted. They drank two coffees, one long and decaffeinated, the other dark and bitter in its tiny cup. The weather was cheerful, but Knapper remained agitated, brooding. Jim invited him home for a meal, but unusually his friend declined. Instead, he announced he'd given up drinking alcohol, somehow implying that his over-indulgence had been Jim's fault. Knapper added that he'd been unwell, and referred to a counsellor. He was vague about symptoms, but they were clearly mental as well as physical. Work was worrying him, especially his teaching. He was being watched, he said. Jim asked how and why. Apparently, management monitored his lessons weekly, demanding plans in advance for each class, but as to why he refused to discuss the matter. After a short silence, Knapper tried to explain his idea for his next lesson plan, for an upcoming class that week. Jim could scarcely follow the reasoning, or the examples, troubled as Jim was by his father's decline in health. 'I'm not sure,' Jim responded to a query concerning the viability of enacting dramatically some aspect of Marx as a role play. Alienation was referred to. The concept's vagueness perturbed Jim, faced with Knapper's fervent conviction about the idea, as did the oblique references to *Das Kapital* and *The Communist Manifesto*. Neither made much sense in the current context. He couldn't fathom how Knapper imagined he might shape his forthcoming drama class, and as a role play?

'That's what they need,' Knapper explained of his students, 'with alienation they'll grasp where I am . . . why they're after me.' It was nonsense. Jim wondered what he meant.

'So, who is after you? Management? What's going on? Are they hounding you?' Knapper just ignored his friend's queries.

'Or maybe surplus value might be a better concept?' Knapper added, lapsing into what appeared to be a befuddled silence.

'What do you mean?' asked Jim, but his friend looked away.

'Surplus value, I have a passage that's perfect. He passed Jim a paper drawn from his bag. 'Here, you can keep that' he said. Jim started reading. 'The rate of surplus-value and the length of the working day depended on the magnitude of this prolongation. Though the necessary labour-time was constant, we saw, on the other hand, that the total working day was variable.' Jim was confused; how weird this would seem to the drama students.

'Look,' said Knapper pointing several sentences highlighted in yellow which he asked Jim to read aloud carefully, slowly.

'Let the whole line a c, a—b—c represent, for example, a working day of 12 hours; the portion of a b 10 hours of necessary labour, and the portion b c 2 hours of surplus-labour. How now can the production of surplus-value be increased, i.e., how can the surplus-labour be prolonged, without, or independently of, any prolongation of a c?' Jim sighed at his memory of the utter incomprehensibility of Knapper's part in the exchange, their last apart from final pleasantries, Jim letting it go, not pursuing the threads. As Knapper snatched back the paper, with obvious disappointment, they'd parted for the last time, with an urgency on Knapper's part that seemed inexplicable. If it were to be written up, thought Jim, how could anyone encompass or even approach such an overwhelming madness? The thought made Jim shudder, as did the memory of that awful phone call, telling him of the suicide.

After those two deaths in as many weeks, in truth Jim just about managed to cope at work, clinging on as best he could, lesson by lesson, essays marked one at a time. He realized at this juncture maybe his professional sea-change had begun, that feeling of being adrift, with the threat of being swamped, often fearful, always tired. Jim hadn't published much in that first year of bereavement, just a few articles already in the pipeline and virtually nothing since. Unusually he'd attended very few conferences. In truth, he'd slowed somewhat. He paused at that thought. He realised he wasn't sure he felt he could recover any of his previous capacity in terms of engagement with writing or research. If he were to be honest he'd lost direction. His motivation had declined. This new reality troubled him, but he decided, scholarship could be displaced by writing fiction, and yet . . . . Maybe he could talk to David on Skype, about work and the issue of being pestered by emails from the girl . . . . And there was his draft novel, or more accurately his ongoing attempt to think about one.

Although it had been enticing and exciting at first, the act of getting together the ideas for his novel, *Gin & Tonic*, also seemed arduous in the early light after dawn broke through that Sunday. Even the rewriting of the first notes set down rapidly in several short bursts of energy was proving so very difficult to sustain. And he faced a heap of other far more boring work-related tasks that he'd have to complete first, he thought, looking down with a frown at the list he'd made while trying to clear some time for his fiction. Having noted all his professional commitments, and when scrutinised together they looked daunting just in themselves. And he was too young to retire, not enough in the pension pot. As to the novel, he'd written only a few short sections of several episodes, it wasn't flowing, not even in his head. When he'd charted the plan offered to Alfred it seemed easy but wasn't so on the page. Not a single scene was anywhere near complete even in his head. He thought of the task, realizing there was so much more to add. Looking over the grass at the grey sky beyond, he was thoroughly dispirited. Where was his previous enthusiasm, found earlier in life when he'd finished three whole drafts of novels, although admittedly they remained unrevised, unpublished? And given lately he'd also stalled in terms of planning any new academic publications. Maybe he'd lost the knack of writing? He pulled himself together. Today though, letting Gabi have a lie-in, he'd come down early to put things back on course, intent on reviving his enthusiasm. He'd just think of new ways through the difficulties that he'd sensed, but as yet hadn't fully defined. Just why over the past few weeks was he so sluggish?

He might seek the advice of Graham Joyce, a friend from their postgraduate days together at Leicester University, when they'd edited an arts section of the student newspaper, *Ripple*. Still living in the city, near where Jim had once lived when married, Graham was now an established and successful novelist. He lived the life which Jim had once dreamed of, writing for a living, fantasy fiction with a touch of horror, having sold his first book in the early nineties. He was a good writer, committed, professional. He'd a beautiful wife and two children. When Jim worked at Wrottesley he'd found Graham his first job teaching Creative

Writing, which he still taught in Nottingham. Graham might be exactly the man to enthuse him. Jim liked Graham, even envied him a little. If anyone could help with *Gin & Tonic*, Graham might well be able to. However, it was far too early to call anyone on a Sunday morning about such matters. And as much as he admired Graham, Jim wondered whether he could really match his friend's dedication and professionalism. Could Jim ever find time or the energy required, after the earlier rejections still weighing on his mind so many years later? Why had he sent out what were essentially first or at best second drafts, inviting failure. Looking back, perhaps he'd been too eager, overly optimistic, naïve.

Gabi slept upstairs in his bed, alone, undisturbed. He daren't ask her advice, seek her support. She complained bitterly if he woke her too early on a Sunday, so he let her rest after her sixty-plus hours the previous week, labouring for her investment bank. Jim had eaten breakfast earlier: three sausages and fresh white bread, and his usual decaffeinated tea by the generous mugful, skimmed milk, no sugar. The day before he'd cut the lawn, if it could be so labelled, infiltrated by so much moss, sprouting so many dandelions. Yet, whatever its failings, the garden seemed verdant, especially the trees and bushes to the left that he'd planted four years previously to divide him from the neighbours. Jim liked his privacy. He'd just rebooted the computer that crashed during a Skype conversation with a younger friend, David, who was working currently over three thousand miles away at a private university in Kurdistan, a low-tax state, the post's prime attraction, that together with a certain excitement, the buzz of a war-zone. According to David, the institution where he taught was chaotic, its president obsessed with students cheating during the examinations, paranoid, but disorganised too, no timetable, questions written at the last moment, different tutors in the same subject setting completely different exams at a whim, no coordination.

Waiting for the reboot to end, an incredibly slow (and annoying) process on his machine at times, Jim felt angry about the crash since he lost a whole thirty minutes of writing. The malfunction meant irretrievable time and effort, yet another hindrance, one more impediment to finishing the novel, about which he was so confident when he spoke to Alfred on that sunny day in April. When he was younger Jim always finished his writing projects, or, at least he completed a first rough draft: the short stories, novellas, and novels. Once everything had a conclusion; life seemed simpler, less freighted with worries, uncertainties.

Recently Gabi took to reading his early efforts on her train journeys to and from work, and she liked them. 'I might be biased, but I think you should have persevered, carried on. I love your writing. It just needed more effort, a little more polishing,' she'd said, part of the reason he'd been continuing with his ideas for *Gin & Tonic*, still the working title for his interlinked stories of premature death, despite Alfred's objections. Titles were never his strong point, *Swallows in the Sky* coming to mind.

'I didn't ever publish anything, not properly,' he responded to Gabi's enthusiasm. 'They're drafts, bound as manuscripts. The truth is I wasn't a real writer, just a novelist manqué.'

'Yes, you are a novelist, this proves it,' she insisted, flourishing the soft-bound typescript she'd just read. 'Under communism people passed around books bound just like this one. They were popular, influential. No one cared that the state wouldn't publish them. To not be accepted ideologically that was a badge of honour. You need more courage, more determination,' she'd added. He knew she was right, but he felt aimless. Gabi even liked what he'd shown her of *Gin & Tonic*, the notes, two or three short passages, except she too hated the *utterly silly and stupid* title. That was no real problem, Jim reassured her. And she added, 'There's not much to go by yet.' She demanded he write more for her. 'Try to finish this one, get it all down!' Only that wasn't anywhere near happening. He'd still only jotted down plans for three chapters, admittedly sketchy, but the rest remained just ghostly fragments in his mind. He'd a list of nine draft chapter titles, with two hundred words in drafts, maybe three, and a hundred more notes. He set those down, looking at a few lists of potential ideas, some typed but mainly written. Plus, he gathered a few clippings, with downloaded photos and online sources he'd printed, including a street-map of areas of Leicester. Together, this amounted to the makings, if expanded, of almost another chapter, so three were in the bag in total if he could find the time, energy and focus to write them up. However, even if he did finish this, he was still stuck. Everything else was totally unfinished. At best this remainder could be said to be radically under-developed, but the reality was that it wasn't even started. He sighed. He'd never encountered anything like writer's block in his life before. Now he was deep into such an impasse, suffering the syndrome of the blank page. He was dissatisfied with whatever he tried mentally. He thought of Jack Nicholson as the would-be writer in *The Shining*, a film Jim found deeply disturbing on four counts: the horror, the spiritual link with the dead, the power of prescience, and naturally, above all, the writer's absolute failure to write.

Given his impasse, he was distracted further from his task, as yesterday there was a Skype message (after all the emails) from Eileen Beckett, the daughter, as she explained in more detail, of a woman who'd died, aged fifty-nine, telling him again of Lauren Beckett, whom he did remember, resident of Newcastle, which reminded him of all that happened on the Bunting trip, all that youthful commitment, which resulted in one short profile and interview. That trip was the one chapter for which he made the most notes earlier, but this morning's efforts were apparently lost in the system crash. The daughter asked him again if he'd known her mother himself at the very beginning of the eighties, during his visit to the city. The very specific request from this stranger caused Jim to worry, even panic, as he did whenever events span out of control. Never as badly as Howard, but clearly it was a trait he inherited. Jim was discussing the approach from the daughter earlier with David in Kurdistan, just before the computer crash, which was why he hadn't backed up his files, fiddling rather with the Skype connection. Jim wore his headset with tiny mike attached to headphones, telephonist-style, redolent of his youth. He outlined the basic scenario, the woman's first email approach, repeated, followed by Facebook, messages about her mother's death and asking if Jim had known her in early 1980, a very specific period. Jim couldn't discuss the matter with Gabi yet, but felt he needed advice, hence his online discussion with David.

'Well, first things first, did you know this woman the daughter has mentioned, and what was her name?' David asked.

'Lauren. If I think back I did know her. Lauren Beckett, from a London Irish family, pretty in a very seventies way. We were involved briefly. So yes, I had a fling with this woman, this Lauren, on one single occasion.' He thought again. 'Well possibly on two. So, there were maybe two one-night stands separated by about fifteen months, or maybe it was just one, possibly.'

'So, why only say *possibly, maybe*? Why so equivocal?'

'The first was a definite, since I know we shagged, but when I saw her after that when she was with someone else. And on that second occasion I was pissed, I'm really not sure anything at all happened. I couldn't even make up my mind at the time. All I know was I woke up, her in my bed the next morning, after drinking.'

'So, didn't you try to find out whether you'd . . . you know . . . had . . . been . . . done . . . something?' David requested in an exaggeratedly hesitant tone, laughing, so as to tease Jim.

'Had intercourse, had shagged her, you mean? Sure, I asked her, but she was being totally elusive at the time, very enigmatic, you might say almost playful. She was more concerned that her bloke, the one she lived with, might catch us together.'

'Oh, he was there?' David reacted with surprise. 'The partner on the premises at the time, *in situ*?' He was enjoying his interrogation.

'Yes, in the same house, but totally stoned. The boyfriend got wasted with a friend of mine, a guy that's now dead, Chris Challis. He died in 1997, big pal of Sue Townsend's back in the day.'

'You knew her, didn't you?' David commented, having been a big boyhood fan of Adrian Mole, an enthusiasm Jim didn't share, despite having been friends with the author years before.

'Yeah, I did, quite well in fact, but do you think it's at all relevant?'

'No, but I really liked Adrian Mole as a kid,' David added.

'I know, you told me ages ago.' Jim had actually forgotten.

'I presume you know that she died very recently?'

'Sure, I've been trying to write about her,' Jim admitted.

'Article?'

'No fiction.' Uncomfortable about this further admission, Jim shifted the subject abruptly. 'Dave, what do I do about this woman from Newcastle, the potential daughter? Do tell me,' Jim pleaded.

'Oh, look here, folks, just see before you the sins of the sixties and seventies generation coming home to roost in the new millennium, now they're approaching and some have even gone past their sixtieth and seventieth birthdays, still vigorous, youthful, every one of them,' David said in a mocking voice, as if a fairground barker, then, laughing more, he savoured the ironies of Jim's predicament. Jim couldn't see him on his screen, enjoying his crisis from 2500 miles away, but he knew he would be. 'This is all typical baby-boomers stuff, Jim, the past catching up with them. No wonder the country is in the state it's in. Me, I blame the idiocies of all you sex-mad, self-obsessed baby-boomers.'

'Look, I'm not arguing with you, am I?' Jim responded.

'When did this all happen, this . . . what would you call it, dalliance. When was this possible or potential conception?' He laughed. 'Rather than being immaculate this is Jim's potential conception.'

'Oh, very funny, I don't think. Just laugh at my expense, won't you? If it happened, it would have been early January 1980. I can't remember the exact date, but I could look it up, an old diary or journal.' Somehow his humour calmed Jim, as did the potential narrowing of possibilities, his idea of seeking concrete evidence.

'So, it was a long time ago, which makes me ask, why are you so worried?' David asked. 'You won't have to pay her university fees or anything like that, no alimony, no child support. You need to look on the bright side. And how likely is it anyway? If there was a partner at the time he'll think he's the father.'

'It's just a shock, the possibility, I found it unsettling.' He stopped, thinking again about the trip with Challis, about Bunting, about Jim's life back then, so different, so improbably distant that he was hardly able to remember what it was like. 'Well, I suppose you might be right. I don't know how old she is currently, but there must be at least an outside possibility at the very least that she could be my daughter, and if she were, she'd be just a little younger than Will, by about three months. Why else would she get in touch? If she is my daughter, she would have been born in . . .' he paused, calculating on his fingers, 'around about October 1980, I think.'

'Look, it's obvious you have a number of options, Jim.'

'Which?'

'Well, first you could ignore her, hoping that she goes away. She doesn't have your address, or phone number, and I think you can block people on Facebook. Second you could talk to her, but my advice is that you do so on Skype. And you could block her if you changed your mind later. Unless she's some kind of computer genius, surely, she can't track you down.'

'She could do so easily via the university website, or via Amazon. My name's uncommon, and I'm a published author.' Jim referred to his academic scholarship, the monographs, edited collections.

'That's true. So, if she's an obsessive, then you're buggered. The computer liberates the maniacs, you know, sets them free. Although, let's face it . . . .' At that moment, the sentence hanging, Jim's computer crashed again, and waiting for it to revive he was now faced with two problems, first the woman from Newcastle, and second, it appeared, he'd no access to his server, so was frozen out of online communication, which felt somehow like being exiled, reduced in some awful fashion, a social exclusion that he could never have imagined even ten or fifteen years previously.

He thought about writing, continuing with his new novel, since Word still functioned, but there was a hurdle: all those scenes he'd avoided to that point which thwarted him somehow, because he'd made no real notes, despite Gabi's encouragement the day before. And there were some required chapters he doubted he could ever face head on. The first was the death of his father, aged eighty-three on 21st June, followed by that of Steve Knapper aged forty-eight less than two weeks later, both in 2012, the anniversaries of which he pondered earlier. Subsequently Jim had attended two funerals in quick succession, giving speeches at both, formal orations, and elegies. The only other real difference was that he organized the whole of the first event for his father: the coffin, flowers, music, catering, everything. Together they'd been just too much for him, and afterwards Jim was ill, nothing drastically serious, but debilitating at the time. Something profound had changed inside of him too, he admitted.

In May 2014 he couldn't bring himself to write anything about any of them, the period of their deaths seemed so dark, his malaise of that time aggravated by chronic toothache. The removal of the offending tooth was painful, as was a complaint from a postgraduate student who argued with him in a pub close to the university after a postgraduate evening. She was full of a sanctimonious illusion about the moral primacy of the individual, the right to take offence and regard it as a public and social issue, exhibiting a rampant individualistic notion not only of identity, but her right to reshape the social fabric in her own image. In Jim's opinion her evident stupidity was thrown into the mix. And to recapture his feelings, her asinine arguments compounded the existing conjunction of occasions he found so utterly awful. He put the night in the pub out of his mind. He couldn't contemplate such radical nonsense, it was too hard. Like all the rest he was trying to write, this seemed doomed to incompletion, existing only as fragments.

In May 2014 later after lunch at Gabi's, a weekly routine shared by Jim's mother, he sat at home again in his office, staring at the computer screen, blinds down again against the glare, trying again to write since it would please his partner. Nothing came. He looked at Challis' book on the Beats that he'd found. 'A work of criticism that shares features of the travel book and the picaresque novel . . . ,' claimed the back cover. Maybe Jim could combine his criticism with fiction, but he couldn't imagine finding a publisher in the contemporary world for such self-indulgence on his part. Jim flipped through Challis' *Quest for Kerouac*. In the countryside on the route from Philadelphia in a roadside diner Holly combines cigarettes and coffee, the book's author reluctantly drinks coffee for breakfast. Thirty miles from Denver he orders more coffee for Holly, making Jim yearn for a cup. However, Gabi would be at home cleaning vigorously, her monthly sprucing-up undertaken like some fervent revolutionary commitment, so completely useless to suggest a jaunt to the retail park for supplies.

He went back to his untidy pile of old notebooks and magazines in the living room, going through them, marking out sections with post-it notes. He was trying to inspire himself, find a way to continue writing drafts for the novel, but still after an hour he admitted he'd stalled. He took a break, making a mug of tea. The previous day, sweating profusely, Gabi's son had retrieved all of these items including Challis' book from the loft under Jim's instructions, shouted from below, relayed in Hungarian by Gabi halfway up the loft ladder. She passed down various boxes, some returned immediately, others treasured by Jim. And on the next morning he looked up Richard Caddel. He'd never met him during his trip to the north-east, nor subsequently, despite him being the conduit to meeting Bunting. Jim was shocked to see Caddel, a poet and university librarian, died in 2003 aged fifty-four suffering from leukaemia. There was a Wikipedia page dedicated to him, telling Jim about the press Caddel founded in Durham, detailing the innumerable pamphlets of poetry he'd published, as well as collected poetry in three major volumes. Additionally, Caddel edited Bunting's *Uncollected Poems*. All his publication served as a concrete and lasting memorial to his creative commitments in life. Overall Caddel was considered a key figure in the British Poetry revival. He mattered. He'd served as Director of the Basil Bunting Poetry Centre at Durham University prior to his death. Jim read Caddel's obituary in the *Guardian*. 'Most of all, he knew how to live life in the present. As he put it, "Each day now/ I leave the house as if I'll never return."' Sad, Jim thought, and what a dreadful fate, to die so young with a wife and daughter left behind.

As the afternoon lengthened, Jim went through those mostly unpublished papers, poems, journals and notebooks of his own, ones he'd selected to help him write *Gin & Tonic*, although this authorial task still seemed so mountainously off-putting. He read another passage from the manuscript of his first novel, *Swallows in the Sky*, using a smudged carbon, the top copy having long ago been unreturned by some forgotten friend or acquaintance. The protagonist having escaped to London was being told by the police that his wife's body had been found in a canal in Leicester, murdered while walking home from a job as a waitress at a nightclub. The younger Jim took his imaginary revenge on his real wife in his various fictional accounts. Here the wife had been called Mrs Carol Winifred Want. Jim wrote that first book in summer 1979, which, together with his current preparation for a new novel, brought him back to the facts of his disastrous marriage. That was at the heart of all that he did *and* wrote at that time at the end of the seventies and maybe during the next two decades. He was stuck in the past. Another key coordinate was Jim's relationship with his father, fractured, confrontational, with memories of year upon year of being bullied from early childhood, of being screamed at, threatened, and dismissed.

In Jim's notebooks in his own scrawl and in print in a few stories he'd published, he recovered the fabric of his past life, in fragmentary form at times, a strange distant territory, both familiar and utterly alien. Jim had blanked out many of the people alluded to, expunged from his consciousness long ago. As he read, other aspects were resuscitated, becoming familiar again after some thirty-four years. 'Free Issue Number 1, *magazine*, Leicester's only arts magazine,' he repeated the red lettering on the cover, thinking how naïve they'd been to have given the whole thing away *gratis*, no real business plan, no strategy for a readership, just a buoyant hope that was to be deflated by financial failure. His mother-in-law had loyally subscribed, he remembered. The cover art of *magazine* stood up well, featuring a male head, a version of Medusa, snakes instead of hair, fearsome looking. Jim opened it up. 'Editor, Rod Macpherson,' he read. Jim looked him up, googled the name. The first one was a banker, in asset management. No, he'd been educated at Aberdeen, so he could be eliminated. And far too young, Jim thought. Roderick J. in a Faculty of Environmental Studies was doubtful, the page refusing to open anyway, Jim fearing another crash. There was another Rod at Ryerson University, a food policy analyst. It was definitely not him. There he was, Jim thought, head of his own communications consultancy, formerly at Greenpeace, at ITV, and BBC Radio, editing *Start the Week*. That absolutely was him, the same guy, thought Jim, the photo confirming Jim's hunch, same face, blonde hair, prominent chin, just older, late-fifties, he must be. His firm was concerned with environmental and green issues, sustainability and the low carbon economy. Jim wondered what he was like, what cards he'd been dealt in the intervening years, whether he was happy. Jim pondered whether Macpherson had ever referred to Adrian Mole, of having been the first editor to discover him, whether he too mourned Mole's creator's passing. And there he was himself, Jim thought, his own name listed as poetry editor. The *magazine*'s film editor, Jane Guys, now appeared to be a writer, publishing three novels late in life, living in France, near Perpignan, a profile on a webpage for the British ex-pat Community of the region, *P-O Life: Life in the Pyrénées Orientales*. He presumed they were self-published, vanity projects. He turned to page ten of *magazine*, headlined 'Teenage Rebellion.' Between the pages was a single sheet of lined paper, with Sue's name printed and her Leicester phone number, both in a large bold hand. He remembered the journal being signed. He made notes about that for the relevant chapter, but he'd forgotten the address and number left in the issue, untouched since he last met Sue in Enfield. Why on earth did he fail to contact her? Sue had written on the page of her first published Mole story, 'To Jim, This is the first Mole. It's great to see you and it. Love to you from Sue T. (52 11/10).' He read an entry in Sue's short piece, for the Monday: 'I think I am turning intellectual. I have grown fond of rain and the light classics played by Richard Baker on radio four,' Small beginnings, Jim thought, such small steps to greatness. In contrast, he himself was now stymied; suffering writer's block, his last chance tentative, for already the project seemed enfeebled.

He put down *magazine*, issue one, and picked up another thin magazine, *Fix*, Issue Two, undated, similarly coloured cover, red on white with black drawing. It was much cruder, really hideous in fact, and from the ads he calculated it was the journal of its students' union, UWSU, and had been published when Jim had been working at Wrottesley. He wondered why he'd kept it until he discovered the poetry on page thirty toward the back of the issue, where he spotted his own name. Embarrassing, he'd submitted a poem to a student mag, vaguely recalling a pretty young student girl metaphorically twisting his arm. Later they'd indulged in passionate sex together in her rented room above a shop. Jim had written about this episode in a novel entitled *Call Me Horse*, another story of revenge, with a wrongly punished, guiltless murder. He read the earlier poem, appalled. Entitled 'a schoolteacher's morning journey (2)' it was utterly uninspired. Why two, he pondered, but nothing came to mind, unless he'd published another version elsewhere, which was a most troubling thought. His verse had no punctuation, no capital letters and was centred on the page for some reason, although that was the case of most of the other featured poems, so maybe Jim didn't need to censure himself for the layout, a choice probably made by the young woman poet. She must have included a poem herself. That was logical, for why else would she have gone to all the effort? Helen, Lisa, and Katie were the feminine contributors. It was the last, his paramour, and her untitled poem was perhaps worse than Jim's. At least she had the excuse of youth, of being at twenty seduced by clichés, both verbal and actual, one of which had been her fling with a lecturer, then acceptable, now *verboten*. Jim was nearing forty when rewriting this poem. He read the opening:

> Armful with books
> I arrest my morning journey
> entranced:

Jim groaned. In 2014 this seemed terrible, truly bad. He'd put his name to this drivel. His younger self next described workmen cutting limbs from a tree with a power saw. He was probably trying to capture the dignity of labour, hardly an excuse for such awfulness. Jim read to the end, increasingly disappointed with his younger self. Maybe Virginia was right and he'd been completely wasting his time, whiling away his youth on a dream that would remain unfulfilled. And it was too late now at over sixty. The verse continued:

> & I sense the weight of rain
> where spectral treetops sway
> & finger a grey-washed sugar-paper scene . . . .

Instantly he remembered the forgotten occasion, in the street where he lived, on his way to school, about to teach, driving when he might have walked. He watched one workman at street level, another up a tree, boots with nail-like protrusions, a hoist affair around both him and the trunk, chopping off the lower branches with a chainsaw. The sound had been deafening, which the poem simply noted with 'now the busy saw chatters.' His poetry was grim, a parody, almost comical, if it hadn't been testimony of his utter lack of poetical talent. What on earth had he been writing about, and what had he been trying to say? Well, at least later it led to sex with several good-looking women, which was probably his major motivation, dusting off some old rubbish, submitted to impress a naïve, denim-jacketed, brunette would-be poetess, aged about twenty. There was a picture of her somewhere in the loft, looking sexy. He kept his past in the loft, apart from a few framed family and graduation photographs. He never displayed pictures of women, apart from his mother. He looked too at a poem of Cedric's he'd found in online, a PDF entitled *Once a Caian*, issue 10, Michaelmas 2009. On a single page there was an article that commenced, 'Caians, partners and friends gathered at college in September 2008 to formally remember Cedric 'Buzz' Biddwell who died in February 2003 and launch informally the publication of his written works.' There was a small photograph of Cedric from 1993, hair curly, brown and full, in a shirt, jacket and tie, exceedingly and improbably smart. At the bottom of the page Jim found a single poem extracted from a volume compiled from his friend's notes and manuscripts, the first Jim would read, over a decade after his death. There were two versions in adjacent boxes, both at an angle, one set out in Cedric's unmistakable calligraphy, the other typed up from that original.

Kensal Green
My ambling corpse
haunts the boneyard – apt icon –
I pace, inward eye dries
the flora, swept by wind to rot,
Gaia absorbs all; wreaths, headstones,
translucent after cloudburst –
light's soundless epiphany – sun,
sky, merges, eternal,
precipitation vanquished;
I regard the remnant: chapel,
catacombs, mud, weeds,
abandoned obelisks, faded chiselling,
tilted gravestones littering

silence, ghostly notes of oblivion.

Well, for Jim, that certainly seemed more like a real poem, his view affirmed after his second reading, the verse overshadowing his own efforts. After all these years he wished Cedric took him far more into his confidence, that they were closer. Jim only ever saw that bedroom-library that annoyed Islington Council so much, on one occasion. He re-read the PDF about Cedric more thoroughly. 'Formal studies took second place in his college life and when undertaking these he adopted his own unique approach to literary criticism. His real focus was on creative writing, especially poetry that won him the College poetry prize in 1978, and this continued to be his raison d'être throughout his life.' Yes, that captured something of Cedric. And now he'd his own posthumous book, a hundred and four pages, with its own ISBN number, and certainly not a vanity project. The article said, 'As a memorial to Buzz a book of his works, assembled from the many papers and paintings collected at the time of his death, has been published by a group of mainly Caian friends.' It was entitled *The Collected Works of C.R. Biddwell.* Jim wasn't jealous, but the fact of this book, all the efforts of Cedric's friends in pulling it together, emphasized the sense of hopelessness and irrelevance that Jim endured.

To distract himself, Jim picked up a dog-eared school notebook kept on the Bunting visit, its cream cover faded. He also found a small yellow and cardboard poster emblazoned with black print demanding 'VOTE, JIM DENT,' a leftover from his long-forgotten student union electioneering days. They had occupations, rent strikes, lots of meetings, drinking afterwards in the bar. On the back was 'TN: Theatre News. The Fortnightly Journal of Leicester University Theatre,' the cover of that journal. Someone helping him, or paid by him had clearly recycled an overproduction of covers, or maybe, like *magazine*, it had collapsed. He searched the web, but found nothing. He tried the university library's catalogue. No matches. Youthful ventures were very much like that, brief, unfinished, disappearing, just like puffs of smoke, ephemeral, which set

Jim off thinking of the unfinished film project and poor old Boris who drowned in Lake Geneva, just as he was reaching adolescence, about to develop as a person more fully, creatively. All was thwarted by the mostly long-forgotten tragedy. Jim realized he might never finish Boris's story, their involvement in the film which long ago disappeared. He would never get these stories out into the public domain, unlike his current rereading, *The Existential Policeman*, which he felt was sad. Thinking of Bunting, he hunted for the relevant journal kept at the time, to read alongside his notes specifically about the visit, made in preparation for the article he co-authored. He found that too. Setting aside the electoral poster, Jim took the three items into his living room, along with the usual non-tea, and read, out of habit scribbling annotations, creating an *aide memoire* on the squared pages of a spiral notebook, pink cover, A5 size.

Later Jim read his cursory notes, checking them against the original documents occasionally. The actual Bunting notebook started with a long, tedious poem about Jim's childhood and adolescence. Actually, his initial literary ambitions had been solely envisaged in terms of verse, and he was faced with the fact that he'd first failed as a poet. Not until university, in the early stages of his Master's degree, had he toyed with the idea of fiction. Earlier he was drawn by the vibrant poetry scene of the era, lots of chicks with fringes, blondes and brunettes in miniskirts, leather or suede jerkins, wearing mascara, just like the ad he read aged about fourteen in *international times*, much like Holly, Challis' *bird*, as the hairy monster termed her. Although back in the day given Jim's taste in women, she was too skinny, overly into dope, always high.

In the notebook one small part of Jim's poetical account of part of his youth stood out. He read it twice, both versions, but found he preferred the revised one, still untitled:

Stornoway stone-walled street
& a drunken driver
flattened our shadows
& butchered our screams
we laughed & cried
our fears, our pain

To Eilean Fladday
grey & green island water
rippled & further on discover
a beached whale, such stench,
its ribs like rafters bleached
residue of rotten flesh
on the rock-strewn shore
& North past Loch a'Squirr
an Arctic sun descends

Clearly later Jim revised his poetic account of these memories
in the year before visiting Bunting, in his mid-twenties, ten
years after the events. By this time, he'd fallen in love with the
ampersand, and yet still in 2014 Jim appreciated this fragment's
immediacy, and it worked, if only on a personal level. For him
it was like seeing his younger self again, inhabiting that earlier
self, the slim, vaguely optimistic boy in love with the idea of
writing, so tentative about life, battered by an awful childhood,
already defeated in many ways by his past. After his reading, he
could remember vividly both occasions memorialized by the two
short verses, with Matt at his side, literally so, two teens, long
hair, scraggy unshaven and drawn faces, stubby roll-ups cradled
from the wind. Such precise sensations were retrieved from the
past, just like all those which he'd scribbled during the pain of his
marriage, the depth of whose anguish and anger he'd recovered
earlier from his journals, both so strong that it had shocked and
surprised him. Jim decided that maybe there had been a residual
talent in him in his late twenties, a very intermittent and uncertain
one, lost among mounds of drivel, line on line of crap where he
churned out by the metre lines evincing his unhappiness, misery.

He dug out another relic, a cardboard covered magazine of sorts entitled *Brown Paper Bag*, the editing supervised by Graham Joyce while at Wrottesley University. As a colleague Jim was persuaded to extend the second verse of the Hebridean encounter, and the whale had been lost, and much added that should have been surplus, his compression lost. Clearly, Jim's tentative literary aptitude was betrayed by him, and since atrophied, lost, as if poisoned in its infancy, despatched during its most vulnerable period. He was beginning to suspect that it might transpire that he was to prove incapable of reviving them.

In the Bunting notes, at the back of the notebook, a jumble of impressions was strewn across a number of pages, next to some more poems folded over, with other reflections of that day stuffed in the book as a bundle, Jim reconstructed a literal, if ragged account of his visit. His reflections on Washington New Town had been scribbled frantically, a large script being the result of rapid transcription. He copied a few elements into his plans for the new fiction:

> Challis asked if *Briggflatts* was about ambition set against an actual life, with an awareness of better things, was about writing.

> Bunting replied ambition was not something that afflicted him much.

> 'It is the very detail of things that matters, but it must be the right and appropriate ones.' Bunting.

> Note: he was drinking Glenfiddich, two very large glasses.

> Note: when we visited, the night before he'd been eating curry.

> Eliot said when asked about Pound (post-war): 'He was as mad as he had ever been.'

> 'Repetition is the biggest sin.' Bunting.

His previous thoughts about the trip hadn't retrieved even half the detail. On one page was a crude, definitely not-to-scale sketch of Bunting's L-shaped living room, labelled, positions noted of a dining table and chairs, sideboard, desk and swivel chair, and one glass-fronted bookcase, mostly his own books. And a random, hopeful thought went through Jim's head, that it hadn't been until Bunting was sixty-five that he managed to write something that just about everyone recognised as worthwhile, his landmark text.

Jim moved to another large hardcover notebook with a maroon cover containing a journal kept during his time in Leicester and beyond, looking for some entries around this period, in 1979 and 1980. On 23rd November 1979 he'd noted 'Yesterday I met Allen Ginsberg!' followed by a long detailed description of events which included a party at Challis' tiny house for the poet. On 27th December he'd written, 'Virginia is pregnant. We've known now for about a fortnight.' Jim saw too that he'd intended to name a son Joel or Jasper, a misguided intention that he'd forgotten. Maybe he might tell Will to amuse him. And there, after perusal, was the part he sought, he'd found it again. He'd 'arranged to go up to Newcastle to interview Basil Bunting on the 2nd or 3rd, but cannot use the tape recorder.' A long description followed, but only a passing mention of Lauren, whom he'd regarded as 'still very pretty,' and whose house the journal noted was 'double-fronted and impressive.' The journal confirmed that in fact Jim drove Challis' car to Bunting's house the day after reencountering Lauren, which he'd forgotten. On arrival the wall to Bunting's front garden was covered with bread for the birds, all frozen solid. When they left the sun had clearly defrosted the food, for it had disappeared. Why had he noted such detail? The journal was full inconsequential matters, but not one clue as to his night with Lauren, his underlying reason for perusing all this old junk.

As the afternoon continued he thought of the task at hand, and as a large cloud darkened the sky that was visible over the box hedge outside, and Jim was moved to admit another larger truth. Writing another novel was well beyond him now, he really couldn't gather the ideas, synthesise them, or find a suitable structure. He just couldn't do it. He lacked the resilience. Jim couldn't bring himself to write another novel that might well be rejected, like the other three in the past. Thinking of all those people he'd known who'd been cut short in their prime, and hence had not succeeded, Challis, Cedric, and all the rest, Jim knew he'd have no such excuse. In truth he was simply a talentless, incredibly lazy failure. He felt so frustrated, stymied by his irresolution. Alfred was probably right. Once-upon-a-time Jim had completed his few hopeful novels and various enthusiastic short stories. Yet they'd disappeared without trace in the real world, existing only up on his bookshelves, stored in temporary bindings like a short row of dissertations not yet ready to be fully assessed, never to be submitted. Their qualities were ignored by various agents and publishers to whom he'd sent them in the 1980s and early 1990s. Sure some of these recipients were initially intrigued, liking his style, the energy and passion, but never the story, and always there came that final lack of interest, the rejection letter, sent in those days by post. That always got to Jim, being rebuffed. Nowadays it'd probably be a bloody email. He couldn't face that eventuality, being brushed-off online. In that moment, with that very thought, he knew with absolute certainty he'd never finish another novel, not even an unpublished one. As a consequence, he'd never ever publish any of his more creative writing, not even the books completed in the past. Unlike Jane Guys, he would never self-publish, a decision which remained a matter of some pride. He savoured the disappointment, another sense of loss, which in fact seemed pretty much like yet another bereavement, followed by a period of mourning.

Earlier he sent his Skype address via Facebook to Eileen Beckett, and so now went back to the office, anticipating her call. That was his other pressing reason for perusing the record of his younger self. He found nothing about that night, his account perhaps censored because of Virginia. Still, there was evidence that his very few draft notes for his novel drawn straight from memory had skewed or even altered the facts. Challis and he'd driven back from the north-east in just three hours, stopping for pints in

Melton Mowbray, followed by even more in the Victoria Jubilee in Leicester, near Challis' gaff. Jim had driven the restored Avenger back home, having retrieved the keys of the repaired vehicle from Holly, with whom the mechanic had entrusted them. Virginia had been at her parents on his return. He'd rung her about a gas fire that should have been fitted, but failed to arrive. Such a fascinating life, Jim thought ironically, no wonder he encountered such difficulty writing in those early years, since he'd been concentrating on all the wrong things, or so it seemed in the journals. There was a great deal about Challis, and his influence on Jim was clear in what his younger self had noted.

Jim revived the computer, launching Skype. At five p.m. as he'd suggested, a call was coming in, from Eileen. Jim felt nervous, and wondered whether perhaps he shouldn't answer, but he did, his curiosity impelling him. 'Hello,' he said. 'Is that Eileen?'

Her webcam was active. She was a confident, pretty-looking dark-haired girl, woman, he corrected himself, brown eyes, all of which possibly derived from his contribution to her genetic markers, common aspects of the code potentially running through both sets of veins. She was in her early thirties, so her chronological age and the insemination period might accord with his brief fling with a twenty-six–year-old Lauren, younger than her daughter currently was. They'd been such innocents, yet felt themselves so knowing, mature, about to change the world in ways dictated by unintended consequences. They were the cursed legacies that they'd left for the future, Jim thought, the fucked-up radicalism of the sixties and the seventies, the identity politics, morphing into political correctness, which he came to hate so much.

'It is,' she said. The accent might even be regarded as posh, refined, but decidedly of the north-eastern part of the country.

'How are you? Sorry, my camera is off, it crashes the machine.' Entirely true, but convenient in the circumstances Jim decided.

'Nervous.'

'Yes, me too,' he replied. 'Could you tell me exactly what you know and want from me. I think I have an idea, but tell me yourself.'

'Well, my mam died eighteen months ago, of breast cancer.'

'I'm very sorry,' Jim said. 'I'm really sad to hear of her death,' and in fact he found that he actually was. He was moved by yet another premature death, of someone he'd known intimately even if it was a fleeting relationship, and he calculated she would have only have been fifty-eight at her death, far too young.

'Thank you. Well, as she was dying, she made some tapes, on a digital recorder, for me, about her life. She put them on some CD-ROM disks. She hadn't quite grasped the possibilities of USB and pen drives. Well, she also left a letter with them, in the bottom of a box, hidden by the disks. She'd already made it clear when she was really ill, toward the end, that Brownie was not my biological father, and that he knew that too. He left when I was nine, but I remembered him. He'd a third family, with a much younger woman, three more kids. But she wouldn't tell me who my real father was, said I didn't need to know, which upset me.'

'Blimey,' said Jim, 'That's seven kids in total from three marriages.'

'Well actually he never married me mam; so only seven if you thought you should include me, as his *step-daughter*.'

'Sure, I see.' Six was enough, compared to his single son.

'Well, to cut a long story short, I'm a writer.' Jim groaned inwardly. Even the next generation could do better than him. In his thoughts he lamented his failure to publish much, nothing much creative, just a few verses in crappy poetry magazines of no merit. 'I write travel guides, books, journalism about travel, and some other factual topics, women's lives, issues, all of that.' In a rush he recalled Lauren's ardent feminism, which was why she'd so disapproved of him, having called him an unreconstructed sexist pig at union meetings at the school where they'd worked. Again, his memory seemed selective, as without this new prompt he'd never have recollected such confrontations. Lauren might have been attractive, but often she'd worn the kind of denim dungarees that had been back in the day a sign of a quite extreme form of feminism, or so he believed. And she'd been an active member of some obscure revolutionary Marxist group, more followers of Mao than Marx himself. He refocused on Eileen. 'I found some time between commissions, and I decided to write a memoir about my mother, her life, our relationship.'

'Did she have any more children, Lauren, your mother?'

'Yes, I have both a younger half-brother and half-sister.'

'So, that's great, I suppose, having the pair, brother *and* sister.'

'Well, it is, but I think first I should tell you why I contacted you. Lauren's letter revealed you might be my father, possibly.'

'Might be, possibly?' Jim repeated her words. He disliked the past catching up with him, like when something shameful or stupid you did was discovered during childhood, something almost forgotten, only to be brought up much later when you thought you were safe, well beyond punishment, home free.

'Well, it's delicate. This wasn't something she was very proud of, to be honest, and she only wrote about in her final letter. She didn't record this in her account. You can tell by her writing that it was composed very near the end, when she was struggling to control the pen, because of the intense pain.'

'Terrible.'

'It was, and to see her go through all of that. It was awful.' She paused. 'I'm over it all, bereavement, coming to terms with everything.'

'That's good,' Jim said. 'My father died two years ago, and soon after my very close friend, I was only thinking of them earlier.'

'So it was a bad time for you, then, two years back?' she added, delaying her need to address the matter of delicacy she'd initiated.

'Yes, it was,' Jim said, thinking of Knapper for a passing moment.

'Well, to be blunt, direct, my mother, Lauren, admitted to sleeping with two men on the same night, neither of which was Brownie. That would be with you and with another man called . . ..'

'Challis, you mentioned him in one of your emails,' Jim said, having realised the potential scenario. Of course, Lauren must have slept with Challis earlier that night, and he should have guessed sooner that it would've been a possibility, for Challis had mentioned that they were to stay with one of his *former babes*. And Brownie must have crashed, passing out before Challis did the dirty deed, the filthy old dog. Then Lauren turned up in Jim's bed. God, looking back at the seventies and early eighties, what had they all been thinking about, Jim asked himself with a touch of retrospective incredulity. David was right in his critique of the period.

'Yes, that's the name. Chris Challis, a poet from Leicester.'

'Well, I suppose you could call him a poet of sorts,' Jim commented, thinking of Cedric's judgment of Challis' output, 'His readership was very local to the East Midlands, not much further.'

'Well, I googled him, and there was very little about him online. But I knew the Challis I sought wasn't the cinematographer of the same name, the famous one, he would have been far too old for my mother's taste. And he wouldn't have fitted the physical description given by my mother. The two of them had a really odd relationship, especially with her being an active feminist and Maoist. Challis persuaded her to pose for naked photos in her first year, plied her with the usual drink and drugs. Next she succumbed to her photographer's advances, on the second shoot apparently.' Jim rolled his eyes at the thought, the situation a cliché. 'She didn't totally approve of him, but slept with him at that time, not for long, about which she was embarrassed, although even so definitely she still liked him. When she writes about her life, she describes him as her *patriarchal dinosaur*. Afterwards he sold those photos to a magazine. However, I can't find any copies, although I did try. You'd be amazed what's sold online. However, the evidence has gone, totally disappeared like so much pre-computer ephemera, and of course there was no digital, online record, whereas now everything might well last for almost forever if it's digitized. I wanted to see how she looked through his eyes, but it's as if all the detail has gone as if it never existed.'

'I knew he did that, in a general sense, the photos. It was one of many ways by which he made a living of sorts. I didn't know your mother . . . .' he trailed off, paused. 'To be fair to him, Challis was a free spirit. He wasn't keen on actual hard work, having a job, and being controlled by a boss.' He wondered whether that wasn't true of many of them in the sixties and seventies. Naturally in this context, he thought too of Cedric, Sue Townsend, Graham, and Jim himself, at least according to Will. Ironically Jim was the one still stuck with having a boss, a particularly awful one like Carlin. Jim subsisted in a university sector that had developed grim managerial structures, huge pay disparities, ever steeper hierarchies, and from the top increasing contempt for those at the chalk-face or undertaking research, those trying to be original in their own modest way, doing the job properly.

'He wasn't the only one wanting that. All you baby-boomers seemed to want the same thing.' She echoed sentiments Jim heard Will express over the years. 'Well anyway, the Challis trail looked like going cold. But, recently I found a page on the Leicester University website, so I knew I'd got the right person. Only he died in 1997, which was a blow, as I thought he might be alive still. He would only be 68 had he lived. So, I visited the library, and by chance I found your piece in some student literary mag or other about the two of you visiting Bunting, but naturally no mention of my mam. You were easy to track down, on the web. Challis was definitely with you at my mam's place, was he?'

'Oh, yes, he was. I was there with him. We drove there together . . . and we did visit her house. I'd worked with her and Brownie in a school in Leicester. We stayed with them in Newcastle.' He waited a moment. 'So, when were you born?'

'September 30th 1980.' From a rough calculation of nine months, Jim thought that a child from their visit would have been born later, maybe in mid-October or later, so he felt relieved.

'Are you absolutely sure you're not Brownie's child?'

'Yes, I am. That much I know. Through family friends I tracked down Brownie's middle child, born to his final partner, a boy aged twenty studying law at UCL. I paid him to have a DNA test, cost several hundred pounds to make it worth his while. Hence I know Brownie is not my biological father, definitively. I could always email you the results if you want.'

'So now you want me to have a test, I suppose?'

'Well, yes, because I can't track down any of Challis' remaining relatives; it's as if he hadn't ever existed, just like he'd been erased from history, well apart, of course, from his library archive and the book on the Beats published by Faber and Faber about seeking the people and places Kerouac knew, which I read.' She paused. 'He dedicated it in part to his mother. I missed tracking her down by about fifteen months. 'Dreada' or Winifred Etheldreada Challis died aged 94 on 9th February 2013, the funeral service at St Edmund and St Mary Church, Ingatestone. I discovered an announcement of her death online, only a passing mention.'

'He did come from Ingatestone. That much I do remember.' He calculated that Challis' mother had been born in 1918, toward the end of the Great War, so she would have been twenty-eight in 1946, the year Challis claimed as his birth year, the one indicated on the University of Leicester Library webpage dedicated to his archive, which Jim too had checked earlier. Jim still wondered whether he might have really been five or six years older, as Sue had speculated, or whether it had all just been so much fairly innocuous gossip. 'An unusual name, hers.'

'So I've got the right man. I did have doubts. I'm excited about tracking him down.' She chuckled. 'I think the name comes from St Etheldreda's Church, White Notley, where some Challises are recorded, married there in the nineteenth century. The records are online. She was perhaps a girl from that area too.'

'So you've done your background research.' She looked energetic.

'Yes, I have. It's part of my professional life, research. You know I'm excited by the Challis connection. I feel I've found part of myself which I was unaware of. It's strange that I now live in Essex just like his ancestors had for centuries. I'd no affinity for Brownie, and so I felt fatherless, even before mum told me I wasn't his. To tell the truth, the idea of your test isn't so much about you, it's more to eliminate you. Your test, if it's negative, in the circumstances, well . . . um, that would provide a way of proving logically that Challis was my father. Mother was totally convinced he was. Yet, she did admit in her final letter that something happened with you on that night, something drunken. She wrote about always pretending to herself that she couldn't fully remember what had happened, but she did. So she had to concede there were in the end two possibilities about my biological parentage.' Jim began to worry that Eileen might consider him some kind of a 1970s defiler who'd preyed upon drunken women, and there would be a revelation, that she was seeking her potentially rapist father, seeking violent or judicial revenge. The ideas swirled in his head, creating a rising sense of panic.

'I didn't take advantage, I didn't f-f-force myself . . . .' he stuttered. What on earth did she think of him, and what were her intentions?

'No, I know; her letter made it clear. In fact, if anything it was the other way around. She writes of taking advantage of you, your state, her shame in doing so. Does that make sense?'

'It sort of does, but why didn't she tell me what occurred?'

'Well, this is the really difficult bit,' Eileen paused. 'I don't want to upset or offend you in any way. How can I best put matters, I wonder? It's oddly delicate.' Jim was intrigued.

'I really won't be offended.' Jim said. 'Why would I be?'

'I do wonder about that. This is really difficult, especially as I don't know you at all. Well, as a committed feminist my mother disliked you, was annoyed by you intensely. In fact, she *hated* you, that was how she put matters: *I really hated that man with utter intensity*, she wrote.' She was clearly reading that sentence out loud from the original. Jim was slightly shocked, and disappointed, although it had all been such a long time ago. He vaguely remembered arguing with Lauren, insisting in those days that without revolution feminism could turn into a negative force, a way of trapping people in the machinations of capitalism. He said nothing, carried on listening intently. There was little one might say. 'I think she thought you far too masculine, too forceful, and argumentative. However, there was another side to her reaction to you back then, part of why she hated you, and she admitted as much. She wrote that she found you incredibly attractive, extremely handsome, and was drawn by that erotically. On a previous occasion, when she first slept with you, she writes of enjoying the sex immensely, far more than ever before.'

'So I had, well, certain, if somewhat limited, charms?'

'Yes, but only physically. Being attracted to you ruined her existing relationship. She later broke off with her French fiancé, Bruno, her partner before Brownie.' Jim remembered him, but he'd thought Bruno merely visiting, an old flame, a hangover from Lauren's year abroad during her degree. 'Well, the Frenchman knew about you: Lauren confessed to him, but he wasn't well pleased, and so he returned to France, broken-hearted. He left her for good. She went out with Brownie on the rebound. You were part of the reason that she wanted to move, change job, relocate to another city. Brownie agreed to do so. After finding new jobs, off they went, leaving both Leicester and you in particular behind.'

'I wondered why the two of them left so abruptly. I thought because of gossip, about her breaking up Brownie's first marriage.'

'Lauren hated the power you exerted over her. When you turned up again in the north-east, so unexpectedly, trailing Challis, that compulsion resurfaced, she said. It wasn't a rational thing, more a strong instinct. Her wanting to be with you in that way troubled her, especially as she wasn't drawn to you in any other way. Such a purely sexual attraction made her feel totally out of control. So, given Brownie was wasted, being drunk herself, she slept with Challis first, for old time's sake she said, thinking it might diminish those cravings. But it didn't. So, well, you know the rest, because you were there. It's old history. I think she was ashamed of what she'd done, not with Challis, but *to* you.' She paused.

Jim hadn't, in truth, suspected anything of the depth of the encounter at all, neither at the time nor since. And Jim had no idea that Lauren had ever been engaged, or that he himself fascinated her sexually. And now it appeared she despised him as a person. Was he to blame himself, or should he be upset about her opinion of him? 'There was also this.' Eileen held up a broach that had belonged to Jim's grandmother, very small, gold, with a single ruby. A shiver ran down his spine. He'd given it to Lauren after their first night together, which he'd forgotten.

The object released a cascade of sensations, images from an unhappy period, aware of being besotted with Lauren, of her apparent indifference to him. Such past emotions, resurfaced, were half-formed, but still painful. And there was the guilt of the time, for he'd been married himself on that first occasion, the first sex with Lauren. She'd known all about that scenario. Of course, she had. She'd bought that ticket for the evening out from his wife herself. And it was the late 1970s after all, it had been the end of an excessively fucked-up decade, full of confusion and bullshit, which on occasion Will was known to reflect upon. 'And what about the test?' Eileen added.

'Do you mind if I think about it all,' Jim asked, still uncertain, 'just for a few hours?' He thought he might even find the courage to broach the topic with Gabi, see what she thought.

'Certainly, but I'd be eternally grateful if you were to agree.'

'OK.' He sounded uncertain about her, or at least her request.

'Look, I'm not after any money or anything like that, honestly. I have a good career and two boys, a partner with a good, well-paid job. I make money with my books, lots of it.' Jim would rather not hear such details. 'We're actually quite wealthy. It's really that I want to eliminate you. If it's Challis, as mam thought, I'd be delighted, a literary father. I'd visit the archive again, do more research, maybe track down his family members, relatives, and write about him, explore my past.   Even the stuff already catalogued online is intriguing. He wrote so many letters, by the yard.'

What if her father were to prove to be Jim himself? What would that entail? She'd probably be disappointed, with a nonentity, a failure for a father. He'd done nothing that might enthuse her, this newly-found potential daughter. His academic work was far too dry, set against Challis' memoir of travelling through the states, his letters to and from William Burroughs, Allen Ginsberg, Carolyn Cassady and others in the archive, all written since their trip. Next, he realized if he were her father, he might even have two more, ready-made grandchildren, worrying what Will might think about that new reality. How would he react? What about Kitty? What might she say? And Gabi?

'Where do you live?' he asked. While they were conversing, Jim looked her up online, where there were several sources: as she said there were two sons, she was educated at Cambridge, published numbers of books, including *Travels in a Fat Country* about the US, and another entitled *Too Close to the Moon*. She was a Fellow of the Royal Society of Literature, no less, a detail which evoked a sharp twinge of envy in Jim.

'Saffron Walden,' she responded. Jim held his tongue with difficulty, their proximity to each other almost blurted out. He felt slightly uncomfortable at the news, her living about thirty-seven miles from where he was currently sitting, about fifty minutes along the M25 and M11 out of rush hour, almost neighbours.

'Let me think it through today. Skype later if you're free.'

'Please.'

'Yes, I promise', he replied, uncertain whether he was telling her the truth. 'You'll be online later, say nine tonight?' he asked.

'Yes, I'm free any time until midnight. Thanks for listening.' Jim ended the call, reading carefully through her profile and interview. She seemed respectable, even had a Norland nanny when travelling for work, according to her website.

Although it was about six p.m. and probably mealtime, Jim rang an old friend, Sasha, a medical doctor. Years before he'd visited his sister, Moggy, who lived on the same road as Jim and Virginia, at Christmas just before the Bunting visit, at New Year. The pair no longer spoke, the brother and sister. Their father had been Ukrainian of Russian stock born in 1928, the same year as Howard. Forcibly conscripted in 1942 into the

Waffen-SS, the Galicia Division, aged fourteen, a big strong peasant boy with blonde Aryan locks who had been living in an orphanage. According to Sasha, his father had undoubtedly been a war criminal, aged fifteen and sixteen; being what would later in Africa be termed a boy soldier. He suspected his father was involved fully in various mass executions, of Jews, of guerrillas from the Ukrainian Insurgent Army, of Communists, of intellectuals, of homosexuals, the usual suspects for the Nazis, the types penciled on their list of hate. His father once managed to escape, and he spent four months working at a remote farm for the harvest, but he was caught, betrayed. The Germans threatened him with execution if he were to flee again. He was terrified. He ended up in Norwich after the war, becoming a watch repairer, dying at about sixty of alcoholism, racked by long-nurtured guilt perhaps.

Jim saw the father only once, a stooped bespectacled, prematurely-aged man with a weird accent, an unlikely mix of Eastern European and Norfolk. After the war he'd married an Irish nurse who Jim had become close to in her later years as a widow, being at the time sweet on one of her daughters, the one who'd go on to marry the carpenter. The initial cause of the conflict between siblings was simple and straightforward enough. Sasha wanted to explore his paternal roots, Moggy to bury that part of her past, which had become the basis of another ongoing family feud that had widened. They hadn't spoken for years. Jim explained to Sasha his dilemma, Lauren's night with the two men, the inquiring daughter, her date of birth. 'But wouldn't a child conceived on 8th January be born later?' he asked, having concluded that it must be so.

'Let me check. I've got a chart that calculates such matters.' Across the ether of the microwaved message on his mobile Jim could hear Sasha rummaging in a drawer, seeking something. He would be in an office in a base. For a few years Sasha had worked as a civilian locum for the military, both the army and the RAF. Sasha far preferred the latter. He'd come to despise the army, most especially as regards their neglect of those suffering from the after-effects of the logistical process of the repatriation of bodies from Afghanistan and Iraq, as well as those dealing with the grieving families. The military bosses expected their soldiers to be tough, just get on with the job, and shake off any feelings. As Sasha knew, many suffered an aftershock, with depression, anxiety, even illness. No one seemed to care, which appalled Sasha. So, he kept moving his base of operations. Hence occasionally Jim was called upon to offer a reference for a new posting. 'Well, it would most likely be a 1st October birth.'

'So, September 30th is within the range of possible births?' Jim was disappointed. Whatever Lauren's conviction, he wanted the baby to be someone else's, conceived after his departure.
'Exactly, it's extremely likely. Are you worried about the possibility, Jim, of a long-lost daughter? Are you nervous?'

'I am. I don't know why. The woman looks wealthy. I suppose it's because I've no idea of what is entailed. It's all come out of the blue. I'm flummoxed. What if it's me and then she's disappointed. She seems eager for it to be this other guy, Challis.'

'I remember him, long-hair hippie type, beard, great big guy.'

'You've got him in one,' said Jim. Sasha had an excellent memory. He was hugely intelligent and empathic. Jim valued his advice.

'So, was she all hairy, huge and with a beard?' Jim laughed.

'No, she's actually pretty, seems to be slim-faced, dark and confident. A Cambridge graduate, so she's probably not dim. How are you? Where are you working currently?' Jim couldn't keep tabs on the numbers of moves Sasha made professionally, but that was the nature of his job as a locum. His wife and child lived in a large house near the Severn Estuary, just above Bristol.

'I'm fine, family's well. Jane's busy.' This was Sasha's wife, who as a Kiwi shared Sasha's grand passion for travel. Their daughter Maya had been so christened after being conceived in Nepal where the name was popular, being another term for the Hindu goddess Durga, considered as the supreme Goddess by some adherents. 'I'm at a base in Cornwall, really nice, near Penzance.' They continued their conversation, swapping pleasantries, but Jim was distracted by his new dilemma, unusual in conversation with Sasha which over the years he'd come to value, even if many of them were disembodied, as if stretched over the phone lines. 'How's your son, Will?' Sasha asked. Jim explained briefly the issue of his only offspring (well, probably the only one) and his departure to live in Congleton, and that Jim's ex-wife had moved to France on retiring about fourteen months previously on a huge pension, or so Jim calculated. However, the Witch didn't appear to want to come to Will's rescue financially. And probably even if she were to do so, she couldn't make up enough of a deposit for somewhere in London where prices were becoming so impossibly high. He explained this to Sasha, reconstructing a segment of his conversation with his son.

'I told Will that I thought we might all help, if maybe we could club together, me, my mother, the Wicked Witch and Kitty's parents. But he reckoned that prices have rocketed so much we'd all be chasing our tails. Even if we managed twelve grand each, it just wouldn't be enough, still short of fifty-grand.' With the failure of Jim's strategy, as he explained to Sasha, his son and family left London for the North. Jim was depressed by reliving that reality, one more of his dreams butchered by the economy.

Afterwards as the evening progressed, Jim took stock, wondering what he should do about the earlier request for testing of parentage, thinking through this new possibility. He sat at his desk. The hot sun went behind a small cloud. In the slight gloom in a garden somewhere someone out of sight was hammering something either into or out of its shape, and the sound gradually became indistinct, torpid. A fly buzzed in his office but was barely audible, and it was as if time had been slowed to an infinitesimal pace, a breeze barely moving the leaves and branches of the shrubs and the tall apple tree to his left beyond the glass, planted by Jim.

Without preamble as if in a trance he thought of Knapper. Jim strongly sensed his presence he could almost hear his voice, saw the spirit of the man Jim knew so viscerally, the highs and lows of seventeen years drinking together, arguments, Jim shoving Knapper across the room, angry his friend had declared it was perfectly acceptable for the Taliban to shoot young girls and women for going to school. Knapper tangled the argument in his drunken state, obstinate, confused, insistent on the logical nature of such horrific actions, a radical resistance he imagined was waged against the West and its dreadful hegemony, somehow retrieving some nobility from all that savagery and murder, delusional.

Jim remembered Knapper's memorial service, Friday, 13th July at 3pm, the Church of the Ascension, deepest south London. He visualised the two hundred mourners, David's speech, one from Knapper's son, Jim's own, referencing Knapper's unluckiness, victim of bicycle thefts, his extreme competitiveness, his research on Commedia Dell'Arte and the masks of Scaramouche, no mention of surplus value, Marx and a confusion so profound it had been alarming. All that was past and now unrecorded too. Jim felt guilt at his abandonment of so much.

As the images swirled, Jim understood more in his body than in his mind that he just missed Knapper so very much, was moved by his absence, which upset him far more than any of the others of whom he'd been thinking recently struggling to prepare ideas for his book: Cedric, Sue, Challis, poor Boris from school who'd drowned before he really had time to develop, and naturally Jim's father. There were others he hadn't included, such as school-friend Fruity who died young of cancer, in his thirties, a frustrated filmmaker, a long-standing devotee of Hitchcock, squeezed out even from the plans for the novel by its author manqué and his idle nature. Jim felt his guilt, a sense of betrayal. And yes, that applied to Knapper too, for whom Jim grieved more than even his own father, far more profoundly in a way. Jim's throat developed the feeling of a lump and he welled up. There were tears, which multiplied. He could feel them streaming down his face. Jim concluded he missed Knapper, perhaps more than anyone about whom he'd intended to write. Yet throughout his plans Jim couldn't fit him properly into the story he envisaged, impossible to focus upon his friend in concentrated fashion, unable to explore the idea of his death, its significance, or detail any of that appalling final depression that had swallowed him and spat out his dead form. Jim was fearful of even evoking in his head the illusions, the voices, the terror, like Jonah lost in his whale, retreating from the maelstrom of a storm, forever, doomed by one's descent.

At these overwhelming thoughts Jim knew once again that come what may, he would fail to finish writing his prospective book. In effect, he'd already abandoned his deceased friends, who were never to be brought to life again, not even in the medium of fiction. He knew for certain that even the scant notes for his narrative about all these lost souls would be boxed up, stowed away, discarded, and eventually forgotten forever. He could imagine his son Will or his wife Kitty jettisoning the lot after he died. Was this failure, the fact of being an uninspired and perhaps insufficiently talented writer, among the very worst fates he might have to endure? Jim's memorial, his swimming against the tide of time proved impossible, much as Alfred predicted. Alfred would be pleased with himself, Jim reflected, as he could point out that he'd noticed the deficiencies in Jim and his plan right from the start.

Jim's inability made him feel bad, defined him yet again as a failure. However, in a curious fashion it made up his mind about his current dilemma, the DNA paternity test. In that instant, impulsively, he decided he would Skype Eileen, agreeing to her request. He would do it before he could change his mind. In a strange way Jim found himself torn, not about his decision, however rash, but the outcome of the test. He might have a daughter, something he'd longed for but had always suppressed the thought. The right person had come along far too late for that aspiration: when he'd met Gabi she felt she was too old for more children, which now she perhaps regretted. Despite such yearning, Jim hoped the child of that rash and drunken night would prove to have been sired by Challis, another legacy beyond his book and the archive of his letters and notes, a flesh and blood continuation of the now deceased self. Bunting had been wrong about one thing, Jim realized, a certain kind of repetition is actually everything, and it is all that really matters,   one's offspring.

If Challis' paternity were proven, Jim would tell Eileen all he knew of her father, show her the few notes for the intended chapters in which he was to feature, offer her unedited photocopies of his journal pages concerning Challis, notes of their trip, the black and white photo on Jim's office wall taken by Challis in 1980, Jim and Holly with members of the visiting Cambridge Footlights Revue, sitting around a table in the Taj Mahal, a much favoured curry house in Leicester's Highfield Street. There was also one short reference to Challis that Jim found online in an e-book published in 2005, written by David Charlson on Charles Bukowski, originally a doctoral dissertation at the University of Kansas. Taken together it hardly amounted to much, was all that Jim possessed, his only mementoes of Challis. He'd three photos variously of Bunting and Sue Townsend, but none for either Boris or Cedric, the former on the lost film long jettisoned no doubt and the latter always camera-shy, and in those days one needed film, real celluloid, and a camera. People and the past slipped away so readily. Jim realised there really were very few monuments to everyday life, or to ordinary people, even to those who were in truth extraordinary amidst all that ordinariness. Their fate was to remain uncelebrated, their talents and ambitions unsung, unknown, forgotten apart from the oral narratives left behind. Maybe there might be an occasional mention in letters, diaries, journals and unpublished novels. Only there did the past truly survive. And in another generation most of that would have been discarded, in ten twenty or thirty years. Nobody wanted the detritus. Although there were the diaries from Jim's ageing project in several archives, where the ordinary of the world had their say and would continue to do so posthumously. Yet sadly no one he knew had contributed to such a store of what was said and written, no record of the apparently inconsequential people, none of these creative souls, the less than successful, and eventually

Jim would join them all. He sighed, thinking suddenly of the possibility that Eileen might be his, that he might be her lost father.

Jim wiped away some tears, no longer mourning the insignificance he shared with so many, blew his nose reluctantly. He put on the headphones positively, moving the mouse, selecting the right page and the correct icon for Eileen, carefully. He wondered what on earth exactly he would do or say if the test went the other way from the outcome she clearly desired, and he was her father, but now wasn't the time for such imponderables. When Jim had finished the call, he would dig out the bowel cancer testing kit and its jolly optimistic leaflet, using the tin foil roasting dishes he'd washed in the dishwasher to, as instructed, catch his crap. He'd prepared three, but he wasn't sure about cleaning them out, what would be the optimum method. Other recommended approaches to the task, which he was torn over, included the simplicity of some toilet paper, or perhaps the small blue plastic gloves, purloined well in advance from the local filling station.

Later over the phone maybe he'd tell Gabi everything, including his abandonment of the planned novel, hopefully much in the manner Cedric would have done, making an entertaining canvas of one's life, the sort of thing readers of novels traditionally liked. Well, they did until the fashion changed among writers themselves, who generally conspired not to write in that manner, adopting different styles. In that traditional fashion Jim would try to inform his partner of all that had happened, or at least he would if she proved to be in a good mood. Otherwise, he might just wait a while, maybe until after the test, see what transpired, what fate might dictate for him, and then think about such unfinished business. He wondered whether he could stomach any more university life, with Carlin near the top, Jim teaching short books because the students were too lazy to read longer ones, the treadmill of tedious work of various kinds that was entailed in being an academic, of student satisfaction, external funding and impact all key priorities. He knew most of the friends he'd been thinking about so intently in recent weeks would be appalled by the prospect of the contemporary university, apart maybe from his father who would have thought the salary made it all worthwhile. Thinking of the future, Jim wondered whether Howard might not have had a point, not everyone left an artistic legacy. In truth, mostly people just did not do so. They left absolutely nothing for posterity, apart from money, which was useful, although many did not even manage this much, like his maternal grandmother, a shoebox filled with detritus, her few valuable possessions stolen by care-home staff. Most ordinary people were simply forgotten. So too would be all those remarkable people whom *Gin & Tonic* might have memorialized, lost souls who never attained the creative recognition for which they craved, friends like Challis, Cedric, all the others, even his poor confused pal, Knapper finally isolated. Forlorn, delusional, he hung himself in a flat visited frequently by Jim.

Jim wondered whether his abandonment betrayed them all, his life yet again defined by incompletion? Sure, the novel was killed off by work, and by his procrastination. All that remained was a residue, a few scraps of paper, some lists, a few scrappy notes and maps. He'd jettisoned those who'd died. None of them would be memorialized on the page, not by him. In his head he'd given them the new life he'd hoped for, however briefly, and would do so every time he recollected those once forgotten years.

Jim thought of a time when their everyday lives seemed far more mundane and pointless without such artistic aspirations, ambitions of the kind he'd shared with so many friends and acquaintances, some he couldn't even remember. Of many literary hopefuls Jim knew by the dozen upon dozen only Will Self, Sue Townsend, and Graham Joyce ever published anything substantial. Of those three only the last two were from ordinary families, working-class children, making it from the bottom without connections or influence. At least they'd done so. Jim tidied his notes away. They fitted in a single plastic blue fold-over file held together by strips of Velcro, one of Howard's favourite materials, using it years before its widespread commercial use, applied to almost everything he could. Jim picked up Challis's book. He read a section toward the end where its author held

Neal Cassady's ashes in a small silk sack, handed to him by the widow, Carolyn, Challis comparing its weight to a bag of bullseyes from childhood, reflecting on its mutability. 'In smoke or to the worms, all of us, books or no,' after which narrative ends with a two-word Latin sentence, 'Hic calix,' which Jim translated online as 'This chalice,' a pun on Challis' last name, making sure everyone with any knowledge could recognize he was still the centre of his work, despite the Beats, and all the charms of Holly, alluded to intermittently, Challis was the book's true lion heart.

Jim's pondered about his situation, his abandonment of *Gin & Tonic*. Were his attempts at memorialization in vain? Was it wasted effort? Could teaching fiction satisfy all those hopes, aspirations and ambitions over six decades of his life? Jim sighed, a grim realization he would not publish any fiction, ever. Yet the thought of Eileen buoyed him. Surely, he'd made a difference by teaching university students about fiction. Did he add to the special quality writing the damned stuff produced? For readers of fiction writers were demiurges. Why so? Writers needed readers after all. Readers needed to be shown how to interpret intelligently, instructed in the critical, creative encounter with a text. He was an educator: educate, derived from the Latin *ēdūcere*, present active infinitive of *ēdūcō*, I lead, draw or take out. Literary meaning was extracted from both text and the reader. Jim might still regard himself as being a legitimate part of the literary industry, vicariously creative, despite his abandoned novel and those earlier unpublished soft-bound ones stood like a short row of impossible, frozen theses, tombstones on a shelf. Jim longed for affirmation of his role as a teacher of readers, including future writers, part of a creative chain. Otherwise there was the terrible conclusion that he'd failed utterly in his life's work. Yet there was Eileen's test and what it promised, whatever the confusion of her conception.

Well, let's see what transpires, thought Jim, staving off any admission of defeat, any sense of a final ending.

Afterlives

Authorial Afterword

After two years of further revisions, finally I have finished this novel, originally part of a doctorate in creative writing, after a plethora of drafts, corrections, editing. I even tried three titles. During my degree, with so many changes one of my tutors called me 'tinker-man' after Claudio Ranieri, so-named when as Chelsea manager he was renowned for constantly altering his team. At this point of completion, I feel compelled to acknowledge the personal influence upon me of two writers, once close friends. I met both during the 1970s. Creatively and commercially they both *made it*. Tragically, however, both were to die prematurely, not so very long ago. The first death inspired me to write fiction once again after a hiatus of twenty years. This narrative acknowledges Sue's example, featuring her as a character in this book (which is in part a fictionalized memoir):

> *Sue [Susan Lillian] Townsend:*
> *2nd April 1946 – 10th April 2014*

Sadly, the second demise occurred as I finished my first tentative draft:

> *Graham Joyce:*
> *22nd October 1954– 9th September 2014*

Admiring Graham immensely, I hoped I might seek his advice, show him my typescript once fully edited. I would never have that opportunity, which I much regret. I recollect them both fondly.

Additionally let me acknowledge others that I've known over the years who shared my largely unfulfilled desire for creative self-expression, friends who all died far too young. They include:

> *Nigel 'Buzz' Burrell; Dr Christopher Challis;*
> *Ian 'Fruity' Graham; and Dr J.C. 'Ian' Hilson.*

Neither of the last two individuals featured as comprehensively in this final version as I intended originally, excised after editorial interventions. I was sad to lose a chapter concerning Fruity's death and funeral, which I removed after advice from my examiners.

My first full draft, entitled *The Gift of Death*, formed the creative section of a doctorate in creative writing (the novel) undertaken at Brunel University London, awarded in 2016. I appreciate the help and guidance from variously: my doctoral supervisors and colleagues, Matt Thorne and David Fulton; research advisor, Dr Nick Hubble; and former Head of Department, Prof Tom Betteridge, who awarded a fee-waiver. Much appreciated (post *viva voce*) was advice offered by my external examiners, with detailed commentary about reshaping this project: so, thanks to Prof Matthew Francis, Aberystwyth University, and Prof Martin Goodman, Hull University.

Much appreciation is also due to my wife, Agnes Bartha, for loyal support and steadfast belief in my creative abilities. She was my first reader, chapter by chapter perused as each was finished on her commute to and from Turkey Street and London Liverpool Street. Fay Weldon was the second, offering most generous encouragement, much appreciated. I was grateful for suggestions from two enthusiastic readers of subsequent drafts: Rev. Andrew Bevan, and Jim Crace. Finally, I must acknowledge my fellow Brigand Press author, Peter Holland, whose enthusiastic response reconfirmed my faith in this project. He, his wife, Fiona, and my son George proofread and edited the ultimate pre-production versions, offering invaluable advice and support, which generous assistance helped greatly in catching my various errors.

Without all those detailed above this book would have never seen the light of day in such good shape, would have stayed incomplete, another unpolished draft like so many other manuscripts begun in my youth, from age twenty-five to forty, at which point I switched to academic life and its associated scholarship. So, after producing twenty-three volumes in various associated fields, finally aged *sixty-four*, I am about have my first (complete and edited) novel actually published, unlike Jim Dent in my novel (a double-irony). Cue the Beatle's song, everyone to sing along. Adapt the original to your own version (I do so partly for copyright reasons): 'When I am older, losing my mind, so many years in time, would you still be sending me my Valentine, birthday wishes, bottle of gin. . . .'

Philip Tew,
Enfield Wash, 5th November 2018.